REALM LEADER

CHRONICLES OF THE CHOSEN

CASSANDRA BOYSON

KINGDOM HOUSE PRESS

CONTENTS

CHAPTER I

Novella tiptoed across the wooden dock until she reached the edge. The lake shimmering in the moonlight made her itch. Water had done that since she was a child. It wasn't until she'd reached twelve years that she learned she was an enigma. She now recalled the day when, after nearly half an hour beneath the water on their seaside holiday shoreline, she'd emerged to find Mother racing frantically toward her.

"*Vella!*" Mother had shrieked, grasping her shoulders in either hand. "Vella, you're alright! Where have you *been?*"

"Swimming, Mother," she answered easily. "You saw me."

Mother bit her lip as comprehension registered on her face. Her eyes shot back and forth between her daughter's. "Come with me," she spoke in a low voice as she turned back for the cottage they'd rented for the season. It was in fashion for well-to-do Victorian families to escape the heat of the city during the summer season.

"Why?" Novella questioned. "I thought we were to spend the day on the shore."

Novella's mother neither answered nor turned back. When Mother or Father demanded a thing, it was to be obeyed without question. She raced after her.

Now six years later, Novella was torn from her revelry by the sound of laughter and music in the distance. She looked back, searching the lights of the house party for signs that someone had followed her. The coast was clear. Swallowing, she restored her gaze to the water, returning to her memory.

Mother had made her bathe, re-dress and enjoy their usual tea before she would return to the former subject. Novella noisily drained her cup. Mother's eyes shot to hers with mild irritation before returning to the fire. The daughter considered her mother's behavior. The woman was often swept up in private deliberation, but this was different.

She was anxious.

"I wasn't hurt," Novella offered for comfort. "In fact, many of the small fish swam with me for protection from the larger ones." She stopped short as Mother's face became nearly mournful. "What... *is* it?"

"Do you know how long Gregory Wetherill can remain under the water's surface before requiring a breath?"

Novella shook her head. She'd never much cared for Gregory Wetherill. He was a snob and couldn't swim nearly as fast as she could.

"Not likely more than a couple of minutes," Mother informed.

Novella smirked. She'd presumed as much. Gregory was a bit of a dandy.

"This is no smiling matter." Mother sat forward, imprisoning Novella in her gaze. "I need you to pay attention."

Novella swallowed. "Yes, Mother."

"I do not believe it likely that any other person on this planet can breathe in the ocean."

"What do you mean? Many of my friends can swim."

"They must hold their breath. The water would choke them."

"I don't understand..."

Mother's face softened with compassion. "It makes you special, Vella... But it also means you must be *careful*. It is vital that we conceal this. If ever I take you to the shore again, which isn't likely, you must play and swim as other children. No more bathing with the fishes for long periods of time."

"But, *Mother*, this was the first time I ever stayed under so long. The fish are my friends!"

Mother pressed her lips together. She contemplated her daughter's face for some time. Abruptly, the cottage door opened. Mother leaped to her feet, twirling to face the intruder.

"Good morning, ladies!" Father called. "We completed the contract in record time. *Now*, I'm free to enjoy that sea with my best girls."

Mother's shoulders slumped with relief as she met him. "We're going home, Harold."

Father froze. "Is something amiss? Isn't Novella well?" His eyes shot to his daughter.

"I'm *fine*," Novella retorted. "Mother didn't like that I—"

"Novella is too old to be parading in bathing attire," Mother broke in. "I hadn't realized until I saw her out there. She's no small girl anymore."

The husband's eyes searched his wife's as their hands clasped. It was clear he didn't believe a word of it. But Father was Father. "When do we leave, Nimua?"

"As soon as possible," she breathed.

That was how things were between them. Everyone in the immediate family knew Mother was a secret-keeper. It was her way. But when she wished a thing, Father trusted she knew best. He couldn't seem to help pleasing her. And he'd never had reason for regret.

"But *Father!*" Novella moaned.

"Will you give us a moment?" Mother asked of Father.

His brows rose to his hairline. "I'll order the carriage ready."

Mother reached for her daughter's hands just as she had her husband's. "You are different, Vella, and that... is a *beautiful* thing. But if this world has shown me anything, it's that it does not respond well to different. My only aim is to protect you. Like your father, you must trust me in this. Can you do that?"

Novella wanted to wrench her hands away, to stomp and shout. But Mother had a way of winning one's trust. With a sigh, she answered, "Yes."

Nimua's hands grasped hers tightly. "Promise me you will take great pains to keep this secret."

The daughter peered up with utter confusion and absolute trust. "I promise."

As Novella's view of the lake replaced that of her mother's face those years ago, she stole closer to the edge. Once again, the sound of the party in the house on the hill made her glance back.

"Novellaaaa!" a man shouted.

She closed her eyes as if it would further conceal her in the darkness.

"Novy, my love!" Gregory Wetherill called again in his playful tone.

Novella grasped her hands tightly together. She hated the pet name. She didn't like Gregory much better. Their imminent engagement announcement was the reason she'd run from the house party, the reason she stood before the beckoning water.

The music's momentary resonance revealed he'd returned indoors. Of course he was looking for her. He had every right. This was their surprise engagement party. None knew it as yet. But they soon would.

How had she gotten into this mess?

When Novella was a child, Mother had abhorred Gregory as much as she did. But he had grown brawn and handsome and was in line to inherit a sizable fortune. Once he'd begun to pay Novella attention, Mother had done the encouraging for her. Novella knew it wasn't for the money—not entirely anyway. Mother wanted her accepted among a society in which she had never quite managed to belong. True, her father's good name scored her invites to the best parties, but she'd never fit in with the other girls. While they were busy mooning over the young gentlemen, all she'd wanted to do was play with dogs and snakes, traverse woodland paths and read about adventurers she dreamed of becoming. When she'd made claims like these, the girls' faces dimmed and they typically made their excuses to depart from her.

Novella Harper was strange, they said. How *right* they were. She leaned over the side of the dock, searching for what, she couldn't say. Every fiber of her person ached to enter the lake. She dug her fingernails into her palms, a layer of handmade lace draped between. She glanced at her party frock—white for the occasion. The girls who'd once avoided her now considered her with envy.

"What a glorious frock!" they'd cried when she entered the Wetherill home that evening. *"French-made!"*

One did not court a Wetherill without one's mother feeling the need to remain in stride with the latest fashions.

"Greg is going to *faint* when he sees you!" one of the girls had declared.

Novella recalled the day he'd fainted on sight of a lizard when they were fourteen. If she looked as fine as the girls claimed, he just might. But a gown like this boded one thing: it was unquestionably not for swimming.

She let one leg dangle over the edge. How she wished she *dared*—

"Aren't planning to swim for it, are you?" questioned a teasing voice.

She spun to face the unfamiliar man. Failing to replace her dangling foot upon the dock, she found herself plunging into cold depths.

CHAPTER 2

THE SENSATION WAS ASTOUNDING. It was just like when Novella was a girl. She could *breathe*. But Mother's warning instantly returned to mind. She must conceal her secret. As her feet hit a dock support, she used it to lunge for the surface. She was drawn back with a jerk.

"What in the *world*—" she began before clasping a hand over her mouth.

She could speak clearly. That wasn't typical, was it? Thrusting such thoughts to the back burner, she attempted to swim up but was held fast. Panic seized her as she fought for freedom. The stranger would surely notice something amiss if she remained for too long. Frantically, she fought the water before realizing her dress was caught in the support.

A splash sent sparkling swirls in her direction. A hand reached for her arm, working to pull her to the surface. She felt the handmade lace of her French gown tear before she wrenched her arm away. The hand reached for her again, a face drawing close enough to reveal a pair of eyes. Surprise registered on his face as he realized she wasn't suffering. Novella only just recalled to hold her breath, sending bubbles floating from her mouth. She pointed down, tugging at her dress to indicate she was caught. The stranger dove down, efficiently managing to release the skirt and send her floating for freedom. She broke the surface with a faked gasp as he appeared beside her.

"Trying to end it all?" he questioned amusedly. "Wouldn't it be easier to just end the engagement?"

Novella swam in dumbstruck silence for some moments before, "You *startled* me into this water, sir! And who told you I wish to be free of Gregory?!" None but her mother and Fannie, the cook, were aware of her abhorrence for her fiancé. Had someone overheard them discussing it that morning? Her heart pounded over the gossip that must have ensued.

"I can recognize a cry for help when I see one," he answered with a grin. "Running away from what I've heard rumored to be the announcement of your engagement is about as big a tell as any."

Novella sputtered, not for the first time finding herself short on words. Turning for the dock, she worked to pull herself up to no avail. In a moment, the stranger had heaved himself up and was offering a hand.

"Why don't we begin again?" he said. "I'm Petyr. That is, Mr. Petyr Tamsen."

Though she was in no way appeased, she allowed him to help her. "Pleasure, I'm sure," she murmured irritably.

His dripping face scanned her up and down with amusement before he planted hands on his hips. "I'd say we have a problem."

Her lips parted in quick question before her eyes flew from his dripping hair to her own sopping gown. She gasped as she tugged at the soggy, imported lace. "Mother is going to kill me."

"And I'd say that's an end to the evening—a *right* pity, to be sure. May I escort you home?"

Her eyes flashed to his. "That isn't necessary, Mr. Tamsen. However..." She hesitated to ask this stranger for a favor. But a lady discovered in such a state would send tongues waggling. A man, however, could only just pass. "I wonder if I might trouble you to call for my driver and send the carriage down for me?"

He replied with an exaggerated bow. "As you wish."

A pair of figures emerged from the darkness.

"Ah!" Mr. Tamsen spoke lightly. "Mr. Harper, I have traced your daughter for you."

Novella did a doubletake. "Father?"

"*Novella?*" Mother gasped. "What are you—Vella, you are *drenched!*"

"Um..." she began, at a loss for words. Things like this weren't supposed to happen to well-bred young ladies.

"I'm afraid *I* am in error, Mrs. Harper," Mr. Tamsen spoke with a respectful bow. "Miss Harper was taking some air on the dock when I startled her into the water."

"And the two of you were skulking about in the dark because...?" Mother questioned.

"*Nonsense,* Nim," Father spoke with a laugh. "I sent my new assistant to fetch her. The hour for the announcement had come and gone and..." He surveyed his daughter up and down. "Is now quite beyond us, it seems."

Was it just Novella or did she detect satisfaction in his voice? Didn't he care for Gregory either? Her eyes flew to his face, which had considerably sobered now his wife was scowling up at him.

He cleared his throat. "I'll have the carriage sent for. Mr. Tamsen, I would appreciate it if you would escort these ladies to that tree just there. I'll see your horse is brought over as well."

"My pleasure," Mr. Tamsen replied.

Mother's glare transferred from husband to daughter. "You knew we were about to make the announcement. What am I to tell Gregory?"

What am I to tell Gregory? Novella pondered. That was the nature of their relationship. Mother was more engaged to him than she was.

"I can have a note sent that Miss Harper was unavoidably detained," Mr. Tamsen offered chirpily. "That should buy time for explanations."

Both Mother and Novella scowled back at him. Neither of them had heard a word about Father's new assistant. Now, he suddenly thought he could run *them?*

"That won't be necessary Mr. uh, Townsend, was it?" Mother answered.

"Tamsen," Novella corrected.

Mother's tight smile was bestowed before her gaze returned to Mr. Tamsen. "We can make our own apologies, thank you. Shall we be going?"

It was a silent journey through the trees before they reached the place where Father awaited with both carriage and horse.

"Isn't this a fine, impromptu party?" he asked as he aided his wife inside.

She raised a brow at her husband. Father liked nothing better than to tease his wife when she was dissatisfied. It was Mother's duty to pretend she didn't like it, or where would be the fun?

"It seems you're the hero of the evening, Petyr," Father spoke with a pat to the man's shoulder. "Can't thank you enough."

Novella was shocked by her father's familiarity with the young man of whom she knew nothing. Moreover, she couldn't help feeling annoyed at Father's apparent pride in the one who'd sent her plunging.

"No trouble at all," Mr. Tamsen answered with something of a sidelong sparkle her way. "Any time your daughter requires a chaperone, I hope you will call upon me." With that, he went after his horse.

"Father," Novella hissed as he handed her into the carriage. "He said himself he startled the life out of me—the reason for my unfortunate state."

Father offered a fairly sparkling smirk. "Remind me to raise that boy's salary."

"Harold!" Mother scolded. "How can you say that? She might have been ruined. Moreover, Gregory will be *irrevocably* offended."

"Our daughter is a well-behaved young woman who knows how to carry herself. *I* sent Petyr and might have explained as much to any witness. As for that young braggart of whom I have the misfortune of naming my future son-in-law, I couldn't give a hoot how he feels about it."

"Father?" Novella questioned with interest. Could it be she had a comrade on her side? All this time, she'd thought herself the helpless victim of her fate. Could there be a way out?

His eyes found his daughter's as his face softened. "I'm afraid I've learned some disappointing news about your Gregory, darling girl."

"By all means, *tell* me," she demanded, feeling, for the first time in many months, a light at the end of a dark tunnel.

"It seems your lifelong friend is something of a womanizer," he explained unhappily. "Has a lady in every town through which he travels, some of whom I'd blush to mention."

"A lady in—" Mother gasped hoarsely. "Harold, that sounds like the rubbish of gossipmongers!"

"I'm afraid not, my love. I've had it this very day from a dependable source: Mr. Locksworth, the boy I grew into manhood alongside. It seems he's heard tales of young Mr. Gregory Wetherill for a number of years but didn't much trouble himself until he learned from my recent letter that *my daughter* was engaged to him." For once, Father was fairly fuming.

Novella wasn't fuming. She rested her head back against the carriage with the sensation that she might manage to sprout wings and fly with relief. Why hadn't she called an end to things sooner? Why had she allowed Mother to push her so long? She supposed it was because she'd truly not thought there would ever be anything better for her. And Mother wasn't often wrong.

"I'm awfully sorry, Vella," Father spoke considerately.

"Sorry?" she questioned. "I'm a new woman, Father! And I... I don't know that I *ever* wish to be married."

"*Ever?*" Mother ejaculated. "Heavens, Vella, you sound like... well, like an old friend of mine."

"Who?"

It was too late. As usual, Mother's face articulated that she was shut up like a trap door. This happened any time something of her younger years was mentioned. "It isn't important," she answered, "though I'll have you know that the woman *did* marry eventually."

"Who cares!" Novella cried. "Father, I feel so liberated just now, I cannot bear the notion of ever marrying. Isn't there something I can do—perhaps down at the paper? I'd start just about anywhere."

"*Heaven forbid!*" Mother nearly roared.

Father rewarded his daughter with a doting smile. "Why don't we take some time to consider your options. You've always been so bright. But you're young yet and there are many fish in the sea."

"The sea..." Novella whispered. "Couldn't we take a cruise through the islands?"

"*Out of the question,*" Mother ruled. "What we *can* do is get home, change you into something dry and consider how to sort out this mess I've made for us."

Novella's eyes went softly to Mother's. She hadn't expected her to take so much responsibility for the engagement.

"It's my fault too," she admitted. "I knew better. I should have said something."

"Yes, you should," Mother returned. "But I imagine you tried... and I did not possess an ear for it. I wanted my way for you. I am *sorry.*"

Novella blinked back. Her mother did not often apologize. Then again, she was not often wrong.

"I forgive you."

CHAPTER 3

NOVELLA WATCHED THE PASSERSBY on the street from where she sat in her nightdress on the second floor of their city house. Awaking that morning had felt like the dawning of a new life after so many months of mental imprisonment. Why she had allowed her relationship with Gregory to progress so far, she would never know. It was as if the situation involving her loving mother and egotistical suitor had placed her under a spell of powerlessness. She'd envisioned her future life as the lady of the largest house on the block with the ghastliest man in her personal sphere. She'd have lived as a shadow of herself, never free to act as she liked or become what she desired.

A yearning churned inside her for something very different from her prior plans. She yearned for travel, adventure, liberty. She needed to find people like herself, who couldn't quite fall into the mold of Victorian London. There *must* be others who felt they could not breathe under society's strict standards.

"Morning, Fannie!" Vella greeted the cook as she entered with a breakfast tray. "You shouldn't have gone to such trouble. I know I slept late, but I might have nabbed a biscuit."

"Biscuit!" the round woman retorted. She placed the tray on a small table and slid it beside the window. "A growing girl cannot live off bread alone."

Novella scanned the tray of bright pink salmon, syrupy brown beans, muffins, jam and butter with a side of fresh cut fruit in the shape of stars. It reminded her of the sky the evening before, when she'd thought herself lost to a loathed fate. She released a contented sigh.

Fannie took firm hold of Vella's chin, turning her head this way and that in examination. "Your color is back. Blushing like a newly bloomed rose, you are." She released her chin and turned for the door. "As I expected."

Novella grinned. Fannie had been one of the few who'd known she hated her engagement. As she scanned the tray once again, she realized the cook considered her freedom a celebratory occasion. The woman had nearly exited when she turned back with an expression that conveyed she had lost an inner debate.

"I'm certain you'll be informed once you're decent, but..." She leaned further into the room to whisper, "Yer father has already been in contact with Mr. Gregory and the ring has been returned. Gregory is to vacate the region before day's end. Any with an inkling of your prior relationship will think the young Wetherill is to blame for its end. It should all be done very quietly."

Vella's mouth dropped open. To think everything had been handled before she'd even changed from her nightdress. More than that, she wouldn't have to face Gregory, nor even *see* his face, for who knew how long.

"*Thank* you, Fannie."

Fannie grinned from ear to ear. "I'd been prayin' an' prayin' from the moment that young braggart entered this household in pursuit of my sweet girlie. Thank the blessed Savior he's gone for good, hey Miss Vella?"

Novella turned to her tray in wonder of Fannie's words as she left her in peace. Did the Lord really care about inconsequential young women like herself? Did he really intervene in such small matters as hers? *Why* should she fall into His estimation of things?

A bright grin stole across her face. Gregory was *gone*—or nearly. She was officially single and ready to fly. To where, she couldn't just say. But the world was her oyster, so long as her parents were willing to send her. Yet, she lacked direction. What she required was *responsibility*. True, she helped her father with his financials. She could read and write better and faster than most. She played piano as well as any well-bred young woman. But aside from these, her skillset sorely lacked.

Taking up a muffin, she restored her gaze to the people below. Everyone was occupied by some errand or other. There was the grocer with a wagon of deliverables, the lady who laundered the apparel of the neighborhood, a pair of gentlemen visiting door to door, attempting to sell something. Now Novella was no longer to be married, where did *her* place lie?

Her gaze followed a familiar set of shoulders beneath a debonair hat that flaunted a small red feather. She failed to determine his identity until he'd reached her own house. It was then he removed his hat to knock upon the door. *Of course*. It was Mr. Tamsen, Father's new assistant. Somehow, she couldn't help feeling the feather suited his disposition. Though he had technically been nothing but polite and helpful, an ever-present merriment glimmered in his eyes. She blushed as she recalled having met him beneath the water. Now it occurred to her that she was to encounter him on the regular, it was humiliating to recount their introduction.

However, it was not until she dressed and descended an hour later that the thorough mortification of the encounter dawned upon her. She was rounding the corner in search of her mother when she found herself colliding with someone. Expecting the maid with an arm full of sheets, it was to her discomfort that Mr. Tamsen graciously apologized for the blunder. Novella stepped back in shock over his use of her first name. Had her foolish incidents made him view her as but a child?

"That is Miss Harper, Mr. Tamsen. I am *above* seventeen."

He stared back with his customary mirth before offering a slight bow. "I apologize once again, Miss Harper. I am unaccustomed to the manners of the region, I'm afraid."

She raised a brow, opening her mouth to inquire where he was from, when her father stepped from his study to find them in the hall. His face grew bright as the noon sun.

"Well, isn't this cozy," he commented. "You young folks certainly don't waste time these days."

Novella stood back in revulsion of her father's insinuation that she'd gone from Gregory to Mr. Tamsen in less than a day. Surely, he was only teasing, but what would Mr. Tamsen think? Certainly, her name wasn't to be coupled with that of another man for some time, if ever. She had only just earned her liberty.

"I'm afraid it was my fault once again—" Mr. Tamsen attempted.

"You know," the father began. "I think we've accomplished quite enough for one day. I wonder... would you mind escorting my daughter into the shopping district? Her mother has informed me she is in need of a new pair of shoes."

"*Father,*" Novella spoke in a low tone, "Mr. Tamsen does not wish to accompany me shoe shopping. I intend to go with Mother."

"Mother isn't feeling well, I'm afraid, so it will have to be Mr. Tamsen for escort. What do you say, Petyr? Have you the time?"

Petyr peered directly into Novella's pleading eyes with, "As you wish, Mr. Harper. Let me replace these papers to your desk and we'll be on our way."

The men returned to the study while Novella was left gaping in the corridor. It simply couldn't be that her father was already attempting to pawn her off on the very first man who appeared. Didn't he *like* having her at home? He'd always claimed as much. Yet, here he was sending her off alone with a gentleman she scarcely knew, who came from a region where men addressed young ladies by their first names. Any who saw them would presume he was either a new butler or she was stepping out on Gregory. Most importantly, Novella was in no wise prepared to be ensnared by another suitor. She'd only just gained her wings.

"Father," Novella stated as she stepped into the room, "I'm afraid I don't feel well. Mr. Tamsen, will you please excuse me for the day?"

Mr. Tamsen's face broadened into a smile. "Of course."

Relief flooded her.

"We can go tomorrow," he added before returning to his conversation with Mr. Harper.

Novella's eyes widened. Her hands tightened into fists at her sides as she strode away. Who *was* this Mr. Petyr Tamsen, who so boldly thought he possessed both the right to escort her as well as to dictate her schedule? As she marched up the stairs, her mind raced for plans she could make in place of his proposal on the morrow.

Aunt Sylvie. She could visit the dreaded woman—stay for the week if she liked. True, she didn't much care for her aunt nor her aunt for her, but she wasn't likely to turn her down. It was typically considered a familial obligation to accept one's relatives when they desired to call.

Novella knocked on Mother's door.

"Come in, Vella! I've been expecting you."

Novella entered the bedroom where her mother sat up in bed, going over her itinerary.

"I'm glad you're here," she went on. "I won't be able to keep our shopping date. It seems I'm a little under the weather and your father thinks it best I remain in bed for the time being. I suppose we'll have to reschedule for some time next week."

Novella relaxed. At least her mother wasn't behind any plot to hoist her off so soon.

"About that," she began, "I was wondering if I might visit Aunt Sylvie tomorrow. Perhaps stay for a few nights. That is... unless you need me here with you." She hadn't thought that her mother might require her care.

"I thought you detested your father's sister?"

Novella shuffled her feet before answering, "I suppose I just feel like getting away for a bit. And she doesn't live so far that you couldn't summon me home if needed."

"*Ah...*" Mother answered with a nod. "I suppose you're hoping to avoid the probable gossip at Gregory's sudden departure. I cannot blame you," she ended with a sigh. "Well, I agree. If you think you can bear your Aunt Sylvia for a few days, I think it would be good for you."

"Good for me?"

"I've pushed you so hard these last months, trying to prepare you to be enjoined with the Wetherills. I was wrong and I see it now. All that to say, the country air will do you good—take the pressure off."

Novella blinked back. It was like a gift dropped from heaven to have both her mother's consent and consideration. Not that Mother wasn't often helpful, simply that she hadn't seemed quite herself of late. It was nice to have her back.

"Thank you, Mother. I'll have a telegram sent for her to expect me and inform Gerald to have the carriage ready early in the morning. I should arrive by noon if we leave at ten, don't you think?"

"It's a good plan. I appreciate your maturity in all of this." She looked her daughter up and down. "You've grown up so neat and collected. I'm proud of you."

"Thank you..." Novella wistfully replied.

For so many years, she'd thought herself the black sheep of society. Of late, her mother's corrections had been frequent due to her impending connection to the Wetherills. It was novel to receive such approval.

"I have long thought as much, you know," Mother continued. "Despite... everything else."

Silence fell between them. Neither spoke what both were thinking. Mother referred to the peculiar scene that had occurred those years ago at the seaside. Novella recoiled at the abrupt reminder of her abnormality. As neat as she attempted to be, she would never be normal.

CHAPTER 4

NOVELLA APPROACHED HER CARRIAGE with a smug smirk. She had done it—outsmarted Mr. Tamsen. Not even her father had time to delay her going, she had found on bidding him farewell. Abruptly, a figure stepped out and removed his red-feathered hat in greeting.

"Oh... Mr. Tamsen," she began with hesitation. "I cannot keep our engagement. It seems my aunt is in need of me just now."

"I am aware, Miss Harper. Your father has asked that I act as your escort to her country estate."

A series of emotions rushed over Novella: disbelief, anger, ending in discomfort. A shopping trip with a strange man was one thing. *Two hours* on a train was quite another. And she'd taken pains to avoid the *former.*

"I thank you, Mr. Tamsen, but that won't be necessary. I intended our coachman for escort."

Mr. Tamsen bowed his head in acknowledgement before explaining apologetically, "I'm afraid your father is in need of your coachman today. He has hired a cab for the journey to the station. I believe they left just before you appeared."

Novella felt her face heat considerably as she allowed him to hand her into the carriage. Father had thought of *everything.* And he really was determined to have her off his hands before year's end. She couldn't help being hurt. He'd always claimed she was so helpful to have about. Ergo, she'd made herself the more helpful. She *liked* to please him. Now, it seemed, none of it mattered.

That didn't change the fact that she was unwilling to forfeit her liberty. If she must endure a train ride with this man, so be it. But she would remain with her aunt for as long as the woman would allow. When she returned, she would simply avoid Mr. Tamsen at all costs.

They'd scarcely descended down the short drive when Mr. Tamsen caught her eye. "I've been searching for you for some time, you know. Feels like a lifetime."

"Mr. *Tamsen,*" she nearly squealed. "For heavens, what a line!"

After some moments, he threw his head back with laughter before moving to sit beside her. "You misunderstand me. As I said yesterday, the customs are different where I come from."

She raised a brow.

With the casual folding of his arms, he sat back against the opposite end of the seat with a smirk. "Novella Harper, you are not who you think you are."

Her eyes narrowed. "And who would you say I am, Mr. Tamsen—you who only met me the other evening."

"I'd say you're quite a swimmer."

She bit her lip as her eyes flashed back and forth between his. Did he know? He *couldn't*. How could anyone in their right mind guess at such a thing?

"Where I come from," he began, "there are many like you."

Her mouth dropped open, closing and opening again before she could formulate her question. "Where... do you come from?"

"The next universe over."

Her mouth snapped shut. This man was in jest and she, like a silly girl, had fallen prey. "Really, Mr. Tamsen, I think the less we speak on this journey, the better."

"When you sleep, what do you dream?"

Her eyes flashed to his face. A knowing glimmer shone in his eyes. But how could he *ever* know a thing like that?

It dawned on her.

"How *much* has my father said about me?" she asked with not a little exasperation.

"Only that you are the best companion one could ask for and I'm a dunce if I don't pursue you. But as tempting as that offer may be, I'm afraid it is of little consequence to my current pursuit."

Novella's face burned crimson with both fury and humiliation. How dare her father be so bold with her? What on Earth had this Petyr Tamsen accomplished to make him so promising a suitor that Father would speak so?

"*When* did he find time to say *that*? And I am leery of inquiring about your pursuit..."

"The day he hired me—about a fortnight ago. I was supposed to lure you away from the dreaded fiancé, but, you see, I restrained myself. It wasn't until you passed me at the house party that I realized *you* were the one I had come for. It struck me like a bolt of lightning. I knew then you weren't destined to be married to that Wetherill fellow. So, when I found you fleeing the announcement, I wasn't in the least surprised."

"Mr. Tamsen, that is enough!" Her eyes flew to that red feather. Perhaps it was less a sign of the boldness and mirth of the man as to his audacity. "I haven't a clue what you could be thinking nor of what you are speaking, but you are hereby officially *relieved* from accompanying me to my aunt's. *Please,* have that coachman stop the carriage and do me the honor of respecting my demand."

Petyr eyed her some moments before, "Water."

Novella raised an irritable brow. What was he on about now?

"You dream of water," he explained, "whole bright blue oceans of it, teeming with all manner of life. And islands, hordes of them, so green and lush they're a paradise compared to this city. Then there are the dragons..."

Novella gasped as if he'd slapped her, sitting up with such force that the next bump of the carriage sent her tumbling to the opposite seat. Righting herself, she turned back to her escort.

"Who are you really, Mr. Tamsen?"

"Tamsen is my father's name actually. We don't have last names where I'm from. I merely took one to score the position with your father's newspaper. I found myself rather lost in your world for a time before I picked up the culture a bit. Lived from job to job before I afforded these fine clothes and landed with Mr. Harper. I had a feeling about him the minute I passed his offices. It wasn't him, but he was close."

"Close to what?"

"I've told you."

"Mr. Tams—that is, Sir, *whoever* you are—why on Earth would you be searching for *me?*"

Really, what was wrong with the man? And how could he know what her dreams entailed?

The carriage stopped with a lurch. Both sets of eyes flew to the train station outside the window. They'd arrived.

"What do you say, Vella?" the mysterious man inquired. "Shall I escort you from here?"

Novella stole swift breaths as her mind raced. It was no secret that this Tamsen, who wasn't really a Tamsen, who, in fact, possessed no last name at all and was aware of what she dreamed, had frightened her. She trembled where she sat as her mouth opened to disinvite him from the journey once and for all.

Listen, a deep, unexpected voice rumbled through her mind.

She stopped short, mouth dropping open as a whole new world of fear enveloped her. Where could that have come from? Was *she* the one out of her senses?

Mr. Tamsen sat forward, resting his elbows on his knees. "Miss, Harper, what was that?"

"What was... what?"

"Your face just paled considerably."

"I..." She swallowed. "It was nothing. I'm afraid we cannot continue together—"

Listen! the voice sounded again, reverberating through her person. She shivered at the sensation.

"You may come!" she cried, leaping from her seat and helping herself from the coach. She stood back breathless and pale as the driver passed her luggage to a porter. Mr. Tamsen gave directions to the man, along with the tip she ought to have given. In silence, she found herself tailing him as he sauntered through the station. The train whistled its near departure as he turned to hand her up into their car.

"Just in time," he said brightly.

Novella stepped up in muteness, waiting for him until he'd boarded where she proceeded to follow him to their seats.

"Window?" he inquired.

"Uh, hm?" she murmured lamely as her mind raced.

His grin broadened. "Window seat?"

She peered into the fairly private section, hoping others would soon be boarding at the last minute but somehow understanding they wouldn't. If she was to listen, as the mysterious voice had demanded, they were in for a long talk in the privacy of this car.

Dazedly, she took the window seat.

CHAPTER 5

THEY SAT IN SILENCE for many miles before Novella brought herself to face her companion. "I am prepared to listen, Mr. uh..."

"Call me Petyr."

She swallowed. "It is forward to call a young man one scarcely knows by his first name."

"It is my only name."

"Even so."

He shrugged. "As you wish."

"Listen—" She cringed as she used the same term the mysterious voice had spoken. "I am prepared to hear you out, but... begin, well, at the beginning. And take it slow. You must understand that you are very different from what I am accustomed."

The corner of his mouth turned up. "I imagine *you* are often considered very different from what the people of this world are accustomed."

"Why, I—" she began in offence before shrugging and waving him on. What was the use of pretending it wasn't so? She simply hadn't realized it was so obvious to a stranger.

He cleared his throat. "I apologize for my abruptness in the carriage. But *you* must understand that my pursuit of you began five years ago, spanning three planets. I was your age when I began and haven't seen my home in half that time."

Novella struggled to take the man seriously. Clearly, he wasn't in his right mind. It was surprising that her father trusted him so much that he was willing to leave his daughter in his care to any degree.

"I hail from a planet called the Greater Archipelagos," he continued. "*That* is the place you dream of."

Novella swallowed hard as her body returned to its trembling.

"It is a planet of many small islands and archipelagos. The water is honey-sweet, our peoples are simple and friendly while dragons fly and swim freely. Most importantly, the planet is governed by a council headed by a single personage called the Realm Leader. Flynn, previously of the planet Kaern, reigned in that position for a number of years before his life was taken by a rebellious sect of society, of whom we were not yet aware was in existence. Thus began my search."

He paused here, scrutinizing her face as if surveying her afresh or awaiting some response. Novella couldn't imagine how to respond. It sounded like something from a fairy novel.

He nodded as if she'd forfeited her opportunity. "I suppose I should go back even before that in order to explain my part. You see, the people of the Greater Archipelagos possess what are called the Great Gifts, bestowed by our one and only god, the Great One. In your world, I've found you merely call Him 'God.'"

Novella's eyes widened. Was this man bold enough to speak vainly of the Lord? Ought she to scold him for telling such tales? But the voice's demand played through her mind. Someone or something would not be satisfied until she'd heard him out. It was the least she could do, she supposed.

"These gifted ones consist of Hearers," he went on, "those who easily perceive the voice of the Great One, Speakers, whose tongues provoke things to occur. There are those with supernatural strength, while others can swim at unnatural rates of speed as well as breathe beneath the water's surface..."

Novella's mouth fell open as a chill coursed over her form. *Was* this man in earnest? In that last description, he had just described her to a tee.

"Among many others, there are *Seekers*. We are those with a fire in our veins to seek out the mysteries of the Great One. Iviana the Glorybringer, the widow of the slain Realm Leader, is the strongest of these and was naturally expected to seek the Great One's choice for the next leader of the realm. But, due to great grief, her emotions clouded her abilities. In the end, I was appointed for the task. Little did I imagine how *very* complex the mission would be at the time..."

His eyes fell on her.

She cleared her throat. "Well... why have you let so much time pass? Aren't your people in need of this all-important leader?"

"They certainly are. I can only imagine how things are going back there. I thought it was a mishap that landed me on this planet in this universe and, to be honest, I hadn't a clue how to return home. That's where you come in."

"Me?"

"I don't imagine the Great One was going to lead me home until I'd called out the successive Realm Leader of the Greater Archipelagos. Novella Harper, you, as I said, are the one for whom I've been searching."

Novella openly gasped before she fell to chuckling. "I'm *sure* this has all been very amusing for you, Mr. Tamsen. But I am no longer a girl of ten years. The very notion of peoples who live upon strange planets! Other *universes!* I can see why you came to work with my father. You must be quite the journalist!"

He shook his head. "I scarcely believe this myself. You don't strike me as a world leader. But while it is man's folly to look on the outward appearance, the Great One's concern is with the heart... Yours must be an exquisite thing."

She stopped short, blinking back as she worked to discover whether she had just been insulted or complimented. In the end, it mattered little. She was through with this game.

"You certainly know how to pass the time of a lengthy journey. Now, why don't you tell me who you *really* are and from where you truly hail?" Indeed, she was more than intrigued by the gentleman by this time, mischievous as he had been.

Mr. Tamsen scowled for the first time, crossing his arms and peering out the window. *"He* must convince you then. I see I have gotten nowhere in my haste."

"Who?" she couldn't help asking.

"God."

She blinked back at him as he glared out the window. His large jaw flexed with irritation, which wasn't entirely fair since *he* was the one pulling *her* leg. Apparently, he couldn't bear that she had not fallen for his jest. It was she who ought to be irritated with him for wasting her time with such fancies.

Yet, as the hours passed and he refused to speak, her mind was left with nothing but to race over all he'd spoken. Most of her thoughts maintained the audacity of the fellow to weave her a tall tale and throw a tantrum after. Yet, when the trail of her thoughts hit upon his mention of those Swimmers, her heart raced with both fear and an inexplicable exhilaration. *Could* it be she wasn't the only one like herself? If so, what could *Mother* possibly know about it? She, who hated fairytales and legends and clung to traditions, who always wanted everything in order, who worked hard to be the perfect wife and mother—an acceptable socialite.

Novella shook her head. It could not be that her mother possessed some secret knowledge of a fantastic world. Yet, was it possible the man had guessed at her well-kept secret? If so, it was cruel to use it in his storytelling, as if she were some peculiar creature of myth. She wished to scold him, but the sight of his furrowed brows gave her pause. He'd been smiling and amused from the moment she'd met him and had quite suddenly given way to sulking? She shook her head. The sooner they reached her aunt's home, the better.

As the train slowed before the nearest station to Aunt Sylvie's estate, Novella's eyes flew to Mr. Tamsen's face. He did not appear to perceive that they had arrived. It was as if he were in his own world, which was somewhat troubling. She must write to her father about his imaginings. Then again, they were likely why he'd hired him. Sensational news sold like hotcakes.

She stood to her feet as the train drew to a stop. Gradually, Mr. Tamsen unfolded his arms and drew to his own feet, opening the compartment with a gesture of his hand to allow her exit. When he wasn't teasing, he had perfectly suitable manners. The problem was that he seemed usually to be teasing.

Before long, he had both her and her luggage tucked into a carriage. To her surprise, he opted to sit with the coachman. She found herself uncomfortable with this. She wasn't accustomed to angering people to the point of shunning. Those she was unable to please simply found her odd. The fact that Gregory Wetherill had wanted her at all had been a puzzle to her. She'd long ago decided he simply liked the challenge, for he had known that she did not like him. Now, as it happened, he'd possessed a *whole line* of lady friends. What would life with him have been like? Already, she couldn't help noticing he wasn't half the gentleman this peculiar "Petyr" was. Gregory would never have taken care of her luggage, paid her tips and quietly transported her even though he was annoyed. Likely, she'd have been toting Gregory around as if she were his nursemaid all her life.

As the carriage pulled up the long drive to her aunt's estate, Novella gazed on the property afresh. For so long, she'd dreaded her trips here. Now, she looked on it as a haven—a place where she would be free to gather her thoughts and determine the course of her life. Also, she could maintain a distance from this playful if helpful young man.

He appeared at her carriage door with something like humility on his face. "As you see, I got you here safely. No harm done, eh?"

"I suppose not," she replied wistfully, not entirely certain if she agreed. Her mind would be spinning with his tale. It was very like the novels she so favored—the ones her mother disapproved. "Thank you for your service. I... apologize I couldn't take part in your joke."

His eyes flew to hers as if he would speak on the subject again. Instead, he stepped away to instruct the coachman about the baggage. As Novella's aunt appeared at the door, she raced to meet her.

"I hope I haven't inconvenienced you, Aunt Sylvie!" she called with uncustomary cheer. It felt good to be with someone familiar again.

"Whatever are you running about like a lad for, child?" her aunt chastised. "For heavens, you're like your father in more ways than one."

She offered her cheek for a kiss which Novella gave against her better desire. How she wished the women in her life were not always so correcting. It was why she favored her father so much and, furthermore, why she was saddened by his behavior of the last two days.

"And who is this?" Aunt Sylvia began disapprovingly as Mr. Tamsen approached with the coachman. Abruptly, her brows flew up as her face softened into a wide smile. "Why, *Petyr!* You look as if you've come up in the world—as I *conjectured* you would."

He replied with an elegant bow before rising and kissing Aunt Sylvie's cheek. Aunt Sylvia actually went so far as to give him a pat on his own cheek as her eyes glowed up at his winsome face.

"But what has brought you back to me, you good boy?" she questioned.

"I hadn't realized until we'd arrived that you were related to the Harpers," he answered transparently. "I have recently come into Mr. Harper's employment and was tasked to see Miss Harper safely to your doorstep."

"Working for my little brother's paper? Well, doesn't that just suit! It's a wonder I never thought to send you his way myself, but it seems you did not require my aid." She took him in afresh. "You're looking so fine and fitting now, Petyr, compared to the half-starved fellow who appeared at my back door in search of work. Well, you must come in and take tea with us, won't you, and you must catch me up after these two years."

"I thank you warmly, Mrs. Merchant, for the offer. But I'm afraid I must be getting back."

"Oooh, surely you can spare twenty minutes?" the aunt begged.

Novella listened on in wide-eyed wonderment. Aunt Sylvia never favored anyone. How had this man managed to so win over both her father *and* aunt? And could it really only have been two years ago that he was half-starved and begging for work like a common tramp? She looked him up and down as if searching for signs of so recent a rise in means.

"I really cannot," he insisted. "But I'll be sure to stop by again in future. How does that sound?"

Novella hoped he did not mean any time within the next few weeks.

"Very well," Aunt Sylvia relented with a squeeze to his hand. "I'm *proud* of you, Petyr. Your manners have quite improved. I see I did you some good after all."

The man's face brightened considerably. "You were very good to me, ma'am. But I'm afraid your niece will have something to say as concerns my manners." He cast Novella a wink.

"As if *Novella* is in any position to criticize," the aunt started in, "the little girl always collecting snakes and snails and puppy dog tales, climbing trees and scraping her knees!"

Mr. Tamsen's eyes turned on Novella with fresh appreciation. "I'm afraid she must have grown out of all that, Mrs. Merchant. Fairytales are quite behind her, so I've learned. Now, I'll wish you two a pleasant visit. Good afternoon, ladies." With the tip of his hat, he returned to the carriage.

Aunt Sylvia's eyes shone as she watched him walk away. "What a *good* boy that Petyr is. It's a pity he comes from so low an upbringing or he might have made a match for you. Then again, there are plenty of fish in the sea and I suppose he has schools of ladies after him, eh?"

Novella opted not to answer. She knew nothing either of the man or his love interests. But was everyone's obsession with her love life? She was *quite* finished being coupled with anyone. She'd just escaped one prison. Leaping into another with a *journalist* was quite another.

CHAPTER 6

Novella tossed for several nights on end. Her dreams concerning what Mr. Tamsen had coined the "Greater Archipelagos" grew frequent and unrelenting. The man's words were playing with her subconscious mind, forming an inescapable experience in the night. And while they began on a blissful beach with golden-blue water waving all around, they always ended with the approach of a menacing older man. At this juncture, she awoke in a cold sweat, assuring herself that it was Mr. Tamsen's fault. It wasn't polite to tell tales of leaders being murdered by rebellious political factions. If ever she spoke to him again, she would tell him so.

"You are ill," Aunt Sylvia quipped after a week.

"I am not, Aunt Sylvie. Only I seem to be suffering from a bout of nightmares. I'm not getting any sleep."

"Mm," the woman mused. "We will have to pray about that, won't we?"

Novella nodded her agreement. She herself never seemed to consider personages such as God or, as Petyr had called Him, the "Great One." Why was it that everyone around her thought to pray but herself? Didn't she believe in Him? Surely, only heathens forsook the Christian church. And her family had attended Sunday services all her life. Perhaps it was Mother's attitude that affected hers, for it was

Father who insisted they attend. Mother, on the other hand, most often seemed to be holding a grudge against the unseen God.

"Thank you, Aunt Sylvie," she answered doubtfully.

As the evenings passed, her dreams were fewer and far between. No longer was she hunted by the menacing man. If she dreamed at all, she soaked in the warm waters of a vast ocean beneath a pink sunrise with rays that shone like a kiss from the heavens. When she awoke, she felt as if she were awaking in the safety of her parents' arms as she had on occasion as a child.

With the sweet relief of real rest, Novella was afforded hours upon hours on the plains of her aunt's vast property. Her soul longed for something on which she could not just put her finger. She was determined to discover it before she returned home. This was her opportunity to regroup and start afresh in order to inform her parents of the direction of her life.

"You need a husband," Aunt Sylvia spoke over another breakfast.

Novella leaped in her seat. "I have only just escaped one engagement, Aunt Sylvie!"

"But it isn't good for a girl your age to sit idle. You require purpose. I've seen how you roam as if searching for some way to vent your energy. I tell you it is dangerous for a girl to remain so unoccupied."

Novella bit her tongue while she worked to dissipate her wrath. She had long learned she gained nothing with a swift retort. "I wish there was something for a woman to do besides just becoming a wife and mother."

Her aunt dropped her cup into its saucer, blinking back at her niece as if she'd used the name of the Lord in vain. "What do you imagine would be more rewarding for a woman, Miss Vella?"

Novella shrugged. "It isn't that I wish *never* to be married. Only that I want to experience something real first."

"And what do you call 'real?'"

"That's just it. I don't know. I mentioned travel to Mother and Father and they didn't much like the idea."

Aunt Sylvia nodded. "A jaunt about Europe wouldn't do you any harm. You could use a little polishing. But I really think nice girls ought to be content to settle down at a young age."

Novella released a long breathe. "I wonder if my distaste is due to the fact that the only young man with whom I have even neared the question was so very dissatisfying."

"Mm," her aunt mused over a sip of tea. "It's too bad about that young Mr. Wetherill. He appeared so shiny on the outside, but the good Lord looks at the heart, you know."

"Does he?" Vella questioned almost breathlessly as she recalled the words that Mr. Tamsen had spoken on the train.

"Fetch my Bible from the mantle and I'll show you."

Aunt Sylvia spent the next half hour dramatizing the story of King David many years before he ever became king. It seemed he'd been a humble shepherd, the youngest of a whole line of strapping older brothers. Yet, the wise old prophet passed by every one of them until his discovery of the boy in the field. This lad he anointed to one day rule as king of his nation.

Novella shivered as she considered what that foolish Mr. Tamsen had attempted to convince her of—that *she* was destined to a similar fate. What nonsense! She was the material of neither kings nor shepherds—just an ordinary girl and not popular at that. She was Novella... the girl who could breathe underwater.

At the end of the account, Novella restored the Bible to its place. In silence, she returned to her seat. Her aunt seemed not to notice her meditation as she finished her tea.

"Aunt Sylvie," Novella began, "how do you think God sees someone like... me?"

Aunt Sylvia considered for many moments before delicately setting down her cup. "Pliable."

Novella nearly sputtered. "What do you mean by that?"

"You're like the clay in the hands of the potter. You're yet unformed, but you possess potential... Perhaps more than I've long given you credit for." She appeared surprised.

Novella raised her brows. "What makes you say so?"

"I've been looking at your outward appearance. He's the One Who knows your end from your beginning. I suddenly get the feeling He quite likes you." Standing from her seat, she added quietly, "And I think you may be right. You *are* intended for great things. But great things take time and a hunk of clay must spin upon the center of a wheel to find its form. Then, of course, there is the pruning, drying, glazing... and the furnace."

The woman stood blinking down as if she'd just returned from another world. Wordlessly, she ventured to the mantle, took down her Bible and ascended the stairs. "I will be praying for you, Miss Vella," she called down before shutting the door to her personal study.

Novella considered her aunt's peculiar exit. The woman was known for her Biblical knowledge and earnestness for the Lord. The niece often presumed this was why her aunt could not seem to approve of anyone. She knew the law aspect of religion a little too well. Yet, she'd liked *Petyr Tamsen* of all people.

With a muted growl at the memory of him, she stood from the tea table and tossed on her cloak. Though it was chillier than usual, she craved her regular breath of air. Aunt Sylvia's home was nothing if not stuffy. But her property was nearly endless. Traipsing about every corner of it helped appease her yearning to journey, especially since this was about as far as she was ever going to get.

Today, it was to be a river walk. She'd perceived its dribbling the day before but had been forced to turn back as it was nearing suppertime. She marched for it directly so as not to lose time. It proved no disappointment as it sparkled under the rays that reached though the shifting branches above. Novella considered removing her shoes in order to dip her feet but knew the temptation to leap in bodily would be too great. This was another reason she'd avoided the river the day before. She'd been well trained to avoid water. But it did not seem to lure her today. She was content merely to walk beside it, enjoying the cool breeze whipping through the trees, watching the golden leaves fall like rain around her.

Watch your step, spoke the voice from over a week prior.

Novella froze. She'd convinced herself that it had been a wild figment of her imagination. Now, she knew it was not so. Or was Novella Harper losing her mind? Perhaps that strange Petyr did not exist at all and she had suffered a kind of psychosis. She'd heard of such happenings.

"Be still, Vella," she murmured to herself.

Of course it was a simple imagining. People suffered them from time to time. With a forced shrug, she walked on. But the patch of bald earth in front of her was soft from recent rainfall. Her feet slipped beneath her, transferring her into the rushing river.

The current was swift and strong. Novella fought to keep her head afloat, but so demanding was the current that she found herself being plowed into rocks and fallen logs. Without warning, she was sucked beneath a strainer – desperately dangerous with the water level so high.

Gracious Lord! she called frantically in her mind. *Help me!*

The water was illuminated by a strange blue light. Her form flooded with energy. She felt herself gain control of faculties. It was suddenly as if there were no current at all. She was *strong*. She flew from the depths of the fallen tree as swift as a gull at the shore. Like a fish with wings, she swam against the river's current, easily dodging obstacles. Before she knew it, she was crawling onto a grassy haven.

Bent over on elbows and knees, she gasped for breath. It occurred to her that she might have breathed the entire time. Her breath had merely been stolen by sheer terror and then exhilaration. Her eyes fell to her glowing veins – their light now slowly dissipating. What was this? She clenched her now ordinary hands into fists.

What was *wrong* with her?

CHAPTER 7

Novella was freezing by the time she reached the house. Her cloak had been torn off in the water she now wore like a garment of ice. The beautifully chill day had become a peril if she did not quickly restore warmth to her bones.

"*Vella!*" Aunt sylvia gasped, forfeiting the always proper 'Miss.' "For pity's sake, child, what have you been playing at?!"

"I s-slipped into the river," Novella informed through chattering teeth.

Aunt Sylvia gasped again, reaching for the nearest quilt and pulling it snuggly about her niece. "After all that rain last evening, you might have been killed! Thank the *good* Lord I happened to be praying for you. Let's get you upstairs and into a hot bath. I suppose water is the last place you wish to be just now, but you'll catch your death if we aren't careful."

Novella allowed herself to be ushered upstairs by the unaccustomed tenderness of her aunt. Never had the woman treated her with such concern. After a long soak, she was tucked into dry garments and a bed heated by hot water bottles.

It was dark when next she awoke. Never in her life had she slept so much of a day away. When she discovered she was wet with sweat, she feared the worst before realizing the fireplace had roared during her nap. By the height of the flame, it had recently been stoked.

Aunt Sylvie soon arrived with a tray of steaming tea, leek and carrot soup and a side of fresh baked pumpkin bread."

"You'll have to show me you can finish this bowl before you may even taste the bread," her aunt notified. With a small smile, she added, "I thought you deserved a treat after your scare. The groundskeeper tells me that river is as high as it has ever been. Claims not even a fish could swim it. It is a *miracle* you returned home alive." She took the liberty of stroking her niece's temple. "How are you feeling, Vella?"

Novella swallowed a mouthful of the rich broth. "As if it never happened. Really, Aunt, I'm hotter than a panting dog and don't feel the least bit weak. I can't believe it is evening already."

Aunt Sylvia felt her forehead, eyeing the girl with doubt before giving way to relief. "Thank heaven. We can't have two invalids on our hands."

"Two?"

"I meant to keep it until tomorrow, but it seems your mother's illness has worsened. Your father sent a telegram asking that you return on the morrow in order to care for her. It seems the servants lack your touch."

"Mother is *worse?* What is it? Does he say?"

Aunt Sylvia clucked. "The common flu, I'm sure. She should be well in a week or so."

Novella was in no way appeased. "I wish I might have gone today."

"Not on your life, young lady. You clearly needed that rest. You'll get more tonight and awake without a fever before I let you travel."

"I'm fine, Aunt Sylvie. But what shall I do for a chaperone? Can Charles be spared?"

"Your father is sending Petyr for you as soon as I send a telegram that you are able to return."

"*Mr. Tamsen?*" Novella groaned.

"Don't you care for him much, Vella?" Aunt Sylvia asked with surprising softness.

Novella was uncertain of how to respond, knowing how her aunt felt about him. "It's only that I do not know him very well, I suppose."

Her aunt nodded with the sudden drifting of her eyes to the fire. It was as if she saw something Novella did not. Aunt Sylvia mused, "He must be a stranger boy than I gave him credit for. You're going to watch your step, aren't you, Vella?" Her face turned to inquire of her niece with concern.

Novella blinked back. This was an abrupt change after the glowing way she'd received him before. What had transpired in Aunt Sylvia's mind?

"I certainly am," Novella promised.

But her aunt seemed to have forgotten all about the exchange when Petyr arrived late the following afternoon. The woman's eyes glowed with affection as he tipped his hat to her, followed by a peck on her cheek.

"I didn't expect to see you so soon again!" Aunt Sylvia cooed.

"I seem to be my employer's righthand man—even afforded the pleasure of escorting his beloved daughter." His eyes went to Novella's as if in search of something. After a moment, he asked, "Are you quite ready?"

Novella nodded as the coachmen took her bags. "I do hope the train won't suffer any delays. I'd like to see Mother as soon as possible."

"She's no worse from what I hear," he soothed. "She only wants for your presence by her side."

Before Novella knew it, she was enclosed in Aunt Sylvia's embrace. "I am sorry our visit was cut short. The two of you must come see me again very soon."

Novella pulled back with a blush at the unaccustomed display of affection. "Thank you for letting me drop in, Aunt Sylvie. I'll write you of how Mother is fairing."

"Do. But I am in no way concerned. She's always been quite strong. Although... she *was* rather frail when first she turned up at our door—not entirely dissimilar to how you arrived those years ago, Petyr."

Novella took a step back. "Turned up... like Petyr?" she murmured. "Is that how she and Father met?"

"I'd presumed you'd been told all about it. She was such a pretty, fragile little thing with such peculiar manners. She was like a kind of fairy creature. But your *father* didn't mind a bit, nor the fact she had no money nor absolutely *any* family to speak of. Hard as she worked to deny him, he was *quite* determined to care for her. The rest is history of course."

Novella considered this. Her mother was so very proper and orderly and *perfect*. Could it truly be she had appeared on Father's doorstep as a homeless tramp, that her father had felt the need to care for her by way of matrimony? Had they even loved each other? It sounded rather as if her father had loved her mother and Mother had lost the battle.

"But... where had she come from?"

"Do you know... she was ill for so many weeks that I never did learn just where. Your father mentioned some island or other. She certainly was brown enough to have lived by the sea."

Novella felt the heat of Petyr's eyes on her. He was searching her again. What could he think of a young woman whose father had married her mother because she was beautiful and helpless?

He cleared his throat. "Our train is due to leave in less than twenty minutes. We really ought to be started."

"Oh, so soon again?" Aunt Sylvia complained. "I had a whole tea prepared for your arrival—with *crumpets.*" She spoke the last as if it had been an old weakness of his.

His brows flew upward. "If you had any idea how much I've missed those, you would understand my regret."

Nothing lost, Aunt Sylvia raced to the kitchen, returning with a basket. "For your journey home. I had Cook throw in some muffins as well, Vella."

Novella beamed up at her aunt. Things had changed between them, though she couldn't just say why. "Take care, Auntie."

Novella hadn't even realized she'd accepted the offer of Petyr's arm until he was handing her into the carriage, so engrossed was her mind in the tale that had just been revealed. She scarcely noticed the carriage ride before they arrived at the station. If only her mother wasn't ill, she might race home and inquire of the truth. No wonder her mother was always so secretive about her musings. She was *not* the woman she pretended to be on a daily basis. But if it was true, *who was she?*

It wasn't until they had boarded the train that she noticed Petyr observing her again.

"What *is* it, Mr. Tamsen?" she pressed.

"I was just wondering if you were working it out."

"Working what out?"

"Your heritage."

"Am I to understand that you know more about my parents than I do?"

"I know very little, but I conjecture much."

"You think my mother was some fishmonger's child, don't you?"

He released a chuckle. "I couldn't say just *whose* child she was, but she may well have been that."

Anger churned in Novella as she redirected her attention to the window. How dare he conjecture anything about her family? He worked for her father but had no business delving into their family history. Without a doubt, she must speak with her father about him. He had often taken her advice in past.

"I don't suppose anything interesting happened during your visit?" he next inquired.

She narrowed her eyes on him. "What are you getting at?"

His shrug was all innocence. "Nothing. I only hoped."

"Hoped?"

"That He had troubled Himself to reveal the truth."

"Who?"

"The Great One."

Novella groaned, smacking a hand to her forehead. "Not *that* again, Mr. Tamsen, *please.*"

"You're glowing."

Novella opened her mouth to correct his boldness when her eyes flew to her hands.

"Not again..." she murmured in disbelief. "Not *here!*"

In place of the blue glow the day before, her veins now shone a vibrant crimson. With an abrupt lurch of the train, she was tossed to the floor. Petyr dove to help her back onto her seat, inquiring of her wellbeing.

"Yes, yes, I'm fine," she retorted. "Don't trouble yourself." Her gaze flew to her hands to discover that all evidence of the light had vanished. Her eyes flew to Petyr. How was she ever to explain?

"Miss Harper..." he began calmly, "I'm afraid you've just placed us in a complicated predicament."

"Excuse me?"

His eyes flew to the window.

Novella followed his gaze, instantly leaping to stand before the window. No *wonder* the train had stopped so hastily. Not only had they run off the tracks, they had entered a kind of *desert*, if her father's encyclopedias had taught her anything.

"What on *Earth?* How could the engineer have got things so very wrong? Where *are* we, do you think?"

"You'd know the geography better than I, but I'd say we're not in England anymore."

She spun to face him. "How ridiculous! What can you mean?"

"It wasn't *my* doing. You were the one glowing."

"Wha—you think *I*... What an impossible notion! How could *I* have—" She sputtered before stopping short and falling into her seat. Stealing a few long breaths, she regathered herself. "*Mr.* Tamsen, won't you trouble yourself to inquire of a porter just what the trouble is?"

He folded his arms. "I'm afraid they'd know far less than we do. They didn't witness your display."

"B-b-but..." She glanced down at her hands, turning them over and again. The day before, she had cried for help and the light had come. She'd then managed the unthinkable. Today, they'd glowed again and... now this lunatic was suggesting she'd somehow derailed their train in the middle of the Kalahari. The very idea!

Mr. Tamsen leaned forward to rest his elbows on his knees. "I told you you're not from around here," he spoke in a deep voice. "If I'm right, you'll experience even stranger occurrences than this. I imagine, now that I've found you, your giftings are blooming. After years of buried, pent-up power, we could have a real mess on our hands if you do not allow me to accompany you to where you truly belong."

Her mouth dropped open. He really believed his story. As a tear drifted down her cheek... she realized she was coming to believe it too.

"What is *wrong* with me?" she whispered.

"Nothing at all. You're just not entirely descended from around these parts."

"Well, how are we to get *back?*"

He sat against the seat rest and folded his arms. *"I* didn't do a thing. Moreover, I can't. Not my area. I'm afraid it is entirely up to you."

It was Novella's turn to sit forward. "I didn't *intend* to do it in the first place! I can scarcely believe it *was* me except for my..." She eyed her hands as if they were an enemy.

"I'll admit this is a pickle," he said with a sigh. "But, you see, He had to get your attention somehow. I do wish I'd been better acquainted with a Transporter... Of course, I've never known one capable of hijacking whole *trains.* But I suppose we must try. So many people lost in a desert... could make for a regrettable condition."

Novella eyed him with numb impatience.

"Picture the tracks we were on," he directed, "and... *will* us back there."

"Picture the—How very *childish...*" Yet, she did as told, wishing with all her heart that they were back, that this impossible incident had not taken place, that she was *normal* and that Petyr had never entered her life.

"Open your eyes," he ordered.

She blinked out the window in disbelief. Though the train wasn't moving as yet, the scenery was undoubtedly that which ran between her aunt's estate and home. A chill coursed through her.

"You know what this means, don't you?" he questioned with his customary grin.

She gazed helplessly back at him.

"You are *definitely* my ticket home, Novella Harper."

CHAPTER 8

A KNOCK AT THE compartment door sent Novella bolting to her feet. Were they come to lock her away for commandeering the train? How could she ever explain?

"Be seated, Miss Harper," Petyr directed as he rose to answer.

The conductor appeared dripping with perspiration, his gray hair askew. "Eh, we apologize for the delay, folks. Not sure what happened there, but we're having the train examined before we move on. I'm afraid we're in for a long wait, but we'll do our best to get things moving as soon as possible." He turned with hat in hand before looking back with, "Eh, er, uh... thank you for your patience."

"Of course," Petyr answered easily. "We appreciate your thoroughness." He handed the man a sizable tip. Novella realized that Petyr must feel some responsibility for their circumstances. She rose too and added her purse to the offering.

"Sorry..." she murmured without thinking.

The conductor blinked down at her before bowing his thanks and going his way.

"*Sorry?*" Petyr questioned with amusement as he closed the compartment. "Do you feel the need to present your blunder to the engineer as well?"

Novella stood before the window with arms wrapped about herself in self-protection. She scanned the horizon. As she'd feared, it seemed there had, indeed, been a delay on the train. She'd simply never imagined it could be due to her own incredible blunder.

She turned to face Petyr. "So, I am…" She swallowed almost painfully. "That is, *you* are… an extraterrestrial?"

"*No*—er, *well*… I don't know." He appeared bewitched by the idea. A mirthful smirk communicated he thought her charming for having posed the question.

"If you're going to laugh at me all the time, I shan't speak again!" she admonished as she returned to her seat. Things were complicated enough without always being made to feel herself the center of a joke.

"I apologize, Miss Harper," he replied as he retook his own. "I am unaccustomed to sensitive, offendable young ladies such as the ones of this world."

Novella flashed fire with her eyes.

"Where I'm from," he continued, "women slay dark dragons, invent unique mathematics, design portals to other worlds—which is how I happened to come to this one in the first place. With *them,* one does not feel the need to watch one's expressions quite so carefully."

Novella worked to remain offended with him but hearing of such women was entrancing. It made her blood burn for what *could* be. Swiftly, she glanced at her hands. With a shriek, she discovered they were glowing once again. She proceeded to pat her hands against her skirts as if to put them out.

"What *is* this?!" she cried as if harassed.

"That is the fire of the blood of one who contains a Great Gift. Or, in your case, a number of them." He knelt down on the floor before her to take control of her fidgeting hands. Once she had relinquished them, he proceeded to examine. "I will say…" he spoke thoughtfully, "I have never seen this hue."

"Wh-what do you mean?"

"I mean, I've no idea which gift this signifies. It is neither the color of a Swimmer nor a Transporter, which I think we have concluded you are both. This color means you've another gift and a unique one... one I cannot name." He looked up at her and dropped her hands. "Anything might happen now."

They watched one another as if awaiting the culmination of a ticking time bomb. Quite suddenly, the typical pink of her hands was restored.

Petyr returned to his seat. "You are more interesting than I gave you credit for. Perhaps you *will* prove as impressive as the women of my world."

As Novella gazed down at her hands with relief that she hadn't landed their train in the ocean, she worked not to feel gratified by the comment. "But *how* can I descend from this other planet you've named? I was born *here*, have grown up *here*."

"*Someone* in your line was of the Greater Archipelagos."

"My father can trace his ancestry back to Queen Elizabeth I!"

"And your mother?"

She hesitated as her blood turned cold. "I am not certain," she skirted.

He chuckled warmly. "I think it is clear that she is our track. You must inquire of her when she is well enough."

"I shall do as I please," she answered haughtily, unable to keep from feeling offended that he thought her mother not what she seemed even if it was entirely plausible. Still, her mother *couldn't* have come from the place this Petyr described. She was so very... *English.*

The sun had already completed its retirement by the time the train pulled into the London station. The car was immediately flooded with employees, who doubtless had heard of the strange derailment. When Petyr lost no time in spiriting Novella into a carriage, she put up no fight. Not only did she fear being found out, her anxiety for her mother was at an all-time high.

"You said she was no worse?" she questioned as they rode.

He nodded. Eyeing her fidgeting hands, he added, "Why don't you relinquish the matter to the Great One?"

He was right. It seemed everyone but herself thought to speak to God. After all, she had cried out to him for salvation from the rushing river and had emerged a miracle story.

Ignoring Petyr's attempts to aid her from the carriage, she rushed to the door. She had scarcely taken three steps before her father appeared, stopping her in her tracks. A solid grip on either shoulder detained her while she took in his face. Her eyes questioned him. He shook his head as his sad eyes met hers.

"She isn't managing well, Vella. The doctor claims she... may not make it. We must be very careful of her."

Novella bit her lower lip as tears flooded her eyes. She wrapped her arms about his torso, imagining how he had been suffered without her in the face of such news. His arms encircled her. It was only the breeze from the open door that alerted her to Petyr's presence among them before her father spoke.

"I appreciate your service," he spoke over her shoulder. "And I regret you two endured that train derailment. I am glad to see you are both well. I hope you will remain as our guest for the evening."

"I appreciate the offer," Petyr answered.

Novella wished he would leave. His presence in the midst of her home only spoiled any sense of normalcy. He knew better than she what she was and she wished she was merely a typical English woman. She pulled back from her father's embrace.

"I must see her now."

"Of course. Keep quiet in case she is asleep. She requires all the rest we can manage."

Novella raced silently through the halls of her home. It wasn't until she'd turned the knob and cracked the door to her mother's chamber that she realized Petyr had taken the liberty of following her.

"What are you doing here?" she whispered in frustration. Couldn't the man afford them a little privacy in their hardship?

He opened his mouth to answer when his eyes froze on something in the room beyond. Her eyes followed his gaze. Mother lay sleeping while beside the bed knelt a woman near her mother's age with her mother's hand grasped within her own. Her head was bent as if in prayer. Another woman, somewhat younger, stood in watch. Her eyes were locked on Petyr.

Novella entered in confusion. "I'm sorry," she murmured, catching the sudden attention of the woman kneeling beside the bed, "Father didn't mention any visitors. Are you from the church?"

Her question was answered as she took in their clothing. They were dressed something like the Grecian warriors of the history books, if somewhat more feminine. Decidedly, they were not from the church. They were *not* English.

"Petyr!" the woman on the floor exclaimed, flying to her feet. "Where have you *been* all this time? We'd begun to believe you were dead."

Petyr bowed his head reverently before stepping forward. "It's a *long* story... but I've found her." He gestured to Novella. "Though only just last week."

The strange woman turned to Novella, eyeing her for what felt like an eternity. It was as if all the air had gone out of the room as those bright blue eyes peered into her soul, sifting out its secrets. Abruptly, she approached and, without consent, placed hands on the top of Novella's head. Tipping her chin toward the ceiling, she chanted in an indecipherable language. Novella stood helpless as waves of what felt like invisible oil coursed over her. Instantly, she was flooded with confidence, boldness, certainty. She felt she might take on the whole world if she must. In the next moment, her body glowed, consuming the room with its light. She nearly cried out, fearful she might inadvertently do something reckless. It was only the knowledge of her mother on death's door that maintained her quiet.

Without calamity, the light dissipated. The stranger stepped back and the waves ceased. Even the sensation of confidence lessened. Yet, as Novella stood gazing back at the woman of the blue eyes, she felt herself buzzing from the occurrence.

CHAPTER 9

"YOU MUST HEAL NIMUA," the woman informed.

"Heal Mother?"

"The Great One has anointed you for the enormous undertaking that lies before you. You have been afforded every Great Gift under the sun. There is very little you cannot do."

Novella stood stunned. Everything Petyr had told her was true. These people must be from his world—the one of which she had so long dreamed.

"I cannot believe all this..." she whispered.

"Well, *do*," the woman insisted with impatience, "or your mother will die. My gifts are waning, or I would do it myself."

"Do *you* possess all these gifts?"

"I used to boast a number of them. Now, do as I instruct and Nimua will live."

"How do you know my mother?"

A spark entered the woman's eyes. "We were the very closest of friends once upon a time. She made me welcome in her world when I first arrived."

"In her world..." Novella gasped disbelievingly. Even this strange woman was not originally of the amazing world from which her mother was supposed to have come. *Who was her mother?* More importantly, how had she ended up here?

"Close your eyes," the woman ordered.

Without understanding just why, Novella obeyed.

"Ask the Great One how he wishes you to perform the healing and do whatever He says."

Novella emptied the forefront of her mind in wait of some occurrence, while the back of her mind expected nothing at all.

Take her hand, the familiar voice reverberated through her form like the surprisingly warm sensation of a lion's purr. It was the one she'd heard thrice before, though far less demanding. She felt the corner of her mouth turn up.

Command her to melt.

"Melt?" she questioned in sudden confusion.

Her heart toward me is ice, the purring explained. *I wish to heal her in more ways than one.*

Novella opened her eyes to find the strange woman watching her with satisfaction.

"Do what he says," she urged.

Novella didn't have to be told twice. She knelt beside the bed. Taking Mother's soft hand into her own, she commanded, "Melt."

Her mother's mouth opened with what sounded like a relieved sigh. Her feet twitched and curled beneath the covers as they often did when she was awaking. Her eyes opened. But instead of finding her daughter, they fell on the blue-eyed woman.

"Ivi?" she gasped like a happy girl.

"Nim," the woman – Ivi - returned with a grin in her voice and the crinkling of her eyes.

Mother's hand slipped from Novella's as she sat up. "What on Earth am I doing in bed?"

"What on *Earth* is correct," Ivi agreed. "Do you have any idea how *long* I searched for you after you leaped into that portal?"

Mother appeared perplexed, as if having trouble remembering. "That's right, I... I was running. I no longer cared what happened to me... Oh, *Necoli!*" Her momentary joy melted into tears as she planted her face into her hands.

Ivi sauntered to the bed to sit on its edge and stroke her old friend's back. "Dear Nimua," she cooed affectionately. "Release it to the Anointed One."

After a good long cry, Mother accepted the handkerchief Petyr offered. Drying her face and blowing her nose, her eyes found her daughter's. The woman appeared liberated.

"Oh, *Vella*," she began, "I suppose you're terribly confused. This is my old friend, Iviana the Glorybringer." For the first time, she noticed the second woman, who had not spoken as yet. "And Era!"

The younger woman approached the bed, bending down for a hug. "You are *wild,* you know it?" Era spoke. "How many people drop into entirely unfamiliar worlds and make a life for themselves?"

"Present company excluded of course," Petyr spoke from the door.

The women looked up as if only just remembering him.

"Mr. Tamsen?" Mother questioned. "What are you doing in my bedroom?"

"He's with us," Iviana explained. "That is, I sent him years ago. This is really quite a reunion."

Petyr cleared his throat. "If you don't mind my asking... how are things at home?"

Iviana's face paled considerably. "They're not great anymore, that is certain. With you gone so long, things began to unravel. Some said you were dead. Others kept up the faith. I... retreated into my grief."

"Your grief?" Nimua questioned with concern.

Iviana nodded, chin dropping to her chest. "Flynn is dead, Nim."

"Oh, *Ivi...*" Mother gasped.

"A fractious remnant was quietly gathering in the shadows. Their first move in the open was to take his life."

Mother gripped her friend's hand. "I don't understand. Everything was thriving when I left. How did things get so wrong? Where is the Great One?"

Iviana released a sigh. "Do you recall what you said when Necoli passed away?"

Mother's eyes darted between hers as if working to remember. "I had a dream... A voice told me that his death signified the emergence of a new dispensation. But if we weren't careful, it would be stolen."

Iviana nodded. "You know Flynn, *dear* as he was, was always faulty. He... made a bad deal when the rebel faction first emerged, promised things he shouldn't have promised and opened a door for our enemy to harass the realm. He was the first victim."

"I am so *sorry* I wasn't there for you," Mother nearly sobbed. Her eyes fluttered to Novella's. "Flynn was Iviana's husband and the leader of the planet. Necoli was... my first husband. My grief at losing him provoked me to do, as Era put it, a wild thing. I leaped into a portal without setting a destination. That is how I ended up on Earth."

Novella looked on her mother with fresh eyes. *Never* had she guessed that Mother had been married before Father, let alone was from another world. She swallowed. "Aunt Sylvia said you turned up at their door out of the blue."

"Did she?" Nimua asked with amusement. "I thought she'd take that secret to her grave. She never approved of your father marrying me and I can't say I blame her. But, you see, he claimed it was love at first sight and... he wouldn't let me go. *Thank God.*"

A smile curled Novella's lips. Her mother *did* love her father.

"Ivi," Nimua continued, "I was so *angry* with the Great One. I hated Him, but He wouldn't leave me. I could feel Him wherever I went. That was why I used the portal in an effort to escape Him, but... He never let me go. I can see it now. He made your Father love me and he thawed my heart enough to love him in return. I don't know what would have become of me otherwise. And this..." She gestured to Novella. "This is the daughter the Great One afforded me."

Iviana's eyes crinkled again. "It is an honor to meet you, Novella. Any daughter of Nim's is a friend of mine." The smile faded as she restored her attention to Petyr. "To answer your question, our world was in nigh anarchy before the Great One awoke me from my self-concern to the needs of those around me. I realized we were in dire need of a leader to restore a sense of unity. I appointed your father to the task."

After some contemplation over these revelations, Petyr merely nodded. "What brought you *here?*"

"For the first time since you left, I felt a stirring from the Great One. In a dream, He showed me this planet and gave me the coordinates to enter into the portal. He said... it was *time.*"

"Time?"

"Time for me to awaken, I imagine. Time for Nimua to melt. Time for Novella here to take her rightful place."

Novella felt her face flush as all eyes fell on her.

"Her rightful place?" Mother questioned.

"I sent Petyr to locate Flynn's replacement... and he has found her."

Mother's eyes shot from Novella to Petyr. "*My* Vella? Are you quite certain?"

He nodded gravely.

"But she... wasn't even born there," she spoke as if in denial. "She's scarcely grown up. She... can't just *leave* me."

"I'm afraid she must," Iviana spoke with decision. "She is the one the Great One has chosen. Flynn wasn't from the Greater Archipelagos either, if you recall. Nor was he our finest leader. Yet, he was what the Great One desired for a season. But now that season has ended and given way to perhaps our darkest one to date. Your daughter is the leader destined to bring calm to our storm."

"Calm to..." Novella began in disbelief, rising to her feet as her body trembled. "Mother is *right*. I'm an English woman of eighteen years. I'm no leader. All I can do is... is knit and keep my father's books in order. For heavens, how am I to restore order to a whole planet! There's been a mistake somewhere."

"Novella!" Mother scolded in her familiar roar. "All your life, you've yearned for and believed in the impossible. You've longed for travel and adventure. Why, when you were just a bitty thing, you used to tell me all that the Great One had been speaking to you and how much you *loved* Him."

"I... don't remember that."

She nodded. "You climbed one of your *trees,* fell head first and never spoke a word about Him again. When I asked, you had no recollection."

"I *have* been hearing someone of late..."

"Then the time *is* now," Mother declared with an abrupt change of heart. "This is the hour for which you were born. Weren't you just confessing you longed for purpose? My girl, if God is guiding you, there is *nothing* you cannot do. Why, giants shall fall before you!"

Novella raised a brow. She had never heard Mother speak so before. Ever. What had the healing done to her heart? And why did her speech sound so strangely reminiscent of King David's victory over Goliath? Novella was no David, no "man after God's own heart." She never even thought to pray these days.

"I can't do any more of this tonight!" she cried of a sudden, turning for the door.

She stopped short as her eyes fell on Petyr. For the first time, he looked to her with understanding rather than amusement. It brought a small measure of calm to her soul.

"I'm sorry, everyone," she spoke softly. "This is... a lot to work out. I need time to hear myself think."

Novella started for her room. She had healed her mother. *Actually* brought her back from death's door. And everyone in the room had acted as if it was an everyday occurrence—scarcely worth mentioning. Meanwhile, her mother was from another planet, had been married prior to being scooped up by her loving husband here in England. Suddenly, all these aliens were popping out of the woodwork to inform her that she was one of *them*.

She fell into her bed with a gasp. It couldn't be true. Surely, she was enduring a nightmare. But her hands were glowing in the dark. She sat up. It was the mysterious hue that Petyr had claimed he didn't recognize.

Anything might happen now.

"Please, no!" she whispered.

With a strange sputtering, it snuffed out. She blinked down. Had it... obeyed her urging? She fell back onto the mattress.

"There is scarcely anything you cannot do now," her mother's old friend had claimed.

She felt herself a monster—a creature of legend—a mutant. Even she wasn't certain what she might do next. Yet... she had spoken and the glow had ceased. There was light at the end of the tunnel.

Petyr's face flashed to mind—that compassionate look he'd given her in her final tantrum. Did he really grasp her situation? All along, he'd been impatient to have her believe his claims, irritated when she couldn't. Did he finally see her side?

Father. Did Father know any of this? That mother had been married, was from another world, that her old friends had turned up at the house and she was now healed? Poor father. She sat up, prepared to find him and put him at ease. Then, she froze. This was mother's secret to tell. It wasn't Novella's place to intrude. What should she do?

CHAPTER 10

A KNOCK SOUNDED AT the door.

She stood frozen for what to do. It must be Fannie come to welcome her home. Her hand hesitated above the knob before turning it.

"Come with me," Petyr ordered with a daring brow.

"Where?"

"You'll see." He turned, disappearing around the corner.

Part of her wished to close the door, while the other drew her after him. It wasn't until he was ascending the ladder that led to the attic that she questioned her decision. She followed him up only to find him opening a dormer window.

"Whatever are you about, Petyr?"

"How very *bold,* Miss Harper."

It was a moment before she realized she'd called him by his first name. "You said it was your only name."

He turned a grin on her in the darkness. "Need a boost?" He gestured out the window.

She approached to find a lower portion of the roof not far below and bit her lip with sudden interest. She'd always wanted to do this but had been caught on the one occasion she'd made the attempt. Dared she now?

"What if someone sees?" she asked with a smirk.

"What of it?"

With a huff, she sat on the windowsill, spun her legs over the side and landed on her feet.

Petyr released a whistle. "The lady knows her way about a roof."

"Trees, more like."

"So I've heard."

She wrapped her arms about herself in the cold of the night, taking in the stars, the cool of the breeze, the quiet.

He passed his jacket. "I didn't consider the weather."

Novella didn't have to be told twice as she thrust an arm into the sleeve. Well-fortified against the cool breeze, she turned to find Petyr sitting on the very edge of the roof with his feet dangling over the side. Swallowing a lump of nerves, she followed suit, not revealing her dread of heights.

"I've been wanting to do this from the moment I saw this house," he informed.

"So have I and I've lived here longer."

"Why didn't you then?"

"English girls don't traverse rooves."

"Those of the Greater Archipelagos do. Well... some."

"Guess I'm not so special after all."

He grunted. "Iviana said you possess every gift known to our people. I'd say you're nothing if not special, Miss Harper."

She released a sigh. "You may call me Vella, if you like."

"That makes us practically engaged, doesn't it?"

She turned a wide-eyed scowl on him.

"Jesting," he answered with an easy smirk. "It certainly took some time to grow accustomed to all the social regulations here. As you see, I never quite mastered them."

"Actually, I think you've done miraculously well, now I know something of your story and believe it. You don't make a half bad escort considering."

"I'm touched." He smacked a hand to his heart.

She chuckled, releasing a soothed breath as she realized the fresh air was doing her good. "Why did you bring me up here?"

"I couldn't stand the thought of you wallowing alone in your bedroom all night. I don't see how a person could sleep with so much on her mind. Let's talk it out."

"Mmm. Like how I would be considered an extraterrestrial by all my acquaintance if they knew the truth? How I am expected to return to your world with you in order to 'calm its storm' when I couldn't even protect myself from an unwanted engagement? Am I supposed to follow up a faulty leader by making a million mistakes of my own? I don't see what you think there is to discuss."

"I couldn't see your side of things until I watched that scene play out downstairs. I was so impatient to get home—more concerned with how much I missed my family than how you might feel about discovering such profound truths."

She turned to study his profile. His shoulders were hunched in relaxation while his legs swayed with restless energy. "And I hadn't considered what it must be like to be gone from home for so long, unable to return. How have you managed it?"

"This conversation is about you."

She shook her head. "I don't know what to tell you, Petyr. I just can't do it. I'm not the stuff of King David."

"King David?"

"From the Bible. Surely, you've read it."

"A little. I've been busy. But I've read enough to learn that our worlds share a God. In fact, that was what helped me to not feel so far from home. He has been faithful to guide me here."

She quirked a brow at him. "I thought this conversation was about me."

"Who's teasing now? But on a serious note, I previously said I did not see leadership material in you, but... your father spoke of nothing but you while you were away. He's determined to make a match of us before the year is out. I think he's afraid you'll entrap yourself with another Gregory Wetherill. My point is that I didn't really know you when I said that. And I still don't, but... Mr. Harper is over the *moon* about you. I think if he knew what you were facing, he'd harbor no doubts that you were capable of more than you realize."

Novella hadn't considered her father's possible motives for trying to hoist her off on Petyr. It made sense now. He'd watched his daughter be manipulated into what would have been a miserable life and felt as helpless as she to stop it. Once she was rightfully free of the engagement, he wasn't keen on seeing her fall into such a foolish trap again. And, for reasons she knew not of, he idolized Petyr.

"Thank you," she answered quietly. "I had not considered what he'd make of all this. I know beyond the shadow of a doubt, if I could ask him, he'd tell me to..." She swallowed, unwilling to speak the words that had nearly slipped from her mouth.

"To go?" Petyr pressed.

Swallowing, she nodded. The impossibility of leaving everything she knew for untold danger didn't feel quite so impossible anymore. In fact, the sudden desire to travel was sparking inside her.

"You should see an evening sky upon the Greater Archipelagos," he commented.

"Oh?"

"It's teeming with stars and galaxies. The moon is a bit closer. It's a sight to see, especially when you're sitting on the beach with the ocean roaring before you, the waves caressing your feet, the aroma of honey in the atmosphere."

"Honey?"

"There's this huge hive at the crest of a mountain that just oozes the stuff into a pool that feeds into the ocean. Ergo, the water smells and tastes of it."

"Can one visit this hive?" she asked with yearning.

He turned to her with a raised brow. "I could take you there."

She turned away. "I really can't, you know."

"Why not?"

"Because—"

Go, rumbled the voice she now understood to be God.

"Can you *swim* in this pool?" she questioned.

"You can do anything you want," he returned. "You're Realm Leader."

CHAPTER II

NOVELLA DESCENDED THE STAIRCASE with precision the next morning, so stunned by her decision in the night that she feared she might take a wrong step. Surely, she wasn't in her right mind. Perhaps the events of the evening had been but a dream.

The resonance of numerous voices in the breakfast room nipped that hypothesis in the rear. Their unusual guests were all too real and still in the house. What must Father think of them? Or of Mother's sudden recovery?

He wasn't present at the breakfast table. Instead, the strange women of the evening before were garbed in some things that Mother had not yet worn. This was likely done so Father would not recognize them.

"Good morning, everyone," she greeted as calmly as she could before the women she'd learned were not of this world. "Where are Father and Petyr?"

"You're up early," Mother chirped like a girl. "Your father had an emergency at the paper and Petyr volunteered to accompany him."

Novella couldn't help thinking Petyr's decision honorable considering he was soon expecting to leave. Though he could have no real interest in her father's paper, he was willing to lend a hand. She supposed that spoke volumes of the Seeker who'd come from another realm in search of, well... her.

"How did you sleep?" Iviana inquired.

"Like a babe after... everything," Novella admitted. "And you?"

"We were up all night talking," Mother divulged. To her guests, she added, "It's so wonderful having you ladies here."

With a pensive nod, Iviana turned to Vella. "Have you considered where you stand?"

Novella nodded as she seated herself. "I have decided that I would like to visit this Greater Archipelagos with you, on one condition: It must be understood that I am going merely to consider the possibility of accepting the position you've offered. It is impossible to make a decision without familiarizing myself with the terrain—both geographically and politically."

Deep down, she knew this was something of a falsehood. Truth was, she'd tossed and turned until she'd acknowledged that she was *dying* to visit the mysterious place from which her mother had come. *No* part of her felt either willing or able to accept the role as its leader.

Mother clapped her hands. "How I *wish* I might go with you all! Vella, you will love it there."

"You aren't coming?" Novella questioned with astonishment.

"Why, I—cannot. Your father would think it peculiar if I travel without him. We've not been separated a day since we were married. He simply wouldn't understand."

"Then you haven't told him *anything?*"

Mother bit her lip as she shook her head. "He's never known a thing. It was a term of our engagement that he allow me to keep my secrets. I wouldn't accept him otherwise and he has never pressed the matter."

"But now it's *my* secret. I don't like keeping it from him." In fact, she was dying to discuss it with him.

"My dear, you do not understand Earth. They believe they are *it* as far as the reaches of humanity are concerned. I can't have him looking at me like some kind of anomaly."

"But it's *Father*. He's not like that!" Although, she had to admit she'd been seeing both Mother and herself as extraterrestrials. Perhaps she was a hypocrite.

"The matter is settled. He knows I have friends staying with us *and* that they intend to take you along for the remainder of their travels. He has given his approval. In fact, he was quite pleased with the scheme."

"Then Father knows you are well?"

"Of course, dear. You didn't think I was going to let him fret all night, did you? No, I popped in to tell him I was feeling better and he was content to sleep. This morning, I informed him of my friends' imminent visit. When he arrives home later today, he will meet them. You, my sweet, will keep mum as concerns *anything* else. Is that understood?"

"You already arranged for my departure?"

Mother shrugged. "I know my daughter."

"If you don't mind me butting in," Iviana spoke up, "I cannot tell you how pleased I am at your decision, Novella. You're a brave young woman. I will do my best to see you protected and cared for."

Somehow, Novella had forgotten just how dangerous this could prove to be. Not only was it nearly impossible to believe that she would actually be traveling off planet to a whole other universe, the very world on which she was to tread was in a state of near anarchy... all because *she* had not yet come.

What was she thinking?

"We must leave early in the morning," Iviana informed.

"I'll have the carriage waiting for you," Mother added. "I presume you can take it from there...?"

Iviana nodded and Novella couldn't help noticing that no one was making eye contact with her. What did this journey entail? What did everyone in the room know that she didn't?

⇶⇶⇶ ⇷⇷⇷

Novella flew to her father the moment he arrived that evening. Throwing her arms about him, she greeted, "I'm so glad you're home."

He chuckled as he returned her embrace. "Ooh, it's good to have you home from Sylvia's. We scarcely had a chance to catch up last night. And *now* I hear you're off again to take on the world."

He didn't know the half of it.

"I don't know if I'm ready to go," she mused into his sleeve.

He pulled back to peer into her face. "Not ready? You've been hinting at this for a year."

"I know, but... it is difficult leaving you and Mother."

"Well, would you like to know the best part about leaving?"

She nodded.

"You can always come *back.*"

Novella swallowed. She certainly hoped she was coming back. "Thank you, Father."

"Now... I have the very worst of news. It's lucky you never took a liking to my assistant, for it seems Petyr must leave us. He gave his notice today."

"How shocking," she replied, not wanting to dig too far.

"I thought as much. It seems he is desperately needed at home. How can I fault a fellow for honoring his family? Ergo, off he goes. And it's too bad. That boy displayed remarkable promise in a number of areas. There wasn't a single witness to a crime he couldn't locate for an interview, nor a politician he couldn't fish out of some devious gutter." He released a sigh. "Not only that, he saved my life."

"How so?"

"I was awaiting a friend at the station last week. Next thing I knew, a crowd of rowdy school boys had surrounded me. They nearly had me off my feet where I would have fallen from the platform and onto the tracks when Petyr Tamsen turned up out of the blue and hoisted me from harm's way."

"How did he happen to be there?"

"Claimed it was an instinct—that he'd had a feeling about me and had to hunt me up to make certain I was well. Can't say how he knew where I was. All I know is he showed up in the nick of time. Your old father would have been seriously injured or worse."

Novella stood in awed silence. Petyr had said he had a gift for seeking things out. She'd never imagined it might help in a case like this. Despite the position he'd placed her in by locating her, she couldn't help feeling suddenly very *grateful* to him. And, truth be told, he'd been good to her. He'd helped her from the lake and had taken pains for her comfort on their journeys to and from her aunt's. Now, as it happened, he'd been keeping an eye on Father. If one was to visit another planet, he was the sort of man one was grateful to have about... even if he *did* sport a red feather in his hat.

"Do you know, Father... I think I might have liked Mr. Tamsen after all."

"Pity, isn't it?" he commented as he reached for his wife's approaching frame. "I'm dying to meet these old friends of yours, my dear. *They* aren't a secret, too, are they?"

Mother patted him on the chest.

CHAPTER 12

FATHER RATHER LIKED HIS wife's traveling friends. He posed question after question about their travels until Mother and Novella were weary of covering for their true whereabouts. Novella thought it proof that he ought to be informed, but it wasn't honorably her place to do so.

The following morning commenced in a whirl of action. There was false luggage to be gathered for Mother's friends, along with no small amount of baggage for Novella. She'd tried to insist that, wherever she went, she was acceptable in her own clothes. But Mother insisted she must dress as the natives. Ergo, she packed merely a small, secondary satchel of personal belongings she couldn't do without. The remainder of the luggage was to be brought back by the coachman and spirited into Novella's room without Father ever the wiser. The coachman was in for a hefty bonus.

As Novella stood in her most sophisticated traveling suit, complete with a sprayed feather hat, Father stood back with tears pricking his eyes. "I almost regret letting you go," he spoke while Mother made her guests comfortable in the carriage.

"I could stay," she offered wistfully.

"As if I could keep you. I see that glimmer in your eye. You're anxious... but exhilarated. I wouldn't keep you for the world."

Novella gripped him in an embrace before he saw the tears pricking at her eyes. She was a grown woman. She ought not to be so prone to weeping.

"Besides," he whispered into her ear, "how else will you discover your mother's secrets, hey?"

She pulled back, searching his eyes. How much did he know?

"Come along, Novella," Mother called, "Mrs. Flynn must be getting on."

A grin spread across father's face as he gave her a wink. "Go on then, my brave girl. Conquer the world!"

Novella could scarcely peel her eyes from him as she allowed the coachmen to hand her into the carriage. *Father knew something*. But how? She supposed he did own the finest newspaper in the city. He was bound to be gifted at picking up riddles. With a growing grin, she waved her kerchief at her parents as the carriage started on.

"Good luck," she mouthed to her mother.

Perhaps Father had agreed not to *openly* pry into Mother's history, but his instincts told him things were not as they seemed. She wasn't his daughter if she did not grasp what her mother was in for. Father had the sparkle of a mystery to be sorted. He wasn't going to rest until he knew all. And what mystery in all the world could be more important to a husband than his own wife?

"*Well,* Novella, we're off," Iviana mused. "How does it feel?"

"Terrifying," she admitted with a chuckle.

"Good! Terror upon leaving one's planet is a sign of good sense. Now, we've just one more stop to make before our final destination."

"Oh?"

"We must pick up Petyr."

"My father is grieved to be losing him."

"Why do you think I appointed him to seek you out? He is diligent if nothing else. Has a passion for seeing a thing through no matter the cost. Why, he even missed out on a pretty girl when he left in search of you."

"He didn't," Vella stated in dismay, somehow feeling it her fault.

"They were engaged when he left, but she wasn't as loyal as one might hope. She gave up on him and married a Swimmer." She clucked. "Swimmers can be flaky fellows."

Novella swallowed. "I am one of these Swimmers."

"No, you are multi-gifted. At any rate, Petyr is better off. Better to be single than attached to anyone unworthy of him."

"Everyone seems to think a good deal of him."

"How could they not?" Era chimed in. "He is a rare young man. Rather magnificent, in fact."

"That is a strong word," Novella mused bluntly.

"It is the one the Great One used in describing him to me when I sent him to seek you," Iviana explained. "He is a 'magnificent gift,' he said."

Novella sat in silence. She couldn't begin to imagine what that could mean. To whom was he a gift—the world? Certainly explained why he sauntered about as if he was God's gift. But she kept her thoughts to herself, especially as they pulled to a stop.

"Morning, ladies!" Petyr greeted as he seated himself beside Novella. "This is a pleasant party, isn't it?" He winced. "I sound like an Englishman. Cannot describe how thrilled I am to be going back home. Haven't seen Wendi in *five whole years*. What does she look like now?"

Novella pressed her lips together as the ladies before them actually appeared at a loss for words.

"She's fuller," Era offered.

Petyr raised a brow. "Well... she always was too slender."

Fuller. Novella loathed to imagine the woman pregnant with another man's child when they arrived. As silence descended, it seemed neither Iviana nor Era was willing to divulge the truth. Novella bit her lip at the sad end of a romance that awaited them. She only hoped she wouldn't be around when he discovered the truth.

It wasn't until they were well into the countryside that the carriage pulled to a stop. She glanced out the window in apprehension at the pastureland on either side. She presumed they knew what they were doing but didn't see how a lot of cows were going to get them to a planet in another realm.

"Thank you, Harvey!" she called to dismiss the driver.

"Safe travels to you, Miss Vella," he called back before turning the carriage about and starting home. She watched him leave with her last hope of relative security. Home called like a baby for its cradle. But she had come this far. She would look a fool if she did not continue.

"Where do we go from here?" she inquired of the company.

All eyes were on her.

"That is entirely up to you," Iviana informed. "As I've lost my gift for it, you're the only one who can transport us. Petyr told me you managed an entire train—passengers and all. So, I trust you."

Novella's mouth dropped open. "You all think... that is, you're all expecting *me* to get us there?"

They nodded in unison.

"I said you were my ticket home," Petyr reminded with a wink.

"The Great One always provides a way," Era added.

"Surely, there is *another way,*" Novella spoke with a disbelieving chuckle.

They all shook their heads.

"Well, how did you expect to get back before you knew I existed?!"

"Never experienced a journey worth taking in which I was informed of every juncture," Iviana replied sagely. "We walk without seeing. It's called faith."

"Ha!" Novella managed in disbelief. "Well, we're all in a pickle, because I don't know how I managed it the first time and I *never* want to do it again. Besides, we're not talking the Kalahari anymore. This is a whole other universe!"

Had that word truly sprung so naturally from her lips?

A patient grin spread across Iviana's face. *"Try."*

"Think back to what I told you on the train," Petyr directed. "Just picture where you want us to go and *will* us there."

"But I've never even been there!"

"Sure you have."

She raised a brow at him.

"In your dreams."

She opened her mouth to argue before realizing he wasn't quite wrong. She was well familiarized with the beaches of another world. She'd been visiting them in her sleep all her life.

"No one can blame me if we end up stranded in a desert again... or on *Mars."*

"Of course," Iviana answered collectedly.

Novella studied her. The woman really did trust her. Either that or she was so depressed over losing her husband that she didn't care what became of them.

Releasing a soft growl, Novella shut her eyes. "Sorry if I leave anyone behind."

"Don't do that," Iviana demanded.

Novella nearly smirked. This dauntless friend of her mother's *could* experience concern.

In the quiet of the country, with scarcely a sound but the roar of the wind through the pastures, Novella returned to her dreams. She could almost feel the soft sand beneath her feet, the pleasant heat of an oversized sun, the roar of the waves as they ebbed and flowed. She couldn't deny her desire to see it in person.

The clapping of hands jolted her concentration.

"I'm afraid you'll have to keep quiet while I attempt this—" She stopped short as her eyes fluttered open.

"*Well done,* Novella," Iviana congratulated with clear surprise. "Not a bad beginning at all."

Petyr fell to his knees, grasping fistfuls of white sand in each of his hands. "There is *nothing* like it back in that country," he spoke with adoration. "Truly *nothing* so velvety and perfect as this."

Novella stood flabbergasted at the world around her. The vertigo of complete disbelief sent her to her bottom. Her eyes wandered from the tropical trees inland to the teal ocean with gleams of gold throughout. The overwhelming aroma of salt and honey permeated her senses while the pearlescent sand gleamed blindingly around her.

"It's *real*..." she breathed in wide-eyed wonder.

Petyr turned to her with a boisterous laugh. "You may as well learn now that I *never* lie."

"It's true," Iviana confirmed.

As if it mattered in any way to Novella just now. She caressed the dreamily soft sand beneath her hands, scarcely able to make her eyes stop roving their surroundings. At any moment, she was to awaken and find it all a dream. Yet, she'd thought this many times since she'd met Petyr and it had not transpired yet.

"Someone pinch me," she murmured.

Petyr dropped beside her, squeezing her forearm.

"*Ouch!*" she squealed, leaping to her feet.

He laughed again. "It's not a dream, Novella. This is the Greater Archipelagos."

CHAPTER 13

"QUESTION IS," IVIANA BEGAN meditatively, "which island is it?"

"I believe it's Atlantyss," Era informed as she squinted inland. "See the glaring glints of sunlight reflecting off the city?"

"Of course it is," Iviana answered. "The Great One always knows. I'm too weary for any more travel after all that." She turned to Novella. "Not that I'd have missed seeing Nimua safe and well after all those years of worrying and wondering."

Novella smiled wistfully as she attempted to view the city that Era had pointed out. To think Mother had grown up in this place. But could it truly be on another planet? She wasn't entirely satisfied on that score.

"Does Wendi's family still live here?" Petyr questioned. He drew to his feet as if prepared to race to her side.

"They do," Era admitted, "but she doesn't."

"Petyr..." Iviana began. "Eh..." She hesitated. "We must speak once we've got our guest settled in."

His eyes darted between hers as if sensing something amiss. "As you wish," he answered with gravity that drove the ecstasy of his homecoming from his face.

Novella found she missed his open and unadulterated joy. Yet, that was life, was it not? It contained ups and downs. And, as she'd been told, he was a bright, courageous young man. He'd survived years in another world. Surely, he could endure this.

"Come along, everyone," Iviana rang as she started forward. "It's time to face the music."

Face the music? Novella mused. That didn't sound encouraging. Could it be they were marching into jeopardy? Even in her trepidation, her feet kept time with Iviana's stolid march. She blinked through the glinting light to survey the great metropolitan that loomed ahead. Buildings soared for the heavens like pointed steeples stretched further than she'd realized was possible. Like a coral reef, they shone in teal, violet, magenta and rose. Everything was accentuated with pure gold. It seemed to be something like the heavenly city she'd grown up hearing about on Sunday mornings. Surely, this wasn't heaven?

Petyr released a long whistle, plunging his hands into his pockets. "She's bigger than the last time I saw her. Who oversaw all this infrastructure?"

"Your father," Iviana explained with a smile. "It was why I appointed him temporary Realm Leader. If anyone could see so much done in the midst of the mounting confusion, they were worthy of holding down the fort."

"How long has he been leader?"

"A year and a half."

"Has he accomplished much as far as concord goes?"

She bobbed her head from side to side. "You'll recall that, before my great, great Grandfather Latos merged the Eastern and Western portions of the archipelagos, they were divided?"

He nodded.

"Well, everything was in an uproar. It was every island for itself. Your father has succeeded in reuniting the Western isles."

"Then the East is the trouble?"

"So, it would seem."

He whistled again. "Hard to believe all that happened in just five years. I can scarcely comprehend it."

Era glanced at Iviana sidelong.

"I know it, *Era,*" Iviana answered with exasperation. "Era had been trying to bolster me to lead the people, but I wouldn't budge. I holed up in my hut on the Isle of Dragons and stuck my head in the ground."

Petyr eyed the woman in disbelief. "What... did you *do* all that time?"

"Knitted," Era explained with mild irritation.

Iviana rolled her eyes.

Novella could only imagine how frustrating it would be to watch someone you cared about live short of their potential... especially when the world was going up in flame. She wondered if that was how *she'd* been living. She had nearly thrown her freedom away on Gregory Wetherill. Now... she was *here.*

She caught her breath as a bird flew low overhead, ducking at the sheer size of the creature.

"What on Earth—or—er... what *was* that?" she questioned.

"Dragon," Petyr replied with a sparkle in his eye. He turned to the elder ladies with, "Her planet believes them a myth."

Iviana grinned. "They're myth and legend in many of the places they've historically traveled. But here is where they chose to settle. She took in the scenery as if with fresh eyes. "Can't say I blame them. I did the same."

Novella's eyes widened with the shock that she was nonchalantly walking beneath something she had long believed to be naught but a symbol for the devil. Moreover, Iviana had made her home here from another planet... the very thing the woman was hoping Novella would do. She shivered at the thought. It may be beautiful, perhaps even prove to be wondrous, but there was no place like home.

"Aren't they dangerous?" she couldn't help inquiring despite everyone's lack of concern.

Iviana quirked a brow back at her. "Hardly..."

Era grinned to soften the blow. "Iviana's closest friend is a dragon."

Novella raised her brows. When was she going to awaken?

At last, they entered the outskirts of the city. Gone were the brick-and-mortar buildings of her home country. Rather, the structures towered in glistening as if built of a single piece of material rather than the typical stacked layers. She touched a hand to the nearest wall to find it cool and smooth.

"That one is ruby," Petyr informed as he drew beside her.

"You're not serious."

"I am. Atlantyss is a whole legend in and of itself but entirely real. Long hidden beneath the water's surface, it was protected by a transparent dome until Iviana drew her to the surface."

"Why was it hidden?"

"I was getting to that. It seems their leader was concerned they would forfeit their passion for the Great One as the remainder of the planet had. He asked they be hidden until the time appointed for the Glorybringer to emerge. That would be a much younger Iviana."

Her eyes flew to the woman with fresh interest.

"At any rate, his prayer was answered, but their time down there did not go to waste. Under cover of water, they became world-leaders in invention and technology. One of the keys they unlocked was how to liquify gemstones for construction."

"This planet is *that* abundant in ruby?"

"The Western islands are."

She raised her brows. "Thus... the historical and now current division between the Eastern and Western archipelagos."

"Precisely," he answered.

"I imagine the Eastern half covets the riches of the West while the Westerners grow greedy of their riches in a time of uncertainty."

"That was certainly how it was before Latos united them. Couldn't just say where we're at now. That's something I'm both dying and dreading to learn."

Aside from the political aspect, the place was something next door to heaven. Yet, there were signs of poverty in many of the children who ran about. What looked to have once been a thriving neighborhood of gemstone now contained dust ridden partitions with lean children. How could a city be built of pure riches while its people were in want? Yet... if the Western islands were refusing to exchange commerce with the Easterners, perhaps the purses of the lesser fortunate were drying up. After all, one could not eat rubies. And one couldn't sell chips of their home to those who were already thriving. The only people who might be interested *would* be the Eastern isles.

They soon entered a lively city market. Bustling with both merchants and consumers, Novella was struck by the fashion of their garments. They looked positively Grecian with perhaps a futuristic flare in accessory. The materials appeared cool and easy to move about in. She took the liberty of feeling a bolt of cloth. It was softer than anything she had felt in her life. No wonder Mother had urged her to leave her wardrobe behind. While the women of her world were slipping themselves into corsets and layers of hot, prickly material, those here dressed for comfort that was no less comely.

"Like what you see?" Iviana asked with a knowing grin.

"I cannot deny the beauty of this place." Abruptly, she sniffed the air. It smelled of caramelized honey. "Oooh, what is that?"

Iviana laughed. "Those are fresh baked honey rolls—a favorite of mine. Petyr," she beckoned, holding up a coin, "fetch us a few."

Novella was soon supplied with what appeared to be but a plain baked roll. However, it nearly dissolved upon touching her lips, flooding her mouth with notes of honey, cream and oats. The experience of eating the food of another planet made the experience suddenly quite real. This bread, along with everything and everyone she saw, overwhelmed her with incredulity.

This was no England.

It wasn't until they reached the center of the city that she beheld the loftiest of all edifices. It was spread out like an advanced palace, composed entirely of clear crystal. Did this land possess kings and queens as hers did? If so, what was the point of a Realm Leader?

"This is the recently built Council Hall," Petyr informed. "It is where the council members of our great planet meet to govern and dictate the laws and sway of the isles. This is also where you will live... should you choose to remain."

"You are to be housed here over the duration of your visit," Iviana explained. "Petyr's father, as current Realm Leader, is occupying the Realm Leader's suite, so you will be afforded second best. I don't think you'll mind too much." She ended with a wink.

"And in case you haven't guessed it," Petyr put in, "the structure is comprised of solid diamond."

Novella's mouth fell open at the towering castle as she entered its courtyard.

She *really* wasn't in England anymore.

"It's Iviana!" a stranger whispered.

Novella watched as they raced to point out her guide to a nearby group. Before she knew it, her mother's friend was swarmed with people questioning her about her journey and asking for wisdom concerning their affairs.

"Can you give me a word of encouragement about my daughter?" one woman asked.

Another broke in with, "I need coin in order to maintain my property. What shall I do?"

"Where have you been all this time?" asked a number of them.

"Did you succeed in locating the rightful Realm Leader?" boomed a voice above the rest.

Everyone turned to find a towering man in beautiful Grecian-like robes standing beyond the group. As if in shared thought, the crowd parted but did not dissipate. They seemed to be waiting with baited breath.

"Realm Leader Tamsen!" Iviana called in comradely fashion. "Let us speak in the convening room, shall we? I will update you on our progress. As you may or may not have noted... we discovered your missing son." She gestured to Petyr, who stood with glowing eyes as he surveyed his father.

Realm Leader Tamsen's lips parted in something nigh disbelief. "Petyr," he whispered, approaching with swift step until he stood before his son.

As he extended his hand, Petyr grasped it with eagerness. "Father," he spoke with his usual chuckle, eyes shining like the sun on the ocean.

With linked hands, they drew close to pat one another on the back before drawing back to survey one another with disbelief.

"I'd heard you were spotted on Kaern," the father began, "last seen in the kingdom of Kierelia. But I'd not heard another word these last two and a half *years.*"

"I'll tell you everything once we're in private," Petyr promised.

Novella felt herself happily invisible as she watched these happenings. At a mere eighteen years of age, she appeared more like sixteen or seventeen. Ergo, none had begun to guess she was the one whom Petyr and Iviana had set out to find. Tamsen's gaze passed her with mild question as he returned his attention to Iviana.

"Let us assemble in the convening chamber," he directed. "I have many questions and... many concerns."

"I imagined as much," Iviana replied. "After you, Realm Leader." She urged him to walk before her.

Novella could scarcely contain the awe she experienced as they entered the Council Hall. Under the light of both torches and what appeared to be electric chandeliers, the place sparkled at every imaginable angle. Though the partitions were built from solid diamond, one could not view the rooms beyond them. She supposed there were layers in between of some other material in order to maintain privacy. Yet, the place was so reflective it made her dizzy.

Petyr came up beside her to take hold of her arms as she hesitated on the impressive stairwell they traversed. "It takes some getting used to," he informed brightly. "Some slip and slide all over the place. You're actually handling it well for a beginner."

Novella couldn't help questioning why these people would build with something that took "some getting used to." Clearly, they valued beauty over serviceability. That was very likely what her father had done. Her mother was nothing if not a beauty. Even in her maturing years, everyone said so.

Upon reaching a long hall, Petyr stopped short. Novella followed the path of his eyes as they fell on an uncommonly goodlooking fellow some feet down the hall. The stranger too had stopped short.

"Petyr?!" he called in amazement.

"Michal!" Petyr shouted as he abandoned Novella's side. The two met in an affectionate embrace. When they parted, it was clear each were fighting back tears.

"I'm going to have to whip your *hide* for taking off so long," Michal voiced mirthfully. "Where have you *been,* brother?"

"You wouldn't believe me if I told you," Petyr replied with a pat to his back.

"*Try* me."

It was then Petyr awoke to the group surrounding them. His eyes fell on Novella.

"Miss Harper," Petyr began before correcting himself. "That is, Novella, this is my big brother, Michal—the best fellow you'll ever know."

Michal's affectionate grin turned from his younger brother to Novella with something of a start.

"Michal," Petyr continued, "as I said, this is Novella."

Blinking as if in disbelief, Michal proffered his hand to her. "Any friend of Petyr's is automatically a friend of mine," he commented warmly.

Novella accepted the hand, which he proceeded to squeeze rather than shake. She presumed this to be the custom until she realized she wasn't being afforded it back.

"Glad to know it," she replied meaningfully. She could use friends in this foreign place.

"Michal," Realm Leader Tamsen broke in with the clearing of his throat, "if you'll escort this young lady to the convening chamber, we can all become better acquainted."

Nothing daunted, the elder brother released her hand in order to offer his arm and did as told. "I suppose you are of some kingdom upon Kaern?" he ventured, surveying for the first time her peculiar outfit. Novella was grateful she'd removed her feathered hat at Era's advice. She'd have looked a fool in this place.

"I do not even know what Kaern is," she answered with a smile.

Petyr sidled up to his brother. "I told you you wouldn't believe me."

Michal surveyed first Novella, then his brother, in question. "Don't tell me you ventured all the way to the planet *Wysteria?*"

Petyr shook his head. "It's a new world for us—Earth. I have much to tell."

"Well, if the ladies of Earth are all like this one, I can see why you took your time returning." His face dropped. "That is... is this young lady your, er..."

Petyr appeared confused before shaking his head. "Her identity is something else you will not readily believe... Give it a minute."

Once they entered what she presumed to be the convening room, Michal ushered Novella into a chair.

Iviana stopped him with, "Please seat Novella at the secondary head of the table."

All eyes fell on Iviana, who merely nodded.

CHAPTER 14

IT WAS THEN THE eyes of the room flew to Novella, who felt her cheeks flush as she ducked her head and slipped into the apparently momentous chair. Michal scrutinized her profile as he seated himself beside her. Did everyone in the room know who she was meant to be merely by the chair she was given?

"Iviana," Tamsen began with incredulity, "are you insinuating that this young woman is the one destined for Realm Leader?"

Iviana nodded. "She is ever so slightly older than she looks if it helps. And she is *powerful.*"

Realm Leader Tamsen's eyes found Novella's, pinning them with his stare. "Then you found her..." he stated with relieved acceptance.

"Actually, Petyr did. It was then we found Petyr. I must presume it was all according to the Great One's timing."

"I don't think she'd have come on my word alone," Petyr added with a wink to Novella.

"And she is from...?" Tamsen questioned.

"A planet called Earth," Iviana informed. "Not a place that has been mapped by us as yet. I do not suppose you were ever acquainted with Nimua, my deceased brother's wife?"

"I've heard of her. She and your brother were missionaries to Kaern. When he died, the wife disappeared."

"To Earth. This is her daughter."

"She was pregnant when she fled?"

Iviana shook her head.

The man sat back in his chair. "Then she is only partly of our blood." Sitting forward, he finally dawned a smile on Novella, "Well, young woman... do you have any idea how in need we are of your services?"

Novella swallowed.

"Actually, the matter is not yet settled," Iviana supplied.

Tamsen's eyes shot to Iviana.

"She was not informed of the Greater Archipelagos' existence until quite recently. Though she was eager to survey our great planet for herself, she does not yet feel in a position to accept her rightful role."

The man's face dawned complete confusion before growing grave. "That is a display of wisdom," he spoke with a nod. "I can well understand your reservations."

"Thank you for your understanding," Novella answered, slightly impressed by her own diplomacy.

"I can only imagine being in your position. Leaping in as leader without taking stock of the situation would be foolhardy... Am I given to understand that this visit is to determine your decision?"

"I suppose that is what it comes down to," Iviana supplied, "even if it is *entirely* unprecedented." She turned to Novella. "No one has ever considered turning down the call of the Great One to this auspicious position."

Novella raised her brows.

"Well," Tamsen chimed in, "we will do our best to acquaint you with the *best* of our fair planet before thrusting you into the gory details. I hope you will make yourself entirely at home."

"Thank you, Realm Leader Tamsen," Novella answered smoothly.

"That said," he continued, "it wouldn't hurt to dip your toes into the water in order to get a feel for things."

"I consider that a shrewd notion," Iviana agreed. "But until she has made her choice, it is best the facts of her identity remain undisclosed to the public."

"Agreed," Tamsen replied. "That goes for everyone in this room. I may not be rightful Realm Leader, but my orders stand until and *if* this young lady steps into position. Is that quite understood?"

Grim nods were the response of the room, including the guard who stood at the door.

"I'm not certain what to divulge to what remains of our council as concerns her presence, but I am certain I will think of something. Perhaps... she may act as my assistant... for reasons I have not yet discerned?"

"Perfect," Iviana answered with a slap to the table before standing to her feet. "I've a number of things to see to before day's end. Era, will you see Novella to her suite. It should be ready by now. Petyr, I hope you'll remain near her quarters in case she is in need of anything and... in case of any trouble. Not that I expect any."

Petyr nodded soberly.

Iviana sauntered for the door before stopping in her tracks and turning back with. "I thank you for your long service to this planet, Petyr. We would not be this far without you."

Petyr appeared surprised before his jaw flexed as if remembering the years of toil and trouble he'd endured. After all, the man had been forced to ingratiate himself into an entirely unknown culture. And had left his disloyal love interest behind.

"It was an honor," he answered with sincerity.

With hesitation, Iviana informed, "May we have that word I mentioned?"

Novella ducked her face to follow Era from the room. She was glad she would not be present when Iviana informed him about his dead romance. Yet, she rather guessed his brother would spill the beans before Iviana ever got a chance.

"How do you like it?" Era asked as they traversed the large corridor.

"The palace—I mean—hall? It's the most beautiful place I have seen in my life. The whole city is. You must have thought London dirty and dull."

"Actually, it was fascinating. The horsedrawn carriages, the food, the clothing. That dress you're wearing is lovely."

Novella glanced down. She thought it rather silly beside the clothes the Realm Leader had worn.

"Michal is *completely* smitten," Era informed.

"Hm?" Novella asked without meeting her gaze.

The woman smirked at her sidelong. "That man has been so busy he hasn't taken the time to fall for a girl the whole of his life. One look at you and he was practically falling over himself. I think we've got a match made in heaven on our hands."

"I cannot begin to agree," Novella mumbled, wishing the woman wouldn't press it.

They fell into silence as they entered a small compartment with a door that slid open and shut of its own accord.

"Is... this my room?" Novella asked with apprehension. The place possessed no furniture whatever.

Era appeared as if she'd be chuckling if she were a more demonstrative person. "This is a mechanical transport... You shall see."

She activated what looked to be a telephone dialer. Novella had been begging father to install one of the new contraptions, but he'd refused on the grounds of not wanting to be bothered with business at home. Instead of sending a call, Novella felt her body jerk involuntarily as she suffered a disconcerting vertigo.

"What is happening?!" she gasped.

"The 'room,' as you called it, is ascending. We'll arrive at your floor in a minute."

Novella grasped the walls until they were softly brought to a stop. When the door opened, the corridor from which they'd come was replaced by one gleaming in pure gold."

Novella stepped out in wonder.

"This is the floor that houses the council," Era explained, "those who live in the city that is. And your room is just here." She reached for a doorknob.

As it was thrust open, an apartment fit for a queen was revealed. The large receiving room was decorated with both luxury and taste. The splendor of it continued into a large bedchamber, fitted with silver and gold décor, with an attached wardrobe. On the opposite end of the receiving room was revealed what she understood to be a lavatory, though the apparatus that replaced the toilet in her world was entirely unfamiliar. Era was forced to walk her through each step of its use before moving on to the cleansing pool and beauty reserve.

Novella's head spun with the novelty and splendor of it all as she stood at the wide window of the receiving room. She was afforded what must be one of the grandest views of the city as it glistened in the sunlight. The variances between this place and her London were overwhelming. And *she* was expected to become leader of not only this magnificent island but every other one on the face of the planet? She shook her head as she fell into the chair Era ushered her to.

"You must be exhausted," Era commented, kneeling to remove Novella's shoes as if she were a mere servant.

Novella's eyes widened at her meekness. "I can manage them," she insisted.

The woman clucked at her. "I know what it's like to be in your shoes—visiting a new planet for the first time. I think it best you make yourself at home in here for a while. I'll have someone fetch you in time for evening meal. How does that sound?"

"Perfect," Novella sighed with relief.

She *was* in overload mode. It wouldn't offend her any if she could be forgotten for evening meal. The ordeal would only be a whole new level of unfamiliarity. All she'd experienced thus far was quite enough for an eighteen-year-old from Victorian England who had been longing for travel and adventure and now found herself in a place of dreams.

Yet, she found she couldn't sit still. She explored everything over again in order to convince herself she was really in the world in which her mother had been born and raised. She shook her head as she re-entered the bedroom to enjoy its view of the outside world. Her mother had known this exquisite place... and abandoned it through something called a portal with no fixed destination. It had landed her on Earth where she'd met Father. The rest was history.

Novella couldn't even imagine having been born anywhere but Earth, having had any other father—which, of course, she wouldn't. She was the result of the good-natured, easy-going Mr. Harper and her formerly protective and uptight mother. But Mother was so different since the Great One had "melted" her cold heart. She had seemed almost like another person. The former version of her mother would never have let her run off and leave them for who knew how long. She would have rather seen her married to the next wealthy man who came calling, if ever another did.

Here, however, she was safe from such a fate. Men were the last thing on her mind. There was far too much else to consider in this new world... even if Petyr's brother *was* stupidly attractive... and, quite mysteriously, seemed to think her the end of all beauty. She bit her lip at the memory. She could not be deemed a conventional woman if that circumstance had not moved her.

With the shake of her head, she fell onto the bed. Her mind spun with all she'd seen and learned. Already, she was homesick, but that was baby-thinking. She was a young adult now. Whether or not she had any mind to accept it, these people thought her *world leader* material. She must live up to it... somehow.

She was jolted from a deep slumber by a knock upon the outer door. It was all she could do to peel herself from bed before stopping short. It was some moments before she recalled her present location. Without a single torch lit nor knowledge of how the electric lighting operated, she felt her way to the door by moonlight.

Era stood by with a smile. "You certainly slept. Come, we must adorn you for evening meal." She let herself in, pulling at a long gold chain that soon sent the oversized chandelier to blazing.

"I've never slept in my corset a day in my life," Novella commented groggily. "Don't see how I managed it."

"I couldn't *wait* to be free of the one your mother leant me... Here." She held up a long violet toga. "It'll bring out your eyes. You've your mother's lavender hue, you know. That is a rare color here."

"It is on Earth as well. Mother was fairly famous for it."

"With your father's dark eyes, it's a wonder you inherited them. You've your mother's golden locks as well. Or, rather, the hue hers used to be."

"The fact that I began to display one of your, er, Great Gifts, aged her. She was never just the same the day I remained in the sea too long."

Era's brows rose. "I hadn't considered what it would be like to have a daughter displaying gifts that would be an irregularity in another setting. I suppose she was rather frightened."

"As was I. I fancied myself... something very strange. Felt out of place wherever I went... It made it difficult to let people in."

Era turned a grin on her. "You're where you belong now. No more hiding."

An unexpected flood of relief overwhelmed Novella upon those words: *No more hiding.* She hadn't considered that she would fit in better here than where she'd always lived—only that she wasn't prepared to leave her homeland forever. Could this place ever truly be *home*?

She stopped before a mirror on her way out the door. It was strange to see herself dressed as the locals. The violet made her eyes glow like stars while the plum sash made her appear almost regal. Era had encouraged her to wear her hair down, pulling back one side with a floral pin. She scarcely looked like herself—which was somehow comforting. It would be easier to play a part if she looked it.

Era soon led her into a chamber with an extensive dining table set close to the floor. It was adorned with fluffy multi-colored cushions surrounding, each bedecked with gold needlework. The light fixtures appeared like dripping threads of glittering tapestry, each of which glowed delicately over the arrangement. She was glad she had not viewed this room before her nap. It would have completely overawed her.

"Novella!" a merry voice called across the room.

Her eyes flew to where Michal stood with Petyr. The latter did not appear pleased. *He knew.* She bit her lip with pity for him as the two approached.

"You look like a resident," Michal commented with approval. "One would think you'd lived here all your life."

"Short of her pale complexion," Petyr added. "What she needs is several days on the beach."

Michal snorted at his brother before returning his gaze to Novella. "My brother isn't in the best spirits just now."

She smiled generously, never having been one for vanity anyway. "I'd like to spend a few *weeks* on that sand."

Petyr offered up a half-hearted smile, as if only really seeing her for the first time. "You'll have your chance," he promised.

"Petyr would live at the beach if he could," Michael put in. "After the years he put in to his last assignment, I'd say he has earned the right."

The younger brother flicked the elder a grin before moving on to converse with another group.

"I don't suppose you've heard about the disloyal lady?" Michal asked.

"I have... and I can't help somehow feeling to blame."

"I'd say things turned out for the best. I never much liked the girl. She'd been after me before giving up and turning to him. In my humble opinion, Petyr deserves better than the moon."

"That seems to be everyone's view."

"But... not yours?" he asked with a quirked brow.

Her eyes nearly popped from their sockets, so caught did she feel herself. "Don't get me wrong... He has taken very good care of me. Only... he *does* like to tease, doesn't he?"

"It is my favorite aspect of his nature," he returned with a playful smirk. "But you should be made aware that he most often teases those of whom he most approves."

"It doesn't feel that way."

"It is his way. Now, shall I take the liberty of seating you beside myself? As the eldest son of the current Realm Leader, I take secondary head of the table. I've been informed things are to be no different tonight in order to maintain your secret."

Novella nodded gratefully as he helped her slide into her cushion. She grinned as it occurred to her that this arrangement would feel something like eating dinner in bed—something she'd not done except when recovering from illness. Of a sudden, her countenance dropped.

"Something the matter?" Michal inquired as he seated himself.

"These cushions have no back support."

He hesitated a moment before his face grew sober. "I presume things are very different where you are from."

"To say the least." She patted the pillow.

"You are very different from the ladies I am acquainted with."

She hesitated to ask, "How so?"

"You seem so delicate and... perhaps sensitive?"

She groaned inwardly. It was just as Petyr had described her—a mere flower compared to the conquering women of this world. Well, she was going to have to toughen up, wasn't she?

"Don't get me wrong," he amended. "I find it charming."

A blush heated her face. Era had been right. This man was nothing if not interested in her. A knot formed in her stomach. Another suitor was not on the agenda—especially one from another world. Wedding someone from this place would thereby ensnare her. And she hadn't changed her mind about matrimony—she wasn't ready. Besides, she wasn't just sure how she felt about someone who had displayed interest in her on a mere first glance.

Realm Leader Tamsen entered the room with the clearing of his throat. All eyes turned to him, rescuing Novella from Michal's awkward gaze. "Shall we begin?" he inquired with the clapping of his hands toward the servers.

A dazzling light illuminated a band of musicians in the far corner. An astonishing tune crescendoed throughout the hall, overwhelming Novella's senses. It was as if they possessed the ability to manipulate her emotions, sending her first up and then down, this way and that. It was all she could do to bite her lip and keep from tearing at the sheer splendor with which she was enveloped.

"You like the music?" spoke the woman beside her. She was startled to find Era seated there.

"Oh, I *do*."

"They are skilled with a Great Gift for composition. *These* are the best in the world."

"I believe it," she breathed, unable to remove her gaze from them until Era passed her the first of the dishes. Her gaze shot about the courses being passed. "Era..." she began as she filled her plate with what smelled of unfamiliar vegetables. "I can't help noticing there is no meat present."

The woman flushed. "We do not consume animals on the Greater Archipelagos." She appeared wholly embarrassed by the notion.

It was Novella's turn to blush. "You must have considered us awfully savage when you were with us back home..."

Though her expression denoted otherwise, Era shook her head. "Every planet maintains unique cultural preferences. In fact, there is only one other within our charted planes that boasts a diet similar to ours."

Novella raised her brows. Were things always to take her off her guard here? Would she ever manage to find her footing? Would she ever manage to *like* vegetables?

Out of nowhere, a commotion ensued. Gasps and even screams sounded from the strangers at the table as it became clear they were under attack. Novella froze as arrows flew about. It was some moments before she realized they landed namely around herself. One had struck the very cushion on which she sat, another the table before her.

As if in answer, her skin pulsed with magnificent light, efficiently disintegrating the remaining onslaught. It wasn't until the arrows ceased and her skin restored to normalcy that she realized a ring of arrows surrounded her. She gawked first at Era, then the remainder of those present about the table.

She undoubtedly had the attention of the room.

Petyr was at her side in a fell swoop. He and Michal ushered her from the chamber and down the hall to a room with no windows. A troop of guards followed the standing Realm Leader not long after. He held a series of papers in his hands, his expression severe. His sober gaze fell upon her.

"I am desperately embarrassed by this, Novella. We should have posted more sentinels outside the dining hall. Perhaps we will install glass in those upper windows. I cannot think how those Easterners managed to enter the grounds unawares."

"I don't understand," she managed beyond her racing heart. "Why should Easterners target *me?*"

He passed her the papers. Realizing she couldn't read a word of the foreign symbols, she passed the parchment to Petyr His eyes scanned them with growing wrath as his face paled.

"They know who you are," he informed.

"How could they?" Michal questioned in a mirrored tone.

Petyr shook his head. "Someone has informed them. Perhaps the guardsman who—"

"No," Tamsen insisted. "Rupa is a vault."

"Please read them aloud," Novella pleaded as Era took hold of her hand much as her own mother might have done.

Petyr swallowed, considering her with eyes that conveyed he would rather not. He shuffled through them with, "This one says it most succinctly. 'The chieftains of the Easterly Conglomeration hereby refuse the leadership of the tiny alien girl-child from an unknown planet."

Novella flushed with humiliation. What a description! But how could they know anything about her?

Petyr gritted his teeth before continuing, "'This is the first in a series of prearranged strikes should the child of distant galaxies remain upon the Greater Archipelagos.'"

Novella leaped to her feet, hands clenched into fists. Quite suddenly, she felt ten times more tenacious than she had the day she'd realized her father meant to marry her off to Petyr and he appeared to be playing along. She wouldn't be hoisted back home before ever getting a chance to really *see* things. This Easterly Conglomeration did not know her, nor she them. They simply had no say in the matter.

"I will ask it again," Michal voiced doggedly. "How did they become aware of her identity?"

Tamsen ran a hand down his face, stopping to rub at his eyes as if from exhaustion. "They've prophets of their own in the Conglomeration."

"Well, where do we go from here?" Era asked calmly. "Ought she return home until we can get things in better order?"

"No!" Novella barked. "I'm not being chased off by these rabblerousers! How *dare* they jeopardize my life when I have not so much as made a move to take the place of Realm Leader? All I'm asking is the chance to experience the place where my mother grew up. I am not in the least anxious to take Realm Leader Tamsen's place. If they could just *step off* for a second, they might learn I'm not a threat."

Petyr's somber face cracked into an almost unidentifiable smirk.

"I take back what I said about delicate," Michal spoke with an open grin. "And what was with the arrow-melting? I've never seen the like."

"Salt," Era informed.

"You tasted it?" Petyr asked with a gleam.

She nodded gravely.

"What's that?" Tamsen questioned.

"She turned the arrows to salt," Era somberly explained.

Novella blinked back at her. "I didn't intend to."

"It was the Spirit of the Great One moving in you." The woman looked to the others in the room. "It is clear he stands with her. We cannot take this assault lightly. Moreover, we must do all in our power to convince her of the import of this call."

"I told you," Petyr whispered over Novella's head.

A chill coursed over her. It was one thing to refuse to be driven out, quite another to be pressured into a role for which she was not in the least suited. She ought to have taken her excuse for an exit when she had the chance. Really, what had she been thinking? She scarcely knew herself.

"Is she safe in her suite?" Era questioned Tamsen.

He nodded. "The windows are of special glass. Still, I'll assign extra guards on the grounds below, as well as outside her door." He turned to Novella with, "Would you like someone to stand guard in your suite as well?"

That sounded like the worst night's sleep of her life.

She shook her head. "I trust your other measures are perfectly suitable."

"Michal and I will see you to your room," Petyr informed as he assisted her to her feet. "Era will bring some food up and make certain you are quite well. You aren't harmed, are you?" He surveyed her with renewed anxiety.

Her eyes darted about the room. "Uh, where is Iviana?"

When no one answered, her eyes sought Era.

"Iviana felt it necessary to return home for the time being," Era explained evenly.

"And her home is...?"

"On another island."

Novella's eyes widened.

CHAPTER 15

"IVIANA *PROMISED* MOTHER SHE'D be watching out for me," Novella accused.

Era nodded patiently. "The Atlantiian population is perhaps too fascinated with her. She wasn't just ready to face her public, so she assigned Petyr and I to mind your care and safety."

"So, she abandoned me." What *wouldn't* Mother say to that?

"No," Petyr insisted, "she placed you in the very best of care—mine. Now, come along." He spoke as if she were a child as he took her hand into his.

She tore it from his grasp. Iviana's commanding presence had made her feel safe. Now, she felt entirely vulnerable—especially considering what had just transpired. The realization of the episode coursed over her. Why on Earth and not-Earth had she insisted she would remain?

"I can see myself to my suite," she retorted, "as it is clear I am on my own here."

She marched for the door.

At the yank of her sash, she turned to find Petyr behind her. He lost no time in laying claim to her arm and persistently, if gently, ushering her from the room. Michal wasn't far behind, keeping watch as they went.

"You can't act like a Victorian schoolgirl anymore," Petyr hissed into her ear. "If people are discovering who you really are, it is vital you put your best foot forward. Even if you inevitably refuse your role, the people must see you as someone to be trusted. They don't know where you stand just now—that you take your calling so flippantly. We can use that."

Her mouth fell open several times while she worked to stutter out a retort. "I haven't been a schoolgirl for *some* time, I'll have you know. Passed out of my studies years before my acquaintances. As for my behavior, I'll have you also made aware that I am exhausted. This venture is overwhelming to say the least. I took comfort in Iviana's presence and I just endured an attack on my life. So, forgive me, Perfect Petyr, if I am not at my best this evening." She ended with another painful wrench of her arm from his grasp.

The three walked in silence until they reached her door where Petyr coldly directed, "Get your nap in, princess. Perhaps we will both be in better spirits come morning." With that, he turned on his heel for the elevation apparatus.

Michal offered up a feeling smirk. "Eh... as I said, he's not in the best mood this evening. As for myself, I thought you behaved rather astoundingly. You deflected those arrows without placing anyone in harm's way. And your refusal to kowtow to the chieftains was moving. I just witnessed my first glimpse of a Realm Leader down there and I look forward to seeing where all this leads."

Tears instantly flooded her eyes. "Thank you, Michal... I appreciate your support. You weren't fibbing when you said you'd be a friend to me."

"That is certain but certainly not all I hope for. Good evening, Novella." With that, he took his leave of her as swiftly as his brother had.

Novella entered her suite to the presence of a guardsman, releasing a squeal as she flew back.

"I apologize," the tall man spoke with a bow. "I was directed to examine your suite. All is clear."

With an embarrassed nod, she let him pass her.

"I, along with another, shall be just outside should you require aid," he informed as he closed the door.

Era arrived not long after with tray in hand. "Do you realize Tamsen has leant you his Rupa for a guardsman? That is his favored ally. It is clear our standing Realm Leader was appropriately rattled by this incident."

Novella offered a weary smile as she surveyed her choice of fruit and vegetable. Her eyes alighted on a honey roll. "I'll have to thank him," she murmured before biting in.

"He'll sooner be apologizing to you again. We're supposed to be convincing you to remain and *this* happens." She surveyed Novella afresh. "You poor dear. You *are* courageous. Are you quite certain you do not wish to return home for a time at least?"

"No, I am not," Novella tearfully admitted. "Frankly, I don't know what came over me down there, insisting I wasn't to be turned out. I wish... I wish Mother had come along."

Era nodded. "I expected her to wish to return with us. But perhaps..."

"Perhaps?"

"I rather wonder if she feared she would never return to Earth once she got a whiff of home. And she does so love your father."

Novella felt herself melt at that. She loved Father too. "He is the best of men." Her face clouded at the thought.

"What is it, dear?"

"It's *Petyr*. Everyone raves about the fellow while I just can't seem to... quite like him! He outright shocked me into disbelief with his claims about my identity, then proceeded to have himself a tantrum when I wouldn't believe him. Then my gifts began to act up and he spoke as if it was *my* fault. I know he succeeded in saving my father from harm at one time, but his treatment of me this evening was really quite offensive."

Era's eyes shone with compassion. "I cannot imagine what he has been through these last years. I presume he dearly missed home and family... along with that disloyal lover of a Swimmer. Yet, you certainly deserve to be treated with consideration. I will speak with him."

Now that Novella had finally spoken her mind, she couldn't help feeling ashamed. "I wish you wouldn't. I should not have said anything. I'm sure he is a very good sort of person and... well, his brother is very considerate."

Era's eyes lit up. *"Isn't* he though?"

Novella blushed. "I'm really not interested."

"I don't see as it matters much. With a face like that, I've always considered he could get any lady he wished if he had a mind to."

Novella's eyes widened before she relented to a chuckle. "Then I hope he shall *not* be of that mind. I've only just escaped one engagement. And... there's enough on my plate as it is."

"Of course," Era answered with growing somberness. "I am dreadfully sorry for what happened at evening meal. I can only imagine you require rest. And you're quite right that you've enough on your plate. Come, let's get you changed and into bed. Perhaps everything will look different come morning."

CHAPTER 16

NOVELLA AWOKE WITH THE impression that the dearest Personage in all the world had been whispering her name. What had she dreamed? Had it been of that Voice... the One that had been directing her of late?

As her eyes fluttered open, she was surprised to find herself in the secondary suite of another world. She did not seem to mind. The ultra-bright sun gleamed warm rays over the plush bed in which she had enjoyed the sleep of the righteous. She sniffed the air.

Breakfast.

Pulling on her oversized robe, she stepped into the receiving room to find a breakfast tray awaiting her. It was piled with all manner of fruit, along with a generous supply of those honey rolls. She plucked one up and bit down on the hot, fluffy bliss.

Iviana.

The woman had left her behind. That did not bode well. This was the person who had promised to see to her wellbeing. Quite suddenly, peace gave way to doubt. She wasn't safe—that was clear. She had been closer to death last evening than ever she'd expected to be in her life. Her gaze dropped to her hands. Something in her blood had reacted to the danger—one of the mysterious "Great Gifts." Would she ever get a handle on what was happening to her?

"Oh, God," she whispered, "please help me."

She recalled what she'd pled in the rushing river. He had instantly responded. Now, she waited with baited breath.

Nothing came.

"I know," she continued. "You're supposed to have been the One Who chose me for leader of this world, but... do you have any idea what you'd be getting into?"

"Do not despise small beginnings," rumbled a voice like a lion.

Her mouth fell shut. Small beginnings? Had He considered yesterday to be small? It had been the most epic day of her existence thus far.

"Small but significant," he persisted.

Significant was *right*. She'd nearly been killed!

"The small is big."

Her face formed a frown. "What do you mean?"

When no response ensued, she measured the ones he'd already given. It was as if he considered the prior day a success... like He'd *planned* it that way. But she'd been terrified out of her wits! How was she to walk freely in this place knowing something like that could happen at any moment?

"You were never in any danger."

She frowned. It had certainly *felt* perilous. Yet... all those arrows and not a single one had so much as grazed her—even before her blood had boiled to the surface and turned the remainder to salt. She recalled the expressions of those who'd witnessed the occurrence. Era had called her powerful. Michal had gone from calling her charmingly sensitive to astounding in no time at all. Perhaps, as awful as it had been, much *had* been accomplished. She began to grasp the significance of the event. Yet, if the Great One called *that* small... what was to come?

Suddenly, she was having trouble swallowing her pastry.

A knock sent her leaping to her feet. Answering it felt like opening a stranger's door. She must get it into her head that this suite was her home for the time being. It certainly wasn't a bad place to pass the time.

"Petyr..." she greeted coldly on opening the door. She folded her arms in self-protection.

"Change into something you can swim in."

It had been an age since anyone had suggested she enjoy a swim. In fact, it was scarcely considered appropriate for her to do so at her age. Moreover, who was this man to tell her what to do all the time?

"How do you know I haven't other plans?"

"You don't want to swim?"

"I may be otherwise occupied."

"You aren't. I checked with father and Era."

She rolled her eyes.

He released a long sigh. "Vella..." he sighed out, appearing as if he would bring correction before relaxing into something like humility, "I apologize for the way I spoke to you last night."

"Do you?"

He pressed his lips together before, "I was in a foul mood, I'll admit. After what you'd been through... I should have been more solicitous."

"Try solicitous *at all.*"

He nodded. "I have no excuse."

She felt herself soften as her arms relaxed to her sides. "I suppose you have."

His eyes searched hers. "Someone told you?"

She nodded. "I apologize for any part I played in—"

"Are you joking? It wasn't *your* fault. It was hers." Bitterness rose to the surface before he visibly relaxed again. "No, it wasn't hers either. It was the will of the Great One. If he'd willed me to return sooner, he'd have led me to you right off. Nothing is too difficult for him. I... have to believe I spent all that time on Earth for a reason."

"Perhaps he was waiting for me to grow up a little..."

"Perhaps I had some maturing to do of my own."

Petyr was admitting he had room to grow? She inwardly groaned at herself. Was she jealous of the way people spoke about him? She now considered him with fresh eyes. He might swagger and speak as if he owned the world, but he was a remarkable person. She needed to give him a chance. If he failed her again, she could pull away.

"Let me go change," she acquiesced, closing the door to open her wardrobe. It was then she realized she had little notion of what women wore to swim. Returning, she asked, "What should I bathe in?"

"Anything, I suppose."

"I mean, have you specific swim garments here?"

"Swimmers typically just swim in their everyday clothes. It's how they travel, you know. You can't run around everywhere in a bathing suit."

"Hm..." she replied with consideration as she closed the door.

With a shrug, she selected a blue toga. That seemed most appropriate to her. She turned for the door before snatching a look at her hair. It was a disaster. Taking up the comb provided her, she let her long locks fall around her shoulders. For the last few years, she'd been expected to wear it up as a sign of maturity. Ergo, she raced to her bag from home to fetch a ribbon and tie her tresses back into a braid.

With a nod of approval to herself, she joined Petyr in the hall. It was then she recalled the guardsmen posted outside her door. They nodded with assurance. She tried to feel assured, but wondered if she was to be escorted by them wherever she went over the course of her stay, as Petyr's father seemed to be.

"Here." Petyr handed her what looked to be a long scarf.

"Is it cold?"

"It's a garment of mourning for those who cannot bear to be disturbed in their grief. For you, it is a disguise so we can ditch the guards."

She grinned before faltering. "Is it safe to do so?"

"I consider myself guardsman enough, but it's up to you."

She deliberated for some moments. It would be nice to go about without anyone recognizing her. The guards would only draw attention. "How do I wear it?"

He helped her arrange it over her head and around her shoulders. It fell so far over her face that she was certain no one would know her. At last, he pulled the gold chain for the transport. When the door slid open, Michal was revealed.

"What are you doing here?" Petyr inquired apprehensively. "I thought you were busy today."

"I was," he admitted with a shrug. "I canceled my plans. She needs a Swimmer to show her the sights."

"*You're* a Swimmer?"

He bowed. "One in the same... Why does your tone bode ill at the knowledge?"

A chuckle escaped her lips. "I've only heard negative things about Swimmers—how flaky they are."

Petyr released a snort. "I suppose that is true about *most* Swimmers, but Michal is a rock. He goes when and where Father sends him and does what he is told. In a phrase, he is Father's dream child."

"Like you can talk," Michal scoffed. "Petyr just happens to be the most renowned prophet's personal favorite."

"Iviana?" Novella clarified.

They nodded.

"You locate a prophet's long-lost daughter and suddenly you're showered with favor," Petyr explained.

"Lost daughter?"

"We'd grown up hearing tales of how Iviana's newborn child disappeared in the hands of her closest friend, Era," Michal began as they departed from the transport.

"*Era* made Iviana's daughter disappear?" she questioned. "And they're still friends?"

"Let him continue," Petyr urged with a grin. "This is my shining moment."

"Indeed," Michal affirmed with a laughing elbow to his brother's gut. "The tale went that Era had long refused to touch the child. One day, Iviana thrust her into Era's arms. Next thing they knew, the babe was gone."

"How terrible!" Novella gasped. "What had happened?"

"Era's a Time-jumper," Petyr supplied. "She sent the child through time."

Novella eyed them leerily. She could not comprehend such a thing. How could they speak so flippantly? "Era can... do what?"

"She travels through time," Petyr supplied again, "though never of her own volition. It happens of the Great One's accord. This time, however, it was Iviana's daughter she sent off. That had never happened before."

Novella shook her head. It was all quite beyond her. "Go on," she pressed soberly.

"A couple of years passed," Michal continued. "Iviana and Era did not speak in that time, though they each blamed themselves. But *Petyr*, here, decided he couldn't accept the story lying down. He got it into his head that if the daughter was sent *back* in time, she might yet be living in our time. So, to put his Seeker's fire to good practice, he asked the Great One to help him locate her. Aaand *guess* whose doorstep he ended up on?"

Novella was at a loss.

"Era's," Petyr supplied with a grin.

She blinked back at them.

"Turned out," Michal went on, "Era was the babe who'd disappeared. She'd landed in Atlantyss when it was concealed beneath the surface and was adopted by a good couple. She grew up here as an ordinary girl until just before Atlantyss was to emerge. As the Great One developed a bond between her and Iviana, a prophet of that day informed Era who they were to one another. But neither of them ever told Iviana."

"Which is really fascinating," Petyr chimed in. "Era technically wasn't even born when Iviana first met her. In fact, Iviana hadn't even married Realm Leader Flynn yet."

Novella stopped outside the doors of the Council Hall, bracing herself against its diamond partition. "Can you gentlemen repeat all that?"

It wasn't until they'd taken her through the city and reached the shoreline that she was confident she thoroughly understood the tale.

"But why didn't Era tell Iviana as soon as she, as an infant, disappeared?"

"Beats me," Petyr retorted. "Said she wasn't sure Iviana was prepared to accept her as a grown woman after having lost the chance to raise her as a child."

"How did Iviana take the news?"

Michal laughed.

"She fainted," Petyr explained. "I mean, Era had begged me not to tell, but I was ten years. How could anyone expect me to keep a secret like that? Besides, I'm a famed truthteller. So, I found Iviana and revealed everything."

"Oh, Petyr..." Novella groaned. "Those poor women."

"To be fair," Michal spoke up, "the truth healed them. They're closer than ever, as you've seen."

"It was difficult for Era to remain here to care for you," Petyr informed. "She somehow feels responsible for her mother's wellbeing... though they're really not far apart in age."

Novella eyed the stunning ocean before them. She hadn't considered what it meant for Iviana to leave Era with her. She saw now that having Petyr and Era for support truly was Iviana's way of watching out for her. These truly were the people she trusted most in the world.

"Petyr's fame was indisputable after that," Michal explained as he sauntered into the water. "*Everyone* knows about the boy who solved the mystery of the prophet's missing child. In fact, it is how father's notoriety initially grew."

Novella stopped short as her feet hit the water. It was a sensation she had never experienced before—not even at the seaside back home. Its warmth sent soothing tingles up her body, as if flooding her with strength. Her veins burned with teal light while the aroma of that honey-scented water imbued promise into her spirit. It was like returning to her father's embrace: She belonged here.

Instantly, she leaped from the water. This couldn't be home. *Home* was made up of corsets and carriages and mother and father. Yet, the call of that water was like denying herself oxygen.

"Something wrong?" Petyr asked, eyes shining with comprehension.

She narrowed her own. "Nothing's wrong, I—it's cold."

"Liar."

"I'd rather not swim today."

Michal sauntered back up, his own veins glowing mildly with the hue of the Swimmer's gift. "You have *no* idea what you'd be missing."

She shook her head. "I can't go in there. I just... I can't." She *couldn't* belong here. It was a trap prepared to swallow her whole. After all, there were people who'd rather she was dead than remain.

Michal offered up a hand. "Just give me five minutes."

She raised a brow. "You have clocks here?"

She was rewarded with their laughter.

CHAPTER 17

THAT NIGHT, NOVELLA TUCKED herself into bed with a mind *swimming* over the adventures of the day. There were *valid* reasons for Mother to remain on Earth. Now Novella had gotten a taste for this place, she could not imagine leaving—*ever*. The sweet, tangy water was one draw, but all the natural phenomenon housed beneath its surface was quite another. Not to mention being able to breathe *openly* beneath the surface beside another just like her. But it was the moment he had ushered her into a colony of Swimmers who lived beneath the water, with whom she was able to speak with ease, that she understood she could never return to her old life. This place boasted *endless marvels. S*he wanted to spend the remainder of her life discovering them.

Her heart pounded with the truth. It was an exhilarating dream but terrifying in the extreme. Lost was her taste for carriages and social protocols. She felt she would run out of oxygen if she returned to them. Yet, there *was* Mother and Father. They were her world, the people who loved her more than anyone on any planet. Surely, she must return eventually. Father didn't even know where she was or what she was about. But... how could she *ever* content herself to a place in which she had never really belonged? She tossed and turned with these questions, debating with herself one minute, soothing and assuring the next. It was hours before she fell asleep and it was with the nightmare she'd endured at her aunt's home from which she awoke in a cold sweat.

She sat up, working to catch her breath and settle her heart. The stranger with the knife had approached her again. This time she recognized him. But it was only a dream... wasn't it? Could it truly be he boded her harm? She shook her head. He seemed so very *for* her. This comfort in mind, she returned to slumber. The dream did not return. Come morning, she concluded that she would be watchful, but it could only prove a nightmare. After all, he was trusted by Iviana the Glorybringer, the greatest prophet in the Greater Archipelagos.

As weeks passed, Novella grew stronger from her swims, as well as her exploration of the city under the guise of her mourning garment. Her skin became bronzed as brass and her golden hair was now almost white. She had never had the liberty of spending so much time out of doors and found it did her good body and soul.

She'd also been afforded free reign of the Council Hall and knew it like the back of her hand. It was like discovering one lived in a treasury, it boasted such opulence. It sorely contrasted with her second evaluation of the outer region of the city. Once again, she noted skinny people living in riches itself without the benefit of them, aside from a roof over their heads. How could it be that these people lived in a prosperous city with scarcely enough to live on? She couldn't begin to fathom it. She supposed it was thus in England... but no one lived in homes of gemstone.

Aside from that district, the island proved a paradise. Especially as no further attempt was made on her life. When Tamsen discovered she was sneaking off with his sons without guardsmen, she'd heard tales of his anger concerning their decision. Yet, Michal managed to convince his father that she was safe between them and her mourning garment. The Realm Leader let the matter rest in her own hands. If she was willing to risk it, he had no choice in the matter. And she *was*

willing. It was too attractive an island to miss out on any experience the fellows were willing to provide.

"You *like* it here," Petyr stated as they traversed the tropical
forest.

Novella scarcely stifled her grin. "It's not so bad."

He folded his arms. "We really ought to pop back to Earth for
a visit to your parents."

"What? Why?" What if her father shouldn't allow her to leave
again?

"Knew it. You're hooked like a fish at a fishing hole."

She glared at him. "Fine. I *am* entranced with what I have seen
of this planet. But... I will eventually have to return."

"Who says?"

"Well... *I* do."

"*Or* you could consider obeying the Great One's summons. It
is really inescapable, you know."

She shook her head. "I admit I belong here. But to become
leader of the whole planet is unfeasible. And your father seems
to be doing well."

His face dropped into a frown as he stepped in front of her.
"Vella..." he began with intensity, "most of the population is
unwilling to accept a leader who was not discovered by a Seeker
for the purpose. This world used to be *far* greater than it is now.
You should have known it as I did growing up. It was something
akin to heaven, I think."

"It seems like that to me now."

"*No,*" he insisted. "We can be better. You can make us greater
again."

She shuffled around him with exasperation. "Don't you realize
how daunting that sounds? I don't know how to juggle world-
wide affairs!"

"My father does. He would counsel you, as would the world council itself. Better yet, why don't you speak with Father about these concerns?"

She walked in silence a long while before, "I will think about it."

But Novella in no way intended to act on his suggestion. She wanted to go on relishing the place for what it was, not go altering things or trying to fix them. These last days had been like a happy dream from which she could not bear awakening.

"What was that?" Petyr asked as he stopped to listen.

She studied the forest around them that glowed almost golden under the vibrant sun. "I didn't hear anything."

His head shot to the left. "There it was again."

"An animal?" she questioned, not really believing he'd heard anything. He *did* like to tease.

He shook his head. "Wait here. I'm going to have a look around."

Retrieving a dagger from his belt, he vanished into the forest. As a deal of time passed, Novella grew weary of waiting, seating herself against a tree. It wasn't until she'd nearly fallen asleep that she was jolted to total awareness.

"You are Novella?" the low voice of a stranger spoke beside her. It proved a tall woman of about middle age.

Novella leaped to her feet, searching for Petyr.

"He is being led on a fool's errand," the woman explained. "We had to speak with you and knew no other way."

Novella opened her mouth to call out, but the woman was faster than she was. She had her in a headlock with her mouth tightly covered.

"You *must* hear me out," she stranger insisted. "We mean you no harm, but you must come with us now."

Chomping down on the hand, she managed to squeal out, "What do you want me for?"

The hand smacked back over her mouth. "There are those on the Eastern isles who believe you are the true and chosen Realm Leader. We need you there—*desperately*. You are the only one who can make things right."

Their attention was caught by the sounds of approach. Novella stole her moment to lunge from the woman's grasp. Leaping for a large stick, she held it up defensively. "I'm not going anywhere with you! Moreover, I'm no Realm Leader. I would like to help, but I'm not the person for the task. You must see Realm Leader Tamsen about your needs."

"I guess you were right about an animal," Petyr called as he reappeared.

Novella's eyes shot from him to the space where the woman had stood.

She was gone.

Petyr quirked a brow at the stick in her hand before his face grew grim. "*Not* an animal then..."

She shook her head, dropping the stick as she caught her breath. "I think I'll have that chat with your father now."

CHAPTER 18

NOVELLA PAUSED OUTSIDE THE door. She wasn't prepared for a one-on-one meeting with the current leader of the world. Or, well, half of it. Moreover, they were to discuss matters she wasn't entirely eager to get into. Yet, it must be done. That had just been proved quite clear.

"There's no reason to be nervous," Era assured as they approached the door. "Tamsen likes you."

"He does?"

"Says he admires both your spirit to remain here in the face of danger and caution to carefully consider your role."

Novella was bolstered by that. It was a new picture of herself. She rather liked it.

She tapped at the door.

"Yes, come in," the Realm Leader called.

Era gave her a final nod of assurance before opening the door. Novella wished she'd accepted the woman's offer to sit in on the conversation, but she had feared her presence would only increase the pressure of embracing the call to Realm Leader. She was in no mind to debate two at the same time. It happened often enough with Petyr and Michal.

"Novella," Tamsen spoke with a smile as he turned from a stack of parchment on his desk. "Please, be seated by the windows. It is so much more pleasant than that old desk. I've taken the liberty of having quincea tea sent up. Will you take a cup?"

Novella had no idea what quincea tea was but nodded just the same.

"I'm glad you requested this meeting," he continued as he fixed her drink. "I'd been meaning to schedule one myself, but other matters got in the way." Passing her the cup, he seated himself to look her over like a proud father surveying a favored daughter. "But seeing as how *you* made the arrangement, why don't you begin?"

Novella swallowed, stealing a sip of the direly bitter tea to clear her throat. Setting the cup down, she planted her hands in her lap. "I previously expected to remain on this planet no longer than the span I have already spent."

"But now you're here... you want to see more," he ventured.

She bobbed her head. "The trouble is, much as I'd like to extend my stay, I in no way feel prepared to fill your shoes... I don't see how I ever could."

He considered her for some moments before, "I don't see why you should not be granted all the time you need to make your decision."

She released a sigh. "I'm not entirely certain just how much time I have. Not only did we experience that attack my first evening here, I was approached by a woman from an Eastern island in the forest this morning. She expected me to accompany her to her home as rightful Realm Leader."

He drew to his feet. "Where did this occur?"

"On the southern tip of the island."

"I thought Petyr and Michal were to be with you at all times on these *jaunts?*"

"Michal was unable to accompany us this time. The woman insinuated that Petyr had been lured away so she might speak with me."

He smacked his fist against the wall. "I *told* those fellows it was foolhardy to show you around without a proper guard." Dropping into his seat, he looked to her with pleading eyes. "I can only do so much if my orders are not appreciated. Whether you like it or not, the Greater Archipelagos *needs you* to unite them. We can no longer toss your safety around like so many marbles."

"Realm Leader Tamsen," she began after clearing her throat, "I apologize for the concern I have caused you. I take responsibility for our rash actions. I'd... not realized you felt this way."

His face softened. "That is well-said. I see glimmers of why the Great One must have chosen you every time we meet. Yet, I do not in any way place the blame on anyone but my own sons. *They* know better. You are an entire stranger here."

She released a sigh. "I caught a glimpse of that today. From now on, I will gratefully acquiesce to your security measures."

He raised a pensive brow at her. "Would you... *also* consider allowing me to coach you for your destined position, even if you inevitably defy the Great One's desire in the end?"

That was quite a way to put it. It left her with little room to negotiate. In fact, she began to feel ashamed. "What would this training entail?"

"To begin with, I would like to have someone tutor you on our geography, culture and judicial practices. But since it is clear we haven't much time, I think it judicious to send you on a diplomatic tour as well."

"A... tour—to see the sights?"

"Yes," he answered brightly, *"and* to meet with some of the surrounding islands. We could begin on a small portion of the Western half. They've been requesting a visit from me in order to hear out a number of grievances. With a few pointers from the council, I think you might appear in my stead."

"Go... in your stead... to handle grievances?"

He nodded firmly. "To only a handful of islands—the mildest of them. You would be in no danger. You have exhibited a tactful tongue. And..." he began meditatively, "we must take another direction in our management of the matter of your identity. As it is clear we have failed to conceal it, you must be officially presented to the council. It is they, really, who must release you for the tour."

Now more than ever, Novella regretted this conference. She'd known things would become serious once they spoke, but not *this* substantial. Every fiber of her being rejected the notion of meeting the official council of the world, let alone taking a diplomatic tour. How was she to dictate matters of which she was so ill informed?

"To be honest," she began, "I'm not sure I feel myself ready for all of this."

"It is too late now, my girl. We've been had. The people must see you for themselves on an official level. They must become acquainted with the notion that someone is present whom the Great One avows can bring calm to their storms. If, after this journey, you find you have made a final decision to either remain here or return to Earth, we will discuss how to handle the situation at that juncture."

He stood to his feet, seeming to expect her to do the same. Though she was in no way finished, she found her legs obeyed as they followed him to the door. Before she knew it, he had dismissed her with all the courtesy in the world and she no opportunity to negotiate.

"How did it go?" Era asked with an eager grin.

Novella shrugged. "I am to be presented to the council as the Great One's selection for Realm Leader and then sent on a diplomatic tour of the surrounding islands."

Era clapped her hands. "I knew he would convince you!"

"I'm not sure he has, but he *is* difficult to refuse."

"Why do you think Iviana made him a provisional Realm Leader? He volunteered and she acquiesced."

Novella's eyes narrowed. That was not how she'd pictured that situation playing out. Yet, she was glad to have a man like that on her side. It was better to have him for her than against, that was certain. If she minded herself well and ignored her dreams, she might just manage to keep it that way.

Novella's hands shook as she righted her hair in the mirror. An employee of the hall, skilled in beautification, had seen to her appearance for the auspicious occasion: her presentation before the council of the world. Dropping her hands, she turned to face Era, who'd been tutoring her for the event.

"I can't do this. I honestly fear I'll faint before them."

Era raised a brow in contemplation. "The council is not so plenteous in number as it once was. In the old days, there were about a dozen. Of more recent years, that number grew to nearly twenty. Today, you are to meet but six members. And you must recall that, in their eyes, *you* are the significant one. You are the chosen leader. Though technically they must be informed that you have delayed the event of your acceptance, they will see you for what you are."

Novella released a sigh. "You know I am but eighteen years, right?"

"The Great One is fully aware of what he is doing. It is important to remember that He does not view things as we do. Where we consider the strength and maturity of a person, he sees spirits and hearts. *He* does not fear for you, so why should you or I?"

Once again, Novella was recalled to mind of King David as a mere shepherd boy. He'd been the youngest of his brothers when he was anointed as the future king of Israel. Ergo, *her* youth was of no consequence. She must trust God.

"May we descend now?" she asked. "I cannot bear this waiting."

"Atta girl."

All the way down the transport to the very doors of the public council chamber, she trembled. Era gestured to the guardsman to open the doors, but Novella stopped them. She required a moment. Racing around the corner, she bent over with hands to her knees. *I can't do this. I can't do this,* sing-songed through her head like a mad ballad. This was not what she'd intended in traveling to this planet. She'd merely wanted to see the place from which her mother had come. She'd not expected to suffer such an attraction to the place, so much so that she was willing to honor Realm Leader Tamsen's proposal.

"If I be for you, who can be against you?"

She looked up as the words of her lion-voice echoed adamantly through her soul.

She'd not necessarily expected anyone to be against her. She was simply intimidated by the presentation. But now it sounded like an opposing force awaited her. Could it be that the council was not eager to embrace her?

She stood up straight. Though she in no way wished to be Realm Leader, she couldn't abide the notion that people she'd never met had pre-judged her, as had those Easterly chieftains. And she had always found it difficult to refuse a dare. She returned to Era's side with a curt nod and Era gestured to the guardsman.

To the unexpected accompaniment of trumpets, Novella followed the path of a rolled-out carpet. She marched with all the poise of a queen beneath a ceiling vibrant from draping diamond chandeliers. The room glowed in rainbow hues like sunlight on a diamond, altogether fitting for an edifice built thusly.

At the end of the hall, settled in rows on either side of the mighty perch on which Tamsen sat, were six council members. Era had been right. They failed to intimidate her. Rather, they appeared rather ragtag and lost. This large chamber was intended to be filled with a number of reigning members. What had happened to all of them? Ignoring such qualms, she concluded her entrance with a low bow before the members.

"Novella of Earth," a woman greeted, her dark gray hair streaming long about her shoulders, "daughter of Nimua the Seer, I hereby welcome you to this humble planet with all gratitude." The woman's eyes kindled with startling warmth.

With a bob of her head, Novella studied the speaker with perplexity. She appeared awfully familiar. If it weren't for her clear maturity, she might have reminded her of...

The woman nodded. "Your mother is my daughter."

Her mouth fell open. Meeting not only her mother's relatives but the *grandmother* she'd scarcely heard a word about had not been on the day's agenda. How had it not occurred to her to seek her out?

"I apologize that I could not meet you before now," the unexpected grandmother spoke. "I was on a journey through distant isles and was only informed of your presence in time to appear at this hall an hour ago. In fact, I had not even realized we were to take part in this event until my arrival." Looking Novella over in full, she added, "I must say, you are the spitting image of Nimua."

Realm Leader Tamsen cleared his throat. "I apologize, Naii, but may I ask you complete this conversation after our presentation?"

Naii nodded her willingness, though her eyes hungrily scrutinized her granddaughter. Novella scarcely knew how to respond to this close relation of whom she'd heard so little. Now and then, Mother had gotten a distant yearning in her eyes. Perhaps it was for this very woman who was dressed like a humble queen.

"Novella of Earth," Realm Leader Tamsen continued, stealing her gaze for himself, "I hereby announce the Great One's summons of your leadership to the Greater Archipelagos. It is to be understood that you have not yet acknowledged that call but are, nonetheless, chosen. Will the present company please applaud?"

The poor excuse for an ovation from but six people made Novella feel somewhat embarrassed for them. Out of the whole world, how were these the only members remaining? Surely, if one was lost, another could be appointed. Or was there a reason why so few were either selected or willing to stand as council of the world?

A blonde gentleman to the right of Tamsen cleared his throat. "Are we given to understand that she is not eager to accept the invitation as Realm Leader?"

From the moment Novella had entered the room, this man had been scanning her for weaknesses. Her eyes flew to Tamsen, who nodded for her to respond. She swallowed. Era had prepared her for this. She turned to the man with all the dignity she could muster.

"The invitation to stand as leader of this splendid world is over-whelming in the extreme to one who has only just arrived."

"In other words," he continued, "you're daunted by the challenge of cleaning up another planet's mess."

Heat spread through her blood as her temples pulsed. Even so, a small smile reached her lips. "The Greater Archipelagos merits a leader confident in their ability to honor its adversities. I... feel it nec-essary to better acquaint myself with its hardships before accepting such an auspicious role."

"*Well* put," Tamsen spoke conclusively. Novella sensed he was as proud of her as he might be for his own daughter. It was good to have him with her.

She turned to the entire company with, "Realm Leader Tamsen has suggested a diplomatic tour to a number of the surrounding islands.

I hope in that time that I may better grasp the issues the Greater Archipelagos is facing."

"And then you'll let us know if you feel up to bothering about them?" the blonde man questioned. "I officially *object* to this ridiculous agenda. Clearly, she is but a girl, floundering about like a lost duckling. This is a dire moment for the Greater Archipelagos. Passing the role of Realm Leader from one of experience to one who cannot be bothered could well-nigh send us into pandemonium. I demand we continue under Realm Leader Tamsen's leadership for the foreseeable future."

"I understand that any word from me will come across entirely bias," Naii began evenly, "but I believe that is too hasty, Illiab. Not to mention, it is disrespectful of the Great One's will and wisdom. I stand with Tamsen. A tour is the best policy for introducing her to both the public and the issues of the world. I think we cannot do better than to allow her a little time."

Illiab shook his head. "Who does this young upstart of an Earthling think she is, waltzing in here with borrowed garments and gold jewelry, proposing she can manage even so much as a consular tour among those she fears to govern? Really," he started again, turning to each member of his audience, "this must be a *jest*. How can we be certain Petyr is not telling tales to cover for his inability to locate our *true* chosen leader?

Novella's blood turned cold at that. "Petyr is the very Seeker who managed to locate Iviana's lost daughter," she reminded. "Moreover, he is *famed* for his integrity. If you want to call my abilities into question, very well. But Petyr is faultless in this matter."

Illiab quirked a smirk. "Now, young woman, do not lose your temper—"

"*That* said," she continued without pause, "if the Great One be for me, who dares speak against me? Surely, he stands with me, for I have heard it from his own lips. Therefore, any who accuse me stand in accusation of the God who formed the galaxies. I, for one, would be terrified of being found guilty of such iniquity. Now, honorable council, shall we have the vote to determine whether I be sent?" She eyed them in their turns until she met Naii's proud expression.

"All those in favor?" the grandmother promptly announced.

In addition to Tamsen and Naii, three council members raised their hands.

"Opposed?"

Only Illiab raised his, though his eyes bored into the woman who had not yet cast a vote. Finally, she raised her hand.

Naii rolled her eyes, turning to Novella with, "You are formally released for your tour of the Western isles. The Great One be with you."

Illiab leaped to his feet, wrath rolling from his person in waves. But when he opened his mouth to speak, Tamsen invited him to step into another room. Novella smirked to think of what a meeting with the skilled leader would entail. She wouldn't trade places with Illiab for the world.

"Who is that man?" she asked of Era as they departed.

"I'm afraid that is your great uncle."

"My *uncle?*"

"Your Grandmother Naii's youngest brother. He always was a spoiled boy. Problem is, he's quite a grown man now and still imposes his way. Unfortunately, he typically gets it. There are a great many on both the Western and Eastern sides who follow him. Considering that you are his niece, I had hoped he would take a liking to you."

Novella raised a brow. "Do you think he could get me shipped back home?"

Era pressed her lips together before admitting, "He may, if you do not make a success of this tour."

CHAPTER 19

"THANK YOU FOR ALLOWING me this visit," Naii greeted from her chair in Novella's suite. "I know you must be busy preparing for your trip. But I simply could not let you go without getting a proper look at you."

Novella couldn't help feeling at a loss for how to handle this unanticipated grandmother. "I'm glad you came. I wanted to speak more with you."

"Naturally so. It isn't every day one discovers they've a grand-daughter they weren't aware of... who can now update one on the wellbeing of her runaway daughter?"

Novella grinned. So, *that* was it. "Mother is well, I can assure you. From what I understand, she was not on her own long before Father scooped her up for himself."

Naii's eyes widened. "It is difficult to imagine that she married again so soon after losing Necoli."

"Father's doorstep was the first she turned up on. She was ill and undernourished. The family nursed her back to health, but it was clear she wasn't capable of caring for herself. Father, it seems, fell promptly in love and rather badgered her to let him do the caring before she finally gave in. The only catch was... she was allowed to keep her secrets."

"Hmm," the woman murmured. "That doesn't sound like my Nimua. But... I suppose she wouldn't be the same after such a sore loss, then landing in an unknown world. Tell me, what is she like now? And your father, tell me of him."

"I think she is currently returning to what she must have been before her loss," Novella spoke thoughtfully. "All my life, she was loving but held expectations for me that were sometimes difficult to meet. I think it was because of her insecurity that I was different due to her lineage that she was determined to make a social success of me. Moreover, she suffered bitterness toward God. But the Great One used me to melt her heart and... she was another person just before I left—almost like a young woman."

Naii released a long, satisfied sigh. "The Great One's faithfulness knows no bounds. I knew she had turned her back on him, but he wasn't willing she should be lost. You have no idea what that does for me."

"Father, on the other hand, has always been easy-going and even-keeled with a whole trove of mirth in possession. He kept his word not to pry into Mother's secrets and accepted her as a mystery. In fact, I think he loved her for it. His whole career involved uncovering truth. Yet, he met his match in her. He doesn't even know where I am right now."

Naii clucked. "I don't like secrets between married people. But I am glad to see your mother held to one tradition at least."

"What's that?"

"All the women in our family possess names that begin with an 'N.'"

"Really?" Novella asked with intrigue. "Funny that everyone calls me Vella back home."

"That's pretty too, but I like Novella. And now..." She looked her granddaughter over carefully. "My own flesh and blood has been called to lead our suffering world." She shook her head. "It is an honor and a mystery in itself."

Novella's eyes dropped to her lap. "A mystery is right."

Naii's eyes roved her features as she asked, "May I give you a single piece of advice—as a grandmother?"

Novella's gaze shot to hers. "Please."

"You are incapable of managing the challenges before you."

Novella blinked at her 'loving' grandmother.

"That is to say," Naii continued, "you must cleave to the Great One for all you're worth. The *only* one who can make it possible for an eighteen-year-old foreigner to lead us *is* Him."

Novella's eyes shot back and forth between her grandmother's. This frankness was refreshing. Everyone else seemed to think she could just jump into leading and *be* the right person. This view made much more sense.

"I am not even certain how to 'cleave' to him, as you say."

"Simply put, you must give him your time. Put in the effort of seeking him as a Seeker's fire drives them after a treasure. Let anything that does not align with the Great One fall by the wayside. Take *every* concern to him and learn to trust that he will never, ever drop you, even when it looks as if you're walking through valleys dark as death. Don't look to the right or left; keep your faith in him. With his eyes upon you, there is nothing he cannot do through and for you."

It was clear that there were strong women of faith on both sides of Novella's family. But though the words moved her greatly, she was at a total loss. "How do I even seek him in the way you describe?" Something in her burned to do so. She noticed her blood was glowing green like Petyr's on occasion.

"*Talk* to him, pray, study the hallowed scrolls, thank him for his daily care, worship him in his gracious kindness and majesty. He is a *good God*, Novella. His love is the variety that looks on tempests and is never shaken. When he makes a bargain, he keeps his end even when we do not. He can redeem anything so long as we are living in surrender to his will. I cannot begin to describe all he has been in my life, especially after your mother..."

Naii swallowed as large tears dropped from her eyes. "Your mother was my closest friend—all a mother could ask for and more. I knew she was devastated when she lost Necoli, but... I couldn't seem to help her. Perhaps the Great One used her grief to transport her where she needed to be. She met your father and... *you* were born." She ran a soft hand along Novella's jawline. "You are no accident, sweet girl. The Great One knew you before you were knit together in your mother's womb. His hands shaped your person, inside and out."

She released a sigh. "Forgive an old woman's rambling, but he *loves* us, Novella. It doesn't seem quite possible, but it is so. In the end... seeking him is loving him with *all* your heart, soul, mind and strength—with every part of who you are. Seeking is trusting Him with everything, even when it appears irrational."

The way this woman viewed life with the Great One felt like a whole new world of possibility. Novella wanted it. She would do her best to cleave to the advice or... die trying. "I wish you were coming along with me," she admitted, feeling the first stirrings of affection for her mother's mother.

"I wish I was too," Naii responded with a regretful smile, "but the council would credit me with any successes you make. It is a trial by fire, but you will arise from the blaze stronger than you were before."

Novella released an inspired breath. "I certainly hope so..." Yet, the notion terrified her. Why was she doing this again?

A knock at the door interrupted them with a jolt.

"I'll get it," Naii volunteered as she floated to the door on poised feet so much like her daughter. "Michal!" she greeted with affection. "I haven't seen you in an age. Strapping as ever, I see."

Michal actually blushed. "I hope I've grown in more than my looks."

"I'm sure you have. You are an honorable man. Now, I presume you must speak with my granddaughter, so I will give you the room. Good day to you both and good luck to you, Novella."

Michal raised his brows in Novella's direction. "I hadn't put it together that you were related."

Novella rose to meet him at the threshold. "It hadn't even occurred to me that mother had family. The jokes on both of us, I suppose."

"I suppose it is..." he replied distractedly.

"Can I... help you with something?"

"No," he replied as if torn from his revelry. "It is only... I wished you to take this on your journey." He retrieved a scroll from behind his back. "Petyr told me you possess a hallowed text from your own world, but... I thought it might be helpful to read from one of ours. He says we share a God. There is but one after all. Even so..." He placed it into her hands. "There you are."

"Oh," she gasped as she felt the aged parchment, its crimson seal broken long ago. "How very considerate. I would love to read this, especially as I have recently grasped the alphabet of your people. Why, this is beautiful."

"I asked father if I might accompany you on your journey, but he insists he requires me here. So, I thought I'd send something to help out at least. And... perhaps, when you read it, you will be reminded of me."

Her eyes flew from the scroll to his sober face. His eyes searched hers for an answer she did not have. In fact, his attention seemed only to unnerve her.

"I'm sure I will," she answered transparently. How could she not after he'd said something like that?

His eyes glowed as if she'd knighted him. "I must let you complete your preparations. But I will see you at evening meal and will be present for your send-off tomorrow morning."

Her stomach flipped over. What she'd taken for a passing fancy was suddenly being presented with intention. From such a man, she could not help feeling privileged. Quite suddenly, the walls that demanded she protect her liberty were trembling.

"I look forward to it," she answered with a scarcely concealed grin.

His smile was all the reward required as he bowed his exit.

Closing the door behind her, Novella bit her lower lip. What was happening to her defenses? Could it possibly be that the Great One intended Michal for her in order to assist with her projected role? She shook her head against the thought. Yet, she could not help looking at her future in an entirely different light.

"Silly schoolgirl *indeed,*" she chastised as she recalled Petyr's words many nights ago.

CHAPTER 20

THE DAY WAS WARM and clear, not a cloud in the sky. The world remained lush and magnificent. It had not rained once since Novella had arrived upon the planet. As she sat in her compartment aboard the *Glorybringer*, headed for the Emerald Island, she wondered when the season for rain emerged on the Greater Archipelagoes.

"I hope you grasp the gravity of this undertaking," Petyr abruptly voiced as he poured himself a glass of water.

He had been on edge all morning. Now, Novella understood why.

"*Petyr...*" Era chastised.

"More than you know," Novella insisted with mild irritation. She could not censure his nerves. Her own stomach was turning over like the waves of the sea.

Sitting down beside her, he spoke abstractedly, "You *can* do this. Not only are you sensible and well-spoken, you have the Great One on your side. Nothing is too difficult for him."

"Petyr..." Novella began in astonishment, "was there a compliment in there?"

"Two. What of it?" He appeared at a genuine loss.

"Forgive me, but... you so often remind me of mother—rather disapproving."

His brows flew to his hairline as his eyes darted between hers. "Do you believe I'd have brought you here if I'd been of that opinion?"

She and Era exchanged a glance.

He fidgeted in his seat before rising. "I'm going to check on our progress."

Novella looked to Era with wide eyes. "What's eating him?"

Era's eyes glowed with surprise and gratification. "I have a guess, but I'm not sharing it... I *am* fascinated to see how this plays out, though."

Novella released a sigh. The company she'd hoped would be a comfort was only feeding her nerves. Petyr may be even more anxious than her. It did not bode well for their first landing, that was certain.

In a moment, he returned with, "I do not intend to behave as a kind of mother hen, Vella. You are a grown woman who simply needs to start believing in herself, as well as the one who selected her." With that, he was gone again.

"Don't let him get to you," Era consoled with a knowing grin. "He is perhaps too invested."

Novella couldn't blame him for that either. Already, he'd been accused of simply picking her up because he could not find the true Realm Leader. That notion only contributed to the pressure she suffered. She couldn't let him down. Somehow, some way, she must prove that he was right... even if she *really* wanted him to be wrong.

"Get out here," Petyr demanded, disappearing as swiftly as he had reappeared.

Once again, Novella and Era exchanged glances before rising. They found Petyr leaning against the rail, eyeing the horizon.

Novella's stomach turned over again. "The Emerald Island, I presume?" she questioned with a shaky voice.

He turned to consider her. "Depend on the Great One. He will never fail you."

"You sound like Naii."

"Profound minds think alike." He ended with a wink.

A smile broke across her face. It was good to have him teasing again. *That* was the Petyr she knew. Though it had worn on her in past, it was preferrable to his uncustomary anxiety.

"You'll step from the gangplank first," he directed. "You must walk with head high, like you own the world. To them, you do."

She swallowed. Waltzing about like she owned the world wasn't exactly her style, but she would do her best.

"Era and I will be right behind you. If you need anything, listen for our cues. You are well-spoken, so I've no qualms on that score. I suppose that is one of the benefits to having been raised in England. You upper-classers are all so very *civilized.*"

She eyed him sidelong. It was clear he hadn't been a fan of her country. So much for compliments...

"Era talked you through the initial formalities, correct?"

She nodded, finding it difficult to swallow. "No one is going to announce me as Realm Leader expectant, are they? It is only rumored?"

He did not answer, instead turning to speak with one of the crew.

"I've just had the trumpets called off," he informed when he turned back.

Her eyes grew big as saucers.

He flicked her chin. "Pulling your leg, Miss Harper. He just informed me that we should arrive within ten minutes."

The mention of her formal name back home recalled to mind Petyr's red-feathered hat. She grinned as she took in the clothes he wore on his home planet: *red*. As in her world, he wasn't afraid to stand out in a crowd, nor could he help it as he sauntered about like a king, barking orders to whoever passed. Who had died and made him Realm Leader?

Swallowing back her natural dislike, she reminded herself that she needed him on this journey. She could use all the council she could get, especially from one whose father was currently acting in her stead. Yet... it might have been pleasant to have Michal along. He had no trouble helping her feel confident without also teasing and making her ill at ease.

The minutes that followed felt like an eternity. But, at long last, the *Glorybringer* was docked and a crowd subsequently gathered on the shore. Novella's fingers trembled as she doublechecked her ensemble. Everything must be in place. First impressions were vital, so Petyr had informed.

"You ready?" Era asked with a smile as she escorted her to the head of the gangplank.

Peering down at the muted crowd, Novella was certain half the island must be present. Ironically, they were all dressed in green—a nod to the emeralds they mined in plenty. The edifices, too, were of emerald, while even the plant life boasted of the island's wealthy resources. She glanced down at her clothing again—a white toga with green sash.

"Am I dressed appropriately?" she questioned of Era.

"The sash is enough. You don't want to look like you're trying too hard."

Novella nodded, licking her lips. Era stepped back beside Petyr, who nodded to the captain. Novella's heart dropped when the captain stepped forward, cupping his mouth with his hands to proclaim, "Please honor... Novella of Earth, Realm Leader expectant."

She cast a sound glare back at Petyr, whose face only hinted at a smirk, the old glimmer returning to his eyes.

A half-hearted applause commenced. By the faces in the crowd, it was clear they would celebrate her as she proved her worth—not before. In truth, she thought it judicious, but it didn't make for a very warm welcome.

Novella nodded her head in place of a bow and found herself lacing her fingers together before her as she descended the gangplank. She knew she appeared unpretentious, but she couldn't seem to help herself. She only hoped Realm Leader Tamsen had selected an easy island to win over, for she *was* floundering like a lost duck, as Great Uncle Illiab had denoted.

When she reached the end of the plank, a man in cascading emerald cloak stepped before her. With a half-bow, he spoke, "The Emerald Island welcomes you, Novella of Earth."

She answered with another nod of her head. "I appreciate the support of the populace on my landing."

He eyed her some moments, taking in every facet of the face she knew to look even younger than it was. "Did you bring it?" he asked bluntly.

She blinked back at him. "Bring... what?"

"The emerald scepter. We were promised its safe return on your arrival. You would not have been received otherwise."

Novella was certain she felt her heart stop. She turned back to Petyr in confusion, who stepped up beside her.

"Island Leader Rancho, I'm afraid no one informed us of this promise."

The man took two large steps forward until his eyes were bearing down on Novella. *"Trickery.* I knew a girl from another planet would prove untrustworthy."

Novella swallowed hard. This was her moment—her first test. Recalling the advice Naii had given, she cried in her mind, *Great One, you have to help me!*

Almost without realizing it, she approached the captain. "I must beg you return to Atlantyss and fetch the emerald scepter forthwith. We've a bargain to keep."

The captain looked first at her, then Petyr, who nodded gravely.

Novella turned back to the Island Leader with a deep bow. "I must apologize for our grave negligence. A lack of information on our part is no excuse. If you were pledged the emerald scepter, you must have it. I will not depart from your island until the agreement has been honored."

The Island Leader's eyes narrowed on her, nothing swayed. "I will personally make certain of that. The scepter was stolen in a raid by the Easterly Conglomeration, then rescued by Atlantyss but never rightfully restored to us. It has taken all my authority to keep my captains from raiding the Council Hall in order to retrieve it. I will look the jester if you fail me, *Realm Leader expectant.*"

"I give you my word," she answered soberly, turning to Petyr with a glance that commanded he be certain the errand was carried through.

Petyr's brows rose slightly before he turned on his heel to follow the captain up the plank.

"Now, Island Leader Rancho," Novella continued cooly, "may I see something of this beautiful island?" With a small smile, she added, "Green always was my favorite color."

For the first time, something of a smirk was returned her. He turned on his heel to speak to their audience. "I ask all curious parties to return to your business. Any concerns for the Realm Leader expectant must be filed through the island council. Thank you." To her, he directed, "Follow me."

CHAPTER 21

THE EMERALD ISLAND PLAYED up to Novella in various emerald hues as she traversed its city streets. She was relieved by how careful its citizens were to allow her distance. This Island Leader Rancho must rule them with an iron fist. Considering how things had begun, she had much ground to cover if she were to follow in his footsteps.

As they approached a cottage planted directly on the shore, Rancho turned to her with, "This is where you and your party shall reside. It possesses four sleeping rooms. I hope it will successfully accommodate your needs."

"I am certain it will. It looks perfectly charming!"

With the raising of an austere brow, he eyed her like she was a silly woman. "It was constructed with practicality in mind. We do not boast any of your Atlantiian towers here. It is not natural for man to tread so far from the ground."

"Of course," Novella amended with all the dignity she could muster. "I find it charming *in* its practicality, you must understand."

"If you require anything, send one of your innumerable guardsmen—if you think one can be spared." He shook his head. "I've never seen such an entourage in all my life." With that, he turned on his heel and sauntered off.

Novella turned to Era in her misery. "This is an unfortunate beginning."

Era pursed her lips before, "I cannot disagree. But come. Let us explore our accommodations."

Novella followed her in, neck deep in discouragement. What could possibly have happened with that scepter? Had she been set up in order to make a poor impression? She shook her head. It was simply a mistake. Miscommunications occurred. Yet, though she was almost certain the Great One had answered her plea for help on the docks, she could not help feeling she lacked his blessing. Everyone had promised he would make her path straight, but it seemed curvier than ever.

"Well," Era began as she surveyed the place, "it is safe to say you haven't lost much."

"What do you mean?"

"It is clear by this accommodation that they weren't expecting much from you. Although leaving behind the scepter succeeded in affirming their expectations, I'd say you never had anywhere to go but up."

Novella cast her gaze about. Though it was nothing to the Council Hall of Atlantyss, she thought it rather charming. "It reminds me of the cottage my family used to vacation at. It will certainly do for me." She thrust open a pair of white curtains. "Just *look* at that view. From my windows in Atlantyss, I can only see a sliver of the ocean. Here, we're practically swimming in it already."

Era turned to her with an approving grin. "That's the spirit! Perhaps we'll have time for a dip before your council session."

Novella's stomach dropped. She'd almost succeeded in forgetting about the session. Though the pressure had been high enough, it had only just begun. This session was to prove a trial by fire. At this rate, it would take an absolute miracle to win the approval of these people. As she was to leave for another island the following day, there wasn't much time for one.

"I need some time alone," she spoke quietly, feeling the weight of the world on her shoulders.

"That is a good idea," Era agreed. "Take the large room."

Novella shook her head. "The guardsmen should have that. I won't use much space."

"I disagree. Only a couple of guardsmen will be sleeping at a time and you must look the part you are playing."

Novella pressed her lips together a moment before, "The Island Leader is right. We don't require half a dozen guardsmen at a time. Two or three are sufficient to warn the rest should anything ensue. Give them the large room. The second largest will do for my purposes." She stepped into the room and shut the door softly behind her before falling to her knees beside the bed and pulling a pillow into her arms.

"Great One, my grandmother says I'm not capable of doing this on my own. How right she is. You've got to help me."

She listed her misgivings, her apparent failings, her uncertainties. She heard Era leave the cottage for who knew where. Petyr had not yet reappeared. She absently wondered if he'd returned to Atlantyss to see to the scepter himself. It wasn't until she opened her eyes to check the time that she fell back with a start.

There was a peculiar personage standing in her bedroom.

"What-*who* are you?" she nearly squealed.

She discerned eyes that glowed flame, bronze arms and torso and... his bottom portion was pure fire. A shift had occurred in the atmosphere. All was muted, as if nothing in the world existed beyond what was between her four walls.

"I am Help," the personage returned with a voice like a lion's purr.

Her open mouth fell shut. It *couldn't* be... "You aren't *the Great One?*" she questioned with wonder, eyes like two hotcakes.

"I am his third part," he answered with a nod, "his Spirit-essence. I am, as I said, the answer to your prayers. Moreover, I am the guide of your life and the power in your veins. We've really been acquainted for ages."

The third part. She was somewhat familiar with the notion. But she'd never heard of anyone who looked like *this*.

"I am come with a message from the Anointed One," he announced.

"The Anointed One?"

"The One who shed his blood upon a tree, who bore torture and treachery in order to win your soul. Surely, you consider yourself acquainted with *him.*"

"Jesus," she whispered.

His eyes shone like glowing embers. "One and the same."

She licked her lips as waves of wonder stole over her. "What... does he have to say?"

"That he is with you, even to the end of the age. Moreover, he is for you. He will not permit his chosen to be moved. All he asks of you is *willingness*—a boldness to surrender to His movements."

Her mouth fell open again. Willing was precisely what she had *not* been.

"How could I perceive his movements?"

"It is his leading," the Helper spoke softly. "He will guide you where he desires one way or another, so long as you are willing."

She shook her head, chin dropping to her chest. "I don't know how to be willing. I am so *afraid.*"

"Then I suggest you make fear your companion as you step into the intrepid places. One day, you will find it has fled you."

"I do so *hate* to be afraid," she admitted with a pathetic smile.

The Helped folded his arms, rising as if on invisible feet. "Novella, you must stop living like you are trying to reach death *safely*. Do you know what F.E.A.R. is? False Evidence Appearing Real. Living a life of faith is the only way to banish it, for the two cannot abide together."

Her brows flew up as the words played over and again in her mind. Was that what she'd been doing—living safely? For so long, she'd dreamed of *adventure*. True, she'd taken the mighty leap to this planet, had even allowed herself to be suckered into this tour. But it was true that her eyes darted about in hopes of avoiding danger at every turn.

"Things have started so poorly here," she complained.

Abruptly, her vision went dark. She felt as if she was either out of her body or so far in it that she was lost to the world. She groped about in her mind for something to hold on to, but all she found was inky blackness. Not even her voice would come. She felt herself giving way to panic before a small light shone in the distance. With all her might, she hurled her consciousness toward it.

As if she'd taken a literal leap, she found herself floating before a dreadful scene—one she had envisioned many times but never in such detail. The man who hung from the cross looked scarcely a man, so swollen, bruised and bloody was he. The cry that emerged from his lips as he writhed in agony made her wish she could shut her eyes. Her heart sobbed with him, the more so as it occurred to her just *who* this was.

Abruptly, he froze. His head turned to her. His eyes only just connected with hers beyond his swollen lids, effectively doing something to her heart. All at once, she was thrust back into her room on the Emerald Island. She bent over, clutching her gut with frantic sobs over the scene.

It was some time before she was able to gasp, *"Why* did you send me there?"

"I needed you to get a taste of what he was courageous enough to endure for you," the Helper explained. "It will make everything before you look quite manageable in comparison."

Her sobs quieted, giving way to hiccupping gasps as she took in his logic. It was true. He wasn't asking for the moon. He'd already died to give her that. All he asked was that she let him use her.

"*Why...?*" she breathed. "Why does he want *me?*"

"He has *great* plans for the Greater Archipelagos. And though it is true that he does not need you, it pleases him to use you. You will confound the wise, my girl, conferring glory upon his ways. Furthermore, he recalls the heart you had for him as a young girl who could hear his voice and love it. Though you forgot, he never did. He never abandoned your friendship. So, you see, he knows your heart and he *dearly* loves it. Is that not affirmation enough?"

She became very still as assurance swept through her. It was like an embrace from her father after a good cry. She was safe here and always would be... even to the end of the age. Wiping the tears from her face, she returned her gaze to the Helper.

He had vanished.

CHAPTER 22

NOVELLA DREW TO HER feet at the sound of Era's familiar step in the outer room. She'd sat alone long after the Helper was gone. For some time, she'd tried to convince herself it had only been a strange dream. But now that she had learned her mother was of another world, anything was possible. Ergo... she had been visited upon by the very Spirit of the Great One—had been given a message and vision of the Anointed One. He was with her. All she must offer now was willingness.

It was the least she could do.

Opening the bedroom door, she asked, "Is it time?"

Era nodded with eyes that scrutinized her pupil. "You are not the Novella who went in there hours ago."

Novella shrugged. "That's probably a good thing. Shall we depart?"

It was peculiar how eagerly her legs moved toward the thing she feared. The anxiety remained, but it was only background to her determination to do as the Anointed One bid. Even if none else be for her, her heart pounded with the desire to watch His will made manifest. Something told her this was only the foremost rumblings of a growing passion. For now, she had what she needed.

Together, they entered a glistening emerald-columned expanse. With no roof, the sun glowed in generous rays, causing the emerald floor to spark like glass. A surprising number of citizens and island council members were present. Like her presentation before the world council, they watched as she sauntered down the center aisle until she was standing before Island Leader Rancho. His eyes scrutinized her as Era's had. He, too, sensed the shift in her. With the raising of a brow, he gestured for her to take the seat beside him. She decided it was an extension of trust.

She must now live up to it.

He stood to announce, "May the consultation commence. Errald, we shall begin with you. Please stand and state your business before the Realm Leader expectant."

Errald was bald with a long white beard. His pale blue eyes met hers without duplicity. With a short bow of humility, he inquired, "Now that trade with the Eastern islands is at a standstill, many of our inhabitants have almost completely lost their source of income. Does the council have any plans to amend this mounting concern?"

It was a very good question. Novella had asked it of herself many times but never thought to inquire of Realm Leader Tamsen. She regretted it now.

"I have seen this," she began. "It saddens me to see those who, not long ago, were thriving now living without..." She paused as the voice directed her next words. "Though the world council currently has no workable strategy to amend the issue, the Great One is not only using this time to build faith and unity between the citizens of the world, he promises that not one who plants their faith in his provision shall go without. Furthermore... this cessation should not last much longer. He has a plan. We must only be patient. Our *best* days are before us."

The gentleman appeared as if her was weighing her words. Finally, he offered a nod of quiet acceptance before retaking his seat. She was certain it was not the answer he had hoped for. But if his years had granted him wisdom, he must realize that a promise from the Great

One held realms more worth than one from mere man. It blessed her to think of the promise the Great One made the people of this planet. Surely, his heart was *for* them. Not only did he see their struggles, he was using them. That, in itself, was *riches*.

The next spokesperson stood to his feet. "Many of us cannot help but notice the rampant sickness that has swept across the islands since the death of Realm Leader Flynn. We on this island have endured more than our fair share of grief. Does the world council share our concerns? Is there something that can be done?"

Involuntarily, Novella stood to her feet. "Bring your infirm to me, please."

Realm Leader Rancho looked to her with wide eyes. "You do not understand. When he says we suffer with more than our fair share, there are nearly fifty currently struggling with a mysterious illness. What is it you hope to learn? We had not heard you were a healer..."

"I am," she replied simply, concealing her trembling hands behind her back. "Is it possible for them to be brought here or shall I go to them?"

His eyes darted between hers before he turned to a guardsman. "Have them brought," he commanded.

"Everyone?" the man whispered in amazement.

Rancho nodded with a low growl.

The guardsman leaped into action, calling out orders to his men to fetch the infirm. In the meantime, the next woman in line stood to voice her question. It was all Novella could do to nod for her to speak while her mind raced with what was soon to occur.

"The Western islands nearest the border live in constant dread of raids from the Easterly Conglomeration. Can Atlantyss spare us watchmen to help ease that burden?"

Novella nodded to the Helper in her head. "I will speak to the council about it on my return, but I must remind you to seek the

Great One in constant prayer. I strongly counsel you to appoint people to intercede with interchanging shifts at every hour of the day and night, that the fragrance of your needs will never leave the Great One's throne. In a time of such uncertainty, he is the only force we can depend on. We *need* him... And he likes it that way."

A hush fell across the expanse. Even the island leader looked to her as if on tenterhooks. Suddenly, all eyes flew to him, as if awaiting his response. Swallowing hard, he finally nodded.

"Let it be as you have said," he consented in a low voice. "My council will discuss it on the morrow."

Novella had no time to consider whether her response was truly pleasing to her listeners as the first of the guardsmen appeared with the infirm in their arms. A pair of women were laid at her feet. It was abundantly clear how they suffered due to sallow faces, sweat pouring down their temples. Unexpected tears filled Novella's eyes. She knelt beside the first. Touching a hand to the woman's forehead, she closed her eyes and repeated the Helper's command, "Be well, daughter of Alpha."

Immediately, the woman's eyes opened and connected with hers.

Novella nodded, biting her lip with satisfaction. She helped the woman to her feet until it was obvious she required no aid. She ran to a man in the audience, who enveloped her in his arms. Novella turned to the next woman and repeated the exercise. As the remaining infirm were presented to her, she healed every one as the Helper directed. Before she knew it, she was finished. Curiously, she felt herself sweating. She was *warm*—as if power had passed through her over and again. Patting her slick neck, she retook her seat.

She turned to Rancho with, "I will have a Healer sent to live among you for situations such as this. The Emerald Island shall no longer suffer as you have. But because you have been tried so severely, you will reap a mighty harvest when the day of renewal dawns."

Truly, she had no real conception of what she spoke, only repeating the words that flowed into her mind.

Rancho's eyes glowed with rapt attention. He nodded, turning from her to gaze at the healed as if in a state of ecstasy. He sat forward in his seat as the next spokeswoman launched to her feet. Novella consulted the sun's placement, realizing it was to be a long evening. But watching the Great One's will made manifest was surprisingly satisfying. With a smile, she nodded for the woman to speak.

It wasn't until the sun had nearly vanished beyond the horizon that Petyr returned from Atlantyss. He appeared as if breathless at the far end of the expanse. Though Novella was exhausted, she pulled herself to her feet, darting through the people to meet him.

He held the scepter in his hands, whispering under his breath, "It was a battle. Father had in no way attained permission from the council for its return, which means someone sent a false letter. We threw together a council session with the members who were present to have the transfer approved. They have also launched an investigation into who sent the promise to Island Leader Rancho."

Novella took it from his hands, thanking him with her eyes.

Falling to her knees before Island Leader Rancho, she offered it up with shining eyes, "I hereby restore the emerald scepter to its rightful place."

Island Leader Rancho surveyed her with a grin that spoke volumes. If he had taken a dislike to her, his opinion was transformed. Standing to his feet, he thrust the scepter into the air. An uproar of woops and cheers were released in celebration of the scepter's return—like a prodigal restored to his family. Knowing how much the island had suffered in recent years, her eyes sparkled to see the assemblage so pleased. Yet, there were so many more who required encouragement.

This was only the beginning.

CHAPTER 23

THE EMERALD ISLAND BEGGED her to remain for the week, but her agenda was too full to consider it. She and her party departed the following morning with a vast sea of citizens gathered at the docks to wish them farewell. Her eyes watered as she waved goodbye to those she knew had not initially wanted her. Now, they seemed almost to love her. But it wasn't her they loved. It was the one who had used her. He had refreshed their hope for the future and granted them keys for victory.

"Wish I'd been there for the show," Petyr murmured as they sailed away. "Rancho couldn't stop singing your praises to me this morning. He plans to demand that the world council have you take your place as Realm Leader directly."

She spun to face him. "Did you tell him I wasn't ready for that just yet?"

He smirked.

Her eyes narrowed on him before she turned back to the Emerald Island for a final wave of farewell. Things had turned out well here, but there were a number of islands yet to be visited. There was no telling what they might face. What if this one had been the easiest to win?

"This isn't your story, Vella," she chastised herself under her breath. "You're not the author."

Clearly, the author of her life liked *drama*.

Her reception on the Isle of Jubilee was a night and day difference from the previous. A crowd cheered as she waved from the vessel. Island Leader Kenna raced up the gangplank to meet her on board the ship, speaking speedily of how grateful she and her citizens were to have been afforded a visit from the Realm Leader expectant. Novella was enthusiastically ushered from the vessel, through the town, where she and her entourage were placed in a sizable dwelling, befitted with all manner of gifts and delicacies.

"This is certainly a generous people," Novella commented as she cut into a fragrant fruitcake.

"I always liked Island Leader Kenna," Era answered. "Her life is a walking, talking example of *joy* in the midst of every season. I imagine her people cannot help but be affected by it."

"I wish you'd have told me that on our way here," Novella returned with a grin. "My stomach was in knots."

"Like you should worry," Petyr grunted as he stole the slice from her hand with a wink. "If you managed to nail the last island, the rest will be a breeze. They haven't suffered as much."

Novella sighed with relief as she cut another piece, stealing a bite before it could be snatched. "Thank the Great One."

"You're quite the native," Petyr commented with a grin.

She raised a brow in question.

"You call God by our name—not Earth's."

She weighed the comment for some moments. It was true that this world had gotten under her skin. If indeed she ever chose to return home, it would pale in comparison. She was clearly at an impasse. Especially when she considered that the Anointed One had requested her willingness to follow his movements. Where he went, she most now go. According to her heart, there was no other way. Did that mean she must really and truly accept this position as leader of the world one day? Would she *ever* be ready? Despite her recent success, the notion of becoming Realm Leader made her dizzy.

"When in Rome," she answered with a shrug.

Era looked to Peter with a questioning brow.

"Do as the Romans do," Petyr retorted as if it was explanation enough.

"I think Earth left an impression on you as well," Novella pointed out.

His eyes met hers. "Undoubtedly." Swallowing, he added, "Sometimes, I still find myself craving those peculiar crumpets at your aunt's."

"I can make you crumpets, Petyr," she answered with a laugh.

His eyes broadened. "What would you need?"

"I'll make up a list."

"Will they be as good as your aunt's?"

"They will not."

He grimaced.

A knock at the door sent the three to their feet. Petyr took the initiative of answering. It was Island Leader Kenna.

"Shall we commence with the session?" she asked. "The people cannot seem to content themselves to wait and we've really only got the remainder of today."

"Of course," Novella agreed, launching to her feet to follow the woman. "I'll see you two at evening meal."

Petyr and Era watched as if they scarcely knew her.

The session was shorter but no sweeter than the last one. To witness the transformation of the Emerald Island had been a wonder. Here, the citizens were far more content. It wasn't until after the feast they threw in her honor that evening that she learned why. Sensing that the meal was at an end, a weary Novella stood to her feet, hoping to turn in early. But with the shaking of Petyr's head, she dropped back into her seat.

"What now?" she questioned as the first strings of the peculiar band in the center of the dining area began to sound. Her eyes flew to the musicians as a tune even more beautiful than what she'd heard at the Council Hall of Atlantyss commenced. Though not nearly as polished, it possessed an almost wild quality. There was something about the way they played that connected with her spirit. Perhaps she herself wasn't polished enough for Atlantiian music.

Before she knew it, the entire assemblage was singing. They followed neither the same words, nor even the same tune. It was a crescendo of impromptu vocalization that rose like the broadening of the dawn. The atmosphere shifted. It did not take long for Novella to recognize the presence she'd felt when the Helper had entered her room. *He was here*, with these people, in the midst of whatever was occurring.

It dawned on her. This was worship. But it was unlike any she had ever experienced back home in her family's church. As she caught first one utterance, then another, she was moved by the deep affection rising from these citizens. This was where their contentment derived from—gratitude. Island Leader Kenna's joy sprang up from *this* fount. She had fostered an appreciative people, who honored the Great One for his daily care. But the inhabitants did not remain in their seats. Many rose to their feet, arms extended to the sky. Others clapped and danced in time to the music. Some even twirled ribbons in the air while others waved flags.

Waves of the Helper's presence washed over the expanse until Novella dropped to her knees. A natural worship rose from her own heart for the one who had been so faithful to her these last days, the one who had deigned to visit her and even to choose her for this world. Gratefulness coursed through her with overwhelming bliss as she relished the worship to the one who had created all things and loved them. Who was this God who heard the cries of his people and answered them in his perfect time and way? She'd had no idea she possessed a friend quite like this.

Novella stood to her feet some hours later, wiping tears from her eyes. The music had long since ceased, but she'd been unable to move. She had never experienced anything like this. Most had returned home, but some, like her, had remained for hours. She turned to find Petyr awaiting her. His eyes surveyed her with surprising warmth, looking her over as if only seeing her for the first time.

"Ready to go?" he asked quietly.

She nodded, letting him plant her arm in the nook of his.

"You're different," he commented as they walked.

"It's true."

He peered down into her face. "What happened while I was gone yesterday?"

"The Great One came to see me," she answered with a satisfied smile.

His eyes widened. *"You're jesting?"*

She shook her head.

He turned from her to survey the path. "Novella, you are nothing if not completely astonishing."

"So, I'm not just a sensitive Earth-girl you have to tiptoe around?"

He released a chuckle. "I still think you're sensitive, but... I no longer consider it a failing. You naturally connect with the concerns of others. That will aid you well in future."

In future... when she accepted her rightful call. She gripped his arm all the tighter at the thought. It seemed that every time she found her footing, she felt herself called to a new level. Would she ever feel comfortable again? Or was comfort overrated?

"Why is your father so willing to pass his position to me?" she asked.

He weighed her question for some moments before, "I admit I've lost touch with many things in my absence, but I'd wager it's because he knows what is right. He was not chosen by the Great One to become Realm Leader. He was only temporarily granted the position. To turn his back on that would be to turn his back on God. That is a dangerous place to be."

"As dangerous as refusing to respect the Great One's calling on my life?"

His eyes met hers with gravity. "I think having to live with that refusal the remainder of your days would be punishment enough."

"Would you become the leader of Earth if he asked it of you?"

He released a long whistle. "Never thought of it that way... Leaving home for five years was hard enough. Not to mention the *chaos* of that world. I wouldn't even know where to begin."

She smiled up at him.

"Alright..." he answered with a laugh. "I see your point. But I know that, when the time is right, you will make the *right* decision."

"I wish I was as certain. I don't know that I entirely trust myself..."

"That's alright. *I* trust you. More importantly, I trust the Great One."

CHAPTER 24

WHEN NOVELLA ARRIVED ON the following island, her first order of business was to arrange a time of worship for that evening. But this Island Leader was no Kenna. She looked on Novella as if she were abusing her power. Even so, she alerted the musicians. After the day's session, the island was more than willing to do as Novella bid. The music was far less cultivated than the last, but it was jovial, practically compelling one's feet to move in celebration of all that had been done that day. This island, too, was refreshed by her visit. She was stunned over the three successful visits in a row, wondering if the remainder would feel as fruitful.

By the conclusion of her tour, she had encouraged every island to follow the Isle of Jubilee's example. Moreover, she had obeyed her Helper and seen great change wherever she went. As her eyes now spotted Atlantyss on the distant horizon, she was stunned to find herself disappointed to return. To be certain, a new island every day had been tiresome. But getting to watch all the Great One accomplished had been a beautiful gift. Moreover, she'd discovered more of the Great Gifts that rested within her, from seeing visions to speaking changes into existence.

It occurred to her that the random outbursts of her power had ceased the moment she had agreed to visit the Greater Archipelagos. She understood that the Great One had been frightening her into coming. She could not run from what she was. And she could no longer blame him. Her heart beat faster whenever he came to mind. In the evenings, she dreamed remembrances of her early years of fellowship with him. These dreams infused deeper loyalty into her heart. Whatever was to come, she could not turn from him. She *must* not.

When she found that the world council members awaited her return in the convening chamber, she was overwhelmed by their reception of her.

"We have heard from nearly every island you visited," a woman, who had previously been uncertain of her, informed.

"Indeed," Naii confirmed with pride. "The letters singing your praises have been pouring in." Siezing Novella's gaze, she added, "They are demanding you be given your rightful role."

"Case in point," great uncle Illiab vocalized haughtily, "they are blaming *us* that you have not accepted. May we please dispense with this beating about the bush?"

Novella's mouth nearly dropped open. Her uncle's tune had certainly shifted. Gazing on his haughty face, she blinked.

"*You* are the one who sent the council's 'promise' that the emerald scepter was to be returned," she accused.

His eyes bulged from their sockets. "Who *dared* to speak such *fallacy?*"

"The Great One."

Realm Leader Tamsen flew to his feet. "Guards, escort Illiab to my personal study. Make certain a guard is placed at the door. Illiab, we have much to discuss." Retaking his seat, he turned to Novella with, "You are certain?"

She nodded.

"I will deal with him." Looking her over with confusion, he spoke, "You seem changed. I trust your tour was as satisfactory to yourself as it was to those you ministered?"

"Do you know, it really was."

As his eyes froze on her, she couldn't help noting that his former warmth seemed cooled. Or was it only that he was more haggard this day? Surely... *surely* he wasn't envious of the attention she had received. After all, it had been *his* idea to send her. And he was the one encouraging her to accept the call.

"Does that mean you consent to becoming Realm Leader?" another man asked, breaking into her revelry.

Her eyes flashed to his. Though her stomach immediately knotted, she knew she must accept. She opened her mouth, prepared for the Helper's response in her mind, but none came. Something wasn't right. The timing was off.

She was *glad* of it.

"I request time to seek the Great One on the matter," she replied.

Tamsen nodded. "Granted. All agreed?"

Like the pulling of teeth, they gave their consent.

"Before we disburse..." Tamsen began, turning his full attention on Novella. His eyes scanned her as if weighing something before he continued, "I wonder if, after a day or so, you would handle another matter for me... this time on an Eastern island."

It's go time, the Helper promptly whispered.

She nodded her acceptance. "I'd be happy to."

Tamsen's brows flew up. "Well... good. I will make the preparations."

Michal met her outside the convening chamber with a smile that made his face light up like an aurora. Certainly, he was a fetching man. *And* he was kind and good.

"Petyr's been singing your praises," he informed. "I knew you'd make a success of it. You're the kind of person who surprises people."

She quirked her head to the side. "How so?"

"On the outside, you look like a small teenaged girl, but now and then your insides peek out and it's clear there's a secret weapon inside of you."

"My Great Gifts."

"No, more like your willingness to face that which terrifies you."

Willingness. It was a sweet word to her. It was what she had a mind to be the remainder of her life. It had already brought her far.

"I appreciate that opinion. You are nothing if not gracious. But how have things been here?"

Unexpectedly, Tamsen approached from behind his son. Planting a hand on Michal's back, he said, "It does me good to see you two together. You make a handsome pair."

Even Michal appeared astonished by the bold statement. "Er, yes, we've made fast friends, we two."

Novella herself knew not what to say. It was true that Michal had not exactly hidden his interest, but they'd only been acquainted a short time. What was the Realm Leader thinking?

"Well, we all know where a friendship between those of opposite genders so often leads," Tamsen insisted with a wink.

Michal, nothing daunted, answered, "Then she and Petyr ought to be safely engaged by this time, for they've spent far more time together."

The Realm Leader's face dropped. "Yes, well, we all know Petyr is nursing an old wound. At any rate, I've places to be. Good afternoon, Novella. And fine job on those Western isles. You've managed to impress even Illiab, who has been against you from the start. Keep up the good work."

There it was—the old warmth. Novella was glad to see its return. Even if it did mean he teased her about an interest in his son.

"I apologize," Michal murmured at his father's departure. "He must be awfully impressed with you. He has never coupled my name with another's. He quite depends on me."

"Well, who can blame him?" she answered with a smile. "The way you and Petyr fill in wherever needed makes you model sons."

"Glad you think so," he answered with a grin. "Now, how do you feel about visiting the underwater colony again?"

To her surprise, the days that followed were filled with Michal. Never had she spent so much time with a man who was not her father—not even Gregory. She saw little of even Petyr, who seemed always to be off on some errand for the Realm Leader. Despite her former fear of being tied down, she found her heart opening up to his kindly, accomplished elder brother.

Yet, she made time to enjoy tea and luncheons with her newly discovered grandmother, whom she was swiftly coming to adore. The woman poured forth wisdom that Novella eagerly ingested. If ever she required counsel in her life, it was now. Back home, her own mother had been so consumed with fitting into society that she had spared little advice for other matters. This mother of her mother's easily filled that gap.

"You should hear the way Petyr speaks of you," Naii surprised her one day. "I think you shocked him with the way you handled that tour. He'd expected to have to babysit you every step of the way. From the sounds of it, he enjoyed his vacation."

"Petyr is biased because he discovered me," Novella spoke with a wave of her hand.

"Oh, no," Naii spoke with a sober expression. "Petyr is a known truth-teller. He does not speak a thing he does not firmly believe.

And impressing the son of the standing Realm Leader is no small feat. Surely, the Great One is with you."

Novella's eyes shone with ecstasy. "Yes, he was with me. He sent Help."

Naii eyed her. "In what way?"

Novella pressed her lips together. "I was visited by the spirit-essence of the Great One."

Naii nodded, her face brightening with, "You've met HS. Isn't he a ham?"

"A... ham?"

"He makes me laugh all the time."

"Then... you've met him too?"

"I have." She spoke it with as much adoration as Novella was coming to feel. "We've been acquainted a *long* while."

"But you called him... what was it?"

"HS is what he typically goes by. Apparently, he gave you another name."

"Why... he never just shared a name. Only that he was the answer to my prayer."

Naii chuckled. "And he turned up out of the blue to shock you out of your senses. How very like him."

Novella shook her head. This woman must know him well to speak so. "He walked me through that tour every step of the way. I *never* could have accomplished so much on my own."

"I heard you influenced those islands to take up evening worship. I imagine the Great One appreciates that."

"I suppose that was *one* thing I originated on my own. I'd never enjoyed anything like that before. I was made for it."

Naii squeezed her hand, leaning in close to say, "I can see why he loves you so much, my Vella."

Working to rein in her emotion, Novella reached for her teacup and changed the subject. "What do you know of this errand that Realm Leader Tamsen is sending me on?"

"Absolutely nothing."

Novella quirked a brow. "He didn't discuss it with the council?"

She shook her head. "I was surprised you accepted without further inquiry. In fact, I found it interesting that none of us did. You leave on the morrow, do you not?"

"I do... Only now I wish I'd learned more before accepting. The Helper gave me affirmation, so I answered without thinking."

"Well, I don't imagine he'd send you into anything you can't handle."

"Yes, but... Tamsen said even *he* was struggling with it. What if I can't—"

Naii clucked. "How swiftly we forget the miracles that the Great One has already performed. Do not you see that *nothing* is too difficult for him, nothing impossible? He will never drop you, Novella. Not unless you turn on him in willful rebellion." She snorted. "Even then he'll pursue you."

"I see your point. I will simply do my best and... let him manage the rest."

Naii smirked. "Well spoken, my Vella."

CHAPTER 25

A WELCOME NOTE ARRIVED for her the following morning. It was Michal, asking her to walk the tropical gardens with him before she departed for her voyage. She couldn't help grinning over the invitation. He knew how she loved the gardens as well as a good chat. She wrote her response and sent it back by way of the lad who'd delivered his. That evening, she discovered she was rather content with her life among the Atlantiians. She had trustworthy friends, all the provisions she could ask for, a place to belong where she was no mutant. She was decidedly at her leisure. If only she did not have to depart so soon.

The following morning, she ate and dressed with swiftness in order to keep her arrangement. She'd been raised with the conviction that early was on time and on time was late. Her father was in the newspaper business after all. Time was of the essence when it came to news.

"Good morning," Michal greeted, emerging from the shadows of the garden. "Thank you for meeting with me."

"Did you imagine I'd turn you down?"

His face flew to hers with such swiftness that she wondered what she'd said. "I rather hoped not."

She raised a brow at him. "What is this about?"

Abruptly, he stopped, stepped before her and took her hands into his own. "Novella... from the very moment I saw you, I knew I would never find another who so fitted what I dreamed for in a future wife."

Her stomach flipped. Surely, he wasn't going *there* just yet. Now, she wished she *had* turned him down.

"I know we have been acquainted only a short time," he continued, "but I hope... I hope you will consent to become my wife."

His eyes were locked on hers. She had room neither to breathe nor consider. And what was she to do? Well, obviously answer to the affirmative. He wasn't the sort of man she could turn down. She'd be a fool.

"Michal, I... I was only recently released from an engagement, you know."

"Petyr told me all about it. But I wouldn't ask if I wasn't certain—"

"Does your father approve?" she found herself asking before she had any idea the question was in her mind.

"Actually, it was *Father's* idea that we not waste time," he explained with a smile.

Her stomach dropped. Realm Leader Tamsen had to *urge* him to ask for her hand? That notion stole all the romance out of it. She desired to be wanted when the *asker* desired it, not his father.

"But... why should he rush things?" she asked as she eased her hands from his.

Fear flicked across his face as he grasped what the information had done to her. "Honestly, I'm not certain. He inquired of my feelings for you and, when I admitted to admiring you, he urged me to make it official. But you must understand that I was *pleased* he did so. It never would have occurred to me to take this chance so early in our friendship."

She nodded, brows drawing together. It was awfully flattering that Michal thought her desirable. Gregory had been the only man to show her attention prior and she'd detested her childhood acquaintance. Yet... a proposal that had to be urged wasn't flattering. She felt rather pathetic.

"Novella," he broke into her thoughts, "I harbor greater affection for you than I have for any other woman. I would not be asking if I did not want this."

She offered him a half-smile with eyes she knew shone with compassion for what she was about to speak. "I would be lying if I did not admit that I felt similarly. And I'd be a fool not to consider your proposal. But... I *do* need time to consider. I cannot give an answer at this time."

He swallowed hard, shoulders drooping with dejection. Rubbing the back of his neck, he said, "I seem to have gone about this all wrong. Perhaps I should be grateful you are only asking for time."

"Michal... you really are a charming fellow," she soothed. "Something about this doesn't feel right to me just now."

He nodded. "You may have all the time you require. I apologize for broaching the subject so prematurely. I shouldn't have let Father get in my head. He rather goaded me to man up and take the horse by the reins."

After a moment's silence, Novella burst into laughter. Poor Michal looked at her as if he felt himself an utter dupe. Yet, she could not seem to help herself.

"Oh, Michal, I'm *sorry*..." she chuckled out. "It's only that *I* am the horse in that scenario. The imagery isn't entirely flattering, is it?"

To her relief, his face broke into a grin. "Never have I been so clumsy with a lady in all my life."

Managing to calm herself, she squeezed his hand with, "Do not trouble yourself. I leave on the morrow, so we may take this time apart to... relax, I suppose."

He shook his head. "Do I have *words* for Father..."

"You won't tell him I laughed at you, will you?"

"I'm not entirely certain that I won't."

Somehow, she felt relieved by how things ended between them. She'd managed to essentially turn him down while maintaining their growing friendship. Michal was such a generous man that he did not blame her. Yet, she questioned why she had not simply taken advantage of the opportunity to betroth herself to such a spectacular fellow. It wasn't as if she could ever find better. Yet, when she recalled that Tamsen had pressured him into asking, she felt herself in the right.

To her astonishment, the Realm Leader called on her early the following morning while she was looking over her luggage for her journey to the East.

"What is this I hear about you turning down my favorite son?" he demanded.

She blinked back at him. Did he truly favor one son over the other? Perhaps Petyr's absence had brought the other two closer.

"I, er, did not exactly turn him down," she hedged. "I asked for time to consider."

"Consider *what?* Have you ever encountered a more strapping fellow?"

Her mouth fellow open with hesitation. It was difficult to face such a man over this sensitive matter. "Why... I have not known him long, you know."

"Do you favor Petyr? Is that it?"

With vehemence, she shook her head. She'd refused to consider him in those terms since her father had attempted to set them up.

Rubbing his chin, he contemplated her for some while before, "Your travel plans are to be delayed an hour. I'll send someone up to fetch you when your vessel is ready for departure."

"Has something gone wrong?"

"I've realized there is one last thing to be arranged before you leave. I apologize for any inconvenience." He stalked from the room, closing the door soundly behind him.

Novella's hands fell into her lap. Never in her life had she imagined herself in this position. It was one thing for *Mother* to pressure her into an engagement, quite another for the interested party's father to enact the coercion. Whatever was she to do if she never felt she could accept Michal's proposal? Pressing her lips together, she battled these concerns as she completed the preparations for her journey. As promised, Era arrived to look over her work.

"It seems you've thought of everything," she informed evenly.

"Is something the matter?" Novella inquired. "You seem... put out."

Era planted hands on her hips. "I have officially been *uninvited* to the party this time. It seems Realm Leader Tamsen wants to see how you do without my counsel."

"But... Iviana placed me in *your* care."

"She did. But the command of a Realm Leader is difficult to negotiate. Besides, you'll still have Petyr."

"I suppose, but... he's no you. Though he can be encouraging, he isn't exactly nurturing."

Era raised a brow. "To put it mildly. Yet, he can protect you from danger far better than I. You have not seen him in battle."

Novella's brows rose at that. "Has he seen battle?"

"Just after Realm Leader Flynn passed away, there was a terrible mutiny on Atlantyss. They were swarmed by an undercover political party and it was all the Council Hall could do to fend them off. Tamsen and his sons were on the frontlines of that battle and..." She released a whistle. "Tamsen's long been known for his swordsmanship, but those sons of his are *mighty* men."

It was difficult to picture the fellows who'd introduced her to the wonders of Atlantyss fighting anyone. They seemed so soft and considerate... most of the time. Clearly, she did not know them very well.

"I suppose that was why Iviana appointed Tamsen to Realm Leader when the time came."

Era nodded. "I'm sure it played a part in that. Speaking of, doesn't he seem edgy of late?"

Novella released a sigh. "Perhaps that is my doing. I have not yet accepted his son's proposal."

"Petyr proposed?!" Era nearly squealed.

"*No!* It was Michal!"

"Ah...." Era settled down with a smile. "*That* I expected."

"So soon?"

"Not exactly, but it was obvious he was smitten."

"Well, his father paid me a visit this morning and he was rather cross."

"What has Tamsen got to do with it?"

"He's been pestering poor Michal to ask sooner than later. It was why I could not accept."

"Rightly so. That is no way to begin things."

"*Thank you,*" Novella burst out. "It is relieving to have you in agreement. Michal, though sweet, was humiliated and I do believe Tamsen is offended."

"Well... time heals all wounds. It sounds as if this time apart will be good for all."

Novella nodded decisively. "Thank heaven for that."

CHAPTER 26

IT WAS SURPRISING HOW homelike the *Glorybringer* felt upon boarding. After a week within its confines, Novella found she'd missed gazing out at the open sea every day. She questioned the expected duration of this voyage, especially when she understood she was to visit but one island. Yet, it was to be an island in the East. With brows scrunched together in thought over just where that might be, she entered the tea room in search of Petyr.

Michal alone stood to greet her.

"I hope you do not mind me butting in," he spoke apologetically. "It was father's order."

"Where is Petyr?" she nearly gasped.

"Father believes I can provide better counsel for this trip, seeing as I am better acquainted with issues in the East. He requested Petyr remain to help him in my stead."

When Novella could not immediately find words to reply, he continued, "I know my brother is a rather exciting fellow, but I do promise to make this journey as enjoyable as I can. And, admittedly, I am looking forward to this."

"It's not that," she answered softly. "I am accustomed to Petyr, of course, but... he *is* a blunt fellow."

Her trouble was that she knew precisely why Tamsen had altered the arrangement. It had nothing to do with Michal's experience with the Easterners. Apparently, Tamsen was not a truthteller like his younger son. Yet, she had felt the momentum of the *Glory-bringer's* departure on her boarding. And Michal *was* undoubtedly pleasant company. She must make the most of the alteration.

"He is famed for it," Michal replied with a nod.

"Er... can you tell me where we are going?"

"You don't know either? My attendance was determined so last minute that I neglected to ask Father. I assumed you possessed the details. I'm sure Petyr is thoroughly informed. Father really ought to have sent both of us, but he does like having someone close whom he can trust entirely. At any rate... I *am* aware that it is an Eastern island with an issue that Father says only *you* can handle. He must have great faith in your abilities after your latest success."

Novella bit her lower lip. This was beginning to seem *awfully* irregular. But she reminded herself that it had been the Helper who'd eagerly urged her to accept the mission. If he was for her, who could be against her... right?

When an entire day passed before they reached their destination, Novella went in search of the captain. He, of course, was aware of the details. Yet, part of her feared he would not tell her. The location seemed to have been kept so very mum.

"You're not aware of where you're to venture?!" he asked with dramatic concern.

She shook her head, feeling like a child at the mercy of her parents.

He waved her to the window. "You see them distant isles?"

She nodded. It was a number of islands forming an archipelago. A rainbow shone above them from one end to the other. It looked an unparalleled paradise.

"Them is the Easterly Conglomeration," he announced.

She shivered. "I am glad we do not have to land there."

He raised a brow of apprehension that reminded her Father. "The nearest tip is where we are to dock, missy."

She fell back a step as her heartrate pounded into her ears. *Surely,* Realm Leader Tamsen would not dare take the chance of sending her among those who had attempted to take her life on her first night in the Greater Archipelagos. It would be *madness.*

She licked her lips. "Are you... *quite* certain, Captain?"

He nodded gravely. "I was given no order but to safely land you there with a small battalion of guardsmen."

Though her breathing was yet laborious, she felt somewhat comforted by that thought. "How many?"

"When I say small, I mean small. You've got but five guards... with the addition of Michal, who's worth twenty men." After a long pause, he added, "I can offer you my men as well. They are no weak fighters."

She watched their approach to the last place she'd expected to be sent. What had the Realm Leader been thinking? Had her victories been so great that he thought she could fail nowhere? So much trust was flattering, but she was seriously considering turning back.

"*If* we remain, I would appreciate that, Captain. I must speak to Michal forthwith."

A curt nod was his response. She got the feeling that he himself would guard her with his life if he must. She'd spent a deal of time inquiring about his vessel on their last journey. Thankfully, she seemed to have won his loyalty.

"Michal!" she declared as she found him on the hull of the vessel. "Have you noticed where we're headed?!"

He gazed into the distance, shading his eyes. "I do not imagine we have reached our destination as yet. That is the Easterly Conglomeration. We really shouldn't risk sailing so close. Those chieftains are the ones who desire your life."

"The captain has just informed me we are about to dock there."

"Why would we do that? This vessel is equipped to sail a week if we must."

"That is where your father has sent us!" she fumed.

Never in her life had she experienced fury like this. Once again, she questioned what Tamsen could be thinking. Was he *trying* to get her killed? That would certainly defeat the purpose of all he'd been training her for.

"There's no way," he spoke with confidence. "I'll speak with the captain myself."

"There is no need," she insisted. "I have fully grasped the matter. The question is what we are to do about it."

"Well, *turn back*. Whatever issue he wishes you to negotiate isn't worth your life. Nor is it honorable to send a defenseless maiden into certain death. There must be some misunderstanding."

Novella felt it again—the sensation of being *dared*. Her response was never quite wise, so she worked to remain calm. "What do you mean by defenseless? *I* protected myself from their assassination attempt."

He eyed her as if he feared she were a ticking time bomb. Calmly, he answered, "That is true... but it wasn't really of your volition, was it?"

"I thought you said I'd impressed you that evening."

His jaw flexed before, "It was your determination to remain that astonished me. Something that I am beginning to fear at this moment..."

"You should. Because if I survived that attack, I can survive this. If the Great One be for me, who can stand against me?"

"The chieftains of the conglomeration for a start, along with probably most of the planet considering your age and stature. You look like a teenaged girl. It doesn't bolster a great deal of confidence."

Novella felt her own jaw flex as she ground her teeth together. *Yes,* she'd been dared. Spinning on her heel, she marched for the captain's deck, sensing Michal in her wake.

"We are to continue as planned," she barked to the captain.

"We're turning back," Michal directed from where he towered behind her.

She placed her hand on the captain's where it rested on the helm. "I am Realm Leader expectant. Not only that, this was the standing Realm Leader's order. *I'm going.*"

"She cannot," Michal spoke as if it were a jest that would soon be sorted. "I'm not about to allow a young maid to go galivanting through the conglomeration. We could kiss this planet's future goodbye."

She spun to face him. "*You* are not in authority here, Michal. If your father thought it wise to send me, he has reasons of which we are not yet aware. Perhaps the conglomeration has changed their tune after hearing what I accomplished in the Western islands."

Michal peered back at her as if she were a jester of the hall. "The likelihood of that is slim to none. I care too much for you to take this chance. And you can trust me when I say you are no match for them. They boast extremely gifted people among their ranks. You are a mere sprite of a lady who doesn't know the first thing about how to utilize her power."

Novella released a growl, turning to the captain with, "Dock at the conglomeration or it'll be on your head before Realm Leader Tamsen."

She exited the compartment, experiencing rage the like of which she had never been provoked to feel. Realm Leader Tamsen's neglectfulness of alerting her to his plans was more than in question. Now Michal, of all people, treated her like a pathetic child. He had not witnessed her accomplishments in the West. Though it was true she knew nothing of her power, the Great One had urged her to take this journey and He knew how to use her.

Falling into a chair in the tearoom, she forced herself to relax. The Helper had sent her. She really must go. As childish as it was... she suddenly felt trapped at the realization. There was no turning back. *Willingness*, even when facing so much as the valley of the shadow of death, was what he had requested. And he was with her. She felt him soothing her wounded pride, settling her anger to the point she regretted her reaction to the dare, just as she always did. Yet, she had done *right*. She must follow the Anointed One's movements. She had witnessed a glimpse of what he'd endured for her. This... was *nothing* to that.

So she hoped.

CHAPTER 27

NOVELLA TUCKED HER TREMBLING hands behind her back as she surveyed their approach. Though the captain's piloting was smooth as ever, every movement increased her nausea. An assemblage of the populace was present to witness her entry, but their expressions afforded no welcome. They truly did wish her dead.

"It's not too late," Michal grumbled behind her. "I can have the captain wheel us out of here in no time at all and vacate the region before they even have time to board their vessels."

Novella turned on her heel, fury rekindled. It was just what she'd needed. She slapped him across the face. "I will not endure another faithless word from anyone in my party. Is that quite clear?"

He blinked back at her, irritation deflated. It was obvious he had no notion of what to make of her, nor how to respond. Ergo, he walked away. Wasn't it *just* like a man to leave her on her own when she necessitated a display of support before the conglomeration? Yet... when she replayed that slap in her mind, she admitted that it had been rather rash, not to mention discourteous. It was not how she was accustomed to treating people, but somehow she'd been unable to help herself.

She returned her gaze to the populace. They had witnessed her action. Many appeared stunned. She released a sigh.

What a beginning.

"I am sending my men with you?" the captain clarified.

"I would greatly appreciate it," she returned.

For the first time in their acquaintance, he smiled. "I am happy to be of service. Great One's fortune to you, Realm Leader."

She watched his retreating frame, noting he'd left off the "expectant." Had it been a mistake, or an indication that she'd won his faith? The show of respect, whether purposeful or accidental, bolstered her to descend the gangplank.

At the end awaited five bulky men dressed in garb that reminded her of the natives who dwelled in the distant Americas she'd heard so much about. It wasn't that they wore cowhide or feathers. More that their stonelike faces indicated a lifetime of war against the surrounding islands and beyond. From what she'd learned of late, it wasn't far from the truth. These people were almost bloodthirsty.

She had only reached the halfway point of her discomfiting stroll when the middle man stepped forward. "Novella of Earth, we *appreciate* your courage to accept our challenge... unanticipated as it is. You will be escorted to your dwelling posthaste, where you will remain the evening." He gestured to the largest man among whom she presumed to be the chieftains. "On the morrow, you will face Chief Xax, chief of the foremost archipelago. Er... *good luck* to you." He ended with a laugh that rippled across the entire assemblage.

Laugh with them, the Helper directed.

A true belly laugh escaped her lips. Humor she in no way understood flooded her until she was patting her belly with enjoyment over his statement. The assemblage ceased while she was wiping tears of mirth from her eyes.

"I thank you for your *warm* welcome," she chuckled out. "And I look forward to becoming better acquainted, Chief Xax. Let the games begin."

While Novella scarcely knew what she was saying, the chiefs did not seem to know how to proceed. They'd not expected her to accept their challenge, whatever it may prove to be, let alone that she possessed the gall to either laugh with them or at them, for she presumed it was difficult to tell.

"Show her to her dwelling," the main speaker demanded of the woman who stood behind him. "This circus is over." Raising a hateful brow at her, he added, *"For now."*

As if practiced, the chiefs disappeared around the nearest structure. Now she'd managed to laugh at them and live to tell, they did not appear quite so fearsome to her. Truly, the Great One worked in mysterious ways.

The woman to whom the chief had assigned Novella bowed low before her. "Welcome, Novella of Earth. That was *something*, to be sure." She rose with a brow of intrigue. "If you'll follow me. I shall get you and your men tucked safely away from any rogues who might wish to do you harm."

Novella hadn't considered that the populace might go "rogue." That put an entirely new spin on the situation. She had no idea what awaited her the following day but understood they did not intend her any goodwill. Meanwhile, she was to sleep through the evening knowing she was in danger from any and all sides at every given moment. Now more than ever, she was grateful for the captain's offer of additional guard. Apparently, she was to be afforded the remainder of the day to work out why Tamsen had sent her, let alone with so little protection. Perhaps it was to have made her appear intrepid. If that was the case, she'd unfortunately foiled his intentions.

The woman sped through the gravel streets of a rougher looking village than ever she had seen as yet. The buildings were of mere clay while the vendors and merchants sold nothing like the riches that the Western islands boasted. Why had the Great One seen fit to enrich one side of the planet while the other was so underprivileged in comparison?

"You're *nothing* like we expected," the woman informed when they reached a quiet section of the city. "My husband will be in a mood the remainder of the day."

"Your husband is... the chief who greeted me?"

"Do you call that a greeting where you are from?" she asked with a small glimmer.

Novella shrugged, affording the woman a small smile in return.

"He is my husband, but that does not mean we share a thought in common. We are typically at odds. I requested the responsibility of your care when we received word you were actually to appear for the competition."

Competition. What a word. And what did it forbode? "About that..." Novella began with hesitation. "This may sound silly, but... what exactly does it entail?"

"You were not fully informed of the logistics? Oh, dear. I hope that will not alter things."

"Not in the least. But it is wise to seek an insider's view."

The woman raised a brow before thrusting out her hand. "I am Ajax, wife of Chief Morse."

Novella shook her hand, feeling the woman was, for whatever reason, not entirely against her.

"A communication was sent to Realm Leader Tamsen, demanding he send you to appear for a duel of the Great Gifts in order to assess whether you are the rightfully chosen of the Great One. Tomorrow, you are to face Chief Xax, our most gifted chieftain and, in fact, the most powerful of the those gifted in all the world. He has never lost."

This was what the Helper has urged Novella to accept? She was to go head-to-head with a veritable Goliath? This was the "issue" Tamsen had sent her to deal with? No wonder he'd said she was the only one who could handle it. *She'd* been the one they'd demanded. It struck her that it did not seem at all like Tamsen to deal so haphazardly with her. Did he truly believe in her to this extent? Or... had she managed to offend him somehow?

"Ajax, how does this duel end?"

"The death of either you or Chief Xax. Unless, of course, you are willing to sign an agreement, promising to return to Earth and never so much as set foot in the Greater Archipelagos again."

With that download, the woman continued on, leaving Novella to wallow in her miserable thoughts. She couldn't understand it—*any* of it. Why were these people so very certain she had not been chosen? Didn't they trust Petyr? She pressed her lips together. Of course they didn't. If they would not submit to Tamsen's leadership, why would they kowtow to his son's claim concerning who she was.

It was only once they'd entered a small, one room abode that the woman closed the door behind them and turned to her with, "I have dreamed of you often over the years, from the time you must have been a mere babe. Though my husband does not believe in my dreams, I know better. I cannot go shouting it from the rooftops for fear of what he would do, but I want you to know that I believe you *are* the chosen of the Great One... even though you are so *very* young."

"I thank you for that faith," Novella returned with meaning. "I must admit that I had no idea of where I was going. I assumed it would be like my visits to a number of the Western isles. What I have walked into is quite beyond me. I hope you will keep me in your prayers."

The woman nodded. "These people who think they rule the world so often neglect to consider what is right and just. It was wrong of the Realm Leader to send you here without your knowledge. Yet, you anchored. I admire that. On the morrow... we will all witness what you are made of."

Novella swallowed back tears, silently nodding as the woman started for the door.

Ajax turned back once more with, "If you need anything, send one of your men to the hall. I have commanded our servants attend you as if you were a *guest* of the conglomeration." With that, she took her leave.

The eighteen-year-old from another planet fell into the nearest chair, pressing fingernails into her palms in an attempt to keep from crying. This was not what she'd signed up for. There had been some mistake. She must have imagined the Helper's direction, or misunderstood it. What exactly did "go time" indicate? Perhaps it had had nothing to do with Tamsen's request. She should have taken a moment to learn more from both the Helper and Tamsen. Surely, a duel was not the way the Great One had intended the Great Gifts be used. Michal was right. She didn't know the first thing about the gifts she boasted. In fact, most of them seemed rather harmless, aside from the salt thing. But she wasn't about to turn Xax into a pillar of it.

Then again, this was a duel to the death...

"*Why* didn't I listen to Michal..." she grumbled under her breath. "Oh, Helper... please come. Tell me what I am to do now."

She waited expectantly before calling again. As time passed, she realized he wasn't going to appear. But he'd been with her through thick and thin on her last voyage. Why should things be different now? Had she offended him?

Or was it a test?

Her head shot up. That was it. Her aunt had often spoken of such things: the trials that purified one like silver. She was meant to prove something here. Her willingness? She was here, wasn't she?

"Faith."

The whisper was so subtle she wasn't even certain it wasn't of her own mind. But it rang true in her gut. And he had already been clear, so why repeat himself? If the Great One was for her, *who* could be against her? She did not put her faith in horses, nor chariots, nor even princes, kings or *Realm Leaders*. He had shown himself faithful in past. What reason did he have to forsake her now?

It was hours she spent enjoying the holy text that Michal had given her before her previous tour. She'd not been spared a moment to open it before, but now she drank it like sweet nectar. She was surprised to learn it was a copy of the Psalms from the Holy Bible in her world. She had no idea where or when this planet had gotten their hands on it, but its words afforded peace as she had not known before.

"Enjoying the gift I gave you?" Michal commented quietly from the threshold.

She flicked him a glance. "You really should knock at a lady's door before entering."

He cast a gaze around. "I'd not realized your accommodations were but one room. This is unacceptable."

"What are you going to do? *Demand* they alter my accommodations?"

Falling into the chair beside her, he stole a bite from the supper that had been provided her. "You really can't blame me, Vella. This is ludicrous."

Her hand shot up as her eyes held fast to the text in her hands. After a moment, she sighed out, "Right as you are, Michal, I cannot hear it. I've got to focus."

He nodded in view of her peripheral, continuing to eat of her bounty while she read. Finally, he stood to his feet, walking softly to the door. Upon opening it, he paused, turning back as if desperate to speak before thinking better of it and stepping out. When the door was shut, Novella fell back into the scroll as if breathing its assurances. Michal's presence stood for fear and uncertainty just now. She would have to request that he remain on the vessel the following day or her faith might waver.

Yet... she had faced sickness, famine, crippling trepidation and faithlessness in her travels. The Great One had seen her through it all with flying colors. He was the same yesterday, today and forever. He wasn't going to drop her. He had a plan.

She just wasn't aware of what it was yet.

CHAPTER 28

NOVELLA'S STOMACH CLENCHED AS she awoke. She'd never been so frightened in her life—not even at the prospect of leaving her home planet for another. She turned over to punch her pillow. What had happened to being awoken by Cook to breakfast in bed because she'd overslept? That life felt eons in the past. Now, every day held some new challenge to her courage. This day was the most trepidatious of her existence... short of becoming engaged to Gregory Wetherill, that was.

With a smirk, she sat up.

She'd been rescued from *that* mess. Surely, her God was big enough for this one. As if from some place outside herself, David's acceptance of Goliath's challenge came to mind. She smiled again as she recalled his stone and sling before a giant and his sword. Dragging herself from the bed, she rifled through her traveling bag until her Bible met her hand.

"Am I a dog that you come at me with sticks?" Goliath bellowed.

A shiver coursed through her. Xax was her very own giant. And she didn't even have a stick. Her eyes fell to her hands as she turned them over. What she *did* possess was what Iviana had described as nearly limitless power. The trouble was that she scarcely grasped the first thing about how it worked. It had never even occurred to her to be trained in her abilities. She'd never expected to face something like this. Moreover, she'd been more akin to running from her abilities than embracing them. She proceeded to go over a list of the phenomena she'd accomplished thus far: healing her mother, seeing and hearing the Great One's direction, transporting a train across the world and morphing arrows into salt.

Her head shot up. The last seemed the simplest trek. But could she manage it of her own volition? She cast a gaze about the room. Her eyes narrowed on a yellow fruit. She held up her hand, focusing on what she wanted to occur.

Nothing happened.

She turned her face to the heavens. "You're not going to make this easy on me, are you?"

No response.

"Great."

A knock at the door made her wish she'd changed her garments. Peeking through the blinds, she found Axis in wait. She answered with a look of apology.

"Oh, have I awoken you?" the woman questioned. "I presumed you wouldn't be able to sleep a wink."

"Slept like a rock," Novella answered cooly.

Axis' expression communicated she was impressed. "I've been dreading this faceoff. You've just managed to pique my interest. At any rate, I've come to see if there is anything you require. I presume you've brought your armor?"

Novella hesitated before shaking her head.

"Just a moment," the woman replied before exiting. She returned again with a mannequin dressed in a fine suit of golden armor. "This is my own. I reckon we are near enough the same size."

Novella brushed the fine pieces, considering the option. Never in her life had she expected the opportunity to appear for battle like this. She longed to see herself in it.

"Let's give it a try," she returned with a smile.

It was some time before Novella was rightly fitted into the suit. But it was to her disappointment that she discovered she wasn't strong enough to carry it on her person. In fact, she was certain it would prove her undoing.

"I thank you, Axis, for the offer. I'm afraid I must appear in but my own raiment."

"You cannot do that. It is suicide."

"Wearing this suit is suicide," she retorted. "I can scarcely lift my arms."

"Do you not exercise?"

Novella bit her lip before shaking her head with a chortle of embarrassment.

Axis did not laugh. "This is disastrous. I cannot allow the rightful Realm Leader to appear for battle unprotected."

Novella stood at her full height. "I transformed conglomeration arrows into salt without the movement of a muscle. I am in no way helpless."

"They *wondered* why not a single one managed to mar you," Axis admitted with a small grin. After a moment's consideration, she nodded. "Let us remove it. It may impress them to see you without. And it will make Xax appear timid in comparison. I recall how you laughed at your mockers when you ported yesterday. That was a brilliant beginning. Though it in no way affected either Xax or my husband, it did make you appear indomitable."

Novella grinned as she recalled that it had scarcely been of her own doing, nor had the handling of the arrows been her volition. Rarely had she been in control of her faculties in those significant moments. As alarming as the prospect was, she must enter into this melee with total dependence on the Great One's ability to display his power through her. She wasn't in control. Surrender was her only option.

"Axis... I wonder if you would deliver a message to Michal for me?"

"I am at your bidding, Realm Leader."

She wrote up a swift note, insisting he give her space. She could not risk seeing his face for even a moment on this auspicious day. It was a matter of life and death—to her faith.

"I believe he is staying aboard the vessel," she informed the woman.

Axis shook her head. "I heard he slept outside your door to keep watch."

Novella pressed her lips together. That was an undeniably *dear* act. How could she give him the note now? "Er... may I see that again?"

Scanning its contents, she added a postscript: *If your feelings on the matter have altered, if you believe that the Great One, through me, can accomplish the impossible, disregard this request. Only meet my eyes with a nod to indicate your support... as well as your faith in the Most High God, for whom nothing is too difficult, nothing impossible.*

"That should do," she commented as she passed it back.

Time would tell if Michal changed his tune. And if, as the Great One willed, she should fail in this task and meet him in paradise... so be it. She had learned such a fate was no great loss. It was *reward*.

Axis soon appeared again with the news that she had not only delivered the note, but it was time for the Realm Leader expectant to be escorted to the tournament grounds. Novella had spent the day without food, eating instead of her Holy Bible. She read over and over again of the shepherd boy's victory over the beasts until she began to *feel* herself indomitable. She was astonished by how easily she sauntered through the crowds on her way to the battleground. They laughed and mocked. Some even spat at her, though most of it hit her guardsmen. Yet, it seemed it was not herself that walked among them. As David was a kind of Christ archetype, she felt herself somehow receiving a taste of the Anointed One's difficult journey through a contemptuous mob. And if she must die as he had, so be it. She was in good company. But if she lived... it would be a sin ever to fear again.

An abrupt skirmish took place between the people and her guards. If it had not been for the captain's offer of his men, she was certain the crowd would have managed to stone her. Thankfully, the sailors were well trained. They handled the matter with surprising ease. She counted herself lucky to have a supporter in the captain of the *Glorybringer*.

Axis pointed out a looming structure. It was what they called the galley. The people of the conglomeration made it a practice to test their finest warriors against one another. It was how the chieftains had won their titles. Chief Xax, in effect, boasted the largest army and greatest authority due to his unbeatability.

Novella gritted her teeth together. She would not tremble. This was not a battle between herself and the unbeatable Xax. This chief was about to face his maker. Even so, she recalled to mind another story in the Bible concerning a man called Jacob who nearly managed to best the Lord in a scuffle. She cast her eyes to the heavens, begging this would not prove to be such an occasion.

As she entered the arena, a ridiculing roar rose up from the assemblage seated in the galley. Before she knew it, Axis had redirected her into a small room beneath the stands. She gripped Novella's shoulders.

"You are so very young... and small," she began. "You possess no body strength."

Novella scowled. Hadn't this woman claimed to be on her side?

"Yet, I *know* you are the chosen of the Great One," Ajax continued. "May his will be exhibited today."

With another squeeze to Novella's shoulders, she left her alone with her guardsmen.

Novella swallowed. If Axis had considered that a pep talk, she needed to work on her delivery. For the first time, her hands trembled. Tucking them tightly together behind her back, she turned to the men who had seen her safely thus far.

"I... realize that letting me face Xax likely feels beyond your purpose," she spoke in a small voice.

The captain's men nodded gruffly, their eyes narrowed on the opening from where a chant had been taken up against her. She swallowed, licking her lips before she felt the words do what they needed to do. She'd been dared. These people did not know her, yet they chose to hate her. They challenged the Great One's will. This day, they must see his support of her... one way or another.

"As I was saying," she continued, "I must request that, no matter how things appear out there, you allow this skirmish to play out as... as the Great One wills. Is that understood?"

The guards that Tamsen has sent merely nodded.

She hesitated. For the first time, she realized they were a ruse. They boasted no real protection. For reasons beyond her, Realm Leader Tamsen had sent her with no covering but his own son, whom he hoped her to wed... if she managed to survive this. She shook her head. There was certainly more to be worked out there, but this was far from the time to do it.

Eyeing the Realm Leader's guard, she quipped, "You are dismissed."

Shuffling their feet, their brows rose in confusion.

"*Now.* Return to the vessel. Only the captain's men may remain."

Even the captain's men appeared perplexed as her official guard shuffled out. Swallowing as she surveyed those who remained, she nodded in satisfaction. "That's better."

CHAPTER 29

NOVELLA SHUDDERED AS SHE perceived Chief Xax's entrance into the arena. The crowd's cheers trembled through her body, making even the captain's men eye the vibrating ceiling with uncertainty. It was clearer than ever how the conglomeration regarded this chieftain. This was the one she must face in order to prove her merit.

She released an unsteady breath.

Once the assemblage quieted, one of the chiefs recited a speech concerning her gall to dare claim the position of Realm Leader, though she was from an unknown planet. He claimed she was the chosen of the Great One. *This day* it was to be determined once and for all where she stood with the God of all creation

The crowd laughed riotously. Novella cast her gaze to the rafters, daring the Great One to stand in her defense. If he truly loved her, and she *knew* how he felt, he would not stand for such ridicule. At the summons of her name, she marched from the room to face her antagonists, striding, she knew, with all the state of a butterfly.

The laughter did not cease until she had taken her indicated position in the arena, while Xax stood erect at the opposite end. The announcer called for quiet, though it was difficult to maintain. The crowd was mad with enthusiasm. They anticipated her demise.

Novella swallowed hard.

"There is to be no interference from either this populace or the Realm Leader expectant's guard," the chieftain informed gravely, "upon punishment of death. Between our participants, anything and everything is permitted. However, the mercy statute is *not* acceptable. Death of one or the other is the only victory... Is that understood?"

Novella nodded, for the first time grasping what that portended. Must she truly take a life to save her own? Would the Great One slay this beast of a man for her sake? Was this an appropriate use of God-ordained gifts? The entire competition was outside the bounds of her sensibilities. She felt as if she had stepped into another world.

As it happened, she had.

Xax's gaze did not break from her small frame even to gesture his agreement. He was a lion on the hunt. Only the whisper of her name from a familiar voice managed to tear her eyes from his. She turned to the room from which she'd emerged. It was Michal. With somber expression, he bowed low.

That was his answer. He stood with her. He believed.

Novella sighed. She could breathe. She *could* do this... That was, she was willing to step out in readiness for whatever the Great One minded.

"On my mark," the announcer began. "Get set...."

"Let's get ready to rumble," the Helper whispered.

"To battle!" the announcer cried.

Xax bounded for Novella as if with wings. On his final vault, he fell to one knee upon the ground. With the bowing of his head, he lifted his arms toward her. Sheer force like Novella had never experienced in half its measure met her like an invisible wave, hurling her against the barrier behind her. Successive waves like the aftermath of an explosion restrained her until she slipped slowly to the earth. Slowly, she tested her appendages. To her complete shock, not a one was either harmed or even sore. Thrusting the hair from her face, she realized her skin glowed like much fine gold. She patted her stomach but felt nothing. It was as if she wore imperceptible armor.

Smiling for the first time since she'd entered the arena, she drew back upon her feet.

A hush overspread the arena. Even Xax gazed back in bewilderment. Novella understood that the blast should have ended her life. Instead, it was only the beginning.

"March," the Helper commanded.

With a nod, she started for her giant, amused when he fell back a step or two before regathering himself. Falling to his knees once again, he sent a burst of flame scorching hungrily toward her. As it enveloped her, Novella felt mysteriously cool.

With the shaking of his head, Xax flew for a boulder that rose taller even than himself. It had been placed as a concealment for the skirmish—likely a mocking nod to Novella. Taking it up into his arms, he managed to lift it as if it were a small child. In the next moment, it was hurdling through the air. As if by instinct, her arms reached to catch it. For the first time since she'd begun her march, she halted. She was uncertain of what to do with the weight in her arms. Despite all else, she could not begin to believe what she was holding. With a shrug, she tossed it back to Xax, who managed to catch it in the nick of time.

It was then that fear entered the mighty warrior's eyes. Cracking his knuckles, he appeared to regroup. This was more hazardous than he had reckoned for.

"Alright, girly!" he shouted. "You've a few tricks up yer sleeve. That don't make you no Realm Leader! Let us finish this." He dropped to his knee once again.

Falling back upon the last direction she'd received, Novella marched onward. There was not else for her to do but continue in obedience to the Helper's movements. If the direction of her adversary was where the Anointed One was treading, she must follow. Already, she had witnessed miracles. She began to look forward to what would happen next.

Out of nowhere, a storm cloud was hurled toward her. In a blink, she mysteriously perceived that it was a combination of every gift the man possessed. She'd not even realized something like this was possible. And it was speeding for *her*.

Her legs stopped as the melee reached her, storming about her as if desperate to make contact. But her supernatural armor was impenetrable. The eagerness of the tempest was like a tantrum as it stirred itself up into an epic maelstrom. It swelled until some in the audience raced from the galley.

But Novella could see very little beyond this desperate storm. She began to feel as if it would accumulate around her forever. She recognized the various aspects of its makeup: flame, water, lightning, strength and so on. As if she possessed knowledge beyond that of her own, she became acquainted with the tempest, reaching out her hands to usurp control of it.

The atmosphere around her cleared as the squall assimilated into her arms. Her heartrate accelerated as she sensed the tempestuous fury within her grasp. It would not be contained for much longer. She faced Xax, whose mouth had fallen open, his eyes grown like the flying saucers of science fiction stories.

"*Release,*" the Helper directed.

Novella did as bid.

As if an explosive had been detonated, the tumult consumed its originator, disappearing into his form. Much like Novella not long before, Xax's body was slapped against the far wall before dropping to the ground in a heap. Novella bent over, heaving for breath as her adrenaline dissipated. She watched the chief's motionless form, awaiting his response.

None came.

Righting her posture, she turned to the silent assemblage. Did they now recognize just who she was to the Great One? Or would they sooner see her dead than allow her to walk away as victor over their beloved hero? Must she fight her way from the conglomeration's shores?

"Restore," the Helper whispered.

Her head jerked in the direction of the fallen Xax. She sauntered toward him, speeding her steps until she had reached his side. Dropping to her knees, she felt his chest. All was still. But not for long.

"Chief Xax of the Eastly Conglomeration," she bellowed for all to hear, "awake!"

As if struck by lightning, the chief's chest popped, giving way to even respiration. His appendages twitched as if greedy for their second chance. His eyes flicked open. He turned to discover the Earth-girl kneeling beside him.

"You have to finish it," he informed. "There is no victory without death."

Drawing to her feet, she held out a hand to help him to his own. "You already died, Chief Xax. The Great One revived you."

He blinked up at her for some time as the crowd remained strangely still around them. Finally, he accepted her hand, allowing her to restore him to his feet. The community burst into uproarious applause. Before long, a new chant was taken up.

"Chief Xax has slayed his thousands, but Novella has slain Chief Xax!"

Novella gazed out at the conglomeration's citizens, amazed by those words. What had been meant as her indisputable defeat had completely altered her relations with the Easterly Conglomeration. Not only had she rightly completed the competition, the Great One had rescued her from her first kill. She silently prayed it would be the last.

"*Do not count on it,*" the Helper breathed. "*This is only the beginning.*"

CHAPTER 30

"HAVE I TOLD YOU how *inconceivable* that was?" Michal reiterated as they sauntered into the Council Hall courtyard upon Atlantyss some days later.

Never in Novella's life had she felt so relieved to return somewhere. She had remained with the conglomeration an extra couple of days in order to familiarize herself with the chieftains and their wives, perhaps more so than she'd ever wished. They were an uncouth lot, who sought recognition via belching tournaments. Despite their crudeness, she developed an affinity with them.

"Michal is to deliver our petition that you take your rightful place forthwith," they informed her at the last. "Our patience for the standing Realm Leader has reached its conclusion."

As she'd stood at the bottom of the gangplank, a garland of tropical flowers had been placed upon her head. Axis announced, "Novella of Earth, though you are the chosen Realm Leader of the Greater Archipelagos, the Easterly Conglomeration demonstrates its endorsement by dubbing you the *Chief* of chieftains."

She shook her head as she now recalled the honor—far superior to the belching tournaments she'd sorely lost. At last, she answered Michal with, "Only about a hundred times."

He shook his head. "I still can't believe what I witnessed—"

The blasting of trumpets sounded through the yard. The two froze upon the steps of the hall as its double doors flew open. Tamsen and Petyr, followed by the world council, descended the steps to meet them. Naii raced ahead, taking her granddaughter's hands into her own, surveying her eyes as if in search of something.

"You *know* now... don't you?" the grandmother questioned ominously.

"Know?" Novella asked.

"Who you are—that you are the chosen of the Great One."

Novella's mouth opened to respond before she was surrounded by the council, all congratulating her over the tale that had already reached their shores.

"The account spreads like wildlife across the islands!" a woman eagerly informed her.

"Come," Naii spoke with the squeeze of her hands. "We must convene in the chamber directly. There is much to be discussed."

Novella nodded wearily. She'd been looking forward to a nice long soak before evening meal. But Michal had promised the conglomeration that he would deliver their demands and now was as good a time as any. Of course, they did not realize that it had been of her own insistence that she wait upon taking her rightful place.

Taking a few steps up the stairs, she stopped short as she found Tamsen's eyes on her. She recalled to mind the nightmare she'd suffered with so often over the last months—the man on the hunt for her life. But Tamsen had been so encouraging up to now. It had been *his* devising that she'd taken the tour and then faced the conglomeration in the East. Her successes were partly due to him. Yet, that glower sent chills down her spine.

In the next moment, he smiled at her. It failed to reach his eyes. Turning on his heel, he sauntered past the rest and through the doors. The crowd elected to follow him.

Novella's gaze flew to Petyr next, who stood with arms crossed and a brow raised. She stopped before him, fearful he had taken a queer disliking to her as well. Surely, not Petyr...

"Is it true?" he asked gravely.

"What's that?"

"You raised the despicable oaf from the dead after soundly slaying him?"

She nodded.

His arms flew around her faster than she had time to realize what he was about. "You *wild* lady," he whispered over her head. "I had *no idea* what you were being sent into or I'd have never let you go... at least not without me."

She awkwardly patted his back until he released her.

"You are well?" he asked with concern.

"Quite." Pointing to the sky, she added, "Who can be against me?"

His anxiety melted into a smile. Planting her hand into the nook of his arm, he stated, "You are to remain in my care for the foreseeable future. I can't believe Michal let you face *Xax.*"

"*Hey* now, brother," Michal chimed in with no mild irritation from beside Novella. "I *tried.* You ask her. There was no 'letting' her do anything. She was quite in control of the situation. In fact, she *slapped* me."

"It's true," Novella admitted shamefacedly.

Petyr shrugged. "What's a slap from a Victorian schoolgirl?"

"*Ah!*" she sounded, yanking her hand from his arm.

"A slap from the slayer of Chief Xax..." Michal reminded.

Petyr smirked down at Novella. "Don't worry, Realm Leader. You're no schoolgirl." Taking her hand back into possession, he added, "You are a warrior." With the shaking of his head, he murmured, "Cannot *believe* you insisted on dueling the chieftain."

She smirked back up at him. "Why? Wouldn't *you* face him? I've heard you're a skilled swordsman."

He frowned down at her before admitting, "Bet your life I wouldn't." He shivered. "You're no Victorian. *Nutty* is what you are. What *would* your mother say?"

Instantly, her countenance dropped. *Mother.* How far away she felt. Yet, this had been her mother's home world. Oh, what she wouldn't give for a mere hour of sipping tea with her parents in her father' study, discussing the politics of the day before the hearth.

"What is it?" Petyr probed.

"It was only... I was wishing I might visit home for an hour or so."

His brows rose. "You can you know. And be back again in time for evening sup."

She shook her head. "I do not believe I can. I think I would lose everything that has been built in here." She pointed to her head. "I cannot afford to look back."

He nodded, searching the floor of the foyer before looking back up. "And that saddens you... that the old life is over. You will never be that variety of Novella again."

She nodded eagerly, thankful he understood.

He bobbed his head from side to side. "Then mourn the end of your fortunate childhood. But look forward to what lies ahead. Your life is really only beginning now. The whole world is opening up before you. You must simply continue your race for your eternal reward, without looking back, nor to the right or left, ever again."

"That was stunningly poetic, Petyr. You sound like an English-man."

He chuckled, patting her back with, "You go on imagining I find that complimentary. I'll just keep my trap shut on that score."

She glared up at him. "What do you make of my father then? Is he some silly, stuffy old Englishman?"

"Your father is a prince among men. And if it helps, I think he'd *love* the Greater Archipelagos. Perhaps he might come for a visit one day."

"Not unless he can convince Mother to spill the beans. She's certain he'll think her an extraterrestrial."

He threw his head back with laughter. "How charmingly familiar."

When they entered the council chamber some moments later, Novella found herself blinking back at a smiling audience.

"I apologize for dallying," she spoke as she took her seat. "Petyr was too busy gossiping." She winked in his direction.

With a grunt, he took his own. For whatever reason, the sons of Tamsen were permitted to sit in on council meetings. As they were two of her closest comrades, she couldn't help being glad.

Naii lost no time in standing to her feet. "Novella, we have just finished reading over the demands of the Easterly Conglomeration. As they say here, 'Tamsen has slayed his thousands, but Realm Leader Novella has slain Chief Xax.' I think that about sums up the way this council feels about it. If even half of what we've been told is true, you are ready to accept your position as Realm Leader."

"Not to mention the fact that," a graying gentleman began, "the conglomeration claims it will go to war against Atlantyss if the Ceremony of Leadership is not performed in all haste."

"Well, we won't have that!" Novella declared with the pounding of her fist upon the table. She understood all too well how serious the threat was.

As silence reigned, Michal explained, "They've made her Chief of chieftains. They cannot make a move like that without her consent."

Naii's face shone with pride. "It is a miracle you have managed to win the favor of those islands. They've been giving this council trouble since before Realm Leader Flynn was killed. Truly, the Great One stands with you."

Novella felt her eyes shining in amazement until they met Tamsen's knitted brows. *Of course.* The conglomeration had ridiculed him in their letter. She wished she'd had a chance to read it before it had been sealed.

"Er..." she began, "may I have a word alone with Realm Leader Tamsen, please?"

Naii nodded her agreement. "Of course. That is right. Let us give them some privacy." She waved Petyr and Michal from the room until it was but Tamsen and Novella left facing one another.

Quietly, she walked about the table until she was sitting beside the leader who had been fighting for the good of the whole world until she had been located. Taking a chance, she placed her hand upon where his lay on the table.

"I admit that I feel myself better prepared for what lies ahead, thanks to you, Realm Leader Tamsen."

His eyes flew to hers as his jaw tightened with restrained emotion.

"But..." she continued, "I cannot relay my willingness to accept the position unless I am certain you are prepared to forfeit it. *You* are the one who trained and tested me, even trusting me to face the conglomeration."

She swallowed, hoping that, despite her nightmares, his intentions *had* been true. After all, it had been her finest achievement to date. She would never have confronted the conglomeration on her own.

"Despite what the Easterly Conglomeration, and even this council, states," she continued, "you have made a *fine* Realm Leader. I would not wish to take this on without you by my side. In fact, I will not."

Her jaw became stone. It was true. She knew she could not dishonor the man who'd been fighting for the planet without thanks, the man who had taught her, believed in her and promoted her. Perhaps the fondness he had once felt for her was waning in the face of her victories, but that did not alter the fact that he had done what none else had. She could not have reached this point without him.

Yet, as certain as she felt at one moment, a sudden dread flooded her system in the next. It was as if it was not her own—as if it stemmed from the voice who had long been in her head, whether she'd known it or not. Did her loyalty to Tamsen trouble the Helper? Surely, it was an honorable attribute, was it not?

Tamsen cleared his throat, covering her hand with his free one. "You are... *above* reproach, Novella." He shook his head. "I admit you've managed to surprise me time and again, including now. While none else seemed to see me anymore, you have." He swallowed before ending with, "I appreciate that more than you know."

She nodded, squeezing his hand with her own. She would have liked to speak further but for the awful sensation in her gut.

"I will stand with you," he promised with astonishing tears in his eyes, "once you feel yourself prepared to file your acceptance of leadership. Take a day or so to consider. Then, call the council to session. I will be in support of you, whatever you may decide. And I will do so *proudly*. For, surely, the Great One is with you."

Novella stole a breath of relief. He was in earnest. It was clear as day. *"Thank you,* Realm Leader Tamsen. God bless you."

CHAPTER 31

MICHAL AWAITED HER OUTSIDE the chamber. "How did that go?" he questioned.

"Very well, I think. We've reached an understanding. We support one another, whatever may come."

He gasped in relief as they started down the corridor. "It never even dawned on me how he might feel about that communication from the chieftains."

"And I never considered how they might word their sentiments," she replied regretfully. "I asked them not to send it along, but *you* were so eager..."

"Of course I was. I was there. It was the most incredible display of power I have ever seen."

"And it wasn't even mine," she answered with determination. She looked up at him with, "You do not imagine *I* was capable of all of that, do you?"

He openly gawked. "Then... how?"

"It was the Great One."

"But... how does he work through you like that?"

"I gave him leave. He asked for my willingness and... I was willing." She smirked up at him.

He shook his head. "Makes little sense to me, but... if you say so. All I know is that you appeared like an aurora borealis as you flung Xax's assault back in his face. Frankly, you were breathtaking."

Novella refused to meet his gaze as it bored down on her. Never in her life had she been so described. It rather took her breath away.

Quite suddenly, he stole the privacy of the corridor to take her hands into his own, compelling her to look him in the eyes.

"I made a mistake before..." he began, "asking for your hand due to Father's badgering. Now, I must put forward my proposal again. I know more than ever how I feel about you. There truly is no one else I could see myself loving in all the world. Novella, with or without my father's blessing, would you do me the honor of becoming my wife?"

Novella swallowed hard. Things felt entirely different this time. Michal was no longer uncertain. He was determined. And he was not concealing it.

"I cannot," she breathed, "give my answer at this time."

He hesitated some moments before, "Don't you understand how I feel about you?"

Her eyes fell to their intertwined hands. "Unless something happens to change my mind... I am about to accept my role as Realm Leader. That will open up a whole world of complication. Throwing romance into the mix might undo us both. I need to focus on this next step. Then, perhaps I can sort out what is to be done about... us."

Despite all she'd said, his eyes lit up on her final word. "I can live with that. And do not begin to think I am finished wooing you. If you do not feel yourself ready, I will pursue you until you cannot help but change your mind. Never in my life have I wanted something as badly as I want to spend the rest of my days with you."

Novella stared back in wonder. It was perhaps the best speech she had ever heard. Butterflies fluttered in her stomach, making her head spin. How she was to focus on the import of her role, she was uncertain. She stole her hands from his, patting them with, "You've just made everything so much more complicated."

"That was the aim. How else will I fool you into wedding a fool?"

She rolled her eyes. Once again, she was battling this concept of marriage. Where would her liberty be? She chuckled at herself. What was *liberty* when one was about to promise her future to the Greater Archipelagos?

"I must rest in my chambers until evening meal." She rather pleaded with her eyes.

He nodded somberly. "Of course."

"But if you see Era, please send her to me."

"I'll bribe her to defend my cause if I do."

"Cute, Michal," she called as she departed. "Very cute!"

"Mm. I feel like a kitten now!" he shouted through a chuckle.

She shook her head as a smirk overspread her face. Michal was a prince among men. It was lunacy to put him off. Yet... off she went.

To her surprise, Era awaited her in her chamber. She leaped from the chair with a gasp and threw her arms about Novella much as Petyr had. "I could have *wrung* Tamsen's neck when I learned where he'd sent you. And without either myself *or* Petyr!" She pulled back with, "Iviana will *kill* us if she learns what we allowed to transpire, so *easily* kowtowing to Tamsen just because he is standing Realm Leader. I tell you, Petyr marched up and down the art gallery the entire time you were away, heatedly pleading with the Great One for your safety. I think, if his father had not sent Michal along for counsel, he would have dared to *have words* with his father. Really, I cannot begin to imagine what Tamsen was thinking!" She fell back into her chair.

"Well, do not trouble yourself anymore," Novella soothed, patting the woman's arm as she sat down beside her. "Everything came out according to the will of the Great One."

"Yes, but Tamsen could not know what would happen!"

Novella bobbed her head. The man had sent her without either of her typical guardians or even a loyal guard. She recalled what she'd sensed from them just before facing Xax: that they had not been sent in honor. She swallowed, recalling to mind the understanding that she and Tamsen had just come to. If any part of him *had* hoped to be rid of her, she had succeeded in restoring his loyalty. And besides, he *had* sent Michal... who had just reiterated his proposal in earnest.

She felt herself blush.

"What is this, Vella?" Era questioned with a growing smile. "Did one of the chieftains' sons pursue you?"

Laughingly, Novella shook her head. "Michal just proposed."

"For heavens, what a determined man!"

"I think he thought it necessary to re-enact the scene under better circumstances."

Though Era's smile broadened, she ended with a shrug. "He is handsome. It would be difficult to do better, especially as he could be extremely helpful in your future role..."

"But?"

"I still think you can do better."

"How so?"

"Not telling."

Novella rolled her eyes. "You're usually so helpful."

Era patted her back. "Come, we must get you into bed. I imagine you're exhausted. In fact, I think I will have word sent that you will not appear for evening meal."

"Can you *do* that?"

"We'll find out," she answered with a wink. "I don't foresee anyone barging in here to carry you down, do you?"

With a smile, Novella slipped into comfortable garments before falling into bed. She didn't care who might turn up to convince her to appear for evening meal. She would sleep a week if Era could manage to keep them at bay.

It was difficult to tell whether it was nightmare or reality when Petyr barged into her chamber with torch in hand, demanding, *"Get up,* Vella! You must come with me, no questions asked."

She blinked against the light. Surely, he had not actually come to drag her down to supper. Glancing out the window, she found the moon high in the sky. It was near midnight, long past the time for feasting.

"What *time* is it?" she asked in confusion.

"Ssshh! We must make haste. *Now."* Starting for the door, he proceeded to pull the coverlet from her bed and shut her into the darkness of the room.

Novella fell back with no mild irritation. She considered ignoring him altogether and return to her blissful slumber before admitting that Petyr wasn't the sort to just let things go. Besides, she *must* learn why on either Earth or the Greater Archipelagos he had barged into her private chamber in the dead of night.

Peeling herself from the bed and onto her feet, she nearly fell back again from weariness. Instead, she lit a candle and surveyed her wardrobe until she located a simple navy toga with brown leggings. It would do for the middle of the night.

With a growl, she ran a hand over her eyes as she flung the door open. *"Now,* will you tell me what this is—"

He seized her head, planting a solid hand over her mouth. "Promise you will not speak a word until I say so," he whispered. "You must *trust me...* Alright?"

Her eyes darted about the room before she was able to twist her head to survey his face. His gaze revealed a depth of concern as she had never witnessed in him before. Something wasn't right. She nodded her acquiescence.

Instantly, he released her and started for the window. Without a word, he flung a leg over the sill, proceeding to climb down from a rope mysteriously attached from her window. She approached, gazing down at the great height, that rope dangling madly as he descended. Unlike other nights, there were no guardsman on patrol to manage her safety. Why was that? And did Petyr seriously expect her to climb down this way? She'd slip and break more than her neck.

When she did not follow, he froze, raising a single brow at her. She had been dared. With a huff, she stepped over the sill. If she lived through this, she was going to kill him.

Even once they'd reached the bottom, he did not signal for her to speak. Instead, he flung a dark cloak about her, took her hand and raced through the back alleys of Atlantyss. She was not afforded a moment to catch her breath until they reached the beach.

"It should be safe to speak now," he informed, "but we must remain quiet." His eyes darted every which way as if expecting followers. "We've got to swim for it. As I do not know who to trust, there is no alternative." He swallowed. "I've always hated this, but... a Swimmer can share his or her ability to breathe beneath the water by maintaining contact with a non-Swimmer. Michal and I used to do it all the time until we were attacked years back and he lost his grip on me in deep waters." He shivered. "It will have to do for tonight."

"Tell me what's going on."

His eyes met her with that great mound of apprehension before he shook his head. "We have too much ground to cover. And no telling when your absence will be noticed. We'll stop on some deserted island on the way."

"No," she whispered with the stamping of her foot. "I'm not leaving unless you give me *something.*"

Releasing a growl, he ran a hand through his hair as his gaze went to the stars. "This *stubborn woman* is who you've chosen, Great One?"

Novella folded her arms with impatience.

He planted hands on her shoulders. "Father came to me tonight, asking after my loyalty. Vella... he wanted my help to end your life."

She stepped back, pulling from his grasp. Why was he telling her this and what did he intend to do to her?

"No!" he whispered hoarsely, lunging for her arm before she could flee. With another glance to the heavens, he pleaded for strength before turning to her with, "I played along, said I was his man. But I am for *you* and always will be." He knelt upon the ground, her arm still in his. "In the name of all that is right and true, I pledge my friendship and loyalty to you, Novella of Earth, now and forevermore."

Novella was stunned by the display. "And I you, Petyr of the Archipelagos."

His eyes shot between each of hers before he released a satisfied breath and returned to his feet. "Now that's settled, we must flee to Iviana for support. Can you trust me that far? After all, my life is in *your* hands on this swim."

Novella felt her lips tremble with emotion over what Petyr had just dropped on her: both that his father had wanted her assassinated and that Petyr had taken her side over his own father. But she'd been *certain* that she and Tamsen had come to a mutual agreement. His desire for her life changed *everything.* What had seemed so certain was now pandemonium. And what was she to do? How she wished she could return home. But she couldn't... could she?

"What changed his mind?" she gasped with emotion. "And why are you choosing me?"

"We can get into all that once we've reached the Isle of Dragons. It isn't far by Swimmer's strength."

She nodded, suddenly feeling quite as eager as Petyr to vacate Atlantyss. No wonder he had been so pushy. He was supposed to be taking her life, not helping her escape with it. At any moment, Tamsen might discover them gone and come searching. She plunged into the water, nearly diving in when Petyr stopped her.

"Don't forget the 'fraidy cat over here. I can't go without you."

She waited for him to catch up, firmly planting her hand in his. It was somewhat terrifying to have a life in her care like this, especially when he had admitted his fear. She sent a prayer to the Great One for Help, knowing he was never far away.

CHAPTER 32

NOVELLA AND PETYR CRAWLED onto shore in utter exhaustion. Even her swimmer's strength had been tested and, though Petyr had been mostly in tow, he'd done some swimming of his own to help out. However, he did not have her strength in the water. They fell to their backs on the beach, catching their breath for some time. The soft pink of early dusk danced on the horizon.

"I'm afraid..." Petyr breathed, "we should go on. I cannot consider us safe until we are tucked behind Iviana's walls. It will be a miracle if we are not spotted even at this early hour."

Novella pounded the ground with her fist before allowing him to help her up, though he nearly fell back in the process.

"You say *I'm* nutty," she gasped out.

His eyes questioned her.

"*I'm* not the one who opted for the midnight swim," she answered with a punch to his arm before starting inland.

"What can I say? I've got a thing for Swimmers."

Gazing up at a quaint seaside cottage with tropical vines enwrapping it, she commented, "This is an *Eastern* island."

"Indeed... and we are *exceedingly* fortunate."

"How so?"

"That is Iviana's home."

She looked up again. It was so small and humble. Was this truly where the impressive "glorybringer" she'd heard so much about resided? She gasped as a large form moved beside the house. It soon proved to be the largest dragon she had ever laid eyes on... and the closest she had ever been to one since her arrival. Petyr and Michal had suggested a flight upon one, but she had insisted against it.

"That's Tragor," Petyr explained, "the Great Dragon of the Ages. He's been devoted to Iviana for as long as I can remember. From his expression, I'd say he considers himself on guard."

"Like a dog?"

"Don't let him hear you say that," he murmured with a wink before wandering from their course to pat the creature. "Just me, fella. And Novella, here, is a friend. You'll see."

He returned to Novella's side as she reached the door, knocking softly upon it.

Iviana opened the door with groggy eyes that widened on recognition.

"Hey, neighbor," Petyr greeted. "Mind if we stop in for a chat?"

Iviana nodded gravely, stepping aside to allow them entrance. She glanced about outside as if sensing the import of their visit. Shutting the door, she followed it with a bolt before striding across the house to bolt the other.

"Follow me," she instructed as she entered a quaint kitchen, gesturing for them to take seats before a small wooden table. "What will you have? Honey rolls and hava fruit are about all I've got."

"Yes, please," Petyr replied. "I don't think Novella's eaten since breakfast yesterday morning."

Iviana turned to survey Novella as she went about preparations. "What has happened?"

Petyr released a lengthy sigh before beginning in his blunt way, "Father came to my rooms early last evening. We'd had such a fine time catching up while Vella and Michal were away that I thought he'd come for a pleasant chat." He swallowed. "I was wrong."

Iviana smacked a plate of rolls onto the table. "Why was she with *Michal* and not you?" she barked. "You promised to protect her in my stead."

"They'd left before I caught wind of it. I suppose I knew father had tricked me, but... I thought it was only an effort to set her up with Michal."

"But Era was with them?" she questioned.

"Tamsen ordered her to remain in Atlantyss," Novella quickly explained.

Iviana shook her head. "Where is Era now?"

Novella looked to Petyr.

"Honestly, Iviana," Petyr began, "I had little time to think before taking action. Just before speaking with me... Father was approached by the rebel political faction. They offered him a deal, and he accepted."

Iviana's eyes fell closed as her lips set in a straight line before, *"This* is why the Great One selected a *woman* for Realm Leader. What is it with you men and your brotherhood?! An agreement with them was what cost me my Flynn!" Her eyes shone with tears.

"Er..." Petyr began awkwardly. "I'm not disagreeing with you, per say. But father did not seem himself. He was speaking like... like a madman, to be perfectly frank. The hatred in his voice as concerned Novella was frightening."

"What does this agreement have to do with her?"

"They want her out of the way, which, to him, meant dead. Honestly... I'm considering she simply return to Earth until we can get all this sorted out."

"No!" both Novella and Iviana exclaimed.

"That is..." Novella continued softly, "not yet. I need to understand this agreement. What are the terms?"

Petyr swallowed hard, pausing for a long while as if he did not wish to speak it. "The baddies are demanding he legally cut ties with the Eastern islands so Father can lead the West in a war against them."

"The aim?" Iviana questioned bitterly.

"Enslave the Easterners to do the bidding of the West."

"What?" Novella gasped in dismay.

"They don't seem to believe that the wealthy islands should be regarded with equality beside those with humbler trade. They consider the Easterners lower class. Ultimately... I think they just want to turn the world upside-down."

"Why would your father *ever* agree to those terms?" Iviana demanded.

Petyr shook his head, glancing hesitantly at Novella. "As Novella has gained praise and notoriety, he has opened the door to envy. I think the council's swift acceptance of her has slapped him across the face as a rejection to all he has attempted for our world. He feels unappreciated and... I don't think he expected the loss of the position to hit him so hard. He's a mess."

"But what do they have to *offer* him?"

"Their support of his leadership. Apparently, their numbers have been quietly growing for a number of years. In effect, he gets to keep his position as Realm Leader."

Iviana shook her head. "If I'd once thought he would fall for something like this, I'd have never placed him in power. Better for the world to be at all odds than for a man with the Western isles in his power to lose his head." She planted her face into her hands, sighing out, "I've failed. And I'm sorry."

Petyr stood to his feet, tiptoeing around the table to place a hand on her back. "That's nonsense. Novella's here. She will put the world to rights."

Novella's mouth fell open on his words. It was a *mess*. She'd been days away from taking her place as leader. Now, the standing leader wanted her dead and the East inevitably enslaved. And Petyr, of all people, expected her to miraculously fix everything?

"What do you expect me to do?" she barked.

The two looked up at her.

"You bested Xax," he retorted with irritation. "The Great One is with you. We'll figure it out."

"What happened to sending me back home while *you* fixed it?"

"Got my head bit off is what."

"Go to the East," the Helper whispered as a breeze from the open window.

Novella froze. The East... Of course. They must be warned of Tamsen's treachery.

"I have raised up the Easterly chieftains as your army for such a time as this."

CHAPTER 33

"What is it?" Iviana questioned with a tone afraid to hope.

Novella's eyes fell on Petyr. "We must go to the Easterly Conglomeration."

His brows rose to his hairline. "You *are* their Chief of chieftains..." he commented pensively.

A pounding ensued at the front door. All three paused before Iviana called out, "What is it?"

"It's me, Ivi!"

Iviana unbolted the door and allowed a large, muscular man entrance before re-bolting it. His eyes fell on the two in the kitchen.

"I was hoping they weren't here," he commented evenly.

"What is it, Darist?" Iviana questioned.

"A fleet of ships approach. Upon the first arrives Realm Leader Tamsen himself. They sent word ahead to have these two delivered upon his landing."

"How does he know we're here?" Petyr asked in bewilderment.

"Unfortunately, you made an obvious choice," Iviana explained. "I would have expected you to come to me in this situation as well."

Darist's gaze fell on Novella. "Is this *her*—the Great One's chosen leader?"

Iviana nodded before leaving the room.

Darist offered Novella a smirking nod. "Wish we'd met under better circumstances, but... it's an honor."

Novella offered a half-hearted grin, mind racing for what to do. Could they swim for it? Or had Tamsen brought skilled Swimmers along? What if, heaven forbid, he'd brought Michal with him? Would the elder son do his father's bidding? She swallowed hard at the thought.

Iviana returned with a sword and scabbard, staring down at it as if uncertain of what to do.

"Are we to fight our way out?" Novella asked with horror.

Iviana ignored her, instead kneeling down and pulling the scabbard about Novella's waist. Standing to her feet, Iviana surveyed Novella with new eyes. She gave a curt nod before taking up a jar of oil and pouring it over Novella's head. "Before the Great One and these witnesses, I hereby perform the right of leadership over this, the Greater Archipelagos. Do you accept, Novella?"

Novella's eyes bulged as her mouth fell open. "I-I do."

Iviana nodded again. "Go and serve your people. Gather your armies. With the Great One's help, defeat this foe."

Novella shook her head. *This* was her inauguration—in a tiny kitchen with next to no witnesses, a fleet of ships in hot pursuit and the former Realm Leader attempting a coup?

"That is a special sword I've bestowed upon you," Iviana explained. "It possesses uncanny abilities. I have not been without it since I was an infant in the cradle. Use it with discretion and it will serve you well. But you must serve it too."

Novella's eyes dropped to the sword. Slowly, she pulled it from its scabbard, surveying a rather ordinary looking blade so far as she could tell. But as she'd had no experience with them other than what she'd read in books, she was moved with awe.

Abruptly, the blade was illuminated in her grasp. Involuntarily, she dropped it. The thud to the floor did not smother its glow. The light flooded the room and, for a moment, the resonance of clashing swords could be heard before a woman's voice echoed out, "By the blood of him who gave himself!" Quite suddenly, the light dissipated. The sword that lay in its place on the floor gleamed crimson. After some moments' silence, Petyr knelt to take it into his hands.

"It's... *ruby.*"

Iviana nodded. "That is its true form. It was placed under a concealment to keep it safe with a mere child like myself. In the hands of a Realm Leader, it has chosen to return to its true form."

"What was with the voice?" Petyr questioned.

"I have heard that utterance in my dreams through the years. I believe it was Jaela of the cavern, the woman who birthed it into being from her strange mouth to be used by the angel, Viijelyk, a high warrior of the Great One. Sometime later, a peculiar man managed to filch it off him and was forced to stand guard over it for a hundred years as punishment. It was then that it was bestowed upon my good friend, Wynn of Kierelia upon the planet Kaern. But, one day, a strange woman called Lady Hazel stepped through the back door of Wynn's cabin, claiming she had passed through time from the early ages of the Kierelian kingdom. Wynn sensed she was to surrender the weapon to her use. It seems that, after Lady Hazel's purposes with it were complete, it was passed on to my infant self by the angel himself... and *now* to you, Realm Leader Novella."

Novella's eyes shot to Iviana's face. "I *cannot* take it from you." Indeed, it seemed too great a responsibility after learning such a history.

Iviana smiled. "It pleases me that you should. Besides, the Great One told me long ago to whom it was to pass. This was the awaited moment, though, back then, I in no way realized what the circumstances would be."

"Open up, Iviana!" Tamsen's voice bellowed from the front door. "We must speak!"

"Now," Iviana murmured irritably, "what to do about the pebble in my shoe..."

"You want me to toss him across the island?" Darist offered with a smirk.

Novella's eyes shot to him, then his muscles. She deduced that he possessed the gift of strength. What she wouldn't do to have a fellow like that beside her.

Iviana shook her head at him. "Where have you even been, Darist?"

"Iviana!" Tamsen called again as his guardsmen beat upon the door.

"Here and there," Darist answered with a smirk.

"I've missed you terribly these last years," the woman admitted.

"And I you."

Petyr cleared his throat. "Not to interrupt, but... Father's waiting. What are we to do with Novella?"

An almost imperceptible knock sounded at the back door before Captain Jonno's face appeared in the window with a wide grin. Novella raced to him.

"Are you for me or against me?" she asked with emotion.

A finger flew to his lips before, "I've traveled with Realm Leader Tamsen, but my intent is to whisk you to safety. Will you trust me?"

Novella studied his face before nodding, but Petyr shook his head. He caught her hand as she reached for the door. "He is Father's favored captain."

"But we have *history*, Captain Jonno and I," she explained.

Petyr's lips set in a grimace before he turned to the captain. "And how do you intend to get her away unharmed with a whole fleet surrounding?"

"Your father is of the understanding that he is acting as a distraction while I fool the girl into spiriting off with me," he answered with a wink. "We shouldn't have any trouble until it's too late. If push comes to shove, my men and I are prepared to lay down our lives for the Realm Leader expectant."

"It's Realm Leader now," Petyr corrected. "Iviana just performed the ceremony."

The captain's eyes flew to Novella, alight with pleasure. "Congratulations, Realm Leader Novella. Wish it was under better circumstances. Now... shall we abscond?"

"Go," Iviana whispered. "I am about to allow Tamsen entrance. The Great One is present. He has a plan."

Novella nodded as Petyr allowed her to exit, following close behind. It was then the front door burst open, having been smashed by the guards. Novella ducked down beneath the window along with Petyr and Captain Jonno.

"Where are they—" Tamsen's voice halted of a sudden. Silence reigned some moments before he began to weep. Novella looked to Petyr, whose brows had reached his hairline.

"Novella of Earth will prove the finest Realm Leader the Greater Archipelagos has ever known," Tamsen chanted as if out of his right mind. "Her influence upon the world will be more powerful than Latos, who once united the archipelagos. And in the coming terrestrial war, her fame will grow to shine like the sun and never blush with shame. Even now, the Great One is leading her out into a *broad* place."

"What is going on?" Novella mouthed.

Petyr shook his head. "Perhaps he has changed his tune?"

It was the captain's turn to shake his head. "The Great One is at work here. I reckon the Hearer's gift is upon him."

"He hears from the Great One?" Novella questioned with surprise.

He shook his head again. "I reckon the Great One spirit has possessed him to buy you time, Realm Leader. Let us depart."

Petyr stole Novella's hand, nearly dragging her across the beach until the three had entered the water. Then, it was Novella's turn to tow him. The captain, it appeared, was a Swimmer—the perfect sailor. In no time at all, they were silently hoisted onto the *Glorybringer*, where Michal stood in the midst of the loyal sailors.

"Didn't think I was going to miss out on the party, did you?" he asked with sparkling eyes.

Novella bit her lip before, "You... are *for* me?"

He bowed low. "My devotion is yours."

With a broad grin, Petyr thrust out a hand. The brother's gripped one another's forearms as their eyes met. Yet, Petyr couldn't seem to help asking, "You are choosing Novella over Father?"

Michal nodded grimly. "I commandeered the *Glorybringer* the moment I caught wind of what was afoot. Father readily presumed I would betray her out of loyalty to him. He and I were all the other had while you were missing..." His jaw flexed before he shook his head. "But he is no longer the man with whom I worked so closely."

Petyr nodded. "He asked me to assassinate Novella."

Michal dropped his brother's hand, turning away for some moments. When he turned back, it was clear he'd fought tears. "Sail on, Captain!" he declared hardily. "We must make haste."

Captain Jonno nodded. "I've sent my best navigator to the helm as we speak. Your father is otherwise detained. If the Great One holds him there long enough, we should be home free in no time."

"To where have you set your course?" Novella inquired.

"Why, to Atlantyss of course, now you are Realm Leader."

She shook her head. "We must return to the Easterly Conglomeration."

"But—"

"It is our best course... especially until we can be certain whether the West will embrace Tamsen or myself. He was the one who successfully united them. And though some islands have lacked, many have acquired great wealth under his reign."

The captain nodded, sauntering for the helm.

"Realm Leader?" Michal asked in confusion.

"Iviana just performed the ceremony," Petyr explained. "Anything Father does now will be considered mutinous."

Michal bowed before Novella. "I wish you a long and prosperous administration, Realm Leader Novella."

She nodded shortly. "Did anyone think to bring Era?"

Michal nodded. "She is below deck, preparing your quarters."

Novella nodded with relief, starting that way. It was an honor to have these brothers for support, but a woman's company was invaluable. How she wished she might have Iviana by her side, but the woman had sent her off on her own... with the expectation that she, Novella, would resolve the bedlam she had inherited. She bit her lip as tears flooded her eyes. She was Realm Leader now. There was no going back. This truly was her mess to fix. And she had no idea how to go about it.

"One step at a time," the Helper whispered.

Her head shot up as she recalled the Anointed One's words, "I will be with you always, even to the end of the age."

She shook her head. This was undoubtedly outlandish. Not long ago, she'd been sipping tea in her father's home in England... upon planet Earth. Now, here she was the rightful Realm Leader, fleeing the former Realm Leader with no idea of how to nurture these wailing, squabbling islands into something advantageous for all. Yet... do it, she must.

Or die trying.

CHAPTER 34

"Never thought I'd see the day we'd be seeking the Easterly Conglomeration for help," Petyr commented as he stood with Novella and Michal on deck. The three gazed at the glorious conglomeration of archipelagos, ten islands in total. A rainbow gleamed over the lot as if signaling promises it intended to keep.

"They used to be rather a thorn in Realm Leader Flynn's heel," Michal explained to Novella. "Always unhappy about something and in possession of large enough armies to be a real threat. They held a deal of sway in decades past. Father, however, had no patience whatever for them."

The three fell silent. Novella couldn't help feeling for these fellows, whom she knew loved their father immensely. What would she do if her parents suddenly turned against all she believed? How she wished things were different. How she struggled to believe they were as they were. Yet, this was their reality. They must make of it what they would.

"As Chief of chieftains," she began, "I am going to entreat their armies for our use."

One on either side, the two turned to her in disbelief.

"The chiefs don't just fork over their men," Michal warned.

"Just filling you in," she answered shortly.

Petyr squeezed her forearm. "I stand with you regardless of how they respond. We will find a way."

It was clear neither expected her to win out. But they were not aware of what the Great One had spoken. Besides, the chiefs relished the notion of a good battle. They might join her simply for the prospect. At least, that was what she'd told herself in order to fall asleep the evening before.

The *Glorybringer* docked. A crowd formed as Novella stood where she could be seen. How they responded would reveal whether they were for or against her in this new juncture. There was no telling what they may have heard.

"It's her!" a man shouted above the gathering crowd.

Novella waited.

"Are we certain we should drop the gangplank?" Michal questioned.

A roaring chant was taken up. "Chief of chiefs! Chief of chiefs! Chief of chiefs!"

The chant intensified like a resounding trumpet blast as the plank was dropped. Novella's hand dropped to the hilt at her waste. She was still growing accustomed to its weight. Even so, it made her *feel* like a chief. She was glad to carry it, even if she didn't know the first thing about its usage. She descended toward the assemblage, whose chant in no way wavered. They were mad with enthusiasm.

At a gesture from Chief Xax, silence reigned. He stepped forward, a fist over his heart. With a bow, he looked to her with expectancy. Novella mimicked his gesture, confident she had done right when he grinned back.

"To what do we owe the pleasure of yer visit, Chief of chieftains?" he asked.

Petyr cleared his throat. "Realm Leader Novella's initiation took place in secret yesterday morn."

Xax's eyes lit on her. He offered a far deeper bow than he'd given before. "Realm Leader Novella, my sword is yours."

"H-how did you know?" she gasped.

He raised a brow. "I do not imagine the ceremony would have been performed in secret if not your life were in jeopardy, nor do I imagine we would be your *first* destination upon your inauguration if all was well in Atlantyss. I cannot speak for the other chieftains, but my armies stand behind you—yours to command."

Novella released a sigh. "I cannot tell you how honored I am, Chief Xax."

He grinned largely. "The honor be all mine, Realm Leader, that you should turn to us in yer need. We've been long overlooked by prior leaders. Now, come. Let us gather the chiefs. There is much to discuss."

Michal released a low whistle as he joined Novella and Petyr. "Pardon my prior uncertainty, Realm Leader," he commented. "I stand wholly corrected."

"As always, brother mine," Petyr returned with a wink.

The next few days were spent in deep debate concerning Novella's next move. As it happened, every chief but one offered his army for her disposal. But when word reached them that Tamsen had put out a reward for her head as an enemy of the planet, the final chief joined their ranks.

The news was a difficult blow to her. After hearing the utterance of his prophetic words under the power of the Great One, she'd secretly hoped he might change his tune. Yet, it was far more difficult for his sons to bear. Michal refused to leave his quarters for days. Novella attempted to draw him out, but it seemed the wind had died in his sails.

"You... could always join him," Novella finally ventured to point out one day.

His eyes flew to hers with fire. "Against you?"

She bobbed her head from side to side. "You might influence him to support me if you returned."

"Fat chance," he growled under his breath.

"All I'm saying is... you love him. He is your father. I don't want you to feel trapped here with me."

"Trapped is not the word. I am in support of you. Even if you were not the chosen Realm Leader, I could not help it. You are *good*, Vella. I like you... That is, you know how I feel about you."

She swallowed, drawing to her feet. "Your support means the world. I thank you for it. But I am sorry about your father."

He stood to his own. "I apologize for my grief. Considering I know Father like the back of my hand, I should be aiding you in those meetings."

"That *would* be helpful."

He grinned. "Did you suggest I return to Atlantyss in order to jolt me from my sulkiness?"

She grinned in return but said nothing.

He proceeded to pull a strand of her hair. "Not too shabby, Realm Leader. I'll be present at the next conference."

Further news soon reached them that the majority of the Western isles were siding with Tamsen. Considering the time Novella had spent on some of those islands, this news hit her harder than Tamsen's prior declaration. As Realm Leader, she'd already lost half the planet. The real question, then, lay with the East. It was true the conglomeration stood with her, but what of the remaining islands?

As she spent weeks training in combat, an answer arrived in the form of a familiar face. The woman who had once startled her within the tropical forests of Atlantyss appeared on the shores of the conglomeration, demanding to be granted a visitation with Realm Leader Novella. In return, the chiefs arrested her with the assumption that she was an enemy spy. It wasn't until Novella finally laid eyes on her that she understood there was no threat.

"Please, have her unchained," she directed with sympathy. "She and I are acquainted." It was interesting how loyalties shifted when one was on the brink of war.

The woman's eyes glowed as she met Novella's. "Then you remember me."

"I thought you were kidnapping me. That is hard to forget."

The woman's head bobbed to the side. "That *was* the plan."

Novella found herself smirking. "How can I be of service to you now?"

"I am come from the Isle of Seekers. Word has reached us that you are assembling an army. We wish to join those ranks."

Novella swallowed. She'd hoped word would not get out so soon. Armies meant war and that was something she was praying to avoid. "What reason do your people have to follow me?"

"You are the chosen Realm Leader," she answered easily. "We've heard you were formally anointed. The people of Seekers follow the movements of the Great One. Where he marches, we march."

Novella's lips curled into a smile. It was so like the request the Anointed One had made of her—to follow his movements. "What is your name?"

"I am Riva."

"Well, Riva... I think I would like to visit your island after all—voluntarily."

The woman grinned largely. "We would be deeply gratified to receive you, Realm Leader Novella. May I make a suggestion?"

She nodded.

"Another tour, throughout the Eastern islands. I think you will find many of the Easterners prepared to assent to your leadership. Those who are not... you might persuade."

"With an army?" she questioned doubtfully.

"Nay. In the manner you treated the Western islands. From what we hear, not a one of them will officially take a stand either for or against you. Their position is neutral. Being so close to Atlantyss places them in an awkward position. To me, that speaks of loyalty well won. I would like to see what you can do in the East."

Novella released a thoughtful breath. Having the Easterly Conglomeration behind her was a great victory, but if Tamsen brought the whole of the Western armies against either her or the East as he had threatened, she and the Eastern isles needed one another. Moreover, until they determined to side against her, she was their lawful leader. She rather owed them a visit.

"I would appreciate it if you would meet with Petyr to lay out plans for this tour," Novella answered. "I've a mind to begin quite soon."

Riva bowed deeply. "I would be honored to be of such assistance, but I must warn you that I am but a potter."

"And why does 'but a potter' take such interest in me?"

"This potter has spent hours in commune with her Great Friend every day for many years. I am my beloved's and he is mine. When one you love so dearly requests you make a perilous journey, you answer no matter the possible or probable cost."

Novella blinked back. Hours in commune with the Great One for days on end? She could only dream of such a life. As it was, her sword had been her master these last weeks and she had in no way mastered it. "Are all the populace of Seekers like you?"

Riva bobbed her head. "Most."

"What makes them so?"

She pressed her lips together before, "We are a community of Seekers... Those who have searched far and wide for answers. We have discovered where the treasure lies."

Novella raised a brow. "Where is that?"

"The love of the Great One, Realm Leader. There is nothing beside it."

Slowly, Novella nodded. She'd been learning to lean on the Great One, his Son and the Helper. She'd even learned to appreciate him with worship. But could she claim to know and love him in such terms as this woman used? Could she claim hours spent seeking this treasure? Not as yet. She'd just discovered she required training in more ways than one.

"Please mark the Island of Seekers among the first of my visits."

CHAPTER 35

"I HAVE GOOD NEWS and bad news," Petyr opened with in the conglomeration's vast gardens some days later.

"Good news first."

Novella was weary of training and meeting with mighty men of war. Where were a good book and a box of bonbons when one needed them? She'd had no notion of how very spoiled she'd been back in England.

"Your tour has been strategized. You may depart as soon as you like."

She sighed. It was true this was good news, but it also meant there was no rest for the righteous. "And the bad news?"

His face became shadow, his voice lowering an octave. "Father is raising his armies against both you and the East. He's using the conglomeration's support of you as his excuse to come against them. War has officially been declared."

Novella sank deeper into her chair. She'd hoped for more time. She'd hoped for no war at all. She was a girl from Victorian London who had spent her days reading and knitting.

"*War,*" she murmured. Her face fell into her hands. "I can't do this."

He slipped into the chair beside her. "You're not alone here. You've got my sword, Michal's, the chieftains' and their armies. Many mighty men and women are behind you."

"But it's not enough. We're not ready. *I'm* not ready."

"I don't know if we ever feel prepared for our day of reckoning. Yet, we must be willing to show up."

"I wish I had more than willingness. I need boldness."

He stole his hand into hers, giving it a squeeze. "All you must do is ask the Great One, Vella. You know that. As for time... Father has just handed you the Eastern isles on a platter. I think you'll find them to be putty in your hands after what he's just done."

She looked up. "I hadn't considered that..."

"And it isn't as if you must enter the battle yourself. Chief Xax has offered himself as head of your army."

For a fraction of a second, Novella felt herself dared. But the sensation faded. She did not want to see battle. The notion terrified her. It did not seem to be her place. Yet...

She shook her head. "I'm not sending my people out to be slaughtered by the West without accompanying them. It isn't just."

His hand became stone. "You cannot face battle. You're our Realm Leader. We must keep you from harm's way."

Her eyes flew to his. "Is that how the leaders of the past handled war?"

"No. But they were typically raised with weapons in their hands."

"And *I* was raised to knit."

He swallowed. By now, he understood how she responded to such insinuations. "You were raised on another planet," he spoke softly, quite unlike the Petyr who was so often bossing.

"And having been raised on Earth, I should not have been chosen to become the leader of another world. Yet, here I am. I must go... if it comes to it."

"You're still hoping to avoid war?"

"Of course I am. Perhaps I am naïve or perhaps I am altogether feminine, but I cannot abide the notion of a formerly united people slaying one another."

"Sometimes the mess is the only way to reach the desired outcome."

She released a long breath, pulling her hand from his grasp to smooth out her toga. "I am aware. Doesn't mean I have to like it."

He stood to his feet. "I will have a meeting scheduled with the chieftains in order to discuss Father's announcement before you leave. How soon can you be ready to depart?"

"Today."

"Er... that seems hasty."

"Time is of the essence. I wish to visit as many islands as possible before things get out of hand."

He bowed deeply. "I will see how soon we can gather the chieftains and have Captain Jonno ready the *Glorybringer*."

The conclusion of that meeting ended in a whole fleet of the conglomeration's finest warriors and seamen for her accompaniment. They insisted on protecting their leader with everything in their arsenal. Novella did not relish the notion of traveling in the company of an army. She wasn't certain it would make the best impression on the islands she would visit. But when an entire room, including Petyr, Michal and Era, was in opposition, she could do naught but forfeit her personal preferences.

"I don't see what good a Realm Leader does if she cannot even have her own way in this," she complained to Era as they packed.

"I'm afraid it is quite necessary when the leader of the other half of the world has put a price on your head, Novella," the woman returned. "Not to mention, when Petyr decides a thing, he typically gets his way."

"*He* should be Realm Leader then, if he is so determined to rule me."

Era chuckled. "If he wanted to rule you, I have no doubt he could. He is that kind of a man. His interest, however, seems merely in keeping you safe. I'm afraid you cannot fault him there, as fond as you are of doing so."

Novella peered up at her. "Is that what I do—fault him all the time?" She dropped the toga she'd been rolling and plopped onto the side of the bed. "He is far too valuable to me to make that a habit."

"I couldn't agree more. Especially at this juncture. Those boys have left all the family they have in order to follow and support you. That is no small potatoes. How you'll pick just one of them, I do not know."

Novella's eyes narrowed. "Petyr is no suitor, Era. Michal is the only choice in the offing and... I still haven't come to a conclusion on that score."

"I wonder why that is."

"As do I. Every time I see that handsome face, I question why I have not accepted."

"I cannot blame you there. And his devotion to you is perhaps even more attractive. But if you cannot feel for him the way you ought, perhaps you should let him off the hook."

"So... I fault one brother and leave the other dangling. It seems I make a muddle of things wherever I go."

"*Nay*, Vella. You are a godsend. All I'm suggesting is, once things have settled down, consider your options."

Novella leaped to her feet to finish the packing. "I know of but two: a singular life or one with Michal's perpetual aid. The latter is the clear answer. I just need time to adjust to the notion."

"Suit yourself. I pray the Great One will clarify the situation in due course."

And, once again, as Novella met Michal's bright eyes on board the *Glorybringer*, she was inclined to accept his offer. True, they were on the brink of war, she was about to attempt a swift tour of nearly every Eastern island and she had only just stepped into her altogether shaky role as Realm Leader. But what was all that to a pair of green eyes that lit up when one entered the room?

"What is on your mind, Realm Leader?" he questioned with an intrigued brow.

"Nothing that concerns you," she returned with a grimace as she realized it was a lie. "I did not realize you'd be traveling with us."

"You think I'm going to let you go traipsing over the globe without a proper escort?" He patted the sword at his side.

Novella raised a brow. She'd witnessed both him and his brother in action. They fought like the fate of the world was on their shoulders. Perhaps having one's father perpetrating mutiny made them feel so. Either way, the chieftains advised they be appointed top generals in her army. If push came to shove, these two could well best a whole squadron on their own. Great Gifts aside, they were two of her best fighters.

"What brought that cloud across your face?" he inquired.

"War. Are the gifts used... or merely weapons?"

"In past, both. That does not mean another agreement could not be reached. I do not imagine Father would turn down an offer to have both yours and Chief Xax' giftings squelched on the battlefield."

"We must look into the consideration. I do not like the notion of someone with naught but a sword meeting someone like, well, myself."

He narrowed his eyes on her. "I admire your consideration of your people, but... you can't be looking at warfare that way. A swift victory would be most merciful to everyone concerned."

"You make a fair point. We will discuss it at a later date."

He raised a brow. "Very diplomatic, Realm Leader Vella."

"I thank you," she replied with a grin.

"I wish the dawn of your leadership might have been spent in ease rather than striving," he spoke softly. "It is good for my heart to see you smile now and then."

"I cannot begin to consider the notion of a better beginning," she answered pensively. "It's all I can do to juggle the one I've inherited. Now... Era told me noon meal was to be served on board. I'm *famished*. Lead me to it, will you?"

His smile faded. "You're never going to accept my proposal... are you, Vella?"

She fell back a step, feeling whiplashed. She'd hoped he'd let the matter slide until she could discover what lay in her heart. All she had time for of late was prepping for a war she did not want while trying to win the people she should be leading by right.

"Michal, if you wish to withdraw your request, I would be neither disappointed nor offended. It... simply is not a matter I can rightly consider just now."

She swallowed back her emotion. Perhaps part of her relished looking to a likely future with Michal as a path of future happiness. The good Lord knew she could not claim to feel especially jovial at this juncture, though she knew she wore his grace for this season like a garment about her. Even so, she had done some imagining concerning a different kind of life one day.

He released a slow groan as he passed a hand across his face. "If I withdrew it, I would only have to extend my hopes again. Though the third time might just be the charm, a man can only be denied so many times before he's putting his manhood into question."

Novella blinked back at him before catching the glimmer of humor in his eyes. "No one would ever question your masculinity, Michal of Atlantyss. Trust me on that."

CHAPTER 36

NOVELLA STOOD AT THE helm of the ship, wind whipping through her hair with a warning. An anxious twinge twisted her stomach. Not only was she concerned about winning her first island as well as gaining warriors, the Helper was in the wind.

And something wasn't right.

"Tiz a fine day, is it not?" Petyr asked as he stepped up beside her.

She leaped to face him, a hand going to her heart. "You walk like a ballerina."

"As opposed to...?"

"A rhinoceros."

He raised a brow. "Not sure what that is, but I'll take your word for it."

She turned back to the forward horizon. "Which island is this to be?"

"The Isle of Merchants. They were one of Realm Leader Flynn's most avid supporters when Island Leader Horren was at the helm. Now, I believe, a woman called Vespa leads them."

"And I imagine they handle a good deal of trade?"

"They're in a good position for it. There isn't another island for miles around. Most every ship that travels this way anchors here."

She shook her head. "I don't like being so close to the Western islands just now."

"Though we *are* near the West, Atlantyss itself is quite far. There is very little chance of issue." He stopped short, stepping beside her to point into the distance. "See there? That shadowy mass in the distance is the Isle of Merchants."

Novella squinted to make it out. Her eyes caught on the skies overheard. Tiny black dots buzzed over it like bees. "What is that in the sky?"

"Dragons, I'd surmise. Many of the inhabitants travel that way. It is a decent mode of transporting wares if one does not boast a sailing vessel."

Novella relaxed. All was as it should be then. "I'm for tea. I don't want to appear famished when we port."

"I'll let you know how things look when we're closer."

"I appreciate it," she returned as she made her way to the sitting room.

It was there she found Era and Michal in deep discussion. She'd scarcely caught a word before silence reigned on her entrance.

"Sharing secrets?" she inquired with a smirk

Michal shrugged. "Era and I often disagree."

"Really?" she asked in surprise as she poured a cup of tea.

Era waved a hand. "Michal is known for his caution."

"Era for her bold faith," Michal put in. "As you might imagine, I often stand corrected."

Era grinned. "Smart boy."

Novella stifled a chuckle with a sip from her cup. "The Isle of Merchants has just come into view. All looks well from this vantage."

"Were you expecting trouble?" Michal questioned.

"Awoke with some anxiety. Guess it's just one of those days."

Era raised a brow. "As Realm Leader, you will grow to sense things around the globe. There may be trouble afoot elsewhere."

She returned her cup to its saucer. "I hadn't considered that."

Unconsciously, Michal's hand flew to the holt of his blade—something he practiced often of late. "I pray Father has not plunged into war already. We have not sent anyone to discuss battle mandates. It is honorable to wait."

Era stifled a smirk.

"What now?" he questioned irritably.

"It is only that you expect the whole world to live as conscientiously as yourself, good Michal. I'm afraid there are not many quite like you. We are fortunate that Novella here has the makings of a knight. Your father, however, is nothing if not a warrior. We've all witnessed that in years past."

"A warrior *should* be conscientious," he insisted. "Especially a skilled one. One should be conscious of one's own power and utilize it only when necessary."

"I like the way you think," Novella put in with a glowing smile. It was conversations like these that made her itch to wear his ring.

"I'm glad of it," he answered with a grin of his own.

Era drew to her feet. "I'm going to visit below deck. The two of you may fit in some flirting while I'm gone."

Novella smirked after their friend while Michal scowled.

"That woman has it out for me," he commented.

"She thinks the world of you as well as Petyr. She is often correcting my treatment of you both."

"Is she?" he asked with a raised brow. "Whatever for?"

"It seems I'm inconsiderate."

"Huh. Well, I've long thought you rather sweet."

"So you've said."

He quirked a brow. "*Is* this flirting?"

She shrugged. "*I'm* merely talking."

"Well, you are sweet, but you are also resilient. I've enjoyed watching you grow since your arrival. It glorifies the Great One."

"I don't even feel like the same girl who transported from Earth. My mother..." Her voice faded as her throat grew dry. It felt as if she was forgetting them.

"You miss her?" he asked softly.

She faced the wall, flicking a tear from her eye. In a moment, she swallowed her emotions and turned back with a smile. "I really cannot bear to think of my parents tucked up comfortably back home, waiting for me. It makes me ache. Let us speak of Merchants. What can you tell me?"

"It is *good* to remember your parents, Vella. It is healthy to recall from where one comes. That is, if you are of good stock, as you clearly are. I wish I could meet them."

Her lips curled into a wistful smile. "Mother would adore your genteel ways. Father loved Petyr like a son."

"He told me. I wonder what your father would make of me."

"You're much like Petyr. He'd take you in in a moment. Perhaps one day we might make a trip."

He raised his brows. "Perhaps to inquire his permission to—"

"Not what I meant. Only... I *would* like you to see where I come from."

"As would I. Petyr tells me of a dish called crumpets. Says I've never lived until I've tasted them."

"Petyr is a lover of simple fodder."

"Too true," Petyr spoke as he entered the room. "But we've got far worse problems."

A sweet and salty breeze accompanied Petyr into the room, causing Novella's stomach to turn again.

"What is it?" she pressed.

"Merchants appears to be under attack, or soon will be. They've got dragons in the sky as a defensive measure, but they're surrounded by Western vessels."

Michal gasped. "I knew Father would go after them in order to spoil Eastern trade, but I'd hoped there'd be more time before he pursued it."

"It was *my* mistake to venture this far West," Petyr put in with a growl. "So many anchor here that I couldn't resist gleaning their support. Now, we're near enough that we're on the radar of those Western fleets. But it isn't too late to turn back." His eyes went to Novella.

She swallowed, turning from the two to close her eyes and listen. With a nod, she spun about. "We must aid Merchants."

Petyr nodded. "It will send a message to Father, as well as hasten the birth of this war considerably."

"He has already sent a message by attacking an Eastern isle. But the East is *mine* until they reject me. I'm not ready to let an island slip through my fingers just yet. How many opposing vessels are there?"

"It is difficult to determine from this vantage. Some may be neutral ships at port. But I'd reckon they've got half a dozen."

Michal released a whistle. "All that for one island?"

"All that for the most successful trade island in the East. As you expected, he's after our purses."

"Petyr, send word to the fleet," Novella directed. "Our course is set. We sail for Merchants."

With a bow of compliance, he exited.

"I will inform Captain Jonno to hang back," Michal informed as he headed for the door.

"*Why?*"

"We're not delivering you straight into Western hands. I've seen you with a blade. You're not ready for battle."

She folded her arms. "I'm not going to sit back like some king in a chess match. It is every ship or none."

"Then we pull back," he insisted. "This was *supposed* to be a political tour, not a battle crusade."

She stepped into his face as flashbacks of the day before she was to face Chief Xax returned. "The Great One is in this, Michal. We will not fail."

"That doesn't mean there won't be casualties. Are you prepared for that, Vella?"

She ground her teeth as the answer wrung through her nervous system. "That's 'Realm Leader Novella' and my directive stands." Her hands were balled into fists as she stepped around him. She intended to deliver her own orders.

Of a sudden, she stopped short to step back into the room. "Michal, have word sent to the fleet that the Great Gifts are not to be used in combat unless first initiated by the Western troops." Spinning on her heel, she left before further debate ensued. She only hoped her order correct, else it may cost them dearly.

CHAPTER 37

NOVELLA EYED THE SHIPS that surrounded The Isle of Merchants through the porthole of the conference cabin. She'd listened to Petyr, Michal and Chief Xax debate long enough. They were far too near the island without an agreed upon agenda.

"I think it only honorable that our first course of action be to send a demand that they stand down," Michal spoke decisively. "Once combat ensues, the war has officially begun. We must give them a chance to avoid that... not to mention ourselves."

"Gives 'em far too generous an opportunity to initiate an attack on our arrival," Chief Xax' retorted.

"Actually," Novella spoke up, turning back to those at the table, "I agree with Michal. It is honorable. They *must* see it is foolhardy to try for Merchants once we have arrived. As they will be well out-numbered, I don't imagine they'll be keen to lose this first battle."

Petyr considered her quietly while Xax spoke up, "Sounds like a child's fairy book when you put it that way, Realm Leader. We must strike while the iron is hot. Go in hard and fast. Trust my experience on that."

Petyr shook his head. "No one can debate your experience, Chief. But I believe, for Realm Leader Novella and Michal, the concern is *how* this war is to play out. They are hoping to wage an agreement upon mercy mandates with my father before things ensue any further. I'm not certain I do not agree with them. If battle can be postponed, it is worth the chance."

Chief Xax' lips formed a grim line as he sat back and folded his arms. He'd offered his wisdom. It was clear he would say no more unless those younger than himself chose to see it his way, or so Novella imagined.

She turned to Michal. "Would you write up our proposition to be delivered on arrival?"

It wasn't long before the message was written out in Era's fine hand. Packaged into a waterproof vessel, a small fleet of Swimmers were dispatched to deliver it aboard the Western flagship. Novella and her council observed breathlessly from the portholes as the Swimmers waved their white flag, communicating that they approached peaceably. But would the Western soldiers allow them to board?

Novella released her breath as a rope ladder dropped over the side of the flagship. Her tongue swept into prayerful intercession. It was a moment before she noticed Petyr blinking down at her.

"What is it?" she questioned with a stomach forming knots.

"Is that a language of Earth?"

Her tongue ceased. She shook her head. "I cannot say. I have never spoken in such a manner before... I did not realize."

He nodded, eyes aglow. "Are you aware that this whole planet was created as a lavish gift for a Firetongue."

"A what?"

"It was a woman by the name of Jaela. She was bestowed with the gift of speaking in a mysterious, hallowed language. Fire breathed from her words. When she spoke... things *happened*. It was her close friendship with the Great One that moved him to create this world of archipelagos. And it was she and her husband, along with those they brought with them, who inevitably populated our islands."

"Are you suggesting that I was using her language? Was there flame?"

"None that I could see. But I felt it."

As she watched the last of their Swimmers climb aboard the enemy vessel, her tongue took up intercession again. She flashed a glance at Petyr as he smiled his secret thoughts at her. She had no time to discuss some mysterious idiom or what it might indicate. This moment may well be the opening of the war she so dreaded.

It was for some time that they watched in prayer, either of a natural or supernatural language. At long last, the Swimmers appeared on the deck again. Without further ado, they leaped from the ship to return to their vessels.

"No military movement," Michal commented. "That is promising."

Petyr merely nodded. Novella discerned that he did not expect a good report. The fact made her stomach flip over.

When the lead Swimmer appeared in the conference room, he bowed low. "I delivered the communication to the captain's assistant. The captain was unable to meet with us personally."

Petyr nodded. It was clearly as he'd expected.

"We are relieved to see you all returned to your ships," he spoke. "Thank you for your service."

It did not occur to Novella that her thanks were necessary until the Swimmer had bowed and retreated from the room. She would find him later... if all went well.

Era's gasp sent her twirling back to the window. She released a growl as she witnessed a cluster of Western Swimmer's approach the Isle of Merchants. In the next moment, the entire fleet of ships pointed their noses toward the *Glorybringer*.

Chief Xax marched from the cabin. Novella hoped it was merely to give orders.

Petyr squeezed her shoulder. "We had to try. It was prudent." He followed Xax out.

"Era," Michal began in a low voice, "will you make certain there is nothing of import to be discovered within the Realm Leader's quarters in a worst-case scenario?"

Era nodded before retreating. Novella looked up into his face with regret. "As Petyr said, we tried. Now, we must face what is before us."

With a grim nod, his eyes darted between hers. His mind appeared to be moving a hundred miles a minute before he took firm hold of her hand. "Come with me a moment."

In confusion, she followed until they reached the ladder that led below deck. She tore her hand from his. "Where are we going?"

He lost no time in sweeping her over his shoulder.

"Michal!" she squealed. "What on Earth are you doing?!"

He marched with purpose until they arrived at her quarters where Era's gaze flew to them with bewildered concern. Without a word, he planted Novella on the floor of her suite and shut the door firmly behind him. Both Novella and Era twitched as the sound of a key turning in the lock resonated through the cabin.

"He wouldn't *dare...* "Novella whispered hoarsely as she raced for the door. As feared, it held fast. *"Michal!"* she hollered. "Get *back* here and unlock this door. You have *no right!"*

Silence was her answer. She hammered on the door, hoping someone might hear even in the midst of their preparations. But her quarters were a good distance from where the soldiers and sailors were housed. Her only hope at this point was Petyr or the chief and they would be with the men and women preparing to fight.

Novella pressed her back against the door and slid to the floor. Her eyes sought Era. "I can't believe he did this. Is he *turning* on me?"

Era shook her head. "He is only doing what he believes is right."

Novella considered that before genuine wrath stirred within her. "He hasn't the authority to do what he thinks is right. I am *Realm Leader*. Or should be."

A tiny smirk reached Era's lips. "You're not wrong. But he believes himself quite in love... and you a mere damsel."

"I defeated Chief Xax!"

"The Spirit of the Great One provoked your Great Gifts to rise to your defense. But if you'll recall, you ordered they should not be used in battle."

Novella's lips shut into a straight line. Perhaps she shouldn't have given the order... at least not with Michal in the room. But she'd not *begun* to imagine he could be so rash. If they survived this and what he'd done was discovered, the rightful Realm Leader would appear a silly fool.

"He is undermining my leadership," she spat. "Who will follow me now?"

Era dropped onto the bed. "The Great One will work it out."

"*Fabulous.* It seems I am completely helpless without him."

"As it should be."

Novella rolled her eyes. She was in no mood to be lectured on the ways of the Great One. What she wanted was to get her hands on Michal and show him what she was truly made of... or at least the Great One she housed. It was true that she would never have made it this far without him.

"We can pray," Era suggested.

Novella nodded. It was the only weapon in her arsenal just now. And it was not long before the sounds of warfare ensued above. She shivered as she leaped to her feet, listening and praying in turns. Yet, as she asked the Great One's favor upon her ships, everything in her told her this involuntary incarceration was wrong. If the Great One was with her, she could enter the melee with the promise of his protection. *He* was the one who had directed *her* to got to battle for Merchants' sake.

"Oh, Helper... help me!" she breathed.

His soft chuckle tinkled on the air. Her hands tightened into fists. *Why* was he laughing at a time like this? She froze. *Of course*. Though she had directed that no Great Gifts were to be used in combat... affecting her door was in no way out of bounds. If he was for her, he would help her escape.

She leaped to her feet.

"What is it?" Era asked fearfully. "Do you hear something? Are they coming?"

Novella locked her eyes on the knob. In mere seconds, both it and its lock disintegrated into small piles of salt on the floor. Casting a wink at Era, she lost no time in thrusting the door open and flying from the room. Her heart raced as she neared the ladder that led above deck. Was she right in this?

With a squeal, she managed to withdraw her blade in time to meet an assailant's blow. She stumbled clumsily back under the force, hitting the floor with a thud that knocked the wind from her. Her attacker chuckled, swinging his sword for a final jab. Once again, she found the wherewithal to parry. The soldier barred his teeth as he pressed the weight of the blades toward her torso. With all her might, she pressed back in a fruitless attempt. Was this as far as she was to reach both as warrior and Realm Leader?

Unexpectedly, her crimson blade burst into a veil of blinding light. The bulk of the blades released as her attacker fell back to shield his eyes. Novella lost no time in crawling to her feet.

"*Bless* you, blade," she whispered out. "That is enough."

Its radiance snuffed out. The assailant blinked back at her in both blindness and bewilderment. She lost no time in leaping for the forward attack. She thrust her weapon in the direction of the Westerner's belly. He only just managed to fling her sword aside. As both their visions cleared, the game was afoot.

Novella fought with a willpower she'd not known in her life. All she could think was that she *could not* let Michal be proved right. But the soldier gained a better footing, forcing her against the wall. She lost her grip on the hilt of her blade. Shutting her eyes to the final blow, she waited for the inevitable but soon opened them to find Petyr standing over her assailant.

Despite her show up bravado, her vision dimmed. *"No..."*

She was no fainter. She *could* not. It would be nearly as humiliating as Michal locking her into her quarters. Yet, she felt herself fall against Petyr as her knees buckled. He lowered her to the floor, ordering her to sit with her head between her knees. With no understanding as to why, she obeyed. To her surprise, the ringing in her ears subsided and her vision was restored.

"You with us?" he questioned.

She nodded, rubbing at her eyes. "I am here."

"Michal told me what he'd done... I was on my way to release you."

She nodded with gratefulness. At least *someone* respected her rights as Realm Leader.

"But perhaps he was right." He patted her back.

Her eyes narrowed on his face. It was happening again: She'd been dared. His face shadowed as he realized what he'd said. Fire flooded her veins. She was tired of these brothers thinking they knew what was best for her. Sometimes, things weren't about being best for her but for her people. If they were fighting, she must join them. Using Petyr's shoulder to push herself onto her feet, she nabbed her sword from the floor. She launched up the stairs without a warning glance in Petyr's direction.

"Vella..." Petyr moaned.

She heard his steps close behind her. If she did not move fast, she could end up back in her holding cell. She supposed that was what happened when a woman nearly suffered a faint.

Weak but wrathful, she instantly leaped to Captain Jonno's defense before a Western soldier could plunge his dagger into the captain's chest. From that point on, she entered the melee numb to both her own emotion and the pain she inflicted, deadened even to the sharp grazes of the blades around her.

Battle ensued for what felt like hours. Always, Petyr was close at hand, aiding her as he was able. She knew he was the sole reason she remained alive, but she didn't care. She was just passively grateful he was not hauling her below deck. Indeed, he fought as she had long heard fabled—as if he were fifty men in one. It would be a sight to witness if it did not make her feel so very feeble. Still, she managed to defend him a time or two.

And then, quite suddenly, the soldier with which she contended narrowed his eyes on the horizon before hightailing it to the edge of the deck and leaping into the waters below. Novella stood in bewilderment as she watched other Westerners follow suit. But what was happening? Feeling a hand on her shoulder, she spun to encounter this unexpected assailant.

"*Woah,* Vella!" Petyr soothed. "It's over. They're retreating. Look."

He pointed to the nearest enemy vessel, gesturing to the remainder. Every one of them was sailing swiftly from the island's shores, abandoning many of their men and women in the surrounding waters.

"We've... won?" she questioned hoarsely, scarcely a sound from her throat.

He nodded, turning from her to order their fighters to arrest every Westerner left behind. The wounded were to be treated while the rest were imprisoned. They would soon take port along Merchants to make certain there were no enemy squadrons left behind.

But it was over.

As Novella's eyes flew to the first prisoner led below deck to the Western vessels in retreat and finally to the bloodshed surrounding, the humiliating vertigo returned. It was Era who caught her this time, wrapping her tightly in a wool shawl. Era's eyes searched her up and down, flooding with tears as she took in the sight that Novella could only imagine.

Silently, the loyal friend escorted her back to her quarters. Planting her into a wooden rocker, she cleansed her with bowl after bowl of hot water before helping her change and crawl into bed. Novella put up no fight. She knew that, as Realm Leader, she should remain alert until everything was settled, but there was no fight left in her. She felt her body give way to unconsciousness as tears passed from her lashes.

CHAPTER 38

NOVELLA SWALLOWED BACK BILE as she awoke from a nightmare concerning her first assailant of the battle. Though she was weak and nauseated, she was not ill. Completely drained and probably starving, yes. But not truly ill. With a shiver, she turned over. She had never known a day like that. And she was changed. How could it be otherwise? She had participated in real warfare—*very* different from training. Lives had reached a decided end. Petyr alone had slain over a hundred, she was sure. *Good,* dependable Petyr, who had remained by her side while she charged into a battle for which she was in no way prepared. But watching him revealed that a great and powerful God dwelt inside him. The way he fought was unnatural. His movements were intuitive and fluid, like a well-accustomed dance—quite extraordinary to a girl with no prior experience.

Michal had been right. She'd *not* been ready. But for Petyr, she'd be dead. But more so than her lack of ability, she'd been neither mentally nor emotionally equipped. She ought to have allowed the other vessels to take on this first battle, allowing her own to hang back. Yet, it wasn't in her nature to let others fight her battles—not when she was the one calling the shots.

The real root of her trouble was that this was only the *first* day of who knew how many they would spend at war. *This* was to be her life for the foreseeable future. How could she ever endure it? It took all her discipline and willpower not to transport herself home, though everything in her longed for it, even if only for a moment. Yet, that moment would not only terrify her parents as they learned what she endured, it would quelch her ability to return to the difficulties of the life she was living. She understood that she would never come back.

Era smiled with satisfaction as she entered with tray in hand. "I was hoping you'd be awake. You require sustenance. I heard a *number* of the men comment on how valiantly you fought. They're quite proud of you. Now, sit up so I can set this tray in your lap."

Numbly, Novella obeyed. But staring down at the bountiful tray only made her lose her appetite. "How can I *eat*, Era?" she moaned. "I know we were successful, but how can I look to more days like *this* without anything but dread?"

Era's eyes locked on hers as she planted herself on the side of the bed, patting her cheek with, "You are weary, Vella dear. But I must make you aware that this was a merciful victory, for it was swift. *Yes...*" She swallowed. "Lives were lost. But not so many as there might have been. You've a *mighty* army behind you."

A tear streamed down Novella's temple. This had been a *swift* battle. She'd heard of confrontations that endured for days and even weeks. Hours were nothing. Yet, it had rocked her world.

Without another word, Era reached for a honey roll, tore off a piece and plunged it into Novella's mouth. *"Chew* or it'll choke you."

As tears continued to stream down her cheeks, Novella acquiesced, chewing and swallowing every bite without satisfaction. Era released a sigh as she returned the roll to the tray. She gazed down at her as if uncertain what to do before they were startled by a knock at the door.

Era rose to meet it, opening it only far enough to allow Petyr's voice entrance. It seemed that a member of the Merchants' island council wished to see Novella immediately. She didn't care if Novella was quite dressed—she was insistent, and so was Petyr.

Closing the door, Era looked to her charge with little hope. "You heard him. He is bringing her down."

Novella pulled herself to her feet. She couldn't afford to be angry with Petyr and he clearly knew it. He'd saved her backside too many times. "Quick, pass me my robe," she directed. "I'll take the chair. Do I look like a fool in my night things?"

"Sit up straight and you'll look but a drained soldier. I'm sure she'll understand." She proceeded to bathe the tears from Novella's face. "There. You're presentable."

Novella nodded, folding her hands together as she awaited the visitor. She couldn't help twitching as the door swung open. She wasn't ready for strangers from the very island she was hoping to win over. Yet, when a head of curly white hair bowed low before her, she instantly felt at ease.

"I am sent with *boundless thanksgiving* from the members of our island council. If you had not happened to be in approach and chosen to stand with us, who *knows* where we would be now? Island Leader Vespa sends her regrets that she cannot come herself, but you must understand that she is quite busy just now. Therefore, I have come in her stead with our deepest gratefulness as well as congratulations on a noble victory."

Novella considered this, almost at a loss for words. This was a view she had not yet thought to contemplate. After all, they'd not attacked the Westerners out of spite. They'd come to the defense of a lone island. Moreover, they had offered the aggressors an opportunity to abscond. Instead, they'd turned attacked.

"I am *glad* we were able to be of service," Novella answered. "I hope to meet with your council soon in order to discuss the matter—"

"Whatever you want, it's yours," the woman insisted. "I think you'll find us more than prepared to celebrate your status as Realm Leader. A feast for your arrival is being planned as we speak."

"A feast is in no way necessary. I—"

"You do not understand just what you've done, do you? Our children would be at the mercy of our enemies this very moment had you not prevailed. We were greatly outnumbered. *Your* appearance was the miracle we were pleading for."

Once again, it struck Novella that *this* was why they'd gone to battle. Not because they wanted to initiate a war, but because Tamsen was determined to defeat the Eastern isles in order to enslave them. They'd fought for the liberty of these people and they'd won it.

Era was right. It was a *fortunate* victory.

She rose to her feet to take the woman's hands into her own. "Thank you, kind lady, for coming to see me. You are a breath of fresh air."

The woman blinked back stunned tears. "You just don't know, Realm Leader Novella... We *need* you."

Novella blinked back tears of her own. "What is your name?"

"I'm just Thilma—certainly the least of those on our council."

"Well, *you* do not understand, Thilma. You have restored my strength with a few words. I hope you will sit beside me at the feast. I'd like to know you better."

The woman's aged face wrinkled into a large grin. "You *dear* child. No wonder the Great One chose you. Now! I see you are resting. I do not wish to infringe any longer, no matter what you may say. We will certainly see more of each other. Rest easy, knowing you have rescued the heart of the East this day."

With that, she retreated from the room. Petyr's eyes flew to Novella's with a knowing smile. He said nothing.

"You did that on purpose," Novella accused with a small smile of her own.

"I know you," he admitted. "We couldn't have a moaning victor on our hands. Feel any better?"

"*Much.*"

"You fought courageously. Shocked most of us. If you were in any way lacking our fleet's loyalty before, you've now earned it."

"It is thanks to *you*, Petyr. You trained me—you and Michal..." Her voice trailed off as what Michal had done came to mind. She could not determine if she wanted to embrace or slug him.

"You won't be seeing him any time soon," he informed. "I took the liberty of suggesting he serve on another ship for a few days. What he did was prohibited by law, you know."

She released a sigh. "I cannot entirely blame him. Certainly do not intend to press charges."

Petyr nodded. "I'll tell him."

"Don't. I'd rather he endure the remorse for a few days."

"As you wish," he answered with a smirk.

"I owe you my life countless times over," she spoke gravely.

"They wouldn't all have proved fatal blows. Sometimes, you merely owed me an arm or a neck." He ended with a wink.

"Seriously, Petyr... Thank you for honoring me by letting me remain even after I nearly passed out. And thank you for remaining by my side. I really do appreciate you. You are a *gem.*"

In fact, she felt entirely endeared to him now that she had witnessed the lengths he would go to both dignify and defend her wishes. He was a friend unlike she had known in her short lifetime. Just as people kept claiming about her, he was a godsend.

Pressing his lips together, he considered her with the releasing of a long, contemplative breath through his nostrils.

"What is it?" she ventured uncertainly.

"It is only that I could not do otherwise, even if you were not Realm Leader. As I pledged you my friendship, my heart will not allow me to act by any other method. So... let us *dispense* with the thanks. I've matters to attend. I will see you either later tonight or on the morrow. Good evening." He took the liberty of closing the door behind him.

Novella turned to Era in bewilderment. Era merely raised a brow. Quite suddenly, Novella's stomach sounded a loud complaint. Her hand flew to it as she returned to her chair.

"Where's that tray, Era? I'm *famished.*"

CHAPTER 39

WITH THE KNOWLEDGE OF how very vital the support of Merchants was, Novella and her outfit remained several days. She endured lengthy meetings with their island council before Island Leader Vespa pledged their support of both Novella's leadership and armies. In fact, they were to depart with over a hundred new fighters, all of whom claimed they'd been prepared to follow the moment they'd witnessed her interference in the attack.

Yet, Novella could not seem to trust the Island Leader. She was decidedly self-centered, caring more about the good of her island than the welfare of the entire East. Novella couldn't help wondering if perhaps that was beneficial. But after their sixth conference with the woman, she could not shake the feeling that Vespa wasn't a friend. Finding Petyr marching across a far lawn one day, she hightailed it in his direction.

He bowed low. "How may I serve the Realm Leader this fine day?"

"I seek your counsel."

"Oh?"

"About Vespa."

"I don't at all care for the woman if that's what you're asking."

"I cannot seem to trust a word she speaks. Can we truly count on her cooperation?"

He released a long breath as his steps slowed. "Only time will tell. She certainly has good reason to stand with you. Her island was nearly hijacked from beneath her. In truth, she needs you. Sometimes, that is all one requires in order to remain faithful."

"Good point. But we also need her. They are the best means we have of rallying those who sail through here."

"For the time being, we share a common aim to survive this war. She will not fail us on that score."

Novella felt herself physically relax as she fell in step beside him. "I am glad you've had more experience in all this. I'd be lost without you."

"True."

Her eyes flashed to his face. "Cute."

"You think? I usually get descriptions like debonair or... domineering."

"Oh, I'm sure you're those as well."

"Very flattering, Realm Leader Vella."

"Are you going to call me by my full title forever?"

"I like reminding you of who you are. Furthermore, I have to remind myself or I *may* become domineering."

"Like Michal at the start of that skirmish."

"Michal doesn't usually act so rashly..." He looked down at her reflectively. "It is clear he harbors strong feeling for you."

She contemplated him a moment before, "Are you not aware he has asked for my hand?"

"I am aware."

"Then I suppose his actions shouldn't surprise either of us," she sighed out.

Uncharacteristically, he merely shrugged.

"Speaking of Michal," she began, "is he still hiding from me?"

"He is. Probably fears you'll slap him again."

"More like he's afraid I'll send him back to the conglomeration."

"Wouldn't be a bad idea if he wasn't so good with a blade."

"Who is better between the two of you?"

"Me."

"And if I asked Michal?"

"Him."

"As I suspected."

"What you should be asking is what I think of the two of you as a pair."

She raised a brow. "Have you an opinion on that score?"

"I have."

"And?"

He ceased walking, turning to her with the thrusting of his hands into his pockets. When his eyes finally met hers, he answered, "No comment." He proceeded his march.

"Then why did you say anything to begin with?"

"To tease you, I suppose."

"Well, it isn't very fair. You know I respect your input."

"It isn't my business to speak into the affairs of a lady's heart, especially as concerns my brother. It is your decision."

"Vella!" Era's voice called from down the path. "Petyr!" She raced to meet them.

"Something wrong?" Petyr questioned.

Era nodded. "Western vessels were spotted not far off. It is said they are headed this way with more than double the ships prior. It is also rumored that they come for *you*, Vella."

"More than double?" Novella questioned before turning to Petyr. "Can we handle that?"

His jaw flexed as he considered for some moments. "We can if the Great One stands with us." He looked to her in question.

Pressing her lips together, she turned away to focus on the Helper. Her heart beat so fiercely at the thought of another confrontation that she could not seem to perceive his whisper. She turned back with a huff. "I require time alone. Let me see if I gain an answer by evening meal."

She lost no time in marching for her large villa, the one Realm Leaders had always been housed on their visits to the Isle of Merchants. She could practically feel the history in the place that had been built hundreds of years before. She froze on the stairs, staring down at the banister. How many Realm Leaders had used it through the years? How many had faced issues such as hers? How she wished she could go to them with her questions. Yet, she boasted a Helper. If she could calm her troubled heart, that was.

Falling to her feet before her bed, she tucked a pillow into her arms. Resting her cheek against it, she stole several long breaths before she felt her body relax. "Great One, soothe me. Bring me peace beyond my understanding. Send the instruction of the Helper."

"You rang?" a familiar voice tolled through the room.

She raised her chin to find him hovering in almost the same position in which she had first met him on the Emerald Island. "Long time no see..." she commented with satisfaction.

"Miss me?" he asked knowingly.

"I did." She swallowed. *"How* I did."

"I've been with you. You've heard me."

"I have, but there's nothing quite like seeing."

"Only if seeing is believing. Now, how may I help my best girl?"

"Tamsen has sent a huge fleet in order to take Merchants on my account. Petyr has indicated we can only conquer them if you stand with us."

"I saaay..." He narrowed his eyes on her. *"Depart."*

"What?"

"I want you to leave."

"Really? But... what was the point of fighting for Merchants the first time if only to lose them now?"

"It doesn't concern you. Your concern is whether or not to heed my decree."

"What... would happen if we stayed? Would you let us fail?"

His eyes became merry flame. "Are you going to remain to find out?"

Slowly, she shook her head. "We will leave, though I do not know what Merchants will think of us abandoning them like this..."

His answering smile was one of satisfaction. "Merchants would have turned you over to the West, Vella."

Her mouth fell open. "And you weren't going to tell me until I agreed to listen on blind faith, were you? *Why* would they turn me in?"

"That specific fleet's task is to locate and haul you back to Tamsen. Once Merchants learned of it, you'd be seized and passed into Western hands in order to win them their enduring freedom."

"After we stood by them?! *Why?*"

"You know why," he answered with a warm smile.

"It would be Vespa... wouldn't it? Even if I told her *you* stood with us, she would not have faith for the victory. To spare her island, she'd cart me off."

He nodded.

"*Thank* you for telling me," she answered with not a little irritation. "Makes it easier to leave. Though I don't know how I'll make my compatriots understand."

"They do not have to. You are Realm Leader. It is *your* obedience I require. I can handle them."

"Vella!" sounded from below. It was Petyr. She flew to the door before recalling her hallowed visitor, but it was too late. He had vanished. Shaking her head, she raced down the stairs.

"What is it?" she asked.

"We need that answer now. The Western fleet is nearer than first reported."

"We're leaving."

He quirked his head. *"Really?"* His hand went to the back of his neck. "This won't look well to Merchants."

"It doesn't have to. We must go."

He raised a brow as understanding struck. "I see. I'll alert the captains to prepare the vessels in order to depart immediately. We need to be long gone from the region before they arrive."

"Has anyone told Vespa where we intend to go next?"

"Not as far as I know."

"If she asks... drop the wrong name—somewhere far from where we are headed."

"As you wish."

She shook her head as she watched him go. She knew running from a fight, even when outnumbered, went against his nature. He'd wanted it, yet he'd opted not to press. His response denoted total faith in either her or their God. She'd have paid money to know which it was. Either way, she was fortunate to have him on her side.

It did not take long to get everyone boarded and the fleet on its way. Novella breathed sweet relief that they'd not been forced to endure another battle this day. If the Helper had not appeared himself, she wasn't certain she'd have believed his voice. She'd have assumed it was wishful thinking. But how did it feel so very right to abandon the very island they had previously rescued?

Inevitable betrayal—that was why. She ground her teeth at the thought.

"How did the island council take our departure?" she asked Petyr as they enjoyed their evening meal aboard the *Glorybringer*.

He wriggled his brows. "*That* is a story. Vespa threw a tantrum while Thilma stood with you. After all, it looked like a losing battle and you *are* Realm Leader."

"Thilma is a good woman. I wish we could have taken her with us."

He shook his head. "They need her. From what I've been hearing from many of their people who have accompanied us, that council is almost entirely corrupt without her. She is a singular voice."

"Mmm. I suppose time will tell where they stand... or *if* they yet stand."

"They do."

She quirked a brow at him.

"Out of curiosity, I left a Swimmer behind. He just reported that the Western fleet altered their course on arrival, headed straight for the Isle of Ferns... which happens to be where I informed Vespa we intended to port."

Novella raised a brow. "So not only is Merchants safe enough, it is clear Vespa betrayed us."

"*And* that the fleet is intended specifically for you, which means we must remain on high alert over the duration of our travels."

Novella released a long sigh. "Well... this is *some* start to our tour."

"Something tells me this isn't a tour anymore." His voice was both remorseful and sympathetic. "Yes, we must gather troops as swiftly as possible, but... my father has surely tasked other convoys to attack the Eastern isles. We're not alone in these waters anymore. And those islands may need us."

Novella's chewing slowed as her appetite weakened. "I see."

"I know this isn't how you wished to begin your reign, but... one day it *will* be worth it. I can feel it."

Hope flooded her—fresh faith in a brighter future than this current season. "Thank you, Petyr."

His eyes shot between hers. "Of course."

"And tell Michal he may return to the *Glorybringer*. I get the feeling I'm going to need all the counsel I can get."

His face dropped. "As you wish."

"Don't want big brother around to step on your toes?" she asked with a grin.

His returning smile was that of bewilderment. "I have always preferred to have my brother nearby. We've been close since we were boys—thick as thieves."

"I believe it, the way you two go on."

"We have never gotten in one another's way."

"As it should be."

His eyes flicked to hers. "Vella... what did you make of me when first we met?"

"Grating," she answered with a chuckle.

A brow of irritation was his response.

"And what did you think of me?" she questioned.

After a moment's contemplation, he answered, "I thought you rather afraid of life."

She scowled. "That's not very flattering..."

"You were also rather endearing," he added softly. "You've a tender heart and it shows in ways you do not realize."

"I had no idea you thought so. You were so impatient with me."

"Yes," he answered as he drew to his feet. "Well, you ought to realize by now that most do—Michal, for instance. At any rate, I'm for bed."

She contemplated his retreating frame. Something about the conclusion of their conversation made her uncomfortable. Perhaps she had offended him by admitting her true thoughts on their initial meeting. He didn't realize she thought him far from grating now—most days anyway. And as she recalled, she had also thought him rather fascinating in the back of her mind. Perhaps that admission would have been preferable. With a shrug, she arose to take herself to bed as well. They had seen much and this was only the beginning. Petyr was for her and that was what mattered. He would not turn on her for a single offense.

CHAPTER 40

MICHAL ENTERED THE SHIP'S sitting room with sheepish step, freezing as he discovered Novella sipping a cup of tea. "Er... good morning," he greeted in a low voice.

"Morning," she answered cooly, relishing his discomfiture.

He sauntered over to the tea things, pouring himself a cup before turning back as if uncertain what to do. Taking a sip, he swallowed it before, "I have dire apologies to make."

"You have."

"Realm Leader Novella... I had no right to take matters into my own hands, especially considering your position. It was mutinous behavior and I... I understand if you command me to take leave of your fleet. Send me where you will and I will go without complaint."

She stole a sip of tea. "I didn't hear an apology."

"*Yes,* that is... I deeply apologize for and regret my rash actions. I beg your forgiveness, Realm Leader."

"You're forgiven. Have a seat."

"You do not intend to send me away?"

She shook her head. "Seeing as I comprehend the heart from which your actions stemmed, it is enough that you recognize your mistake. I appreciate that."

He fell into the chair. "Here, I've been plotting how I might be of help to you from afar, how I might possibly begin to make amends."

"Michal... there is a part of me that wishes I'd have remained locked in that room. You understood I wasn't ready to take a life. Even so... I have seen battle now and I do not intend to run from a fight when one presents itself."

"That is fortunate," Petyr spoke as he sauntered in, eyeing first one and then the other. "The Isle of Seekers is in view. They appear to be occupied by the West."

"*What?*" Novella questioned, leaping to her feet. "Why would your father target them?"

He shook his head. "I cannot say. It is not the fleet that is hunting you. My guess is they're taking islands at random, likely beginning with the simplest to conquer. Seekers are intrepid when it comes to seeking, but they are not typically raised to warfare."

She released a long breath. "That is the place I wished to visit most..." She looked up. "I wonder if Riva is there."

"I cannot say." He hesitated. "Shall we turn away?"

The two fellows eyed her with intensity. She turned to the wall, inquiring of the Helper what was to be done. Would she hear him with her heart pounding in her chest?

A breeze flooded the room from the open door. It washed over her form, clearing away the terror of warfare. She had her answer.

She turned back with, "What are we up against?"

Petyr's eyes gleamed with satisfaction. It was clear he was longing to defend Seekers. "They've got but half the ships we have. I do not believe they expected us to discover them all the way out here. The Isle of Seekers isn't measured as a land of much import. People who spend all their time pursuing the presence of the Great One are not considered a threat."

"*Mistake,*" the Helper whispered as if with a smile.

Novella turned to the wall again.

"My treasures are plotting to take back their island as we speak. At dawn, you and your warriors will send the Western ships to flight. Confront those on land and they will flee as well. And Vella... I believe I hear a melody on the wind."

She grinned at his final statement but could not help asking, *"How will the Seekers confront their conquerors when they are no warriors?"*

"The Great Gifts. Most of my Seekers possess more than one."

She nodded. This meant her hopes of keeping the population's supernatural abilities out of the war was about to be turned on its head. But if this was the Great One's plan, she would get in line.

"We must turn back," she spoke quickly. "Inform the captains."

Petyr's face fell. "I thought you said—"

"We shall return at dawn, but there won't be much to do before we reach the victory. The Seekers have things in hand."

Confusion flashed across his face before he smiled. "Fine by me, so long as the island regains their freedom." He turned on his heel to carry out her orders.

"I have never seen him so swift to follow the commands of anyone," Michal commented with the shaking of his head.

"Excuse me?"

"I only mean he maintains a deal of respect for you. He is typically so self-assured that he puts his own judgement ahead of others."

"Well... I am grateful he is not constantly battling my decisions."

His face dropped. "Like myself?"

She couldn't help but nod.

Drawing to his feet, he thrust out a hand. "I pledge myself to follow the Realm Leader's every whim. If my brother can manage it, so can I."

She accepted his hand. "I'll hold you to that."

Novella was surprised to find herself lively with anticipation the following morning. It was much easier to head into battle when one knew how simple the victory was promised to be. Sending troops to flight in order to aid the freedom of a loyal island was an incredibly satisfying concept. Unfortunately, the first news she received over breakfast allayed her confidence.

"We don't know from where or when they came, but there are twice the number of ships as was present last evening," Era informed.

Novella's face dropped. This wasn't at all what she'd expected. They were supposed to send their enemy on the water to flight with little effort, thereby assisting the Seekers on the island. Had she heard wrong? She shook her head.

"It matters not. The Great One knew what the situation would be when he told me to attack at dawn."

Era raised a brow. "A woman after my own heart. I believe you just out-faithed me. You have grown *so much.*"

"I was fortunate enough to hear his command," Novella reminded. "Our plans remain the same. We will trust the outcome to him."

Yet, her stomach flipped over and again as they drew near the Isle of Seekers. It was deeply surrounded by Western vessels. Why anyone should care to keep them under siege, she could not imagine. What was there to fear from those gifted with locating things?

"They probably wish to use them to locate you," Petyr explained. "I imagine the Western Seekers are coming up short in their gift as concerns that task."

"You believe the Great One is clouding their abilities?"

"Of course, else we'd be had by now."

"*Can* they use these Seekers?"

"A good question. They are the most ardent Seekers in the land. I find it difficult to imagine the Great One stifling their abilities. I suppose the real question would be whether they were willing to be used for such a purpose in the first place."

"And?"

"I am of the opinion they'd sooner forfeit their lives."

Novella gritted her teeth together, all nerves taking flight. If these good folks were willing to die rather than do her harm, she was more than prepared to defend their freedom. "How much faster can we go?"

"Ha-*ha!*" he bellowed with a smack to her back. "I *knew* you'd get a taste for battle when presented with the right conditions. I'll direct the captain to approach at top speed."

Novella smirked over his gratification of her readiness. She couldn't help feeling she'd been knighted by his pride. After all, he was not a fellow to be easily impressed. She physically sensed the vessel's acceleration, glancing back at the ships that followed.

It wouldn't be long now before the Western vessels took notice. Would they put up a fight or hightail it before her fleet had a chance to show what they were made of? Cracking her knuckles, she itched to give them a taste of the power she housed. Fire tore through her blood, alighting her veins with rainbow effect that shimmered under her skin. Clearly, the Helper was eager to go to the aid of those he considered his closest friends. And she was eager to become acquainted with such people. Her heart stirred with exhilaration at the thought.

CHAPTER 41

NOVELLA WATCHED AS THE Western fleet released a rapid battalion of Swimmers in response to their approach. Their ships followed in hot pursuit.

"What is the order, Realm Leader?" Petyr inquired from beside her.

"Tell our men to stand down," she informed with a smirk.

If the Great Gifts were to be used after all, she was well-endowed. Power mounted within as she spoke. Michal peered down at her, shutting up his mouth as if fearful of speaking a wrong word. Petyr gave the signal to the captains and their men, eyeing her with curiosity.

Without further ado, she thrust her hands toward the Swimmers. A wall of water swelled up until they were no longer seen. She pinned it there some moments, allowing it to mount. With the flick of her fingers, she sent it cascading over the Swimmers, deftly succeeding in sailing them back toward their vessels. It was not her intention to slay them—merely to make it clear that they were outmaneuvered. She tossed a cocky brow at each of the sons of Tamsen. Michal appeared mystified while Petyr merely chuckled. Out of nowhere, a corresponding wave rushed toward her fleet. It was fortunate the Swimmers were gifted with breathing beneath the surface, for they were batted about like rag dolls by their own Gifted.

"They've someone powerful on board," Novella commented as she batted the wave back, propelling it over the enemy ships.

"Radian," Michal supplied in a low voice, "an incredibly gifted Swimmer who possesses the ability to manipulate water... as apparently you have. But if he's smart, he'll let those Swimmers reboard or they're going to lose soldiers."

In the next breath, a whirlwind of water developed over the sea, mounting until it grasped the skies. It intensified in width and power as it careened toward the Eastern fleet. Momentarily taken off guard by the sheer spectacle, Novella thrust out her arms to gain control, feeling for the first time her own will making use of the gift inside her. Her focus was on unfurling the typhoon. She'd not anticipated anyone with such strength among the Westerners. And she'd been promised a simple victory.

She sensed Radian combatting her efforts until the twister halted between the dueling fleets. It proceeded to quiver while the will of each gifted one labored to overrule the other. The skies darkened overheard, inevitably pouring forth their substance that fell like billions of tiny daggers.

At long last, Novella released her grip. Narrowing her eyes, she stole three steps forward, pointing a single finger toward the heavens.

"Be still!" she commanded.

The skies cleared and the funnel of water disintegrated. She watched as the Western Swimmers fled for home like rats from a terrier. She eyed their vessels. Had it been enough to send them to flight? As no movement transpired, her impatience mounted. Finally, she swept her arms forward to launch a great wall of water after the fleet. In a matter of moments, the Western ships were effectively washed from the island's shoreline. She sent subsequent surges on every side of the fleet until they had careened a safe distance from the vicinity.

"Now, *that's* a victory," Michal declared as the ships slowly right themselves in order to abscond.

"Take port," she directed. "We must help the Seekers finish this."

Against the partition, Petyr rested with arms crossed, shaking his head in uncharacteristic wonderment before motioning her orders to the captain's men.

"What is it?" she questioned self-consciously.

"Only that the West doesn't stand a chance. Their only boon is the mercy in your heart."

"No pressure then..."

"No pressure," he chuckled out. "The Great One is guiding you. As for me, I've just seen all I needed." The consideration of his eyes provoked a blush across her cheeks. She turned to face the island, searching for signs of conflict, finding none.

"Where *are* they?" she mumbled to herself.

"Who?" Michal inquired.

"The Seekers. They were plotting an attack at dawn."

"It is probably taking place in the mountains yonder. There is a complex labyrinth within."

"Sail for the mountains!" she hollered out.

Unconsciously, her hand reached for the hilt of her blade. It sparked within her grasp, eager for action. Problem was, she did not actually intend to use it. If her gifts could spare lives as well as gain triumphs, they must be her foremost weapon.

"Easy, fella," she whispered to her sword.

It did not cease its stirrings. Rather, as she traversed the island and entered the mouth of a vast cavern, they intensified. The resonance of combat echoed throughout, but locating from which of the three tunnels it derived was another matter altogether.

"We must split up," Petyr directed. "Are you agreed?"

She nodded, standing back as he and Michal barked orders. Chief Xax marched through the largest of the openings as if itching for blood. She was fairly certain he did not share her concern for the lives of their enemies. And perhaps she was wrong to feel so. Yet, as her heart must, in truth, be for the welfare of the entire planet, it was difficult to see the Western troops as anything more than pawns in Tamsen's game. She wanted these people—*all* of them. But if blood must be poured to make it so, she would surrender to the will of the Great One.

As she entered the far most passage, a tune danced through her mind. Involuntarily, she began to hum. It wasn't until Michal halted at the front of the party that she realized something unnatural was transpiring.

"What is that music?" he inquired apprehensively.

"Er... it is me," Novella admitted as she gazed down at the sword glowing in her scabbard. "I apologize."

"Was it just me or..." he began with hesitation, "did anyone else perceive a peculiar kind of wind pass through them with that tune?"

As they stood in the silence that followed, the melody could be heard echoing into the distance. Cries and gasps abruptly sounded in unison. Michal lost no time in racing on. Before Novella realized it, she was humming. Unexpectedly, the light of her blade gleamed from its scabbard and a tangible force surged beyond her. When cries sounded in response once again from down the passage, Novella flew past her fighters.

Michal stood frozen at the end of the tunnel as she reached his side, causing her to collide with him. He caught her with an unconscious arm as his eyes surveyed the scene within a massive cavern. It wasn't until Novella regained her footing that she perceived the provocation of his incredulity. Western soldiers dangled from the grip of tree roots that had plowed through the mountain. Her tune seemed to resonate through them as they pursued the Western troops. Those in Seeker's attire merely stood in wonder of the spectacle.

Novella's eyes fell to her crimson sword. Could it be that it had inspired her song and sent the instruction to the trees above? She shook her head. It was an improbable notion. She'd never heard the like. There must be some feasible explanation.

With an involuntary burst, her mouth opened in song - this time with lyric. *"All who agree to hightail it and flee, these roots shall detect and set you all free!"* But rather than from her throat, the music resonated from the luminous ruby weapon that had mysteriously found its way into her hand. When her mouth clamped shut, she blinked back at the enemy soldiers who peered down in sheer terror.

After a moment, a number of the roots summarily uncurled, releasing their captives. The Westerners whose hearts had determined it best to take their leave lost no time in flying from the cavern, eyeing her warily as they took to the tunnels.

Without asking, Michal stole Novella's blade in order to examine it. "This is no ordinary blade. It... amplifies your voice?" He shook his head as he slid it into the scabbard. "I have not seen or heard of anything like it."

"Well, there *are* the legends," Petyr spoke from behind them.

Michal turned back. "You believe it to be *the* Jaela's blade of old?"

"Actually, Iviana claims it was birthed from her very tongue. I've heard tell that thing can slice through iron bars. Now, it has managed this..." He gestured to the troops yet imprisoned. With a pat to Novella's back, he added, "Don't ever forget you've an angelic sword in possession, originated from the language of a powerful Firetongue."

While Novella's troops cut the remaining prisoners free in order to properly incarcerate them, the Seekers within the cavern raced to her side. She was flooded with thanks and questions, none of which she could hope to follow. In the end, however, she learned that though they'd been holding their own, they would soon have wearied had she not appeared.

"Tiz a miracle of the Great Friend," Riva announced, effectively parting the crowd with her approach. She marched through her people in order to throw her arms about Novella. Pulling back, she added, "I praise the Great One for sending his beloved, for that is clearly what you are. The gifts you display are fierce, my friend. And you *will* be leader of this *Greater* Archipelagos one day. I can feel it." She pounded a fist over her heart.

"It was the sword, really..." Novella answered with embarrassment.

The crowd responded with laughter, taking the liberty of guiding her through the tunnel system. Everyone, it seemed, had a story to share. Novella could scarcely make out a word as their voices echoed madly. She reached for the hilt of her blade, wishing it might help her now, but it sat cold in her hand.

Thanks for nothing, she thought grimly, leaping as a spark went through her hand. Rolling her eyes, she released a sigh as the light of day shone in the distance. The breath was stolen from her as they entered a village of soaring pyres and domes, looming like the most intricate of cathedrals in London. Their white stone faces glowed under the light of day while their multicolored windows displayed various depictions of a hallowed Treasure, sought by many, found by few.

"You admire our little village?" Riva inquired above the voices of the fray.

Novella nodded mutely as she was arrested by the sheer presence of one she recognized. It was clear that the Helper resided in this place to such profuse and palpable degrees that she expected at any moment to be rewarded with the vision of him rounding a corner.

"You sense him, don't you?" Riva asked with a small grin.

Novella nodded again, searching in every direction.

"You are not likely to see him," Riva explained, "but he *is* here. He loves this place."

"How long have you experienced him like this?" she asked breathlessly.

"A few years ago, he appeared at the summons of a young female Seeker who yearned for his presence and, with the very longing of her lovesick heart, simply bid that he come. Those who dwell here have developed habits of steadfast friendship that rather pin him in place. When he asks a thing that is unexpected, we do not question it. We bend to his ways, working to grow more like the Anointed One, that we may never lose our Prize."

Novella shook her head as tears pricked her eyes. This was a sensation she had not felt since her final worship session on her Western tour. This, however, was so much stronger and sweeter than anything she had previously experienced. She wished she might tuck herself behind some vacant building and cry her heart out for him. She wished she might never have to leave, hating the war that would inevitably wrench her from this aroma.

"For everything, there is a season," Riva spoke into her ear. "You will remain here for a short time, but it is true you must continue the course he has set for you. Even when the seasons do not taste as sweet, the satisfaction of following his call is no less pungent."

Novella nodded, working to withhold emotion that mounted like the waves from the battle that morning. She longed merely to soak in the freshness of this presence. Though she'd been unable to eat a bite at breakfast, she felt no physical hunger as a new thirst pervaded her system. When Riva dismissed the crowd and filed her into a simple white edifice, Novella dropped to her knees before a stained-glass window, collapsing into sobs of a mysterious lovesickness.

It was hours before she became aware that she was the only one in the small chapel. She had laughed and cried within its confines, the affection of the Great Friend having effectively washed through her until she felt she could fly. Yet, she was weak from weeping and loving and was surprised when she became aware of her empty stomach when earlier it had seemed of little import. She stole a long breath, releasing it with satisfaction, feeling herself drunk with friendship, yet peculiarly spent as well.

As if on cue, Riva returned to the little chapel. "Had your fill?" she asked with a grin.

"*Can* you have your fill?"

"A mortal vessel can only house so much at once. Moreover, it is clear by your face that you have poured out a deal of adoration. You must rest now. Moreover, Petyr has insisted that you require sustenance."

"I cannot deny it," she admitted as she rose up on shaky feet.

Riva laughed. "You have worshipped through noon meal, I'm afraid. But come to my house and I will provide a little something before evening meal."

"It seems strange that I can even worry about eating."

"He relishes your delight in Him. But He also leads us to lie down in green pastures and beside quiet waters. The time we take to rest is just as important. He wants us strong. He wants us blessed."

Novella released another long breath. "He is such a *good* Friend," she whispered.

Riva grinned as tears pricked her own eyes. "He is at that."

CHAPTER 42

MUCH OCCURRED IN THE days that followed. Novella learned the joys of dwelling in the perpetual presence of the Great One. She laughed more than she had in her life and relished discussions about the character of her God and the faithfulness of his purposes. Nearing the end of three days, she felt emotionally prepared to return to her mission of gathering troops and combatting Western assault. Though she had once believed she could not bear to face that future again, she had gained a confidence in the one who stood with her. If this war was his will, she would walk through it. She might even discover *joy* in the storm.

As if on cue, word reached them from a spy that Michal had sent to track his father's movements back in Atlantyss. The Western islands that had opted to remain neutral concerning Novella and the East were now occupied by Tamsen's troops. This news struck Novella's open heart perhaps as painfully as any Western sword.

"What can be done for them?" she asked Petyr.

His eyes searched her face up and down. What passed through his mind, she could not begin to imagine. He swallowed hard before, "I will lead a fleet against father's militia. And I will work to gain the aid of the loyal Western islands for our cause."

Novella's mouth dropped open as her cheeks heated with anger. "You're *not* serious..."

"Why shouldn't I be?" he retorted with frustration.

"You'd just up and leave me on my own?"

His eyes dropped to the ground. "You would not be on your own. Michal is here. As well as Chief Xax and the captains."

"But Petyr... *you're* my right hand. I'd be lost without you." She shook her head. "No. You're not going."

Michal stepped between them. "What if I should go...?"

"No," Novella and Petyr spat in unison, eyeing one another with intensity.

"I don't want *either* of you to go," Novella added emotionally.

Petyr stepped back, swallowing as if she had pained him. *"Novella,* I would be honored if you would send me to win this victory... Please."

Her eyes narrowed on him. "Why do you want to leave so badly?"

"I simply want to see this thing through and I feel strongly that I can manage it proficiently."

Anger toiled within Novella. He had sworn to stand by her. She had assumed that meant physically—not symbolically. "You really want to go then?" she asked with scarcely concealed distress.

Gradually, he nodded, swallowing back what emotion, she could not determine. Clearly, he was perfectly comfortable deserting her. She didn't care that it was for a righteous cause. He had entered her home planet and drug her here. The only time they'd spent apart since that time had been by his father's finagling. But apparently, he was no longer worried about her.

"I know Michal is perfectly able to protect you," Petyr spoke calmly, "as well as to provide counsel." He nodded at his brother. "I will entrust you to his care while I work to free those islands, Realm Leader Novella."

Novella ground her teeth as she scrutinized his face. Something wasn't right. He had not changed his mind about her, had he? Was he regretting his decision to follow her to the ends of the world? Well...

obviously. But he was Petyr. If he promised to liberate and win the loyalty of those Western islands, he would manage it at all costs.

"Go then," she answered flippantly. "Take whomever and whatever you require. I will not stop you." Turning on her heel, she vacated the room, marching through the streets of the village as tears pricked her eyes. When at last she found her tiny chapel, she fell through the double doors and to the floor before the stained-glass window.

"Why does he want to leave me?" she called to the presence in the atmosphere.

No verbal response came, but perfect peace flooded her system. Everything was going to be alright. The Great One was well able to take care of each of them—together or apart. If her best friend desired to leave, she could not stop him. He had done too much for her. In the meantime, she had this sweet friendship that would *never* leave her. She could rest on that. And perhaps it was he who moved Petyr to go. Perhaps the Helper was jealous for her trust, that it should rest solely upon him. She could certainly afford him that. When Era informed her that evening that Petyr's vessel was due to depart, Novella raced to the harbor. She only just caught him as he approached the gangplank.

"*Petyr!*" she shouted as she raced to his side.

He twitched as he turned to face her, as if fearful she had come to stop him.

"Rest easy, my friend," she breathed. "I have come merely to say farewell and... to wish you a protected and blessed voyage. I will be praying for your triumph."

He stared back in silence some moments before reaching to wrap her in an embrace. At last, he stepped back a step or two. "I will be praying for none but you, Vella."

"Thank you, Petyr. But do not forget to care for yourself. *Safe* travels to you."

Mutely, he turned away, not looking back even once he had arrived on deck. Releasing a regretful sigh, she turned away, glad that she had made herself say goodbye. After all, if anything happened to him...

She stopped short. *Nothing* could happen to him.

"Great One," she whispered to the sky, "you keep him *alive,* you hear me?"

The only response she received was the brush of the breeze through her hair. He was in the breeze, but he gave no verbal promise. She released another sigh. It was a faith walk she was leading. Trust was all or nothing.

"I surrender him to your will, Beloved," she added meekly. "Have your way."

She stopped to watch his vessel depart. For a moment, she thought she saw him standing against the rail, watching her own departure from the docks. Did it not hurt him to be separated as it did her? Even with the peace of her Greatest Friend upon her, she felt an unnaturally painful wrench of her soul.

Perhaps it was her femininity that made her feel needful of his constant assistance. Petyr had fought battles before and would again. He was not in need of the perpetual, thankless presence of a girl scarcely eighteen who was attempting to save the world. She decided the separation would do them good. She would learn to appreciate him as she should and he could get some air. She would entrust their reunion to the hands of the Great One.

"Hey," Michal spoke with surprise as he came upon her. "Have you just come from the docks?"

She nodded. "He has just departed."

"Oh... I was going to say goodbye."

She raised a brow at him. "You haven't already?"

"Well, we did this morning. I'm just... not relishing his absence. And I worry for him."

A broad grin stretched across her face as she planted her hand in the nook of his arm to turn him back for the village. "We can mope together."

"Actually," he began in a brighter tone. "I don't suppose I'll mind having you to myself. Petyr seemed always to be around."

"Oh, some brotherly loyalty *you* boast."

"Can you blame me?" he asked with a roguish smirk.

"Depart," the Helper's voice whispered on the wind.

She stopped short as she took in the command. Releasing yet another sigh, she peered into Michal's questioning eyes with, "It is time to continue our tour. Prepare the captains to leave early tomorrow morning."

A corresponding sigh was his response. "This place feels too akin to my notion of Paradise."

Yet, when they departed in the morning and the Island of Seekers was but a speck in the distance, Novella found she carried the Presence within her. How long the sensation would remain, she was uncertain. As they were taking a number of the Seekers along to join in the fight, she planned to seek them for counsel. Yet, she understood that, for everything, there was a season.

CHAPTER 43

THE FLEET HAD ONLY spent a day on a cluster of islands called The Isle of His Glory when bad news caught up with them. Novella had been basking in a river formed from the sheer power housed within Iviana once upon a time—the very reason she was called the Glorybringer. It was formulated of water combined with the pure *glory* of the Great One. Many received visions of times to come when they swam its waters. What Novella saw made her fall back into the depths in wonderment.

It was a wedding. *She* was the bride, draped in white, walking toward her beloved. She could sense the ardency of her affection for the man whose face she could not see for some time. It was when he turned to face her with eyes aglow that she sunk with a start, instantly tearing herself from the vision. Drenched in the glorious liquid, she sat herself on the edge of the shore, staring up at the sky with wide eyes.

"You *cannot* be serious..." she voiced to the Great One. Not once had her mind thought romantically of Michal's younger brother. How could she ever feel thus about *Petyr?*

Yet... she accepted it as a blessed boon. It meant he would survive his current mission, that they *would* meet again. But as to meeting him down the aisle for such a purpose... she could not begin to fathom. She stared down at the river, tempted to re-enter it in search of an explanation. But Era's voice calling for her sent her in the direction of the city.

"What is it, friend?" she inquired as they met.

"I do so hate to interrupt your repose."

"It is what it is when one is at war. Go on."

"Well... I don't know how they managed it, but the Western search convoy has discovered us. I'm afraid we must battle our way off the island."

Novella nodded with defiance. "With the Great One, we will prevail." She'd just been shown she was to be married after all. One must be alive for such an event.

Era smiled, linking her arm through Novella's. "Everyone should boast a friend who speaks as you do."

"You are that friend to me, Era. Have been from the beginning. Have I ever told you how I cherish your friendship?"

It was true Era was years older than Novella, but she had been a refuge of peace and steady counsel for so long that Novella quite depended on her. If she thought she had mourned Petyr's exit, Era's would be unbearable.

"I don't know what I'd do if you forsook me like Petyr."

"Forsook? Are you jesting, Vella? He did not abandon you. He was fleeing from you."

So much for their wedding.

"What can you mean? Have I hurt him?"

"You *have.*" Era paused some moments as if carefully considering her next words. At last, she declared, "He knows you are intended for his brother, therefore he must fend off the feelings he is developing for you."

Novella halted. It couldn't be. Petyr never spoke as Michal did, nor looked at her in that way. "You are mistaken, Era. Petyr sees me as... as..."

"It is true he cannot show what he feels out of loyalty for Michal. Often, in a season of waiting, there is bewildering obscurity as feelings are harbored but must remain in concealment. But Vella... he has come to appreciate your good qualities. I have closely witnessed how his devotion to you has grown beyond mere friendship."

Novella shook her head. It was too much to juggle: an approaching army *and* this new concept? "He simply *cannot...*"

The woman shrugged. "I have always spoken what I've seen. You may take it or leave it." She narrowed her eyes with concern. "For now, let us drop the subject. You'll require all your focus for the task at hand."

But it was difficult to forget Era's divulgence. Could it really be that Petyr had chosen to leave her out of a devotion to his brother? What had he said some nights back... that he and Michal had never gotten in one another's way?

She gasped as the truth fell on her like an avalanche. She carried the weight of it onto the *Glorybringer*, questioning how she had not picked up on his subtle queues. He had been dying to admit his feelings, but she had unintentionally evaded him every time. Now... he had chosen to leave her side. Possibly, he was hurt that she did not feel the same. And why didn't she? Petyr was a person worthy of honor and admiration. She had long thought him the best of men, despite his past imperiousness. In fact, she rather marveled at his boldness in life, his fearlessness in battle, yet his willingness to yield to her authority as Realm Leader, though she was nothing so impressive as he.

Thanks to her divided focus, the battle was not so swift as it might have been. She found it difficult to release herself to the Helper's use and was inevitably forced to fend off their opponents with the blade—something she had not done since her first battle. Only this time there was no Petyr by her side. Thankfully, there was Michal, who fought just as intrepidly.

At last, they managed to cripple their opponents enough to hightail it from the region. Captain Jonno suggested they alter their course in the event that someone had divulged their agenda. It was awfully suspect that, in such a wide-open sea, the Western fleet had managed to track them.

Even in Petyr's absence, there were plenty about to care for and counsel Novella. This proved necessary as the weeks passed and the search vessels remained in hot pursuit of her, managing always to be either a step ahead or behind. Her convoy was dogged at every turn. Yet, the Great One remained faithful to aid them. And as her focus returned, she was able to use her gifts in order to gain victories with greater ease. Sometimes, she wished she might simply sink those ships. But, as Petyr had once intimated, her mercy was their boon. She simply did not have the stomach for it.

They encountered further warfare as they went to the defense of the islands they navigated past. But with each triumph came troops and alliances. Slowly but surely, she and her sailing army were making a name for themselves among the Eastern islands. When she arrived at each one, they cheered her, chanting her praises, calling her *Realm Leader*. They accepted her, believed in her, wanted her. If only the East were all she must win, the war could conclude. But there remained almost the entire Western portion of the planet.

Word eventually reached them that, though Petyr had managed to liberate the Western islands as well as establish armies willing to fight for Novella's plight, he had gone missing after a recent skirmish. Novella could not help fearing the worst but thought it more likely he had been taken prisoner by his father—not a pleasant notion but at least he was family.

As the days passed and she longed for better news, she found her heart almost entirely wrapped up in anxiety for him. He did not leave her mind a moment. She could not help questioning where he might be and if ever he thought of her. If he did, could he manage to think fondly? As for her, he was becoming a perfect hero, almost as if he were dead. But she shrugged off the terror of that fear. She had seen him in her vision on The Isle of His Glory. She seized it in faith that the Great One was caring for him. She would sooner marry Petyr than lose him forever.

In the meantime, her daily life was taken up with war efforts. Her hands were bloodied, her power often drained. But when she was afforded time in her cabin, she pursued the Great One with all her heart. Without fail, he came to strengthen and imbue her with fresh measures of his essence. Despite her troubles, she was *surrounded* by love—an affectionate care that was more than enough. If it was all the love she ever knew, she would die well satisfied. Yet... the promise of that wedding gown could not help invading her thoughts. Could it be that the Great One intended more and better for her than she'd ever been wise enough to desire?

CHAPTER 44

"THINGS CANNOT GO ON this way," Novella declared to a hand-selected counsel comprised of Michal, Captain Jonno, Chief Xax, Era and Rye, an avid Seeker that Novella had befriended. "Every moment, our army is hounded by Tamsen's search fleet. Our troops are desperately weary."

"What do you suggest, Realm Leader?" Captain Jonno inquired. "We cannot throw you overboard," he added with a wink.

Novella smirked as she recalled Jonah's tale from the Holy Bible. "No, indeed." Her eyes flew to Rye. "I don't suppose you've an idea?"

He bobbed his head back and forth. *"Actually*... I have."

"And?" Michal sternly probed. It was clear he did not relish the addition of Rye among this inner circle.

"There is an island not far from this vicinity," Rye began. "Though large, it is not widely inhabited. You, Realm Leader, and a number of your troops might dwell there in concealment for a time. It boasts a number of hills and valleys and a range of mountains available for refuge. I've found it to be a pleasant place in my travels."

"And our offshore ships that our enemies would obviously detect?" Michal queried.

Rye seemed to gather himself before divulging, "They leave—separate. The captains and their crews continue to tour Eastern islands in order to gather troops. After all, not an Eastern province has failed to send word that they embrace Novella as Realm Leader. In the meantime, we might manage something of a reprieve by breaking up the convoy."

Michal drummed his fingers on the table's surface, frowning back at Rye. At last, he spoke, "What could have possibly inspired such a reckless plot in your imaginations?"

"Michal!" Novella chastised with a gasp. Must he experience jealousy for every younger man who dared come near her?

Rye shook his head. "I cannot blame him. It sounds like utter lunacy in comparison with remaining a formidable host. But I must admit that I received the plan in a dream... I believe it was from the Anointed One."

The room fell silent. There was really no questioning a Seeker when they claimed to have heard from the Great One. They were proved entirely too keen in their spiritual understanding—the very reason Novella had opted to include him in the meeting.

"Allow me to seek the Helper myself," she suggested. No one could question *her* if she managed to gain confirmation.

All but Michal agreed, who glowered in his corner while the room cleared to allow her space. Novella shook her head as she considered him. Why was it they seemed rarely to be on the same page when it came to grave matters?

"Michal..." she began, "you are jealous."

He leaped to his feet. "It is only that we are well-fortified as we are and that *Seeker* suggests we cripple ourselves and tuck you into the mountains. What use would that be?!"

She released a sigh as she dropped into the chair nearest his. "We have not agreed to the suggestion as yet. As I said, I will go to the Helper."

"And what if your Helper confirms this batty plot? Will you let yourself be cornered without a proper army?"

She was stunned by his attitude. Clearly, she'd been correct in voicing the exhaustion of their crew. "If the Helper advises me to follow Rye's plan," she began calmly, "He has good reason. He is wisdom beyond wisdom. Surely, you have witnessed that in our travels."

After some quiet moments, his eyes met hers with a nod. "I *have*... I have. And I... apologize once again. I will trust the Helper to advise you rightly."

He stood and sauntered from the room. Where he went, she did not much care. All she knew was... she could never marry him. To have her faith constantly questioned would cripple her for life. She would be always fighting off his doubts. It was true his fear typically stemmed from concern for her, but this was no excuse. She could not bear to deal with his questions and moods for a lifetime. Not to mention, there was her vision about Petyr...

Question was, how and when to finally refuse Michal's proposal.

Once she had spent time pursuing the will of the Great One, it was decided that she would take refuge on what was called the Silent Island, named for its small reclusive population that scarcely visited upon one another, let alone bother with an army encamped on their island.

"This island will not prove a refuge for long," the Helper cautioned. *"Tamsen is on his way."*

"Tamsen?" she questioned with astonishment. *"Personally? How will he find me?"*

Of course, the voice did not speak again. When had she begun to think she couldn't walk if she couldn't see? If she was aware of every step along the way, her faith would not be tested and thereby matured. She was learning that the Great One fed off faith like it was all the nourishment He required. When she maintained it, he was delighted. But when she failed, he did not.

Arriving on the Silent Island, she turned back to the vessel one last time to bid Michal farewell. He stood at the top of the gangplank, brooding because she refused to keep him with her. He had once offered to take his leave of her without complaint and she had reminded him of it.

"I need you out there continuing the mission if I am to be afforded any kind of reprieve... I *really* need this." She got the feeling she needed to be refreshed for a new season of her leadership in the near future, though she was uncertain of what that entailed.

It was only then he had softened. He'd attempted to draw her into his arms, but she had avoided him by stepping toward the window and spouting off a lengthy speech about all she required of him. In the end, she had failed to reveal the truth about her feelings. Now, as he waved goodbye, she was fairly certain he knew it was forever... at least as concerned his hopes of wedding her.

Returning her gaze to this new island, her attention was diverted by an elderly man watching from within the tropical forest. He dodged behind a tree. The foliage beyond continued to twitch and sway, indicating he was vacating the vicinity. Well, if the forest was *his* turf, she would turn her army for the hills. She had no intention of stepping on toes—only to rest for as long as she was afforded and to do the will of the Great One.

Yet, it would prove difficult to relax when she knew Tamsen was on his way. She would soon be forced to face the man who sought so desperately to destroy her. Would he, heaven forbid, succeed? She inquired over and again of the Helper, who divulged nothing more. In the meantime, she kept her troops on the move. They developed various campgrounds and haunts that, once the seditious leader of the West appeared, would not be easily discovered.

Before she was quite prepared, the island was invaded—not by Tamsen's fleet but a small Western convoy who'd been assaulting

Eastern archipelagos at random. As the inhabitants allowed themselves to be captured in total surrender, Novella was forced to take it
upon her army to conquer the invaders. The Great One stood with
her in great strength. He poured forth power through her and her
Gifted Ones in order to send them to flight. But as she watched them
sail away, it came to her.

"*This* is how Tamsen will find me," she realized morosely.

Now she had revealed herself, these aggressors would report to him
when he reached their waters. She smacked her forehead with regret.
If only she had allowed her troops to go it alone, they would not have
witnessed her gifts in action. Yet, the Great One had stood with her
in the battle. He had already warned her Tamsen was coming. This
was his will. Whatever happened, she was in his hand... even unto
death.

A long quiet followed. There were no more Western ships spotted
on the horizon. No one came to report of vessels in hot pursuit of the
rightful Realm Leader. Now and then, Novella nearly forgot she was
in hiding. Perhaps the invaders would never meet Tamsen's fleet in
order to divulge her whereabouts. Or it might be *months* before they
met. Who was to say where Tamsen was at any given time, far or near?
Upon every dawn, she awoke well rested, ate of the land and drank
of the many brooks that ran through these hills and mountains.

The inhabitants, she knew, rather dreaded her presence. Bizarrely,
they had not minded coming under Western rule. They were, as she
soon learned, a rather batty lot of folks. It was no wonder no more
than this small population ever came to live on the expansive piece
of land. Yet, it was her own beautiful haven for the time being and
she was grateful for it, despite the anxieties determined to pursue her
each day.

"Do you suppose, Era, that any new word has been heard concerning Petyr's whereabouts?" she asked late one afternoon.

"Concerned about your lover boy?" Era murmured over her basketweaving. The woman's hands were never still.

"Of course I am," Novella answered sternly. "I consider him my closest friend... aside from you, of course."

"Of course."

"I simply cannot help worrying, especially if you are right in that it was *me* who sent him to flight."

"Well," Era sighed out, "I wouldn't worry. If something happens to Petyr, there is always Michal..."

Novella cast her a scowl. "You know what I have determined on that score."

"Question is, does Michal? Oughtn't you to have informed him before you parted?"

"I suppose I should have..."

Era's gaze shot to her face. "I agree wholeheartedly with your decision by the way. Especially as concerns your reasons. *You,* Vella, deserve a champion of faith."

"If you're referencing Petyr, he was not always so certain about my decisions either."

"Perhaps. But he did not question them in the end. He had guts enough to trust both you and the Great One with the outcomes."

"Era..." Novella began with exasperation. "I care deeply for Petyr. But I never saw him *that* way."

"Yes, you did."

Novella raised a questioning brow.

"In your vision."

Her mouth dropped open with a retort as Chief Xax lumbered into the tranquil clearing. "Ships spotted on the horizon," he announced. "My scouts claim their flags indicate a Realm Leader aboard."

"Tamsen," Novella breathed grimly. She could not claim she was surprised. "So, it begins."

CHAPTER 45

"MY SCOUTS REPORT THAT Tamsen's troops are searching homes as we speak," Chief Xax informed many hours later. "Not long after entering the first, they were in hot pursuit of every one of our typical campgrounds. I'm afraid the inhabitants have been keeping tabs on us."

Novella ran a hand through her hair. "Why did we not consider that possibility?"

"They seemed genuinely unconcerned about us so long as we stayed out of their hair," Era reminded.

"It only takes but one," the chief reminded. "We ought to be moving or they'll catch up with us soon enough."

"Where do you suggest we go?" Novella questioned.

"One o' them mountains boasts a small cave with a slim crevice leading to an enormous cavern. I've long thought it might make a fine refuge."

"Wouldn't we be entombed if discovered?"

"Nay. There's another concealed crag in the big 'un we could abscond through."

She nodded. "You're the expert." For a moment, she closed her eyes, forcing herself to relax in search of the Helper's voice.

"It is there you will shine like the sun and never blush with shame."

"Let's move out," she directed.

It wasn't long before they were nestled away. They spent two days in seclusion, scarcely the sound of a human call in the distance. The chief's scouts informed that Tamsen had not so much as winked at the mountain. Novella slept all she could, in perfect trust of the Great One, who was worthy of nothing less. All he'd told her was that Tamsen was coming. Now that he was here... perhaps he would simply give up and leave.

"Hush!" Xax hissed the following day.

Silence fell as footsteps in the cavern beyond echoed back. A body plopped to the ground. Likely, one of the troops had become overheated in his search and opted for the cool of the cave. But that placed Novella's company in an awkward position. No less than a swift inhalation might echo beyond, informing of their refuge. It was a tense evening. None could move to eat. Stomachs growled and still the body in the subsequent cave did not stir.

It was the dead of night when Rye crept near Novella with, "Perhaps we might venture out to see what we're dealing with. It may be they've left and here we sit starving."

Novella quirked a brow, slowly rising to her feet. Silently, she lit a torch, creeping toward the tunnel.

"I didn't mean *you,*" he hissed into her ear.

She shrugged him off. She was sick of hiding. If she was discovered, it was in the Great One's hands.

Silent as a snake, she traversed the tunnel, gesturing for Rye to remain behind and keep silent. Deep breathing met her when she reached the outer cavern. She knew she should turn back. She'd learned what she needed. Yet, her feet unswervingly approached. It was all she could do to suppress a gasp when none other than Tamsen lay sleeping at her feet. She held her torch over his form. Here he was, entirely at her mercy, not a defender in the vicinity. She could take him out and bring an *end* to this war once and for all. Power sparked in her blood. Her veins lit hungrily.

But this was Petyr and Michal's *father*. How could she face them knowing she had murdered him in his sleep? Certainly, they were a family at odds... but this was no different than opting not to topple over enemy ships. Her stomach wouldn't allow it. Her heart leaped into her throat at the thought.

At one time, this man had been her avid supporter. He'd honored and tutored her. Ironically, she would not be where she was this day without his aid. For what reason he had been swayed against her and the East, she could not grasp. But she knew that, illogically, she harbored reverence for the person who had stood as Realm Leader while she remained to be found.

Her eyes fell to the sword in his scabbard. In a breath, she stole it up into her hands, retreating to her company. Her eyes flew to Chief Xax, who looked on her with amazement at what she had dared do.

"That be *Tamsen's* blade."

She nodded.

"Then he is within our grasp!" he nearly shouted. "The Great One has afforded us this chance to end things once and for all!" He nearly stumbled over her to reach the man, but Novella shoved him back.

"He *lives*, Chief Xax!" she commanded with a growl.

"*What?*" another of their fighters questioned. "That criminal is enemy number one!"

"He's not my enemy," she answered truthfully, "even if I am his."

The chief raised a brow. "What you be saying, Realm Leader?"

"I am choosing to honor his position as leader of the West."

His face fell. "Makes *no* sense, girly. Has the man ensorcelled you?"

"He is the father of my closest friends. He held this planet together before a strange evil possessed him. We owe him the honor of a safe slumber this night."

"Realm Leader Novella..." the chief began in quiet rage, "this is childish. You are acting like a... a—"

"Woman of honor?" she ended with a smirk. "I certainly hope so. And I thank you for the compliment, Xax. That will be enough for this evening."

She tucked herself back into her corner with Era and Rye. None bothered her again that evening, nor could she sleep. With Tamsen's blade in her hands, she was lost for what to do. Why she had taken it, she wasn't certain. Once he discovered it missing, her location on the island would be confirmed.

Her head shot up at the resonance of birdsong. The Helper brought to mind the story of David slipping into the cavern in which his king slept, proceeding to pinch a piece of his garment. What he'd done next was her directive. She marched straight for Chief Xax.

She kicked his foot. "I'm going to speak with Tamsen. I need you to be at the ready... just in case."

He shot to his feet, planting firm hands on her shoulders. "I hold a deal o' respect for you, Realm Leader... but this be *sheer lunacy.*"

She winked up at him. "Trust me, Xax."

When she turned from him to slip through the crag, she was in no way certain of just where this was leading. She walked in blind faith, precisely where her God wanted her. Though she was sick to her stomach, she must obey and trust him to protect her, no matter how things turned out.

This is on you, Beloved, she whispered in her mind.

There Tamsen lay yet. She wondered if his men had any notion of where he was. Likely, he'd not meant to stay the night. Perhaps the Great One himself had delivered him to her for such a time as this.

Sitting down cross-legged before him, she shook his shoulder. "Tamsen!"

He shook his head, sitting up before he opened his eyes. Rubbing at them, he groaned out, "What is it, Ferdin? Has she been located?"

"She has."

His eyes shot to her face. He backed away, hand searching the ground around him.

"Your sword is in the cavern beyond, along with my company of mighty men and women. I'm afraid, Realm Leader Tamsen, you are quite at our mercy."

He glared up in dumbstruck wonder. "Why don't you finish me off then, girl?! Or didn't you have the guts to finish me while I slumbered?" His tongue dripped with a loathing unlike the Tamsen she had known in former days.

Novella narrowed her eyes, quirking her head in thought. This wasn't Tamsen. It was true he had unwittingly allowed the evil in, but the father of her friends was a *kind* man. What she was dealing with here was something unnatural.

"I speak to the daemonic spirits inside of you..." she began, "*depart!*"

Tamsen's face grew utterly still before a great roar resounded and a shadow fled from him. The former Realm Leader froze many moments as if stricken. It was then Novella stepped forward.

"Realm Leader Tamsen, I am come now to plead with you to end this war, if for no one's sake but your sons. They *love* you, though they have not felt able to stand with you at this time. This war could very well tear the world apart. No one wants that. *I* do not want that."

With a blink, he croaked out, "Go on."

She nodded, eyes dropping to the ground between them. "I am prepared to honor your position as Realm Leader of the Western isles if you will agree to honor the East by calling off your conspiracy against us. I understand that ruling half the world isn't as ideal as conquering and enslaving the other, but... you must realize how my men pled that I bring an end to your life last evening. I myself considered it before I realized that I am *not* against you. You were good to me at one time. I cannot seem to forget it. In honor of your position, I allowed you to rest in safety... Let the *Great One* judge if I have acted righteously."

Tamsen's mouth fell open a number of times. Finally, he stopped, swallowed and searched her face. "Surely... you *are* an honorable woman, such as I have *never* known."

"I appreciate that."

It was certainly a start.

When Tamsen suddenly drew to his feet, it was all Novella could do to stay her ground. Would he turn and rend her? In the next moment, he plopped back down beside her as a chum.

"This is *not* how I envisioned our first meeting after all this time," he admitted.

"Nor I," she agreed with relief.

He stole one of her hands into his. Looking into her eyes, he spoke, "Despite what you are offering, I must confess that I was *wrong*, Realm Leader Novella."

She blinked back. Had he really just called her that?

"The war is *over,*" he continued with emotion, "as is my reign. You are the chosen of the Great One. How I ever thought otherwise, I cannot begin to fathom. Except that I was so terribly *envious* of how readily you won the people from me."

"I never meant to win them *from* you, Tamsen—"

"I know it. That was difficult as well. You were so blasted innocent and naïve yet blessed with such *power*. I had never seen anything like it." His eyes darted between hers. "But you must swear an oath."

"An oath?"

"You must be merciful to me and my sons, and to those who have stood with me."

Did he not yet perceive her heart and motives? Did he truly think she would *ever* make an enemy of his sons?

"That goes without saying."

His relief was evident as he released her hand. "...Was that a daemon sprite you cast from me?"

"Seemed so." Though she'd never expelled such a thing from anyone before.

He shook his head. "I had... *no idea.*"

"Envy is hazardous. It leads to hatred, which is a wide-open door to your soul."

His eyes returned to her face. "You are different, Realm Leader Novella. You are so very grown that I scarcely know you."

"Thanks to you and your deviltries, I reckon."

"Can you ever forgive me?"

"I already have—last evening when I saw you after all this time. You are Michal and Petyr's father. I *pray* that you and I remain at peace."

"There is much to be done. I must return and face the rebel faction, dismantle their forces on the capitol island and prepare it for you."

"Be *leery,* Tamsen. I believe they were a large part of instigating the harm to your soul. That was how Petyr saw things anyway."

"*Petyr...* and *Michal.*" His eyes rose to hers with longing. "How are my boys?"

"You don't know of Petyr?"

"He isn't...?"

"No one seems to know just where he is," she answered with mounting concern. "I thought perhaps you had incarcerated him."

He shook his head. "I knew he was standing with a small number of the Western islands. We hit them hard. But I heard no further word of him after a time. It was believed he had returned to you."

Novella swallowed. Where was *Petyr?*

"Do not you worry about my youngest boy, Realm Leader," he spoke as if reading her thoughts. "He is a champion among men. Wherever he is, he is alive."

She smiled weakly. Had Tamsen, of all people, just attempted to comfort her? Why had no one endeavored to drive off that daemon before?

"I suppose it was the invaders of this island that sent you to me," she answered casually.

"I received no reports from my fleets concerning you."

"Then how did you know I was here?"

He swallowed hard, turning away from her. "I have been keeping a... a gifted individual beside me of recent days."

She searched his profile. From where was this guilt stemming? "Oh?"

"She is... a worker of the arts."

Her eyes flashed between his in confusion before it came to her. "You don't mean the dark arts... as in *witchcraft?*"

He nodded, chin dropping to his chest.

"Oh, *Tamsen*... you know the Great One forbad the planet from ever dabbling. What were you thinking?"

"That you were doing everything in your power to destroy all I held dear and... I *had* to find you." For a moment, it was as if a shadow of all he had felt returned. Almost instantly, his face softened. "And *now*... I am going to declare you Realm Leader. I am going to end this war and I shall tear down the rebel faction." He leaped to his feet. "It is all that I might do to make amends."

She searched his face again. Could it really be so easy? After all this fighting and all those lives lost, she had a single chat with the man and all their problems were solved?

"I thank you, Tamsen, for honoring me as such. You do not have to. You know what I have offered."

He shook his head with vehemence. "I *told* you... I was wrong. Now, I am going to do all I can to make things right. You shall see." He helped her to her feet. "Watch my ships for proof that we have abandoned our prior aim. When we leave, you will know that I mean what I say."

"Safe travels to you, Tamsen."

"And you, Realm Leader. Give me time to settle things in Atlantyss. When you receive word that I have announced my support of your leadership, it is safe to return home."

Was Atlantyss her home? Inwardly, she shook her head. The East was where she belonged. If she could manage it, there would be a new capitol island—the Easterly Conglomeration, without whom she could not have made it so far.

She shook her head as she watched Tamsen make his way down the mountain. The ease with which she had just made peace with one who had come to slay her made her dizzy. It seemed impossible.

"Nothing is impossible," the Helper reminded.

"Thank you, Great One, for causing me to shine like the sun and never blush with shame."

Footsteps sounded through the cave. There stood Era, Rye and Chief Xax, followed closely by the remainder of their company. Xax appeared humbled.

"I presume you caught all that?" she asked.

He nodded. "It must be a trick... He was desperate."

"Nay," Era insisted. "That was an act of the Great One."

CHAPTER 46

TAMSEN'S FLEET DEPARTED FORTHWITH. Chief Xax had his men comb the island for hidden enemies but nothing turned up. The voyage that Tamsen must make to reach Atlantyss would take weeks at best. Moreover, it was some time before the *Glorybringer* was scheduled to return. All they had to do was wait, rest... and dream. It appeared they were liberated from their adversaries. Novella must trust the Great One to see it through.

"What will life be like not constantly on the lookout?" she asked Era as they lounged on the beach one afternoon. It felt nearly sinful to relax, but what was there to do?

"Something like paradise for a time," Era answered dreamily.

"What shall we do with all our free time?"

"Put the world back in order."

"There's that."

"*That* will be the fun part."

"It will, won't it?" Novella bobbed her head to the side. "Seems like I've been fantasizing about it like an impossible dream for so long."

"Nothing is impossible with the Great One."

"I *know,*" Novella answered with awe. "Isn't it wonderful to have it proven so many times over? It seems one could never entertain doubt again."

"One would think. But it is important to *remember.*"

"Perhaps we might erect a monument," Novella suggested.

"It's a keen notion. He does like his faithfulness to be recalled."

"That will be the first order of business."

"I like it," Era agreed.

"For the time being, why don't we hold a feast? We never rightly celebrated our victory."

"What shall we have?"

"Everything! I don't care. *Honey rolls.*"

Era drew laughingly to her feet. "I shall see to the arrangements. Honey rolls are foremost on the menu."

"And we might send a party to fetch those java berries from the top of the mountain."

"I can make a java cake the likes of which you've never tasted."

Novella grinned. "I'm looking forward to it."

At long last, the *Glorybringer* arrived. The party had not heard a word of how matters lay until their arrival. It was left to Novella to inform Michal of the exchange she'd shared with his father. He was infuriated when she admitted she'd offered Tamsen half the realm but amazed to hear that his father insisted she take her rightful place across the globe.

"But... can he be trusted?" he questioned as if afraid to hope.

"I think he can," she answered softly. "He is no longer under the control of that wicked sprite."

He shook his head. "It's a pity it was not handled sooner."

"Indeed. But I recall myself back then and... I'd have had no clue what to do. That day in the cave, the answer came naturally."

"That is because you are no longer sweet, scared little Novella of Earth. You are a force to be reckoned with."

As he eyed her with admiration, her chin dropped. Was it time to share her decision concerning his proposal of marriage? It seemed a pity to spoil this good news with bad...

He cleared his throat, growing somber as he asked, "What do we do now?"

She scanned his face. If she didn't know any better, he knew where her feelings lay. But he was no more ready to hear it spoken than she was to speak it.

"I was thinking I'd like to return to the Easterly Conglomeration. That is where I intend to set up headquarters. As the East has already accepted me as their leader, why not begin now?"

His eyes grew wide. "You do not favor the shining city of Atlantyss?"

"It was beautiful for a time. But it is not where I belong anymore. I wish to be among those who have supported me all this time—those who wanted me *first.*"

"Fascinating resolution. Wasn't expecting it. I will miss my suite in the Council Hall."

"You may still—"

She stopped short. What was there to say? Was his assumption of moving to the conglomeration to wed or support her? Would informing him that he may return to Atlantyss without her sound like a blessing or curse? And she may require his counsel now more than ever.

He drew to his feet. "I will inform Captain Jonno of your decision. When would you like to depart?"

"On the morrow."

As they sailed from the Silent Island, she bid it good riddance. She would not soon forget the inhabitants' treachery. Though they were an Eastern island, they'd possessed no loyalty to speak of. Yet, the island itself had been a blessed haven. It was where the West had been won.

For now, she cast her eyes to the conglomeration. She was itching to get back and meet with her friends there, to learn of all the chiefs' battles over the course of this considerably short world war. More-over, she required their agreement to her living arrangements among them. If they were made the new capitol as she planned, they would grow into an even larger metropolis than Atlantyss. Perhaps that was not in their interest.

Their arrival, however, was direly postponed by a storm that not only threw them off course but left the captain at a total loss as to their location. As misfortune would have it, it was many days' sailing that they failed to meet with an island to either point them in the right direction or replenish their supplies, which were growing scarcer by the day. In the end, all they were left with were humble root vegetables, rationed prudently.

Every day that passed, Novella and the Seekers sought the Helper for aid, but he remained remarkably silent. Could it be they had angered him? Would he allow them to remain lost and run out of supplies, left to starve to death after everything they had been through? Surely, they were not reaching the end of their woes only to die of hunger.

"Tiz a bad omen," Captain Jonno voiced. "Never in my life have I traversed a course in which I failed to come upon some shred of land." He shook his head. "It is uncanny."

"Do you *see* us!" Novella cried to the heavens in her cabin that evening. "You know our straights and you *know* how to deliver us into a land of plenty! *Help us, Beloved!* We need you."

Another week passed before the announcement came that an is-land was spotted in the distance. Novella, Era and Michal raced to the deck. It seemed the most beautiful island in all the planet.

"The Isle of Merchants," Michal breathed. "What better place to stock up on supplies?"

"Not only that, but they rather owe us after we rescued their hides," Era added with relief.

Novella's lips straightened into a line. She'd never shared what the Great One had told her concerning this island's inevitability of betraying her to the West. "We also abandoned them on threat of the second attack," she warned.

"They won't hold it against us," Michal retorted with the wave of his hand, "not after the Western fleet failed to attack once you were away. You rather saved their hides by leaving."

Novella nodded. It was so. And after all, they were Eastern. Not an Easterly island but the silent one had failed to send word of their support. That included Merchants.

The crew cheered as they ported in the harbor. Novella, realizing how shabby she appeared after so many weeks aboard, sent Michal to beg supplies until they could send remuneration. If the fellow was anything, he was handsome even when he hadn't been afforded a bath. Once Novella was clean, Era helped her select a fine garment for the feast they were likely to enjoy that evening. As she was Realm Leader, the island could not fail to offer their best.

"It is so peculiar to be dressed like this," Novella spoke cheerily. "It seems I've been dressing in soldier's garments all my life."

Era surveyed her with satisfaction. "It isn't the garment of a Realm Leader on the brink of uniting the archipelagos, but it will do."

A knock at the door sent Novella racing to answer. "Tell me you brought honey rolls with you!" she demanded of Michal with a wide smile.

His face was sober. "I've got nothing, Novella."

"What...?"

He shook his head. "Island Leader Vespa sends word they've nothing to spare us."

Her face dropped. "How... can that be? Were they raided in our absence?"

"Not so far as I can tell. In fact, she was feasting with her friends when I met her."

"You're jesting, Michal," Era scolded in a motherly tone. "It isn't funny in the least."

His jaw flexed before, "I *wish* I were joking. The Island Leader refuses to send so much as a loaf of bread."

Novella's nails dug into the palms of her hands before tightening into fists. "She's avenging our abandonment, I'd wager."

"But we also saved them," Era reminded. "And you are Realm Leader!"

Rage washed through Novella. The Island Leader must be shown the error of her ways. This was not how she intended to begin her peacetime reign of the planet. Vespa must be made an example. Her veins sparked beneath her skin as she exited the room, marching for the ladder.

"What do you intend to do?" Michal probed as he worked to keep up with her.

"I'm not certain," she retorted evenly, "but I do not imagine it will be pretty."

He did not attempt to stop her. Rather, she perceived the reaching of his hand to the hilt of his blade. He was as angry as she—perhaps more so.

Helper, guide me, she called inwardly, fearing what she may or may not do. If she had her way, the Island Leader and her feasting cronies would end up at the center of a hurricane. But that was just her preference.

"Vella..." a deep voice spoke from the top of the gangplank.

CHAPTER 47

NOVELLA'S HEAD SHOT UP. For some moments, she was frozen in disbelief. "...Petyr?"

Not much time had passed since last they'd met, yet here he stood with a beard and a crutch. He looked older and somewhat sickly. His face was scarred. Yet, he was alive and he was *here*. She raced to meet him before stopping short. Her heart pounded fiercely as an inexplicable timidity overcame her.

"Where have you *been?*" she gasped.

"*Petyr?*" Michal questioned, looking his brother up and down. "You've certainly been through it." He flung his arms around his brother, who gripped him fiercely with eyes that never left Novella.

"I was gravely wounded in Father's final attempt to regain control of the islands who agreed to stand with you," Petyr explained to Novella as he and his brother parted. "My righthand man thought it best to tuck me away somewhere safe while he worked to nurse me back to health. He brought me here where I survived my wounds only to come down with a blasted illness from which I have only just begun to recuperate.

"Yet, here I am out of bed because I received word that the poor excuse for an Island Leader refused to send supplies to our Realm Leader." He gestured to the train of men and women lugging baskets up the gangplank behind him. "Our old friend, Thilma, and I swiftly worked to have these things gathered and sent aboard. It should be more than enough for whatever you've planned next."

Novella's heart flipped and flopped with every word. *Of course* good, faithful Petyr was there for them when they most needed him, when she'd been prepared to wipe the island off the map in her fury. But observing his sickly, scarred face as he described what he'd endured produced a mysterious tenderness in her heart. She only hoped her multitude of emotion did not show. After all, Petyr was all business, showing no signs of a man in love except for the gaze that would not leave her face. Disturbingly, she felt a blush creep across it.

With the clearing of her throat, she answered, "I am *grateful* to the Great One that he has kept you alive. And you have certainly turned up in the nick of time. I am not certain what I would have done if..."

"Think nothing of it. Thilma and I have stirred up a coup that is taking place as we speak. Island Leader Vespa is to be overthrown and a new leader voted in before evening's end."

"You're joking!" Michal declared in disbelief. "Just like that, eh?"

Provocation, the Helper whispered.

Novella's brows drew together. Had the Great One allowed them to endure weeks out on the ocean with no aid so that their rations would run low and this coup upon Merchants would take place? Had he used Vespa's disrespect in order to provoke the island to overthrow her?

"Just like that," Petyr answered wearily.

Novella's eyes shot to his. He was desperately fatigued. She stepped up beside him, planting an arm under his. "Let's get you back to bed. You should be resting or you'll catch your death yet. Where are you being housed?"

He did not resist her as she guided him back down the gangplank and onto the island. Something in him seemed to soften at her care. She could sense it in the way he received her aid.

"I can't believe you did all this," she murmured as they went, "brought us supplies, staged a coup of the island."

He offered up the first trace of a cocky grin. "Guess I still got it."

She chuckled softly before it gave way to an emotional hiccup. "I've been *so worried* about you. No one knew where you were and... it was difficult not to imagine the worst."

What were these feelings bursting up like an enduring wellspring unexpectedly unearthed? For how long had she harbored elusive fondness for this man? How had she *ever* considered wedding his brother?

Petyr flicked her a sidelong glance, licking his lips as if, for the first time in their acquaintance, he was uncertain of what to say. "You thought I'd let myself be taken out that easily?" he ventured at last.

"It sounds as if you nearly did. But the war is at an end. After your long journey to find me and all we've been through these last months, you are due a much-deserved *rest.*"

He froze, turning to search her face. "The war is at an end?"

"Haven't you heard of it by now? I can't imagine your father hasn't reached Atlantyss. But he did bid me wait until he'd had time to settle things."

He withdrew his arm from hers, shaking his head in bewilderment. "You spoke with Father? *When?*"

"Many weeks ago. He came in search of me, but I found him first. We had a little chat, I cast a daemon from him and, lo and behold, he resolved to pronounce me leader of the realm."

Petyr dropped to his knees.

"Are you alright?" she squeaked as she dropped down beside him.

He shook his head, looking to her with great sorrow. "Father..." He swallowed. "Father was assassinated on his return journey to Atlantyss some days ago."

"Oh..." she gasped as if the wind had been knocked from her sails. "Oh, Petyr... how terrible. I am so *sorry.*"

"It was one thing when I believed he'd died your enemy. But to learn he had come to think differently... It seems too *great* a pity to have lost him before I could—" His voice cracked.

Novella rested her cheek against his shoulder. *"Petyr...* I have no words. I don't see how this could have—" She stopped short. The sorceress with whom he'd been traveling had learned of his change of heart. She'd used her advantage in his life to curse him. His assassination was the result.

A tear dropped upon her head, followed by another. She peered up to discover Petyr in open anguish. She could not help wrapping him in her arms and weeping beside him. She could not imagine ever having to face her parents' passing, or having endured *all* that Petyr had in the last months. How she wished Tamsen had flung the sorceress straight off the vessel and renounced any and every agreement with her. Perhaps then this would not have occurred. But this portion of the story was in no way a detail she would ever share with Petyr.

"We must get you inside," she spoke as she drew to her feet, lifting him to his own. "I've no intention of losing you after all this."

He peered inquisitively into her face for some moments. She'd expected him to be entirely drained after the revelation. Instead, there was a leap in his step as he started on. Upon reaching the small building in which he'd been staying, she lost no time in fixing him a meal. Her champion was due that much. At last, she sat down beside him, working with all her might not to wolf down her meal like a vagabond.

Still, a glimmering eye was upon her.

"What?" she barked.

"How long have you been low on rations?"

"A few weeks," she admitted softly, working to slow her eating.

"And I suppose you ate the least of anyone in an attempt to reserve it for your crew." When she did not answer, he added, "As I expected."

"And just as you'd have done."

"Just so."

Hearing shouts without, Novella raced to the window to witness the passing of a crowd.

"You should remain here for the time being," Petyr directed. "No sense in getting caught up in the dramatics."

"But what if things have gone wrong? Shouldn't I be of assistance?"

"In a coup... as Realm Leader?" He shook his head, patting the seat beside him. "Stay with me until the coast is clear."

Novella bit back a grin as she returned to the chair. Was it a girlish fancy that he wished her to stay simply because he'd missed her and wanted her company because she was... just her? But what if it were so?

"I suppose you've been lonely tucked away here," she commented.

"Been too ill to be lonely. What of you? Been lonely yourself?"

"Not particularly. Always surrounded with friends and fighters."

"I see."

"That doesn't mean it was the same without you. Not by a longshot."

It was some moments before he swallowed his food to answer, "I know the feeling."

CHAPTER 48

NOVELLA REMAINED WITH PETYR through the afternoon. It was then she learned that the rebellious faction had taken up both the war effort as well as leadership of the West since Tamsen's passing. Not only was the war *not* over... they vowed it had only begun.

"What does that mean for your plans, Realm Leader?" Petyr questioned.

She released a long breath. "Our course remains the same for now. We are going to the Easterly Conglomeration. We shall discuss with the chieftains where to go from there."

"We?"

"Well, I will wait until you are well enough to travel, of course."

He pressed his lips together before, "Vella, I..." His voice trailed off.

"You what?" she pressed.

"I wonder where Michal has been all this time. I don't suppose he missed his brother a bit with your company all to himself."

"We haven't been together much of late," she answered perhaps too quickly. "I told you I was hidden on the Silent Island for a time."

"Michal did not stay with you?"

She shook her head, dying to inform him that she had denied Michal's proposal. Problem was, she hadn't.

"I am surprised he would leave you so unprotected..."

"Since when do I require his protection?"

He raised a brow. "Feisty much?"

She couldn't help laughing. "Oh, I'm sorry... It seems so wrong to be laughing when the reprieve from this war is no more."

He bobbed his head back and forth. "Now that the rebel faction is in control of the West, I've heard word they plan to regather their forces for an all-out assault against us. No more of this 'dabbling,' they claim. So, we've some time yet before then."

"How *relieving*," she answered sulkily.

"I know... It is difficult to face war again, but I think now is as good a time as any for you to officially take your place as Realm Leader of the Eastern portion. Declare that these are a united archipelagos. It may just plant a little fear into our enemies."

"It's not a bad notion at all, Petyr. But it also means I should be heading to the conglomeration sooner than I planned..."

"I don't see why I can't recuperate aboard the *Glorybringer*."

Her eyes flicked to his. "You think so?"

"It would do me more good than harm, I think."

It was then the knock came. Novella gestured for Petyr to remain seated while she went for the door. There stood Thilma beside Era.

"May we come in?" the elderly lady inquired with a grin.

Novella reached her arms about the woman. "It is so *good* to see you. How can I ever thank you for supporting Petyr in getting supplies to us? Not to mention the issue of Island Leader..."

The ladies stepped inside and the good woman waved a hand at her. "Stuff and nonsense. I've been *looking* for an excuse to unite the council against Vespa for years. Do you know, I think she was working with Tamsen under the table. Er..." Her eyes shot to Petyr. "May he rest in peace."

Petyr shrugged.

"*Wonderful* to see you, friend," Era called warmly. "You certainly don't look the worse for wear."

"I know how I look," he answered evenly.

"I reckon those scars can still win favor with the ladies."

Her wink was pointed at Novella, who swiftly changed the subject. "You must tell me what has become of Vespa. Were you successful?"

"She and those loyal to her are to come under trial for negligence to the Realm Leader," Thilma declared.

"In the meantime, a 'temporary' fill in has just been appointed," Era put in.

"And that would be?" Novella almost feared to ask.

"Thilma."

Novella released a breath of relief. "Just as I would have had it myself. And once Vespa is found guilty, they will request that you maintain your position."

"We shall see," Thilma answered meekly. "I certainly never thought I'd be in this position at *my age*. But it seems wonders never cease!"

"Wonders?" Petyr questioned. "I've heard the way these people talk about you. You've been working for their welfare behind the scenes since before you were appointed to the island council."

"Well," she began with a shrug, restoring her focus to Novella, "I can tell you that our first order of business is to beg that you name the date of your official acceptance of leadership over the East."

Novella nodded. "As soon as I arrive at the conglomeration, everything shall be arranged."

"*Thank* the Great One," the woman sighed. With the shaking of her head, she continued "Do you know I have been *praying* for this day since Realm Leader Flynn's passing? The only day that may outshine it is when we finally win this war against the West."

Thilma took Novella's hands into her own. "I give you my blessing, such as it is." It was then she closed her eyes and uttered a language that Novella had only ever heard from her own lips. This time, it was accompanied by flame that washed over her form, imbuing her with a strange sense of nobility. She felt herself prepared to take the helm of the East and, moreover, face whatever the West brought before her. It was her *right* as Realm Leader.

"A Firetongue..." Petyr murmured from his chair. "I didn't realize there were any left with that strain."

Thilma bobbed her head. "I am descended of *the* Jaela. It seems her anointing opted to rather pop up in me, you might say. I've kept it secret long enough, interceding for my people and planet for so many years. But I don't know... today feels like a *new* day, does it not? Things are different... and perhaps not at all as they seem."

Novella eyed her with question, but the woman swiftly took her leave, claiming she had many matters to attend now she was Island Leader. Era's gaze shot from Petyr to Novella with an expressive brow. Novella swiftly guided her friend to the door.

"You and I should be heading back to the *Glorybringer*. We'll need our beauty rest, I wager." She turned back to Petyr with, "You'll move aboard tomorrow?"

A solid nod was his response. "Sleep well, Vella."

"And you," she answered with such feeling that it was all she could do to conceal it.

Once the door was closed and the two women traversed the path, Era lost no time in bursting with laughter. *"Oh,* I apologize. Vella. But it is so good to see you finally realize how *right* I've been all this time."

"I know no such thing," Novella returned irritably.

CHAPTER 49

ERA HELPED PREPARE NOVELLA for what she'd have called back home "her coronation." Yet, she was in no way royal. She was a servant of the world... who carried authority. After Thilma had prayed over her in that strange tongue, she no longer felt intimidated by the position. Rather, she coveted it. It was hers by every right of heaven.

As a knock sounded through the room, the corners of Era's eyes wrinkled into a grin. "I'll get that."

"Who could that be so near the ceremony?" Novella questioned with irritation.

When the door was thrust open, none other than Iviana the Glorybringer was revealed, along with Novella's grandmother, Naii, and Darist, the strange strong man who had appeared to warn them at Iviana's seaside cottage.

Novella raced to the door. She grasped first her grandmother's hands, then Iviana's, with deep affection. Though she'd not been afforded much time with them to date, the impact they'd made on her early days upon the planet was yet strong.

"What brings you here?" she asked with excitement.

"Why, the Ceremony of Realm Leader, of course," Iviana answered pleasantly. "Who did you presume was to perform it if not myself and your granny?"

Novella's eyes flew to Era. "You told me it was to be the chieftains!"

"I thought this surprise would be better pleasing," she answered.

"Besides," Naii began, "did you think I'd have *missed* this day? In fact, I haven't a mind to leave your side until this blasted war is at an end."

"Good," Novella returned warmly. "I've been missing getting to know my grandmother."

"Oh," Iviana spoke up, pulling her strong man up beside her. "You remember Darist, don't you?"

Novella nodded. "I deeply thank you for your warning that day on the Isle of Dragons, Darist."

He offered a bow.

"We've been married," Iviana blurted with unadulterated joy.

Novella's mouth fell open.

Iviana nodded like a much younger woman. "It seems to me I've loved him forever, though I didn't know it. He claimed the same, so... here we are. We are to depart from the Greater Archipelagos at the close of the ceremony to go portal-hopping, as I've long dreamed."

Though Novella wasn't keen on the woman abandoning the realm, she couldn't help grinning. "I wish you both all the happiness the Great One can afford."

"Request accepted," the Helper whispered.

Her grin broadened to the point of pain. "And you *will* be so very happy—I know it."

It wasn't long before Novella entered the finest hall the conglomeration had to offer, decked in gleaming gold even to the point of a gold-leafed band about her own golden hair. Her curls hung loosely down her back, pulled back to make her appear older than her natural years, for she felt as much within herself.

In the moment that Iviana completed the rites, declaring Novella as Realm Leader of the East, the congested room erupted with applause that caused the rafters to shake. Novella's thoughts turned to her parents, wishing they might have been present. *Her parents*... a peculiarly faraway consideration. Not long ago, she'd felt herself but their little girl. Now, she was Realm Leader of the Eastern isles.

Immediately following, Novella secreted herself to her chamber. She fell to her knees with elbows resting on the bed in order to cry, *"Oh,* Great One, you've done it! You've won me half the realm and I can feel you're just getting started. Praise be to you and the Anointed One for standing with me all this time, to the Helper in my ear for always speaking when I need it most!"

"No trouble at all, my heart," spoke a familiar voice from across the room.

She leaped to her feet, subsequently flinging herself at his fiery ones. *"Thank you,* Friend, for all you've accomplished thus far! Thank you for being *such a friend!"*

She felt his arms pulling her to her feet. "How could you imagine any less for one I love so dearly? I want only the *best* for my best girl."

She wrapped her arms about his torso, breathing in the intoxicating aroma of his presence, so very like what she'd experienced on the Island of Seekers. Only this... *this* embrace was something she wished *never* to be parted from. All at once, she felt entirely whole, accepted, seen and awed. This was God. And he loved her... *so very much.*

Before she was in any way prepared, he pulled back with, "You must get to the party, dear heart. It is no celebration without the star of the performance."

She nodded regretfully. "I wish we could just stay like this forever." Narrowing her eyes on him, she spoke an epiphany, "You are just *everything*... do you know it?"

Soberly, he answered, "As are you."

Those words echoed through her mind through the festivities of the day. Her heart beat with the truth of his. Though the Great One was, in actuality, the prize of mankind, humanity was *his* prize—one the Anointed One had surrendered his own life to win if they would but accept his sacrifice. But not only were they beloved of him as a whole, each jewel on the chain was uniquely prized. It made her choke up whenever the notion returned to her. By the end of a very late evening, she cried herself to sleep with the knowledge.

Not many days passed before Petyr and Michal visited her with a formal communication. It was a missive sent from the entirety of the Western province. Novella's hands trembled as Petyr read it aloud. She sat back in complete shock at the conclusion.

"The islands are officially renouncing the rebel faction and begging that you take your rightful place as leader, thereby reuniting the realm," Michal spoke like he would burst.

When she did not immediately speak, he questioned, "Don't you see what this means? *The war is no more.* They want you. We are united as *the* Greater Archipelagos once again... or very soon will be."

Petyr eyed her with consideration. "What are you thinking?"

After a blink, she turned to Michal. "Write up a reply that I will be satisfied to accept their plea once they have thoroughly conquered the rebel faction in their midst."

"I like it..." Petyr spoke pensively. "Make them work for it after most of them sided with Father against you."

"I am not feeling heady," she explained. "I merely wish them to display their desire for unity with their brethren across the planet. I think they owe the East that much."

"Very well..." Michal spoke with some dissatisfaction. "But we are so *close.*"

"We *are,*" she agreed. "But why bother sending our troops to take out this enemy that the West were so easily conquered by? They've more than enough power to take down this small faction."

With a shrug, he answered, "I will see to it."

Merely a week later, Petyr approached her with a broad grin. "You'll never guess the word we just received."

She faced him with mirroring joy. "The West has overthrown their conquerors."

His face dropped. "How did you know?"

"The Helper told me this morning. I've just been sitting here mapping where to go from here."

It seemed to her that every anxiety she had suffered since transporting to the planet had just been resolved by the great mercy of the Great One. He had furthermore informed her that they were entering a time of his great favor, that the future looked a *festival* in comparison with all the planet had endured in recent years. She, herself, was due *multitudes of joy* to dilute any and all hardships that may come. It seemed there was nothing left to be done except... Her eyes caught the wave of Petyr's hair as it fell in unruly fashion between his eyes. He searched her for an answer as to her thoughts, but she wasn't quite ready to speak.

"Now that's settled," she began with resolve, "I must see your brother about that proposal. *Don't* go anywhere."

"Oh, *no* you don't." With a tug, he twirled her back into the room. "Look, Vella, I love my brother... but you cannot marry him. *I* found you first and, if I'm honest with myself, I loved you first. Moreover, it is clear now more than ever that the women in your family need caring for. So, like your father, I'm quite determined that I'm the one for the task and, like your mother, you're just going to have to learn to love me."

"Petyr..." she began with a poorly concealed smirk, "I just united the whole world. I possess every great gift under the sun. And you think you're the one to take care of me? You think you can handle *this?*"

"Oh, I can handle it," he answered adamantly. "Don't forget I've been behind you every step of the way from day one. I don't care how gifted you are. Someone has got to think of you while you're busy thinking of everyone else."

"Besides that, you're in love with me," she reminded.

"Exactly," he agreed as he caught the amusement in her eyes. Taking her hands into his own, he added, "And you'd be crazy not to fall for a fellow like me."

"Crazy," she reiterated with a grin.

"Then... you weren't going to accept Michal's proposal?"

She shook her head.

"So... I could have gone about this in a more debonair fashion at a later date?"

She nodded.

"Well," he began, reaching into his pocket to pull out a brilliant gold band. "Will you wear this?"

"Put it on."

Sliding it onto the appropriate finger, he grumbled, "I feel like an idiot."

"A very *fortunate* idiot," she reminded.

"Just so."

"Now, I must *seriously* speak to your brother."

The clearing of a throat from the open door sent them both spinning to face the unexpected visitor.

"No need for that," Michal voiced with a good show of bravado. "I've seen this coming from day one too, you know. But you can't blame an older brother for imagining he could win out over the younger, can you? Well, *congratulations* and good riddance, you turtledoves. I'm returning to Atlantyss. I've received word they require an Island Leader and desire none other than this *elder* brother for the job."

"Congratulations!" Petyr called to Michal's retreating frame.

"Oh, *shut up,*" he called back with perhaps a glimmer of humor.

"That might have gone better..." Novella spoke with a twinge.

Petyr shrugged. "He'll get over it. As for you and I, how does home sound to you?"

"Home?" she began in confusion before she caught his meaning. "You mean...?"

Afterword

CHILLS COURSED THROUGH NOVELLA as she and Petyr transported into the tea room of her parents' home in London. It was like being wrenched from a dream that had just begun to get good, only the best part was still standing with her.

"This is *wild*," Petyr whispered as he gazed about. "Seems an age since we were here."

She nodded. "An age since I considered you the projected thief of my liberty."

He chuckled softly. "Shall I take the ring back?"

She clutched it with her other hand. "Not on your life, Mr. Tamsen. Now... *where* could they be?"

It wasn't until they reached the door to her father's study that she perceived her parents' murmurs. It seemed Mother was Father's new bookkeeper. They were having an argument about the numbers. Novella bit her lip as she wrapped on the door.

"Come in, Cook!" her mother called. "You're early, but *just* in time. It seems we..." Her voice trailed off as her eyes widened at sight of Novella in the doorway. With an emotional gasp, she flew across the room to envelope her daughter in her arms. Father lost no time in breeching the expanse to embrace his ladies.

"I thought perhaps you would *never* return..." Mother whispered into her hair.

"I loathe to admit that it was Petyr's idea," Novella admitted through her tears.

The parents pulled back long enough to recognize Petyr watching from the hall. Father stepped toward him and thrust out a hand. "I trust you've kept a good eye on my daughter?"

Petyr hardily shook it. "I'm afraid she doesn't require much protection these days. But as for caring, I quite intend to see to it the remainder of our lives. That is... if you'll grant us your blessing?"

"Vella!" Mother cried with a wide smile. Her eyes dropped to her daughter's left hand. "You're *engaged?*" Tucking Novella's hair behind her ear, she continued, "Why, you scarcely look like yourself. *My little girl...* you're no child anymore. You look like a—a queen."

"Nearly that," Petyr explained. "This is the Realm Leader of the reunited Greater Archipelagos."

"Then you *did* it," Father spoke with nigh disbelief.

Novella couldn't help shaking her head. "If you knew the whole story, you'd understand that it was not due to me. The Great One has orchestrated *miracles* and I get to reap the benefits."

Petyr released a long whistle. "Don't let her talk herself down, Mother and Father. The Great One certainly had her putting her work in. Yet, he *is* to be glorified, even if only for the work he has accomplished in Vella... to say nothing of myself."

Father pulled Petyr into the circle. "As for blessings, you've had mine since before my daughter would deign to acknowledge your interest. Match made in heaven, I said! Although... you might have told me you were from another planet when I hired you."

Petyr raised a brow before catching his former employer's smirk. "You'd have sent me back into the streets more like."

"But Mother," Novella spoke up in astonishment, "you've *told* Father?"

Nimua nodded. "Did you think he was going to let things rest for a minute when I wouldn't identify just where I'd allowed his daughter to travel? Old promises or not, it wasn't long before he managed to wheedle the whole tale from me."

Novella's gaze shot to her father. "What did you make of it?"

"I'll be honest," he spoke with a laugh, "it wasn't in the least what I'd expected. It took some time to stomach the notion of other realms from which someone like my wife had come. But after all these years of mystery, I'd presumed there was quite a tale behind her peculiar appearance at my back door all those years ago. Now, here *you* are, Vella girl, leader of that strange place. What I wouldn't give for just a *glimpse...*" He ended with a yearning sparkle in his eyes.

Novella's smile was broad as a mountainside. "What do you say, Petyr? Think that could be arranged?"

With a wink, he answered, "I was rather wondering what we were waiting for."

DEAR READER...

If you enjoyed this book and would like to encourage likeminded readers to give it a read, I would sincerely appreciate it if you would consider leaving a review wherever you shop for books!

ABOUT THE AUTHOR

Cassandra Boyson is older than she looks but younger than the sum of her years dictates. Based out of the Dallas, Texas area, she is author of Amazon bestselling Christian Fantasy series, *The Seeker's Trilogy*. Her books focus on inspiring the supernatural walk every Christian is destined to live out as Jesus did, as well as the only means of salvation and the matchless, intimate friendship of the Great One.

CassandraBoyson.com

www.ingramcontent.com/pod-product-compliance
Lightning Source LLC
Chambersburg PA
CBHW031649210626
46816CB00023B/1594